a novel obsession

a
novel
obsession

A NOVEL

Caitlin Barasch

DUTTON

DUTTON

An imprint of Penguin Random House LLC
penguinrandomhouse.com

Copyright © 2022 by Caitlin Barasch

DUTTON and the D colophon are registered trademarks of Penguin
Random House LLC.

LIBRARY OF CONGRESS CATALOGING-IN-PUBLICATION DATA

Names: Barasch, Caitlin, author.
Title: A novel obsession / a novel Caitlin Barasch.
Description: New York: Dutton, [2022] |
Identifiers: LCCN 2021013418 (print) | LCCN 2021013419 (ebook) |
ISBN 9780593185599 (paperback) | ISBN 9780593185582 (ebook)
Classification: LCC PS3602.A7528 N68 2022 (print) |
LCC PS3602.A7528 (ebook) | DDC 813/.6—dc23
LC record available at https://lccn.loc.gov/2021013418
LC ebook record available at https://lccn.loc.gov/2021013419

Printed in the United States of America
1st Printing

For my late grandmother

Joan Cameron,

the most enthralling and

theatrical of storytellers.

a novel obsession

chapter one

MY BOYFRIEND'S EX-GIRLFRIEND, Rosemary, has the same thickness to her eyebrows as I do. The same wavy auburn hair and pear-shaped hips.

I'm standing across the street from her office in a chunky maroon sweater and sunglasses, watching her leave. I want to know if she's the type who heads out at five for a gym class or a happy hour, or the type to send emails until eight, adrift in a sea of empty desks.

Watching her exit the building at 6:35 p.m., I've now discovered she's neither.

I note the *New Yorker* tote bag she carries, which to me suggests unoriginality, conformity. She crosses the four-lane street with only two seconds left on the crosswalk's countdown. Cars honk, she pops a breath mint.

I know it's a mint because I stand close to her on the Fulton subway platform and breathe it in. I resist the urge to touch her. To see if she dissolves.

Up close, Rosemary looks different from her Instagram photos. She must use a variety of filters, excessive shadow and saturation. She has a flatter stomach than I do, but much smaller breasts. Smooth and glowing skin, but a square and masculine jaw. In the pictures I've seen, she presses her lips together rather than flashing all her teeth, as I do.

But now, finally, I have a rare glimpse of her teeth. The canines are jagged, protruding like fangs. This might mean I'm prettier than Rosemary, but who knows? Maybe her vampiric teeth appealed to Caleb.

On the train, when she shoves tiny white AirPods into her ears, I mimic her with my bulky noise-canceling headphones. Even though seats are available, Rosemary leans against the door and closes her eyes and taps her feet. I prefer to stand, too, but only ever with my eyes open. Hidden behind dark oversized sunglasses—similar to the kind celebrities wear when evading paparazzi—I'm able to hold prolonged and one-sided eye contact with strangers. Successful surveillance relies on anonymity.

A platoon of bodies in two-piece business suits shoves into the train at Wall Street, and those huddled near the door squeeze closer together. Despite October's cold snap, the subway cars aren't heated yet. I manage, in the scuffle, to stand next to Rosemary. When the sleeve of my sweater grazes her denim-jacketed elbow, I wonder if we'll look at each other. But her gaze never rises. Being two inches taller proves advantageous—I'm able to peer at her screen as she scrolls through artists, albums, finally settling on Hiatus Kaiyote's "Breathing Underwater." With a twinge of discomfort, I realize Caleb—my boyfriend, her ex—has blasted this song every time we've cooked together the past few weeks, chopping onions to the smash of a cymbal.

Next, I observe Rosemary tweet about a novel she edited, which was apparently reviewed in the *New York Times*. She deletes and rephrases so many times that I'm tempted to rip the phone from her hands. *I know you're aiming for pride and humility*, I'll say. *Let me.*

I study her face until she exits at Atlantic Avenue near Brooklyn's Fort Greene neighborhood. I follow her. She walks down the street, takes a left, a right, then punches in a code to enter a modern, industrial-chic building with floor-to-ceiling glass windows. It's an eyesore among the quaint brownstones.

I can't follow anymore. I go, instead, to a biergarten a few blocks away. Order a pretzel the size of my face, drink seasonal beer that tastes of banana bread. Then I call Caleb and ask if he wants to meet me here.

"Where?" he asks.

I cover the mouthpiece and ask the bartender to tell me where I am. He whispers the name of the bar and winks conspiratorially. I repeat it for Caleb.

There's a decided pause. "Why are you in Fort Greene?"

"I'm writing a scene that takes place here. Research."

His voice softens. "Be there soon."

Once our call ends, I scribble down some details—the crosswalk, the tweet, the tote bag, her denim-jacketed elbow brushing against the sleeve of my sweater. The beginnings of a book—my book. I've found, I think, a story worth telling. Until now I've written only short fiction, twenty pages or less; I haven't been intrigued enough about anything to sustain an edifice of words. But life has finally begun to interest me. To prove the believers right and the nonbelievers wrong—I fall into both categories, depending on the day—I will write a novel.

When Caleb arrives thirty minutes later, he gazes around the bar uneasily, as if expecting a ghost. I call him over.

"How's that scene?" He settles onto the stool beside me. "Trying to describe a slant of light hitting a fancy brownstone?"

I force a laugh, unsure if I'm being mocked. "Exactly."

"Work was mental, I've been eyeing the bar across the street practically since the day started. This was a more ambitious trek than I was anticipating, though."

Caleb lives in Washington Heights, while I reside two hundred blocks south in Greenwich Village, conveniently nearer to his office in the Financial District. Would he want to see me as often if I lived elsewhere?

"You must really like me," I say.

"Obviously." Caleb brushes a strand of hair off my forehead. It's movie stuff but feels nice. "I've actually been here before."

I choose to look surprised. "Have you?"

"Well—my ex lives in this neighborhood." His hand is still on my forehead, still playing with my hair. "We came here a few times."

"Oh, shit. I didn't realize—you think she might randomly walk in?"

"God, I hope not." His hand moves from my head to wrap around the beer glass the bartender has brought. "There are a zillion other bars around here."

"It won't happen," I say, more confidently than I feel, and touch his arm. Anchoring him here, with me.

TWO DAYS LATER, on my day off, I return to the corner where Rosemary works and locate a bench where I can read. I'm carrying a book she edited called *One of the Herd*, an essay collection by a woman who grew up on a Wyoming cattle farm. I took it from a box of forthcoming releases in the storage room at the bookstore where I work. The publication date is still a few weeks away, but I've promised myself I'll skim quickly and carefully, without damaging the pages or the spine, and then slide it back into the box before it goes on sale. I want to claim this physical manifestation of her, if only for a short while.

Between surveillance of the building's revolving doors, I manage to digest thirty-two pages before Rosemary emerges, rummaging in her *New Yorker* tote for her Ray-Bans.

She turns west at the corner. I slip the book into my own tote—its illustration a bespectacled woman carrying a teetering stack of Jane Austen novels—just in time to watch the back of Rosemary's royal-blue cotton dress disappear inside a café. I'm thirsty, too, I realize, and in need of caffeine. So I follow her inside.

Rosemary ponders the chalkboard menu. Does she read every item but then order the usual? I peg her as a nonfat latte kind of woman.

"I'll have an iced dirty chai, please," she tells the barista.

"That's what I always get," I murmur, more audibly than intended.

Rosemary turns.

I'm mortified but also electric. Words bubble up. "I rarely see anyone order it," I blurt out, as if to explain. "But I know people like it, that's how I found out it existed." I can't seem to stop. "Espresso in chai."

Furious at the brutal mundanity of what is now officially our first encounter, I blush a deep crimson. Then Rosemary says, "Yeah, it's pretty good." Her gaze sweeps over me. "Cute tote, by the way."

Her voice is raspy, lower than I expected. Alluring.

I glance down. "Thank you so much."

I want to hear her again, but she ducks her head to check her phone, signaling the end of our conversation. The espresso machine gurgles. The barista hands her the chai—Rosemary's fingernails are violet—and then her mouth encircles the straw. I order the same, still vibrating with nervous energy, and step into the bright October sunlight.

Rosemary is gone.

I was prepared to wait all day for her emergence. Now I don't know what to do with all this extra time. I walk a few avenues over and sit alongside the Hudson, zipping my floral-print bomber jacket up to my chin. The seasons are changing, ushering in peak foliage. Golden leaves litter the sidewalk. The wind is biting when it blows. I no longer apply deodorant to the insides of my thighs to prevent them from chafing.

In my iPhone Notes app, I document a few details—the blue cotton dress, the raspy voice, our dirty chai, her violet fingernails. Later, I'll sculpt a scene.

It's only a few minutes before eleven; apparently, Rosemary takes early coffee breaks. Maybe she brewed her first cup around dawn and drank it slowly in her kitchen, savoring the steam. Maybe her routine involves grabbing another coffee before boarding the subway and then attempting to drink it jostled against the other commuters. And finally, when pre-lunch fatigue sets in, she ventures out for her third cup. I drink coffee all day, too, hoping it will successfully jolt me into action. Perhaps we also have dehydration in common.

Or it's possible Rosemary enjoyed a late night with friends yesterday, maybe even a date. She might have been naked in another man's bed this morning. But I can't imagine why a woman in love with someone else would send her ex-boyfriend—Caleb—an email asking if he was well, asking to see him again. What could require they meet face-to-face, other than a desire to repair and rekindle?

That's partly why I'm here. To find out. A narrative is beginning to form, one in which I am braver, bolder, more reckless. Observations are useless without accompanying actions. Maybe I should have spilled coffee on her tote, cried uncontrollably about a pretend breakup to elicit her concern, stolen a bag of coffee grounds and made a run for it. Motivated by a commitment to my craft, I'm free now to make strange decisions emancipated from social convention. Welcome to my intellectual experiment, welcome to my ambition. Who would dare fault me for my ambition?

I MET CALEB nearly six months ago, back in May, on Tinder. I was twenty-four and had never been someone's girlfriend. Now it was time. I wanted to become worthy of love and well-equipped to describe it.

In my Tinder profile, I revealed I was a writer and native New Yorker with a literary tattoo and an orange tabby cat named Romeo. (Some men took it upon themselves to make the same bad joke about whether I could make room for another "Romeo" in my life; those men were swiftly eliminated.) In photos, I showed off my toothy smile with a Rocky Mountain backdrop (outdoorsy-ish) or holding a beer (low-maintenance; "chill") or peeking through the shelves of a bookstore wearing my tortoiseshell reading glasses (nerdy-chic).

Caleb's Tinder profile mentioned only that he was a mathematician working in catastrophe modeling who had moved from the

UK. He provided just one photo—one!—of himself, standing in a beautiful wool coat and scarf on the Brooklyn Heights Promenade with the Manhattan skyline twinkling behind him. I rarely swiped right on men who provided fewer than three photos, but something about Caleb's open, easy, almost sheepish smile endeared him to me. It would be fun, I thought, to share my city with him, experience it anew.

Before Caleb, I made aggressive eye contact with handsome men at the bookstore, gazes that were long and hard but never led to anything real, and so I'd come home hungry, already swiping on my way through the door. I sometimes went on as many as three Tinder dates a week with wannabe singer-songwriters and actors and filmmakers and poets. First dates were enjoyable because I could be anyone, and so could they; we performed our parts well. There was laughter and long lingering touches and cans of cheap beer and self-congratulatory conversations about "making art." Then we would fuck. In bed, I gave each man whoever and whatever they wanted. It would lead to a second date, and to a third. But then they'd stop texting me back. I suspected it was because we could no longer convincingly validate the roles we were each attempting to play. I told myself not to take it personally—if they didn't truly know me, if I hadn't let them in, then the person they were rejecting was definitively not-me.

Maybe now it was time to try someone sweet, straightforward, foreign. Good with numbers, definitively non-artist. Caleb was a solid candidate.

Our first date, we met at a bar in my neighborhood, with a jukebox and a fish tank and a collection of dusty board games. He was more attractive than his picture suggested, more attractive, even, than the men who'd ghosted me. His hair was long and dark, brushing his shoulders, and this abundance felt important somehow.

We settled at a table in the back. With other men I'd grown accustomed to the way we monologued at each other, crafting ourselves on the spot. Most of the men I chose were loud and opinionated and arrogant—but at the time I'd been too generous, calling it *confident*. Those men were good talkers but not particularly good listeners. I probably wasn't, either.

But after mere minutes in Caleb's company, I was surprised by how wonderfully rare it felt to be listened to, looked at, questioned; it was generous and thoughtful rather than pointed, destabilizing.

"So, Naomi, please put me out of my misery," he deadpanned as I finished my first pint of beer around the thirty-minute mark. "What's this 'literary' tattoo? Can I see it?"

I laughed and tugged down the back of my shirt, revealing tight cursive letters on my upper back: *and the walls became the world all around.*

"Maybe not as sophisticated as you were expecting," I said. "But *Where the Wild Things Are* was one of my favorite books as a kid. My parents read it to me almost every night."

"Oh, that's lovely. A real homage to reading itself. Cheers," he said, lifting his beer in a toast, "to our imaginations."

Happy to have his approval, I beamed as we clinked pint glasses.

"I was actually pretty nervous about it," I said, "so my best friend, Danielle, forced me to write a list of pros and cons. I think she was worried I'd tattoo my crush's name on my ass or something." (That was one of my clumsiest and most uncool self-deprecating anecdotes.) "But if she approved of the pros, she promised to drive me."

Danielle had sat beside me as I clutched her hand and cursed and counted from zero to ten on a ceaseless loop until it was done. What I had really wanted that day was to experience a tolerable amount of pain. (The first time my body was altered, I was a teenager under anesthesia, and something inside me was taken; for my second alteration, I wanted to *feel* it—a scar I alone had chosen, decorative and expressive and notable, a scar that meant something other than lack.)

"Danielle sounds like a good friend," Caleb said, tracing the letters of my tattoo so softly that I shivered, rendered momentarily speechless.

The pleasing lilt of his Welsh accent, and his smile—open and bright, like a loaf of bread just sliced—resulted in my deviating from all my other planned anecdotes and inquiries, and in the process, becoming more myself.

"I have a lot of anxiety," I heard myself say, to my utter horror, two hours and three beers later.

Miraculously, Caleb's face remained unchanged.

"I'm terrified of being a cliché because I talk about writing more often than I actually write," I babbled, full speed ahead. "It wasn't always like that—I used to write all the time. My brother, Noah, and I both found things we loved and were good at as kids, which is kind of rare, isn't it, so I thought I would've accomplished more by now. Noah has already been in *three* Broadway musicals, and he's only nineteen! It's kind of insane."

I frequently talk about Noah because his life is objectively interesting, and by association people might assume mine is interesting, too. Everyone wants to be famous, or at least fame adjacent, and so I expected Caleb to ask a few follow-up questions about Noah's career, but he didn't. He only widened his eyes expectantly, creating more space for me to speak.

"It's obviously way more common to be a child actor than a prodigy novelist," I continued, "but I still feel an insane amount of pressure pretty much all the time."

"You shouldn't worry so much!" Caleb laughed, not unkindly. "We're still young, aren't we? There's no rush. You're lucky you found something you're passionate about."

I felt a strong urge to reach across the table and clutch his long warm fingers, but I didn't. Why had I told him so much so quickly? On first dates I tended to skew toward upbeat, lighthearted, inoffensive.

Caleb's eyes, soft and searching, and his sliced-bread smile, so open and bright, made me feel new, feel refreshed.

"Okay," I said, sheepish. "I want to hear more about your life now. Sorry for dumping all that on you—"

"Please don't apologize," he said emphatically, and then raised a playful eyebrow. "What else would you like to know?"

Everything, I almost said aloud. "What kind of catastrophes do you prevent?" I asked instead.

"Oh, I don't prevent them; that's impossible. I model equations to estimate possible loss."

"There's a metaphor in there somewhere," I said.

His laugh, when it came again, soothed me. My body loosened as I listened. He went on to describe how his University of St Andrews residential college resembled a castle, and how every Tuesday students attended formal dinners wearing black robes in the grand dining hall. All were required to stand as administrators and faculty processed through the center aisle. Students were not allowed to sit until each member of the procession was seated. I imagined him in his robe, standing very regal.

We wandered into three different bars during our first night together, a pub crawl of our own making. The air was warm—too warm, perhaps, for early May. Pollen floated by. He sneezed twice, so I blessed him twice. "I appreciate it," he said, tilting his head back to prepare for a third, "but you don't need to say it again."

On each short walk between bars, I frequently glanced at him strolling beside me, surprised he was still there.

At our final destination, a dark, subterranean dive, all the barstools were occupied, so we leaned against a pool table no one was using. "So, Naomi," Caleb said, "my next question might come as no surprise. Where can I read something you've written?"

I was hoping he would ask.

Later that night—after Caleb pressed me against the wall of a nearby building for a memorable first kiss, unexpectedly passionate and unrestrained for a man whose first impression oozed rare calm and composure—I emailed him the link to a story I'd published the previous year. Vaguely autobiographical, it focuses on a twenty-seven-year-old jazz drummer I met when I was sixteen. I fictionalized our relationship and its eventual end as if it were equally significant for both of us, giving myself closure. I was proud of the story, and proud of my byline at the popular online literary magazine that accepted it, and proud of having received fifty dollars, the price of eight dirty chai lattes, for having published it.

Days passed without hearing from him, which felt ominous. It was a *short* story, meant to be consumed in an hour or less! Maybe he'd read it and hated it, maybe he'd gleaned something undesirable about me from its subtext, maybe—

When Caleb's email finally arrived in my inbox ten days later, it contained more than I'd hoped for. You perfectly captured the emotional rush that (certainly in my own experience) comes after a breakup, he wrote. There's a sadness to it, but an optimistic and cleansing feel, too. The praise was gratifying, but I was most excited by the subtle revelations of the life he'd lived before me, all the stories worth excavating. Loving someone, I thought, required learning all their stories—a perpetual excavation.

Of course, it helped that his word choices—*optimistic, cleansing*—implied he had moved on, a clean break.

So, after our next date, I took Caleb home and molded him to me. Skinny but strong in the arms, he lowered me to the mattress and pulled off my shirt and unclasped my bra and helped me wriggle out of my jeans. "Why am I the only naked one?" I said in mock-indignation, gesturing at the heap of my clothes. He laughed and stripped and put his mouth between my legs. For the first time I dared myself to look at him, really look at him, without breaking eye contact as I always had with other men. It invited a rush of feeling I wasn't prepared for, had never felt, and so I scrambled onto my hands and knees and stared at the wall, waiting.

My sudden movement appeared to both perplex and amuse him.

"What are you doing?"

"Fuck me from behind," I said, hoping to convey a seductive authority.

When he snickered, I turned around to look at him, hurt and confused.

"Sorry," he said. "Erm, it's just, I dunno, like you're doing some kind of routine? I want to look at you."

I was shocked into silence. He tickled my ribs and tried to apologize, but I shook my head and said it might be true. None of the men who came before had ever cared enough to notice.

Naked and propped against my pillows, we talked. He told me he used to panic about forgetting his dreams and so, during college, he got in the morning habit of whispering what he still remembered into a recording device.

"What did you do with them, did you listen to old dreams, what did they mean for you?" I asked.

He said he liked the act of verbal recounting. "It woke me up," he said.

I told him the stuffed animals in my childhood bedroom seemed to come alive in the darkness and creep closer to me.

"Spooky," he said.

"I liked them," I said.

In the morning we tried having sex again, and this time it was better, it was great. I stopped thinking.

Caleb asked me on another date, and then another and another—until one July morning, after waking up with a sore throat, fever, and chills, a doctor confirmed I had the flu. For six days I could barely get out of bed, which was physically inconvenient at best and romantically catastrophic at worst; because we hadn't yet discussed exclusivity, I feared Caleb would meet someone new while I was bedridden. Someone he liked better. I feared being out of sight, out of mind.

If this was an elaborate ruse to get rid of me, sorry, but it hasn't worked, Caleb texted on the sixth day. **I'm good at making soup and tea and reading bedtime stories (I can bring Where the Wild Things Are). Anyway, let me know if my services are requested.** ☺

I reread the text over and over and felt, for the very first time, that I might be capable of falling in love—despite how the icky verb itself, *falling*, suggested loss of precious control.

Finally, in late July, after almost three months of dating, we entered into an official relationship. My first ever. Just like that, I was someone's girlfriend: Caleb's.

My mother, after seeing a picture of him, said, *Oh, he looks like a model.* My father, after learning Caleb was a mathematician, said, *Ah, a real smarty-pants.* Caleb was an ideal, but also real, and now mine.

At this point, Rosemary didn't exist. I spent the whole summer with no knowledge of her. She came in with the cold.

TWO WEEKS AGO, in the first days of October, Caleb took me to see a relatively unknown band from Wales perform at a small concert venue on the Lower East Side. "They grew up in the next town over," he whispered, swelling with secondhand pride. Afterward, as we wandered onto the sidewalk and toward a nearby bar, it began to rain. "This weather feels like home," Caleb said, and I leaned in the direction of his accent as cold drops slashed through the sky and onto the sidewalk.

In the bar, as our Pacificos dripped condensation and rain droplets slid down the window, I complained about my fluffy, humidified hair. Caleb wrapped my curls around his index finger and said he liked the way it expanded in the rain, like steam rising. Soon after his declaration, I stopped straightening my hair into submission.

Eventually he untangled his index finger and put his Pacifico down on the table. "So, I should probably tell you that my ex-girlfriend emailed me a few days ago," he said. "I haven't seen her in, I dunno, almost a year—last time she was crying so hard we had to leave the café."

My fingers twitched against the glass. "What—what did the email say?"

"Nothing interesting. She asked how I've been and suggested we meet to catch up. I'll probably write back, say something short. But"—and here he held my gaze, searching, perhaps, for permission, or for gratitude—"I don't think I'm going to see her."

"What do you mean? *See* her how? Like when you go home over Christmas?"

He shook his head. "No, she's here. In New York. An American, like you. She studied abroad at St Andrews, that's where we met, but she went to NYU."

My abandoned drink sweat onto the bar. "We've known each other nearly six months and you're telling me this *now*?"

"Well, I thought it was in the past! We weren't in contact until this email, literally yesterday—"

"I could've passed her on the *street* and had absolutely no clue!"

He looked stricken. "I'm sorry! I never meant to hide it or anything."

A St Andrews girlfriend was mentioned a handful of times, true—as was, of course, the *emotional rush* following their breakup—but I'd assumed his ex was safely locked in the past, overseas, with an accent similar to his. A sound he would find ordinary. He never mentioned moving across the ocean to be with her.

But now I knew. Greedy, I shook him down for more details.

"She's actually in publishing," he said. "A big reader, like you."

It was even more likely now that we had been in the same room. "Omigod, what does she do? Where does she work?"

"You know, shocker of shockers, I'd rather not talk about her anymore," he said. "We were having such a good night. I don't want this to ruin it."

I allowed his deflection—for the time being—but wondered if

neglecting to give his ex a name meant Caleb didn't trust me enough yet, or meant he wanted to keep this part of his history—her—to himself. Or maybe to show I was real, and she was only a category: as in math, she had joined a set. Ex-life. But I wanted, desperately, to know her name.

Why, a year after their breakup, did she suddenly have more to say? I wondered how many drafts she wrote and rewrote before sending the email to Caleb. Were her sentences short and staccato, or long, self-justifying, and dreamy? How many times did she use the word *we*? Did she use exclamation points (dumb) or semicolons (pretentious)?

"Why'd you break up?" I asked.

"Pressure, I guess," he said. "After dating long distance for two years, we always knew one of us would have to move. I was finishing up my master's in London at the time, so we were choosing between our two cities."

"So why didn't she join you in London?" I would've jumped at the chance to start fresh elsewhere, especially with someone I loved. The beginning of a great story.

"She said she had stronger ties to her home than I had to mine. It might've been true, I dunno. Once I got a job and a visa, it happened fast—she worked hard to fit me into her life. I worked hard, too, but I wasn't happy. I don't know why, but I wasn't. And she hated my unhappiness; she couldn't understand it. We were apart for so many years, and then we were finally together, and we were supposed to be so . . . so happy."

He flicked some fuzz off his jeans. "I started feeling like the things I said or did were never what she wanted from me. But I still loved her, and she still loved me, and that was the most confusing part."

His use of the word *loved* felt heavy, like a suitcase dragged behind him. I wondered if, not when, he would be able to open the suitcase again. And if he would want my help.

"She wants me to do more, be more, than what I am, but I can't," he said.

I felt a twinge below my rib cage as his tense changed from past to present. "You've never considered getting back together?"

Caleb took too long to reply, and in those few endless seconds, I anticipated being told I was only a placeholder, the next-best-thing, a necessary bridge between their past and their future. No one upends their entire life for someone they don't see a serious future with; there's no way he's just going to *give up*—

"No, of course not," said Caleb, intertwining our fingers.

My heartbeat thumped inside my palms as I realized—with a jolt of nauseous vertigo—that a small or perhaps not so small part of me had *wanted* to be told, definitively, that I was inadequate, because then it would be okay to put a stop to it, to dial back all the inherent risk involved in loving.

"I'm invested in us now, Naomi," Caleb continued to insist. "Don't you know that?"

Swallowing thick mucus that had built up in my throat, I nodded.

Then Caleb pulled my hips toward him, and we kissed for a little while.

"But it's funny, though, isn't it," I said, pulling away, "how I'm the same type of woman?"

The grooves above his eyebrows deepened. "Because you're both, I don't know, into books?"

Miraculously, I laughed. "Yeah, silly, we're both *into books*."

"To be honest," said Caleb, "you're not alike at all."

Unprepared for this, I immediately began wondering how and why—and if that was good or bad. To confront and then squash my own paranoia, I realized I would need to do some research.

Later that night, with Caleb asleep in my bed, I sat at the kitchen table and opened my computer. Using the information he'd revealed, I typed a jumble of nouns into Google: "St Andrews, publishing, New York University." I sifted through names and faces on Facebook until I hit the jackpot: a photo of a woman standing next to Caleb—my Caleb.

Rosemary Pierce.

The thickness of our eyebrows, the wavy auburn hair, the pear-shaped hips, the *books*—but perhaps it was true our similarities ended there. How could a Naomi Ackerman compete with a Rosemary Pierce? Her name felt smooth and tasted sweet. I pursed my lips to utter it. I was so kissable, mouthing her name.

The publishing house she worked for was listed in her Facebook profile—she was an editor at a major imprint, requiring her to cart stacks of manuscripts home on the subway. The reason for her tote. Meanwhile I sat at a bookstore register most days, selling books with sentences Rosemary might have edited—different links in the same chain. But Rosemary's link in that chain was unquestionably superior.

Aside from a few more basic details (including her birthday, May 29, '91, which made her Caleb's age, twenty-seven, three years older than me—*and* a Gemini, which felt significant), her privacy settings were otherwise airtight. I could only access three of her profile pictures. In the current one, Rosemary posed with an older woman—her mother, as revealed by the caption—in front of the Grand Canyon, a place I had never visited. In the second, uploaded around the same time as her breakup, Rosemary was the only flash of auburn in a group of blondes; all had their arms around one another on a rooftop somewhere in Brooklyn, backlit by a sunset (purple) with glasses of white wine aloft. So basic.

In those two photos, her lips pressed together and curved upward only at the corners—but in the third photo, uploaded a year after she met Caleb, Rosemary stood tucked under his arm in a purple graduation gown, her mouth blurry white as if in the process of showing a rare openmouthed grin. He wore a charcoal suit, and although his hair was shorter, his face was unmistakable. They stood under the arch in Washington Square Park, bursting with joy and pride as if they alone had built it. He must have flown to New York specifically to celebrate her.

It hurt to imagine it. I was surprised by how much.

Next, I managed to find and read the archived Tumblr blog Rosemary kept while abroad. I wanted to know if she boarded her flight to the UK with the same naïve hopes I had when I flew to study abroad in Australia—irrevocable change, upheaval, a story worthy of being told.

She began her blog writing about the scenery—moors and mist—and about her literature courses before eventually veering into romantic territory by describing a certain Welshman who lived next door in her residential college. From that post on, the blog detailed only the café she and Caleb frequented; the pub they sat in for hours when it rained; the secret, hidden passageways around St Andrews that Caleb shared with her; and the surrounding Fife countryside—Anstruther, Elie, Edinburgh—where they *frolicked* (Rosemary's word) on weekends. Her prose, though sharp and clean and rigorous, lacked a certain singularity of voice. This knowledge was a relief. Although she was clearly intelligent and well-read and could string sentences together far better than most humans, she certainly wasn't a writer, at least not in the way *I* was; writers have *voices*.

I scrolled through the blog for hours. But as Rosemary's abroad experience stretched on, relationship descriptions got increasingly spare until the day they ran out altogether. Was her daily life simply too good to be captured? What began as a story, worthy of being told, became real. Caleb exceeded the expectations of her fantasies.

Thrown into crisis mode, I began to mentally restructure. Needing something (or someone) new to write about, I had chosen the newness of love. (I was experienced with and quite good at writing about rejection; the two stories I'd published so far were angsty and depressing—but relatable, too, according to strangers on the Internet.) Since love is supposedly a universal human experience, and writers are often encouraged to *write what we know*, I hoped to undergo it at least once. When Caleb offered to bring soup to my sickbed back in July, I'd thought, *This is it*, surely before long I'll know. I already sensed it growing inside me—looking directly into Caleb's eyes had begun making me feel like I was about to either laugh or faint, what else could it mean?—but now I was being confronted by a different story, perhaps even a parallel one, that had nothing to do with me at all. What I'd imagined was rare and special—a Welsh mathematician and a bookish New Yorker! with nearly nothing in common! becoming inexplicably drawn to each other!—was actually a pattern of his, and I slotted right in. A duplicate.

How could I rewrite our story, reclaiming it as mine?

Clicking around the Internet's bowels, I found Rosemary's Instagram account. It proved difficult to access, locked and private as it was. My account was public. I knew Privates sometimes looked down on Publics, assuming a shameless need for validation, but private accounts, one could easily argue, smack of elitism, exclusivity; was it wrong that I liked being scrolled into existence by a stranger, rebuilt inside their head?

The morning after finding her Facebook, I vaulted into action. As customers trickled in and out of the store, I sat behind the cash register and created an anonymous Instagram account called @Language_and_Liquid. It would feature photos of coffee and books. I skulked around the shelves in search of a generic, unidentifiable backdrop for my first shot. The bookstore was warehouse-chic, high-ceilinged with exposed brick. Six shelves of fiction and nonfiction stretched along the back wall, but the rest of the space was occupied by wooden tables piled high with fragrant candles, literary-themed mugs, fridge magnets, greeting cards, coloring books for anxious adults. When I was safely ensconced in an empty aisle, I positioned my iced dirty chai on the shelf and took a few artfully angled photos. After applying the Gingham filter, I uploaded with book-related hashtags (#bookstagram #bookblogger #booklover). After forty-five minutes, I gained thirty-seven new followers. Now the account looked legitimate, and harmless, enough to request Rosemary. (Since she identified herself as a "book editor" in her bio, it shouldn't come as a surprise.)

I put my phone out of reach, facedown, so I wouldn't be tempted to check every few minutes, and used the desktop computer to find, on the publisher's website, an abbreviated list of books Rosemary had edited. I Googled them all, tracking her tastes.

When my coworker Luna arrived for her shift, I took my lunch break at the pizza place across the street. I bit into a slice and checked Instagram and saw Rosemary had accepted my request. Down went the pizza. I wiped my greasy fingers and scrolled into

Rosemary's past. After quick calculations, I realized posts to her grid were more infrequent than my own—on average, every other month rather than every other week. It was possible her life wasn't as interesting as mine (unlikely), but it was also possible she had less to prove.

Searching for signs of Caleb, my cramping fingers spotted cocktails geo-tagged at various bars in Manhattan and Brooklyn and concerts spread evenly across several of the same music venues Caleb and I now frequented together.

I finally found Caleb facing the ocean on a desolate stretch of West Sands Beach. Gray skies. His winter coat didn't look warm enough. The upload was six years ago—the conclusion of Rosemary's year at St Andrews, and only weeks before she returned to New York to commence the phase of missing him. Someone named Marianne had commented: hope you two are having a lovely time! Someone named Elizabeth had added: you better stop in London on your way back to the States xx. The photo's caption read, aptly melancholy soundtrack for our final weekend: "Loch Lomond" by @runrig. It felt like a suggestion, so I put my headphones in and navigated to YouTube. A man sang, *You'll take the high road and I'll take the low road, and I'll be in Scotland afore you.* I imagined Rosemary and Caleb holding hands on drizzly roads or St Andrews parks or windy beaches, her putting a finger on equations in his notebook and asking what he intended to solve.

They were ripening into characters I could write down, and use, and maybe even keep. After all, I'd never intended to safeguard any fragment of my life from narrative scrutiny; everything was up for grabs and could be transcribed, disguised as Story. Their history was part of my history now; we overlapped. By writing something new, all three of us would be revived, recast, in our roles.

And so, for the next two weeks, I familiarized myself with Rosemary. For every scrap of information scrounged up online, I sweated through my sheets. But copious hours of screen-time grew insufficient; I wanted to be close, to breathe the same air.

And so: the breath mint, the tote bag, her denim jacket brushing against my elbow.

And so: all that came after.

chapter two

SEVERAL HOURS HAVE passed since I followed Rosemary into the café and spoke to her for the first time. The beginning of a story—though I'm not yet sure of its narrative arc. I replay the encounter in my head as I drift among Caleb's colleagues at a bar on the Lower East Side.

Drunk or sober, they speak a distinct language: insured loss calculations, probabilistic models, wind speed, storm surge, event generation.

Caleb's colleagues angle their limbs to welcome me into their circles and squares, but I still wonder if they preferred Rosemary's presence at happy hours. Do they compare us and find me lacking?

I take Caleb's hand and interlace our fingers. He glances down with some surprise—usually he's the one to take mine as I cling to him, brimming with gratitude. Before Caleb, I never held hands with anyone.

After three Brooklyn Lagers, Caleb enters a heated argument about politics. I hear the words *Brexit* and *Trump* a few times, but

I'm hardly listening. (What are most of us prepared to *do* other than wax poetic about how monstrous Trump is? Probably nothing—it's pathetic; we're all pathetic.) But still, this is the first time I've heard Caleb properly raise his voice. I like that he can, but it doesn't suit him—he usually speaks so softly that I need to put my ear near his mouth, always desiring to listen. To prove I deserve to be told.

Later that night, on the subway from the bar to my apartment, I attempt as casually as possible to unearth more information. "So, I have another question about Rosemary."

Startled, his head turns toward me. "How do you know her name?"

Fuck, clearly not casual enough. I realize, too late, that he has only ever referred to her as "my ex." I somehow still manage to look sheepish and innocent.

"Oh, um, I looked her up. I was curious which publishing house she worked for." I stroke the skin between his thumb and forefinger. "Is that weird? I hope it's not weird. It's pretty normal to be curious."

He picks at the scruff on his chin and lets his hands fall into his lap. "It's fine. I just didn't know you were still thinking about it. What's your question?"

"What happens if you're both invited to the same party?"

He lets out a bark of laughter, as if I've said something blatantly absurd. "We don't have any friends in common, Naomi, at least not in New York. We hung out with *her* friends on weekends, but I didn't fit in—especially not with the guys. I couldn't quite pull off their particular brand of American humor. I believe the term is *bro-y*." He cracks a weak smile. "So when we broke up, no one took sides—they were already on hers. My social life revolves entirely around work happy hours now—and you, of course." He looks at me. "You're my best friend."

Unprepared for candor or vulnerability, I'm rendered momentarily speechless and manage only to kiss the knuckles of his right hand. Communicating, hopefully, a mutuality.

Then I pass him an earbud so we can listen to the same music. "It's on shuffle," I say, even though it isn't. I warm him up with a few Mount Kimbie songs, and when his head begins to bob, I tilt the screen toward me and click on "Loch Lomond" by Runrig. I search his face as the music plays, but nothing is revealed.

"Ooh thanks, Shuffle Gods." I gesture toward the ceiling, the sky, the heavens, whatever will help me stick the landing. "I love this band. Sorry if the song makes you homesick, though. Do you know it?"

Caleb must be exasperated by but also accustomed to my constant need to nudge him at any mention of the UK, but since he never explicitly communicates his exasperation, I haven't stopped.

"Well yeah," he says. "It's famous."

Unable to elicit more of a reaction, I switch to something upbeat and try to capture his gaze. It's elusive. He yawns and closes his eyes and doesn't open them for the whole ride home. I stare at my reflection in the subway car's dark, dirty window instead.

We get off at West Fourth and move through the darkness toward my brownstone. In the hallway outside my apartment, I don't put the key in the lock. I yank my tights down instead, shoving my dress aside. Caleb's mouth falls open in surprise, but his fingers know to move instinctively toward the place where I'm already wet.

This isn't a moment to be cautious. Bending over, I silently count some of the riskier places we've done it: a secluded section of River-side Park in swampy August darkness; the handicapped bathroom at a concert venue; the trailhead of a Hudson Valley hike we took in September after I rented a cherry-red Zipcar and drove us north. After the hike and the sex—pants around his ankles, my palms pressed against tree bark—I plucked a hungry tick off Caleb's calf with tweezers, its globular body engorged with blood.

In bed, Caleb usually initiates sex by putting his mouth between my legs—it occurs to me now that Rosemary might have taught him this. But was she ever as spontaneous or adventurous as me when initiating sex? Was she louder? Quieter? Did she prefer lying beneath him, or straddling him, or moving onto her hands and knees? Did she disassociate with the men who came before him, and had he pointed it out to her, too? Or was she the one who demanded more from him, who changed the way he knew how to love?

I've known Caleb for six months, and neither of us has uttered *I love you* yet. Each morning I search the contours of my body for signs that I might finally be in love, as if checking for bumps or bruises.

I will become worthy of love, and well-equipped to describe it.

Caleb is capable of the kind of love I want—he crossed an ocean. Can it happen again for him on the same magnitude? Do I have to leave? Does he have to follow?

DANIELLE BRINGS PIZZA to my apartment after work. Once we each demolish our first slice, she asks how Caleb and I are doing. *I like him for you,* she said a few weeks ago. *He's sweet, such a calming presence. You need that.*

I do need that.

I need a lot of things.

"We're doing well," I say, lips covered in pizza grease.

Danielle and I have always talked about men too much when we're together. After forty minutes or so, one of us always says something like, "Fuck men, let's talk about something important." Then we discuss our ambitions and our families. Eventually, though, we end up talking about men again.

"How's your writing coming along?" Danielle asks, reaching for a second slice. A glob of cheese slides off and plops onto wax paper.

This is the part when we talk about our ambitions.

"I finally have an idea for a novel! I'm pretty excited about it."

"What's it about?" She pops the rogue glob of cheese into her mouth.

I make some quick calculations. To tell the truth, or—

Danielle has always believed in me. By all accounts, she is a very good friend. We met during our first week of college in Colorado and ultimately bonded over feeling so suddenly out of our league. As native New Yorkers who yearned to escape the city, we liked the outdoors, but not enough to sleep in tents and shit in holes and toss bear bags into trees during backpacking trips. We weren't compelled enough, either, to join hard-core skiers or rock climbers on their adventures. Instead, we took Danielle's green Subaru Outback on day-trips to Garden of the Gods or Cheyenne Mountain or Red Rock Canyon Open Space, where we would walk and talk for hours about what the ideal version of our lives would look like once we graduated and moved back to New York and became who we felt we were destined to be: a writer, an actress. We thought it would be seamless, becoming these ideal versions of ourselves, though I suppose out of some sort of kindness (or was it fear of puncturing our shared idealism?) I resisted reminding her how Noah, despite early accolades and obvious talent, was still forced to wait in windowless audition rooms with dozens of boys who looked exactly like him.

I've always believed in my own future. But I'm not sure, yet, how to bridge the gap. So far I have only two publications and a few pages of a novel to my name, while Danielle works as a dental receptionist with no roles, other than a few college productions, on her résumé.

Danielle has always believed in me, yes, and I can trust her, true, but I'm painfully aware of how the premise of my novel will sound. And so I bend the truth, just a little: she'd surely try to dissuade me, and just as surely fail. Why would I want my best friend to worry, or to feel singularly responsible for pulling me away from the edge?

So I experiment by reversing the roles. Wouldn't it be funny if it turned out Rosemary was obsessed with me, too? Our obsessions would cancel each other out—becoming forgivable, inoffensive.

"It's about a woman who becomes obsessed with her ex-boyfriend's new girlfriend. I know it's not the most original idea ever, but—"

She cuts me off. "Is it, like, a horror novel?"

"Are you asking if anyone gets murdered?"

"That's exactly what I'm asking."

"No murders! Unless I need to spice things up."

"I always vote in favor of spice." She points at the space between my eyebrows. "You've always had so many stories in there. What inspired this one?"

I adopt a nonchalance. "Well, so, Caleb mentioned his ex-girlfriend to me recently, and apparently she lives in *Brooklyn*, not in Wales or London or Scotland, like I thought. I sort of—freaked out a little."

"Oh, shit."

"Exactly. So ironically, to self-soothe, I started spitballing possible plots, like—what if she was still in love with Caleb and tried to sabotage us?"

"Well, sabotage can be juicy," says Danielle. "At least you're not working on another story about that jazz drummer."

"Okay, um, rude, those got published—"

"I know, they were good, but he shows up in *all* your stories; you've probably milked him dry by now."

For so long Adam the jazz drummer was my only source of material; I hadn't experienced much else. But I never told the truth, not really. From now on, I'm going to tell more truthful stories—but if I need to lie to dig up something true, so be it.

A true thing, to start: I live in this Greenwich Village one-bedroom apartment for free. My grandmother bought the brownstone in the late 1970s; she has always rented out the first- and second- and third-floor apartments, keeping the fourth empty as a workspace separate from the apartment she lived in. My grandmother remains the original writer in my family—three syndicated television shows and a memoir, *Laugh Medicine*, released by a big publisher—but here I am, trying to be the next one.

"Okay, new narratives," I say. "New narratives only."

"Promise?" Danielle holds out a pinky. "I told myself I wouldn't enable any more unhealthy behavior."

I tear off a cuticle as the phrase *unhealthy behavior* sinks in, then curl my pinky around hers.

Next I change the subject by asking Danielle about her boss, the dentist; she scoffs and relays an anecdote about his insufferable probe-related innuendos. Midway through, I excuse myself to pee.

On the toilet, I watch Rosemary's Instagram Story. Two minutes ago, she photographed her cocktail, smoky orange as if on fire. In the background, a few hands, someone's collarbone. It looks like a group: work colleagues blowing off steam or a birthday celebration. The location is geo-tagged: a bar in Gowanus. I calculate the route, imagining she will be there at least a couple of hours longer. It's too late for happy hour. This must be Rosemary's last stop before bed.

Danielle is scrolling through her own Instagram feed when I return. Avocado toast, glossy actors' headshots, sunset beaches fly underneath her fingertips. It makes me nauseous.

I approach the kitchen sink and splash cold water on my face. "Let's go out!" I say, still dripping. Despite Danielle's admonition, the evening I've planned doubles as research; I have it fully under control.

Danielle folds forward, laying her head on the table dramatically. "Can't we just camp out here with a bottle of wine?"

"Out of the question. It's a Friday! Soon we'll be old. Luna told me about a new place in Gowanus, apparently they make amazing cocktails."

"Ugh, okay, fine." Danielle opens my booze cabinet, extracts a flask, and fills it with gin. "Speaking of going out, my weird roommates are throwing a Halloween party at our place next weekend. Please come?"

Danielle lives with two Craigslist roommates—a graphic designer and a freelance filmmaker—in Crown Heights. They're peculiar and stingy, but not unkind.

"Can't you skip it?"

"No way, I need to supervise and make sure no one, like, trashes my room or anything. But we can celebrate your birthday! Caleb is obviously invited, too."

A true Scorpio, I turn twenty-five on October 29. "All right. I'm in."

"You're the *best*," she says, tucking the flask inside her bra.

We pass it between us on the subway, though I drink most of it. Emerging into the cool autumn air, I don't know how to assemble my features before walking into the bar. Everything is happening too fast. I wish, suddenly, that Danielle wasn't with me. But I need someone to cling to.

Lights are low, tinged with pink and orange. The music is loud, bass-thumping. We wriggle through a multitude of bodies to order a drink, and I'm grateful it's crowded enough to make slow decisions.

I locate the bathroom, and then I locate Rosemary—squeezed between two other people on a bench, her back pressed against the window. She's wearing a cropped turtleneck, forest green. Turtlenecks never flatter me, but she looks great.

I hover behind a bulky man and sip a gin and tonic. When Danielle starts flirting with the bulky man, I'm free to focus on Rosemary.

Unlike me, she doesn't clutch her cocktail like a lifeline. She sips and puts the glass down, allowing for rest. I tend to drink too fast—eager to become the playful, chatty woman everyone thinks I am.

Rosemary doesn't open her mouth for several minutes. She must be the good listener, the person her friends call when they need to vent. But what if Rosemary needs someone to vent to? I could become that person, for her.

Soon Rosemary stands and strides toward the bathroom. I duck my head, fishing inside my purse for a tube of lipstick. When my fingers close around it, I toss a quick, guilty glance over my shoulder to check on Danielle. She and the bulky man are engaged in a spirited conversation I can't hear over the bass as his hand presses against the small of her back. She allows his touch, which means she's into him, and so I feel better about slinking away.

As I enter the bathroom, Rosemary's shoes—brown suede boots with a two-inch heel—are visible under the stall door. Simple but sexy.

The toilet flushes. My cue. I lift the lipstick to my mouth and lean toward the face in the mirror. Slowly I paint my lips red. Rosemary approaches the row of sinks and turns both faucets, hot and cold, to achieve the perfect temperature.

I smear, intentionally, the lipstick. Some of it gets on my teeth. "Damn," I say. "I always fuck this up."

Other women might smile politely, might ignore the sad girl applying lipstick incorrectly in the bar bathroom and talking to herself about it, but maybe because Rosemary is drunk, or because she is kind, or because she was once a sad girl in a bathroom applying lipstick incorrectly, she speaks to me: "Whenever I put on lipstick I always feel like I'm ten again, playing dress-up in my mother's clothes."

There's a silver hoop in her nose. How have I not noticed before? Maybe she doesn't wear it to work for fear of appearing unprofessional.

"I was obsessed with this absurd shade of purple eyeliner in high school," I offer. "I looked like a clown."

As Rosemary lathers soap on her knuckles and turns to face me, I brace myself. How might she react if she suddenly recognizes me from the café? Might she—struck by a justifiable suspicion—choose fight or flight?

We make eye contact. Her irises are a startling shade of green.

"We can blame all those ridiculous instructions in *Cosmo*," she says, smiling at me.

"So true, they're always like *How to give yourself sexy cat eyes!* and *How to master these seven quickie positions!* and—" I clam up, frozen and horrified; did I just utter the word *quickie* aloud to my boyfriend's ex? Oh. My. Go—

But then Rosemary laughs, appearing surprised and charmed and wary and intrigued all at once. "A true bastion of arts and letters," she says. "And indisputably the best mag to read on airplanes."

I rush to agree. "Oh, totally!"

There's a brief pause in which only the running water makes a sound. As Rosemary finishes washing her hands and turns off the faucet, I sense our conversation has come to an end; she's about to leave. I have only one fleeting chance to keep her here. "This might sound crazy," I say, "but I have a weird feeling I know you from somewhere."

She crumples a paper towel in her hands. "Really?"

"Yeah, I'm not positive, but you look really familiar."

I want to say: *We've shared the same man. He once touched you there, and there. He will touch me tonight here, and here.*

"You know, I get that a lot, so either I'm an incredibly generic person or this is classic projection and you're just seeing what you want to see." Rosemary regards herself in the mirror, as if to confirm or deny.

"No!" I practically shout, then recalibrate; I wasn't expecting her to get all weird and philosophical. "Not generic, I mean, sorry, it's just—I work at a bookstore in Brooklyn. Tons of people pass through and usually their faces blur together, but I remember yours."

Rosemary's eyes are narrowing, so quickly I offer an approachable, nonthreatening laugh. "I'm sorry if this all sounds really creepy!"

"A little creepy," she admits. "But I work in publishing, so I've definitely shown my face at every bookstore in the city. Which is yours?"

"Lit House."

Rosemary brightens. "Oh, I love that place, I think one of my authors actually has a launch there soon."

I make a mental note to immediately check our events calendar, which I rarely do. Luna usually reminds me, often the morning of the event, which author we'll be hosting later that night.

The paper towel finally goes into the bin as Rosemary reaches for the door handle. "My friends are probably wondering where I am, so I should head back out."

"Shit, yeah, me too." A part of me hopes Danielle left with the bulky man, because I got what I came for, and I'll feel less guilty if she got something, too. "I guess I'll see you at the bookstore sometime soon."

"You probably will! Oh, and I'm Rosemary, by the way."

Relief rushes in. I no longer need to worry about accidentally saying her name before we've been properly introduced. "I'm Naomi."

"Nice to meet you, Naomi. Hope you have a good night!"

"You too!" The door swings closed, and I put a finger on my teeth, rubbing the red away.

Rosemary has reclaimed her spot on the bench by the time I exit the bathroom, and she doesn't look up when I walk by. I recognize the two blond women beside her from a Facebook photo: white wine, rooftop, purple sunset.

I scan the bar for Danielle but don't spot her.

Checking my phone, I register several missed texts. Ten minutes ago: **Where are you?** Four minutes ago: **Well, wherever you are, that guy invited me to get another drink elsewhere. Sorry to bail, but turns out he's in casting. I hate myself and this stupid business, but a girl's gotta hustle. I'll see you at the party next weekend, yes? Come early! And please respond so I know you're not dead in a ditch somewhere.**

Ahh sorry, no not dead, just felt a bit sick in the bathroom, I reply. **Break a leg schmoozing! Aren't you glad I dragged you out?**

Leaving the bar, I cross the street and stand on the opposite corner. From this vantage point I can watch all the blurry bodies moving in circles and squares. The bodies are all trying to make something happen, trying to find what is missing.

Calling Caleb while staring at the back of Rosemary's head through the window feels risky. I enjoy it. The phone rings, and Rosemary's forest-green turtleneck glows brighter, like a neon sign behind the glass. Maybe Rosemary will sense him; maybe she'll turn around and look at me and know everything all at once. His disembodied voice and her embodied body and then me, somewhere in between.

Caleb answers on the fifth ring. "Hey, you. What's up?"

I watch Rosemary's spine curve as she leans forward toward her friends, still listening hard. More seconds pass. She doesn't turn around.

"I've just left this shitty bar," I say. "The music was so loud, Danielle and I were basically screaming at each other the whole time. I'm on my way home."

"Want me to come over?"

Sometimes he knows exactly what I need. My voice and shoulders soften. "Please."

Waiting on the platform for the express train home, I back-stalk Rosemary's Instagram and discover the nose ring appeared two months after she and Caleb broke up. In my iPhone Notes app, I add to my evolving Rosemary-related document. What kind of impulse prompted the piercing, I type, a sad desperation to move on or a triumphant affirmation of newfound freedom?

Arriving home, I see Caleb before he sees me—sitting on the stoop with a cigarette in his hand, staring vacantly ahead. I once swore I wouldn't date a smoker, but European culture is different, and his connection to the continent is one of the reasons why I plucked him from Tinder.

Before crossing the street and walking over to claim him, I admire Caleb from afar as if he wasn't mine, as if he was someone else's. Then I call his name.

He stomps out his cigarette when he sees me, a goofy smile forming on his face. I've never known a man so pleased to see me. Climbing the steps, I heave my body in his direction and collapse against his chest as he attempts to steady my shoulders. We stumble back against the front door.

"Are you drunk?" he asks.

"No," I say, laughing. "Just happy."

Later, after sex, he peels himself off and reaches for my hand. One of us should say something, initiate pillow talk, but we don't. With a twinge of panic, I imagine a different scene—Caleb and Rosemary engaged in spirited conversation, flowing effortlessly from one topic to the other. Enthralled by each other's way of seeing the world.

To crowd out these thoughts, I start up a new conversation—recounting how, during high school, I wrote a short story about kidnapping Daniel Radcliffe. It was actually pretty funny, if I do say so myself, and I plotted how to get Daniel himself to read it. I was obsessed with him in nearly all forms: naked, violent, and deranged onstage in a production of *Equus*; singing and dancing in *How to Succeed in Business Without Really Trying*, and, of course, as Harry Potter. I once thought of asking the security guard outside the *Equus* stage door to pass my short story along to him, though I'm unsure what that would have accomplished other than a restraining order.

"Wow, I don't understand your type at all, we look nothing alike," says Caleb, playfully swatting my nipple. "So when can I read it?"

"Pretty sure it no longer exists, but I have some of it memorized." I close my eyes to remember and recite. *"The plan is simple: you travel to Los Angeles because the websites that stalk Daniel's every move promised he would attend a fancy premiere. You stake him out from a tree. Climbing the tree is a bitch; you scrape your shins and knees. Your binoculars form a reddish tinge around your eyes, like a rabid raccoon. Your hair frizzes a little, which upsets you, because it was styled in a fancy salon to prepare for the Big Moment. You're wearing makeup. It's a little excessive, but you want to dazzle him."* I pause to search his face for signs of derision and—despite finding none—add: "I know the writing is a bit juvenile, but I was sixteen!"

In reciting it, perhaps an unconscious part of me hoped to craft my own defense, to explain that all my obsessions have only ever been, will only ever be, in the service of art, and so—

"You're a nutcase," Caleb says, laughing. "But I love it."

As a reward for my storytelling, he scrapes his fingernails up and down my back until my whole body goes slack and soft and malleable. I recently told him my mother scratched me like this during childhood to send me to sleep and that I'm conditioned now to crave its relief. Caleb must have listened and absorbed this information because his scratching has escalated, extending to my scalp and arms and rib cage. It's strange and wonderful, and I hope it never stops. Only a few scratches later, it occurs to me that one of the characters Daniel Radcliffe played onstage was also in love with a woman named Rosemary.

Go figure. A romantic name for a romantic lead. I roll over and kiss Caleb, trying to blot her out.

But Rosemary never stays blotted out. Whenever she posts a new Instagram Story, whenever the circle enclosing her profile photo thickens and flames pink, I breathe in and then breathe out, trying to wait a few more hours before clicking on and viewing it, but I can never restrain myself. I self-flagellate for this impatience of mine, this impulsivity; I have twenty-four hours to work with, after all; the best time to view would be thirteen, fourteen hours after she posts it; that way her eye won't be immediately drawn to unfamiliar accounts. Does she notice the quickness and rabidity with which @Language_and_Liquid watches her Story after only fifty-one seconds have elapsed, or is she accustomed to harmless bookish strangers keeping assiduous tabs? How likely is it that she'll perform some detective work?

It's just social media, I reassure myself. *It's not that invasive; she clearly isn't selective when it comes to approving new followers, anyway.*

Still, paranoia manifests as a deep throbbing in my lower back. I don't think it's possible for anyone to trace my fake Instagram account to my real one—I haven't linked any personal information—but I truly can't be certain. I live on the edge of knowing.

———

WE'VE ALREADY SEEN Noah's musical five times, but my family and I manage to snag tickets for the final performance of its Broadway run. There's an after party at Times Square's Copacabana nightclub, of all places, and I've been invited instead of our parents—the latter would be "insufferably uncool," according to Noah. I'm wearing an ankle-length sky-blue gown for the occasion, my eyelids flecked with gold. A silver necklace rests, cold, against my throat.

During Noah's big solo in the second act, I sneak a sideways glance at my mother's expression. Pride mingling with pain. She auditioned for dozens of Broadway shows throughout her twenties, standing on open-call lines in bad weather at six a.m., but despite her talent and her many callbacks, she never booked a role. I suspect that's why she chose to write her own music, form her own rock band, and play gigs all over New York as the band's lead singer. She was creating another life for herself. But she hasn't composed anything new in a long time. Now she primarily fills her days with Pilates, farmer's markets, coffee dates with repressed suburbanites; she has become the type of woman she once, perhaps unfairly, scorned. Occasionally, though, when visiting my parents for a holiday or long weekend, I'll hear my mother belting some of her old ballads. Blended with the piano, her voice remains one of my favorite sounds—reminiscent of childhood, and safety, and warmth. But I never let my mother notice me lurking in the threshold, listening, unwilling to disturb this rare (and becoming rarer still) communion with her keys. I could ask why she stopped, but I'd rather not know. I'm fearful the same paralysis or blockage might rub off on me, too.

During Noah's bow at curtain call, I applaud as explosively as my parents, and after hugging them goodbye, I navigate to the stage door to give the security guard my name. Blowing on my hands to warm them, I watch giggling sixteen-year-old girls and fanatical adults line up, Playbills dangling, behind the metal barriers separating the fans from the stars, the sisters from the brothers. The selfie Noah posted to Instagram—in his dressing room, costume still on—less than ten minutes ago to commemorate "the end of an era" (his caption) has already acquired hundreds of likes. His twelve thousand followers are dedicated and diverse, prone to heart-eye emojis and impassioned pleas for a response to their DMs. His fan base has been accumulating for years—Noah's big break came when he booked the singing voice of a cartoon character at age nine. *The Playground Pals* was a sleeper hit for children and adults alike, the latter enjoying the dirty jokes that flew over the former's heads. But his fan base is on the verge of exploding into even more epic proportions, given that he recently booked a particularly juicy recurring role (two episodes, eight lines) in the second season of the teen dramedy *Ghosts Among Us.*

Despite a shelf weighed down by theater awards (Outer Critics Circle, Drama Desk, even a fraction of a Grammy for a Broadway cast album), Noah spent the last few years coveting the elusive film or television role, desperate to prove himself again and again and again. But rejections flowed thick and fast for a while. The business of art invites an unfavorable ratio, and so we share the need to keep striving, despite me not yet reaching even the bottom rung of my imagined ladder. The day before Noah's callback for *Ghosts Among Us*, he asked me to help him run lines. I've always relished playing different parts: prosecutor, detective, murderer, mother. With someone's else words—someone else's life—in my mouth, I briefly become someone else.

The day after his callback, he booked the role. Every day since, I've practiced feeling happy for him, practiced smiling so wide my jaw aches, practiced my rhythmic wild applause.

After the security guard finally permits my entry through the stage door, I sense dozens of envious eyes piercing my back. Noah greets me in a tuxedo, looking frazzled, and asks if I can help carry his stuff. His dressing room is in the basement, which smells damp and sour. Taped to his mirror are a collection of remarkably detailed colored-pencil drawings depicting scenes from his musical.

"Whoa, these are really good." How is he allowed to be good at more than one thing?

The tips of his ears flame red. "Nah, they're embarrassing. I just drew them to pass the time between scenes."

I shrug and continue to collect his scattered items—stage makeup, headphones, a tin of throat lozenges—for safekeeping in my purse. A few minutes later, when he peels the drawings off the mirror and folds them carefully inside his backpack, I pretend not to notice.

On our way back to the stage door, we climb narrow winding staircases, sweep past coiffed wigs and nineteenth-century hoop skirts, and eventually find ourselves on the stage. The emptiness echoes. I walk to the edge and gaze at the thousands of red velvet chairs. What must it be like to stand here, dead center, and convince everyone out there I deserve their undivided attention?

"Yo, come on!" Noah calls. "I'm already running late."

Exiting, we're overwhelmed by an eruption of noise from behind the metal barricades. Feeling awkward and out of place, I skitter sideways out of the line of fire. They didn't come for me. I wait on the curb, watching him sign autographs and pose for pictures and accept praise until he finally reaches the end of the line.

"Such a *star*," I say as we walk to the Copacabana. "Hashtag *famous*." I never intended to mock him, but here we are.

"You know it," he replies, but it comes out dully and distant. When we arrive four blocks later, I can sense his relief, can sense my own.

Inside the entrance, there's a red-carpet step-and-repeat. After Noah hisses at me, I realize I'm supposed to join him. I put a self-conscious hand on my hip as Noah strikes his pose: unsmiling blue eyes narrowed, one hand in his pants pocket. I've seen him practice it in various mirrors, but it still seems an unlikely choice—he's naturally smiley and approachable. When someone barks at me to "lean in," Noah snakes a protective arm around my waist and mouths the word *sister*.

We then move through the glam and boisterous crowd. Occasionally we stop to converse with gorgeous people in gowns. I lurk by Noah's elbow and get mistaken for his younger sister, his girlfriend, his younger sister again. We both laugh, set the record straight. My mother frequently reminds me that looking younger than I am will eventually be a gift.

"Are you an actor, too?" a slender woman asks, glossy and silver-haired in a mink coat.

"I'm a writer," I say, too sharply. A rebuke, or a defense.

"Oh," she says, taking a small but significant step back. "Well, we actors would be lost without our writers."

"Oh, I'm not a playwright. I'm a novelist."

"That's—lovely," she says hesitantly, then strides away.

Noah turns on me. "Jesus, Naomi, what *was* that? You were really rude."

"I wasn't trying to be," I say, already ashamed. "I only answered her question. When I said I wasn't an actress, she wasn't interested anymore."

"Grace is a Broadway legend! She probably needs to make the rounds."

"Whatever, I'll let you network in peace." As I depart for the open bar, I hear Noah's loud, exasperated sigh. I'll apologize later, maybe. Weaving through actors and their overeager guests, I slurp down a glass of sauvignon blanc and load up on sweet potato fries from the buffet table and plant myself in a corner of the room for a quick perusal of Instagram and Facebook. Photos from the after party have already surfaced. I scroll through until I find our faces. Noah Ackerman and guest, reads the caption. We both look beautiful, elegant. My smile seems genuine, not a mask for jealousy. I prefer myself this way.

I shove through the crowd in search of my little brother. I'm his guest. I'm supposed to stay by his side. When I locate him, he's surrounded by well-wishers—giddy, flushed, in his element. I don't want to intrude; I'll wait.

Eventually we find ourselves back in the same corner, people-watching and trading snarky barbs. Noah, who doesn't normally drink, is drunk after one whiskey sour.

"That old guy I was talking to earlier," he says, "is one of my three stalkers. Have I told you about my stalkers yet?"

My skin tingles. "Define *stalker*?"

"These three people who constantly slide into my DMs. One guy even invited me to have a threesome with him and his girl-friend. They just discovered *The Playground Pals* and have been bingeing it, so apparently their kink is cartoon characters?"

"Or boy sopranos," I add.

"Ew, gross."

As we share a laugh, I remember the moment I first realized how witty he'd grown up to be. During my sophomore year of college, a photo on Noah's public Instagram was accompanied by a caption so hilarious I assumed he must have been hacked and decided to send him a cautioning message saying so. No, I'm just funny, he replied.

"So my second stalker is this teenage girl who sends me postcards from random towns with illustrations of my face drawn on," he continues, "and my third stalker, the old guy, is always telling me how much I look like his dead son and how talented he thinks I am and how he's going to follow my career forever because he thinks I'm going to be *big*."

"The important question is"—deadpan but also dead serious—"are you flattered or freaked out?"

"Maybe a bit of both?"

"It must make you feel special, though, right? Like you've *reached* people?" I enunciate each syllable for emphasis; I need him to understand. "I don't think they mean any harm, they don't know you, you're just part of their fantasy narrative."

"That's very writerly of you," he says.

Pleased with this interpretation, I beam at him. It'll serve as my only defense if my own fantasy narrative goes rogue.

When we leave the party, Noah goes to another bar with some castmates and I stumble home in my too-high heels. Halfway there, I send Caleb a selfie. My eyelids are still gold, the silver necklace warmed by the vibrations of my voice. **I am the world's best plus-one**, I write, wanting to make sure he knows.

chapter three

A⸍ᴛ Dᴀɴɪᴇʟʟᴇ's Hᴀʟʟᴏᴡᴇᴇɴ party on Saturday, I show up as one of my favorite fictional characters, Moaning Myrtle, with braids, a tie, knee-high socks, and, of course, a toilet seat encircling my neck—fifteen dollars on Amazon, and much heavier than I anticipated. Caleb, with his pale Welsh features and long dark hair, makes a perfect vampire. Danielle is wearing a crown and a floor-length white gown, its edges drenched in fake blood. A plastic sword dangles loosely from her fingertips.

"Lady Macbeth!" I greet her. "You nailed it."

"And you, my friend, continue to outdo yourself," she says. "This might even beat Regina George post-bus accident."

"Ooh, when was that?" Caleb asks. "Pictures, please, right now."

"Senior year of college." I present a photo of me in a blond wig with the headgear I fashioned from pipe cleaners and cardboard. During that particular Halloween, as Danielle and I drifted from the lacrosse house's Halloween party, to Sigma Chi's, to the all-male acapella group's, I received dozens of high-fives from people

I'd never spoken to before, despite our living and studying along-side each other for years. It was glorious, being celebrated like that.

"That's bloody brilliant," says Caleb, examining the photograph.

I curtsy.

Danielle hands us red cups sloshing with a dark liquid. "From the witch's cauldron," she says, wiggling her eyebrows. "My roommate spent three hours making it, not an exaggeration."

We each take a sip.

"It tastes good," I say.

"Are we supposed to mingle?" Caleb asks.

"Absolutely not," Danielle says.

After a third person slaps my toilet seat, screaming, "Moan, Myrtle, *moan*," Caleb manages to pull me aside into a private corner.

"Thanks for the rescue," I say. "Your fangs are falling out."

He removes them. "I can't speak properly."

"Naughty vamp, are you trying to blend in so as to attack the unaware and defenseless?"

"Ha," he says, straight-faced. "I wanted to ask you, actually, about your birthday. Do you want to do something just the two of us? After you get off work on Monday?"

My chest warms. "Oh. That would be nice!"

I've been waiting for him to suggest something, anything; this will be the first birthday I've celebrated with a boyfriend.

"Great, what do you want to do?"

My expectations plummet. Is it unreasonable to wish he could intuit exactly what I want?

Or is his anxiety to please me, to choose correctly, its own kind of caring?

I suggest Mexican food, our shared favorite.

"Perfect, I'll make dinner reservations somewhere we haven't been yet." He glances at me. "Is that all right?"

I assume he'll eventually tack on flowers or champagne or a birthday card, as I've often done for friends, but all I truly want is the card. Something to keep, not use, which could double forevermore as a love letter. I'll put it in a drawer for that moment when I need reassurance that his feelings for me are real.

I nod my approval of the plan and remember to smile. He kisses me.

"I have to pee," I say. "Be right back."

Locking the bathroom door requires a delicate jiggling of the knob. Once it's secured, I settle onto the toilet and watch the Instagram Story Rosemary posted three hours ago, hoping for a glimpse of her Halloween costume. But instead of uploading an image of herself, she shot a short video of a man elaborately decked out as the Cowardly Lion from *The Wizard of Oz* standing next to one of Rosemary's blond friends dressed as Dorothy. When the lion twirls his long, cream-colored tail around Dorothy's forearm, I hear the sound of Rosemary laughing behind the lens. I imagine, smugly, that she might be third-wheeling a date. Someone knocks insistently on the door. "Hey, sorry, but you've been in there for a while, and I really need—"

"Coming!" I flush and unlock the door for a sweaty-looking Pikachu before reentering the party.

Around one a.m., even though my birthday won't begin for almost twenty-four hours, Danielle drags me into the crush of bodies and orchestrates a rousing, off-key rendition of "Happy Birthday" that includes the line *you smell like a monkey*. Someone I don't know shouts into the crowd: "You mean she smells like a toilet!"

"Oh, *very* clever," I shout back, downing a shot of tequila.

Caleb and I manage to leave the party, which is still going strong, thirtyish minutes later; en route to the subway, we pass a chalkboard outside a bar that reads: BEER COLDER THAN YOUR EX'S HEART, with an arrow pointing inside. "That's funny," I say, nudging him. "And—accurate?"

He keeps his gaze blank, focused ahead. "Not really. I've seen that sign before. Pretty unoriginal."

Unsure if he meant "not really" funny or "not really" accurate, I immediately regret prompting the ghost of Rosemary to reestablish real estate inside his head. An unwise resurrection. Directing Caleb's attention toward the sign was only my attempt to interpret any emotion caught flickering across his face, but amid his resolute blankness, I've deduced absolutely nothing.

THE FOLLOWING NIGHT, a courier buzzes my apartment to announce a champagne delivery. "You little sneak!" I say, turning gleefully toward Caleb.

He blanches. "Erm, I'm sorry, it's not from me."

"Oh!" I fight to remain upbeat. "No worries!"

It turns out to be from my parents. Sweet, but also disappointing.

Likely overcompensating now, Caleb uncorks the bottle a few minutes before midnight with lopsided enthusiasm and pours it into two mugs. (Does anyone my age actually own champagne flutes?)

"To your happiness and good health," he toasts. It's so earnestly formal that I can't help but laugh and forgive his oversight as we clink mugs.

Later, in bed, once his breathing steadies into sleep, I check Facebook notifications on my phone. The friends I made during my semester in Australia were from all over—Perth, Brisbane, Melbourne—as well as from Ecuador and France and Singapore and Spain and the Netherlands. People around the world are waking up, hours ahead in our shared future, and wishing me well.

I'm still feeling too energized to sleep when a text from Luna pops onto my screen. **Happy birthday, you!! I assume you're still awake ringing it in somewhere, but I'm honored to get to spend tomorrow (or technically later today?) with you, drinking the wine that we're definitely supposed to save for the book launch . . . but fuck it!**

The book launch! Bad habits die hard: I frantically pull up our events calendar on Google Docs to confirm, and, yep, there it is. *One of the Herd* by Sarah Hill.

Rosemary's author. The one she mentioned in the bar bathroom. Of course.

The most unexpected of birthday presents—later today, without interference or manipulation, we'll have another chance to speak. Coincidence or fate?

In the morning, Caleb brings me coffee in bed. "With oat milk," he says. "The way you like it."

I cradle it gratefully, squinting through a champagne-induced headache. The bookstore requires my presence in just over half an hour. It's possible to make it on time only if trains run smoothly, which they rarely ever do. I quickly throw on the birthday outfit I planned days before—a black V-neck sweater, black denim miniskirt, tights, and knee-high red suede boots with a small heel. I look pretty fucking good in my full-length mirror and am gratified to know Rosemary will probably think so, too, when she gets a good look at me.

"I'll text you the dinner details once I figure them out," Caleb says.

I manage to squash traces of disappointment about his last-minute plans as I walk out the door.

At work, Luna gives me a red velvet cupcake from the café across the street and lights a lone candle. "The cupcake is Alex's contribution," she says, "but the candle is mine."

The barista at the café across the street has an incurable crush, constantly showering Luna with free pastries. "I'm *shocked* he hasn't gotten fired yet. Isn't this technically, like, larceny?"

"Well, *I'm* shocked he hasn't figured out I'm gay yet. I flirt with his hot coworker right in front of him."

I laugh and redirect my attention toward the burning cupcake.

"I know you want very many things," Luna says. "But try to think carefully about your wish. Don't screw it up."

"Wow, thanks, so supportive." Inhaling, my mouth forms a wide *O*. What should my hierarchy of wants be? Frazzled by Luna's impatient, too-close face and the line of customers that has assembled behind the cash register, I blow without thinking or wishing for anything at all. Maybe what is meant to happen will. Luna applauds, as do some of the customers. I rush to complete their transactions.

When the store temporarily empties out, Luna and I divide between us the necessary tasks for tonight's book launch. Even though it doesn't technically publish until Tuesday, we've been given the green light to sell books a day early.

"The author's whole team is coming tonight," Luna says. "Editor, publicist, et cetera. I hope they aren't all micromanaging control freaks."

Clutching my copy of *One of the Herd*, which I'll carefully stack on top of the others, my hands moisten the book jacket. I rub the sweat off on my tights and resist the urge to confide in Luna, who still resides in that strange limbo between a real friend and a friendly coworker; I can't predict if she'd find my fixation with Rosemary disturbing or entertaining or justified. Vulnerabilities and secrets have been shared, but only during designated work hours and always punctuated by the comforting monotony of our tasks—reorganizing table displays, sweeping the floor, stacking and stapling receipts, choosing an optimally upbeat playlist for profitable browsing.

I turn to the Acknowledgments page, wanting to be jolted: *And finally, I'd like to thank my inimitable editor, Rosemary Pierce, without whom this book would not be in your hands.*

I wish I had more time to prepare for Rosemary's arrival; today I have only a short window in which to make an impression. Caleb just sent me the address of a bougie Mexican restaurant somewhere in Bushwick that we haven't been to yet. **The Times review mentioned mango guacamole**, he wrote.

I fucking love mango guacamole.

"Um, you *do* know that restaurant is run by a bunch of white guys from Florida, right?" says Luna, raising an eyebrow, when I tell her my dinner destination. "*Please* don't pull a Lit Bro and try to order in Spanish."

"I would *never*."

My other coworker, whom I rarely see—he overlaps with Luna on my days off—promised via email to cover the final hours of my shift so I can leave early. Luna doesn't like him very much—

actually, she hates him—and so we've unaffectionately coined him Lit Bro. Lit Bro's favorite authors include Charles Bukowski, David Foster Wallace, Michel Houellebecq, and Jonathan Franzen, and sometimes Lit Bro speaks to Luna using unsolicited Spanish, hoping to "practice" in advance of astonishingly frequent trips to Cancún ("Mistake fares are actually *really cheap!*" he apparently insists).

Luna's dad is Mexican, and her mom is Israeli. She speaks Hebrew, Spanish, and English fluently, two more languages than I can, and apparently celebrated an "iconic" bat mitzvah/quinceañera hybrid when she was fourteen. "I confuse a lot of clueless white people," she said matter-of-factly to me a week or two after we first met. "No offense."

I remember blushing severely and rushing to say, "Oh no worries it's fine I'm not offended!" with a hysteria that embarrassed both of us.

Customers frequently ask Luna where she's *really* from, a question I've never gotten from any of them. My white privilege is, of course, a simple fact.

"I know it's your birthday and everything, Naomi, but I'll never forgive you for making me spend extra time with Lit Bro," says Luna a few minutes later, staggering out of the storage room with a stack of plastic chairs.

"I know, I'm sorry, hopefully it won't happen again!"

When a customer approaches the register, Luna waggles a faux-disapproving finger at me before turning to face them. Continuing the preparations, I drag two mics from the storage room and stack copies of the book, *One of the Herd*, at eye level by the front door. I set up a folding table and a bucket of ice, then stock it with cans of beer and white wine. As I distribute tiny cups and bottles of red wine across the table, my phone vibrates in the back pocket of my skirt. A missed call from my grandmother.

I take my fifteen-minute break and call her back from the storage room.

"Happy birthday, sweetheart," she greets me.

"Grammie, hi! Thank you. So do you have caller ID now, or were you just hoping it was me?"

She laughs. "I've reluctantly joined the twenty-first century. Your father set me up with a Netflix account. I've been bingeing—is that the word you use?—*The Crown*."

My grandmother, who also happens to be my last living grandparent, moved out of the apartment she once shared with my grandfather and into an assisted-living facility after a low-impact car accident four years ago. She wore a neck brace for a few months, but nothing else changed. She's still old, achy, unsteady on her feet. My father, with a vehement fear he couldn't set down, told her she needed supervision. The facility costs seventy thousand a year, including meals, movie nights, game nights, a shallow pool for physical therapy, and showering assistance.

"Correct use of the lingo," I say. "Welcome to the biggest time suck any generation has ever known."

"Don't let it distract you too much, though. Remember what your professor said? First novel by twenty-seven."

"No pressure or anything," I say through my teeth. My professor's prediction, or demand, was imparted during the English department's graduation barbecue. The mountains cast shadows on the grass, and partygoers clumped together to stand in the shade. I drank too much champagne but distinctly remember my professor approaching to say, "You'll publish your first novel in the next five years," as I dipped a celery stick into a vat of hummus. Taken aback,

I let out an awkward bark of laughter and clinked my glass against his. Even though I was rejected from every MFA I applied to, he still believed in me.

"Oh, don't do it for me, sweetheart, do it for yourself." Chuckling, she adds, "But I *would* like to read it before I succumb to cardiac arrest."

"Stop it," I say, more harshly than intended. "No deathbed chatter, please. That's my one request."

"Well played—invoking birthday privileges."

From outside the door, Luna knocks three times. "Sorry to interrupt"—there's a note of panic in her voice—"but some of our guests have arrived earlier than expected."

"Grammie, I have to go, I'm at work." Lowering my voice, I manage to choke out something sentimental. I can no longer shove worst-case scenarios aside—the only person who truly understands me is getting older and weaker by the hour. "I *really* appreciate your support and encouragement, though. Talk soon, okay? Love you."

"I love you, too," she says as I end the call.

"They weren't supposed to get here for another hour," Luna hisses when I rejoin her. "The author is so nervous she's practically vibrating."

"I've got this." I collect a glass of white wine and a small bottle of water before approaching the author. "We're so happy to host you, Sarah," I say cheerfully. "We're still finishing up with all the preparations, but here, please have some wine in the meantime."

Sarah Hill takes the water and the wine gratefully and wanders over to chat with the posse of people she brought with her. Her book has recently generated some healthy buzz due to an A-list celebrity who, after launching an Instagram book club for her fans, chose *One of the Herd* as the November pick. Sarah doesn't, in my opinion, look like someone who grew up on a Wyoming cattle farm—a leggy woman with glamorous blond curls and a low-cut pink leather pantsuit.

"That can't be real leather," I whisper to Luna. "Is she serious? Is it ironic?"

"Shit, I have no idea. Ask if you can touch it?"

Erupting into indelicate giggles, we disperse to finish our tasks.

As the rest of Sarah's entourage trickles in, I spot Rosemary standing by one of the mics and almost drop the books I'm holding. Carefully I set them down and then smooth my hair behind my ears, waiting for the perfect moment.

The folding table and the wine—placed beside the cash register so people are guilt-tripped into buying the book in exchange for free booze—eventually lures Rosemary. She chooses red instead of white, risky when weaving your way through a packed, well-dressed crowd.

I slink toward her like a big cat. "Bold choice."

Rosemary swivels, startled.

As we find ourselves again face-to-face, I strive to appear impassive and blasé, as if I would have uttered the same remark to anyone. I won't claim to recognize Rosemary until she recognizes me.

"Didn't have time to put on lipstick, so a red wine stain is the second-best thing." She smacks her lips playfully. "Not so bold."

I wasn't expecting to laugh, but I do.

"Hey, I remember you," she says. "From the bar."

Finally.

"Oh yeah! I remember you, too. And it was the bar bathroom, to be precise."

Rosemary grins. "Naomi the bookseller. Of course. It's all making sense."

"That's me." The pads of my fingers are tingling. "You're sure you didn't plan this launch as an excuse to run into me again?" I've used a version of this line before, when flirting with men.

Rosemary plays along. "I don't usually follow up on encounters in bar bathrooms, but maybe I was curious what would happen if I did."

"I thought I was too creepy. Definitely my creepiest moment ever."

"Nah, try harder next time."

I like her bite. "So you're the one who helped sculpt this masterpiece?"

Rosemary glances at the author and then back at me, suddenly uncomfortable, and I realize she thinks I'm mocking the book. Well, maybe I unintentionally am—after all, I certainly wasn't motivated to read past page thirty-two.

To my relief, Rosemary leans in with wine breath and seems to agree: "I'll be honest: I'm so glad it's over. Her proposal was so much better than the finished product. I held her hand through the whole process, but what she turned in wasn't great." She sighs and rocks back on her heels. "At least I can finally concentrate on books I like now. But please help us sell tons of copies tonight, okay?"

Luna interrupts the clamor of voices. "We'll begin in five minutes, so until then please drink more wine and mingle and buy Sarah's book!"

A few people comply and approach the register. Rosemary thumbs her phone screen while I scan barcodes and send sidelong glances in her direction. I have only a few minutes before it's time to leave and meet Caleb for dinner. So it seems a sort of miracle when Rosemary, unprompted, continues the conversation.

"So, to be honest, I spend more time at Greenlight and McNally Jackson. This bookstore has a totally different vibe, I can't quite put my finger on why. But I like how spacious and minimalist it is. Do you like working here?"

I can't tell if her question is genuine, or condescending, or skeptical, so I use my quick canned response. "I'm always meeting new people, and talking about books, and when it's quiet I get to read!" I say brightly. "So, yeah, I do."

Peter, the manager, hired me a few months after my college graduation. (My other job applications disappeared into the void, generating form rejections or no response at all.) I thought I'd move on after six months or so, but two years later, I'm still here. It's comfortable and fulfilling; it satisfies something deep and unnamable inside me. I enjoy punching in and punching out. I'm not hassled by after-hours email; I enjoy Luna's company and the surprisingly stimulating not-so-small talk customers direct at me; I often have mental energy remaining at the end of the workday to write. Customers might observe me repeating, "Sorry, no public restrooms," or doling out directions to the nearest subway station, or picking coins from the grooves in a tourist's palm when they're unsure of the difference between a nickel and a quarter, and assume *bookseller* is a pretentious way of saying *works in retail*; maybe they even sneer behind my back, believing I might as well work at Urban Outfitters, folding clothes people leave crumpled on their dressing-room floor, but they would be wrong, dead wrong. We booksellers keep the wheels turning for the entire publishing industry.

And I'll admit I often imagine what booksellers might say about my own novel when it's bound, when it joins all the others here on the shelf. What sort of person will they recommend it to, and how often?

I don't tell Rosemary any of this. We're not close enough yet.

But maybe, someday soon, we will be.

"Sometimes I fantasize about moving abroad and working in a bookshop," muses Rosemary. "Planning events, inviting authors I love. Wandering through narrow, beautiful European streets after work. Italy is at the top of my list. Have you read the Neapolitan series by Elena Ferrante yet?"

I tell her I loved all of them, but especially the third.

"Well, another major fantasy is moving there and becoming fluent in Italian and reading them in their original language," she says.

"I feel the same way about Javier Marías, I wish I could read him in Spanish," I say. "Anyway, I don't know much about Naples, but there are great English language bookshops in Madrid and Paris and Santorini. You could visit Italy on weekends!" I pause, then add: "It's a little easier to move to Australia or the UK or something, though."

"Definitely not the UK."

I brace for another revelation, but Rosemary offers nothing further, saying only, "I've heard of Shakespeare and Company in Paris! But I'll look into the others for my next life."

"Reincarnation is all the rage these days."

My phone vibrates. Angling my body away from Rosemary, I check it.

On my way, Caleb has written.

Handling the mic again, Luna asks everyone to take their seats.

The crowd shushes itself. I need more time. In the gathering silence my face starts to burn, but—*just say it!*—I blurt out: "We should get a coffee soon!"

Rosemary smiles like she has been offered something sweet and surprising. "I was thinking the same thing, actually."

I struggle to inhale enough air as we exchange phone numbers. If my phone buzzes with an incoming text and Caleb happens to notice her name—well, it would ruin everything. Why would he assume it was only a coincidence? I type "Mary" instead, renaming her.

Out into the cold night now.

I'm twenty-five, and my boyfriend awaits.

THE RESTAURANT, UPON arrival, holds so much potential. The warm-hued light is low. Potted plants and cacti hang from the ceiling. Colorful and intricate murals of a pueblo marketplace cover three walls. Caleb grips my right hand under the table as we order mango guacamole and hibiscus mezcal margaritas.

"How was work?" he asks. "Did Luna spoil you?"

"She did!" My voice veers into a higher pitch. It isn't normal, isn't right, to skip over the most thrilling moment of my day, but I must. "We ate cupcakes and snuck some wine behind the register before the event."

"That's great."

Caleb's hands are still wrapped around mine. Too nice, too good. I pull my hand away and place it, instead, on the menu. And then inside the basket of tortilla chips. What if Rosemary—aka "Mary"—decides to text me tonight?

The waiter brings our margaritas, takes our entrée orders, and departs. As my mouth makes contact with the salted rim, Caleb hands me a brown paper bag. He licks his lips, top and bottom, like a snake. He's nervous—it's a tic I've recently begun to recognize.

"I hid your other gift under your bed. You never clean down there, I knew you'd never find it," he teases. "But anyway. I wanted to give you this one now."

I slip it out of the bag and rip off the wrapping paper and gaze at the gift given to anyone who calls themselves a writer: a notebook, smooth and bare.

It's beautiful. Sateen, lavender-hued, and monogrammed with my initials: N.A.A. Naomi Amelia Ackerman. I brush my hand across the cover and flip through the pages.

I've accumulated, from loving family and attentive friends, dozens of notebooks. And yet it never occurred to any of them to have those notebooks personalized. Caleb will forever be the first person who does.

I slip my fingers back into the paper bag, sifting through air for a card. But the bag is empty. There is no card—unless it accompanies his second gift, the one currently hidden under my bed.

But who needs a card? What is wrong with me?

"Thank you so much! This is a perfect gift." I lean across the table and brush my lips (chapped, scratchy) against his (soft). "I love it."

"I'm glad! I hope you'll like your other one, too." He gives me an exaggerated wink. "It's not exactly eligible for a public unveiling."

The gift turns out to be a thumb-size vibrator with eleven different patterns of vibration and speed. It's playful and sexy and surprising. I laugh as it pulses frantically in the palm of my hand. "Impressive!" I say. "An accomplice."

"Exactly. Not a replacement, just an additive. We'll play with it in a bit," he says, smiling, and disappears into my bathroom to brush his teeth.

As Caleb's electric toothbrush whirrs in the other room, I perform my now-nightly routine of checking Rosemary's social media. Her Instagram Story is a series of close-up videos of Sarah Hill, who is tagged; I navigate to Sarah's Instagram next, clicking on her Stories. After cycling through almost a dozen photos, I spot one from earlier in the night, before the event began. In the foreground Sarah is smiling and holding a cup of wine aloft; in the background I spot the silver flash of Rosemary's nose ring amid the crush of well-dressed bodies, captured in mid-conversation with yours truly. Rosemary must be speaking or about to speak because her lips are slightly parted—when I notice the jagged curve of her tooth, a chill slithers from my scalp down to my ankle. Seeing us together is eerie but thrilling—I can't stop staring at the sight of us and thinking, *Ah, yes, there we are.*

But since when have Rosemary and I, even in my own head, become a *we*?

When the mechanical toothbrush ceases whirring and the bathroom door creaks open, I put my phone away just as Caleb slides into bed beside me and presses the vibrator against my crotch. As he cycles through five variations of speed and rhythm, I close my eyes and picture Rosemary wrapping her legs around Caleb's back as he enters her slow and deep, his lips brushing against her collarbone. It's a fantasy I've recently begun visualizing when touching myself.

Now, imagining it—the sounds and smells—I come quickly, overwhelmed. Bucking my hips to meet his, I demand he put himself inside me immediately. Now I'm the one wrapping my legs around his back and presenting my bare collarbone to be kissed.

"Happy birthday!" Caleb says afterward, tousling my curls, before rolling onto his stomach to sleep.

I WAKE EARLIER than usual Tuesday morning, eager to escalate, to learn more about her. About them. Rosemary's phone number, now in my possession, was openly solicited and voluntarily given. She won't necessarily be surprised to hear from me.

> Hey Rosemary, it was nice running into you at
> the book launch last night. I'd still love to get
> coffee, so let me know when works for you!

One exclamation point, I think, manages to communicate warmth and enthusiasm without being weird.

She writes back around noon. Lunch break. I imagine her forking romaine or kale or arugula tossed in balsamic into her mouth as she sifts through her to-do list and her calendar.

From my seat behind the register at work, my eyes dart from customer to customer before reading it.

> Naomi! Good to hear from you. Yes let's—how's
> Sunday around three?

> Perfect. See you then.

WHEN I ARRIVE at Brooklyn Roasting (her suggestion) in Dumbo on Sunday at three sharp, it's jam-packed. Bodies hunched over laptops occupy all the couches and nearly every chair at every table. On the opposite side of the cavernous industrial space, I snag two tall stools at a counter against a wall. Rosemary and I will have to angle our limbs toward each other, modeling the choreography of a date: side by side, with knees or thighs occasionally touching.

I order an iced dirty chai and wait. Rosemary arrives in a flurry—scarf lopsided, cheeks pink from the chill—and apologizes for being late. "Can you hold down the fort while I grab a coffee?"

I say, "Totally, no worries," and then watch her interact with the barista. He laughs at something she says, something I can't hear, and when she returns I ask what she ordered.

"A dirty chai. I have a sweet tooth, so the espresso shot at least lets me *pretend* I'm prioritizing caffeine."

I gesture at my own cup with mock surprise. "Oh, I got that, too!"

Will Rosemary recall this conversation and understand it has happened before?

"Great minds think alike," Rosemary says, which suggests she doesn't. Probably for the best. I don't want her to become unsettled by too many coincidences.

"How's your weekend going?" I lead with the innocuous, the banal. "Saturdays at work are always madness. All these frazzled parents come in like three seconds after we open, buy a shit-ton of toys and picture books, and then ask me to gift-wrap everything for a marathon weekend of birthday parties."

"Sounds like a nightmare," she says, and then smoothly transitions into talking about herself. "My weekend has been pretty relaxed, but I'm preparing for an intense week ahead. I recently acquired this book I was super excited about—I beat out a bunch of other editors to buy it—but just a few days ago the author dropped a bomb."

When Rosemary pauses to sip her dirty chai, I brainstorm possible bombs. The liquid moves against her throat.

"Someone in her novel is based on a real person, and so now she wants to change some of the best details to avoid detection."

She looks at me directly then, and I look back without blinking, trying not to panic.

"She always planned to make those changes before publishing the book, but everything she's ever been praised for is linked to this portrayal of him, and so she kept chickening out, digging herself into a bigger hole, and now, well, she's desperate—"

I regulate my breathing.

"—and I'm trying to coach her through it, especially since every female writer I work with is asked how much of their book is autobiographical. It's bullshit, honestly, men are rarely asked."

"So true, you're right, it *is* bullshit!" My voice squeaks into high-pitched hysteria. "What are you going to do?"

Recalling Rosemary's quiet attentiveness at the Gowanus bar, I imagine her counsel is calm and slow—*Tell me one more time* and *Are you sure?* and *Don't worry* and *We'll fix this.* I imagine she must be patient and kind but firm, too, with just the right amount of professional steel.

"I've asked her to revise, but if that means the book loses its power, I've suggested she reach out to the person in question and find a solution ending in forgiveness and freedom. That way she can publish the original." She sighs. "I'm mostly trying to avoid getting our legal team involved."

"That sounds incredibly stressful," I say, because it does. "I can't even imagine."

"I know. I'm hoping it doesn't come to that." She effort-lessly gathers her hair into a sleek ponytail. "Okay, now I'm done venting about work, promise. You have anything fun to look forward to?"

Quite the tonal shift, but I keep up. "Nothing too exciting. Mostly coddling the male ego. My boyfriend is in the middle of a huge project at work so he's been in a terrible mood. I basically hand him a beer as soon as he walks in and then nod sympathetically every few minutes."

She snorts. "Oh man, that sounds so familiar. What does he do?"

"Mechanical engineer." Still in a STEM field, close but not too close to the truth. I prepared for this. "But I honestly have no idea what he does, we don't really talk about our work. Only the frustrations or small triumphs."

"I know exactly what you mean. My ex worked in catastrophe modeling." She pauses. "It sort of felt like he was always bracing for something."

Here he is now, in the room with both of us. We are imagining the same face at the same time: Caleb's. A confusing mixture of glee and guilt and tenderness—for him, but also strangely for her—bubbles in my throat. I focus on the guilt, letting it linger and build, because isn't that the most appropriate, the most deserved, response?

"I guess it's true that opposites attract," Rosemary adds.

I push us off the edge, desperate to gather as much intel as possible. Information is armor and ammunition. "How did the opposites attract thing work out for you?"

"Well, I said *ex*, didn't I? So I guess not that well." Rosemary twists the zipper of her purse back and forth between her fingertips, an indentation blooming on the pad of her thumb.

I take note—this must be one of her nervous tics. I keep my fingers busy when I'm anxious, too.

"That wasn't the reason we broke up, though," she says. "Everything was fine for a while—there's a mutual fascination when your partner is good at something you can't imagine doing yourself. I looked at him with a sort of awe." Rosemary gazes somewhere over my left shoulder, even though there's nothing there to see. "And for a while he looked at me the same way."

Caleb often regards me with pleasant surprise, or maybe with amusement. Like I intrigue him. Are those akin to awe?

Rosemary takes another sip of her dirty chai. "So, what's your thing, you know, when you're not busy selling books?"

She has correctly guessed I do indeed have a "thing."

"I'm a writer." My cheeks flush red with—what? The audacity, perhaps, of claiming this vocation as mine in front of someone who is not only the ex-girlfriend of my boyfriend but who also deals with professional writers on a daily basis. "Aspiring," I clarify.

Though we don't make eye contact, I sense her pausing to take me in. Is it possible to accurately evaluate someone's talent based solely off appearances, off a *vibe*?

"That's cool! I thought maybe you wanted to get into publishing."

"Oh no, did you think that's why I wanted to hang out with you? For a job?" I won't dissuade her from this assumption. It's one of the safest.

She lifts an eyebrow. "Well, *are* you looking for a job?"

"I'm not unhappy with where I am right now. But yeah, I guess I'll eventually want a change. Publishing would make sense."

"'Not unhappy' doesn't sound as good as 'happy.'"

This is true—and wise. "I'm also writing a novel," I add, immediately searching her face for clues. "Very early stages, though."

"Good for you." She smiles at me, but it doesn't reach her eyes. "Who knows, maybe your book will eventually cross my desk."

The thought thrills and terrifies me, so I pivot. "Do you mind telling me what you did before your current job? I'm curious about people's trajectories. I feel really behind sometimes."

"Really behind, huh?" She looks amused. "How old are you?"

"Twenty-five." I reveal an even more personal detail. "It was actually my birthday when I last saw you."

"Oh, you're still young, there's no rush. And happy belated! You should have mentioned it."

"It's kind of an awkward thing to bring up out of the blue."

"I guess. How'd you celebrate?"

Your ex took me to dinner.

I finally lend him a new name. "By eating lots of Mexican food with my boyfriend, Lachlan."

It was a split-second decision, choosing the name Lachlan; I knew at least four of them when I was abroad in Melbourne. If Rosemary believes my boyfriend is Australian, we have yet another thing in common: past and present partners with Commonwealth accents and subtle but significant cultural differences.

"Solid choice of cuisine," says Rosemary, setting her dirty chai back onto the counter. "Anyway, to finally answer your question, I was an assistant less than two years ago, it took me for*ever* to get my foot in the door, I was unemployed for seven months, it was horrible. I was in a long-distance relationship, too, so, like, frequently tempted to give up and move there instead—"

"Where was your boyfriend from?" I've interrupted her, but I can't help it, my adrenaline has spiked.

"He's Welsh, but during that time he was living in London getting his master's."

"They have sexy accents," I say, too loudly.

"Obviously agree! I'm guessing you've been to the UK?"

I was ten years old, too young to know what sexy sounds like, when my grandmother took me to London. It was my first international trip, and the fifth Harry Potter book had just been published, and the phrase *Hip, Hip, Harry* was splashed across every double-decker bus, and so I spent most of the trip reading as we waited in long lines for Westminster Abbey and Buckingham Palace and the Tower of London. I wasn't fully present; I regret it.

I tell Rosemary about my grandmother, the double-deckers, the changing of the guards. "I'd love to visit as an adult, too, though," I add. "Experience the pub culture."

"That's such a sweet memory; your grandma sounds awesome." She takes another sip. "Definitely get out of London and explore the countryside next time. I'm biased, but you need to visit Wales and Scotland. They're so beautiful."

My pulse throbs in my stomach and throat. Rosemary seems so at ease discussing Caleb's homeland. Is it because she's over him, bearing no bitterness, no regrets? Or is it perhaps the exact opposite?

"Have you been to Australia? That's where Lachlan is from, and where I studied abroad. The sexiest accents of all, in my opinion."

"Not yet, it's so far, but someday I'd like to. What brought him here?"

"Oh, a job and a girl." Bluntness should capture and sustain her interest.

"Typical." She laughs. "I'm assuming you were the girl?"

"No, someone else," I improvise. "It was over a while before I met him."

A long silence unfolds; I clear my throat, rushing to fill it. "I'm really glad we're doing this, by the way. Ever since moving back to the city, I've been leaning too much on old friends rather than branching out."

I can't simply be a rabid networker in need of a job or a weird girl only capable of forging friendships in bar bathrooms or, god forbid, a writer trying to shamelessly worm her way into an eventual book deal. I need to be *laid-back* and *friendly* and *cool* and *open to new friendships* borne from a perfectly natural desire for *growth and transition*. Plus, as I said it, I realized I'd actually been honest. It was gratifying, truly, to connect with someone new. (Context aside.)

"I'm from the city, too." Her voice softens. "So I totally get it. Where did you grow up? What do your parents do?"

"Upper West Side, though I live in the Village now. My dad is a professor at NYU, and my mom is a singer-songwriter."

As described, we sound relatively upper-middle-class, bohemian, approachable. I don't mention what comprises the bulk of our income because it embarrasses me, but since most people are nosy and suspicious—asking reasonable questions like *How can a bookseller afford to live in a one-bedroom in the Village?*—explanations have become increasingly difficult to withhold.

"I actually went to NYU!" says Rosemary. "Still paying off those student loans. What does your dad teach?"

Duh. How could I forget?

My father teaches literature, so it's not entirely improbable that she took one of his courses as an undergrad. My face flushes with heat as we wade, again, into tricky territory. "He teaches in the math department. Not entirely sure which classes, believe it or not. Math was never my strong suit."

"I bet your dad is thrilled you're dating a math guy now." She makes an ugly slurping sound as her straw bumps up against ice and air. "My parents were psyched Caleb studied something *practical.* The day I chose English as my major was a dark day in my house. I mean, they're big readers and everything, they've been public school teachers for decades, but my parents probably hoped I'd choose finance or law or something—"

I stop listening. She said his name. For the first time. To steady myself, I press each vertebra, hard, against the back of my chair. Might Rosemary use this conversation as an excuse to contact Caleb again? I feel a weird, giddy apprehension before my queasiness returns. Certain events might now be out of my control.

I tune back in.

"Sorry, I know this is rude." Rosemary tips her phone toward her. "But I just have to answer this one text."

"No worries!" I gesture maniacally toward the bathroom. "I'll be right back."

Heart pounding, I lock myself in a stall and immediately change my privacy settings on Instagram and Facebook and Twitter. I've revealed too many facts. People will have to request to follow me now. My profile picture, used across all my social media platforms, is a close-up of me on the Great Ocean Road in Australia, windswept and grinning. I haven't changed it in years; I like looking at it.

In the most recent photo I posted, I'm standing in a cavernous room at the Whitney Museum beside an exhibition of blue suitcases arranged in a tidy row. Caleb and I went a couple weeks ago, and when I asked him to take a picture of me standing beside them, he teased me—a little too disdainfully—about my Instagram usage. I chose to ignore it but wish I hadn't, wish I'd defended myself instead: *It's only one photo, I rarely ask, I'm not that kind of person, shouldn't you know that by now?*

For the caption, I wrote, Posing with all my emotional baggage. It eventually garnered 120 likes, a personal record. The likers must have assumed I was being clever or ironic.

I'll tell Rosemary I don't use social media, if she ever inquires. *It helps me write*, I'll say. *No distractions*.

Caleb has no social media presence at all. His last Facebook post was more than two years ago, and the photo he used for his Tinder profile was taken from that time period. (Months ago, while executing a deep dive into his decade-old photo archives, I was delighted to discover that eighteen-year-old Caleb looked much like the eighteen-year-old boymen who never expressed interest in eighteen-year-old Naomi. Take that, high school boys.)

If Rosemary went searching for scraps of him, of us, she wouldn't find anything. I alone control how our relationship is perceived online, and now I'm private, inaccessible. So far, the only photo of Caleb and me that exists on social media is a selfie taken at Coney Island this past summer. Our faces are large and sunburned in the frame with a suggestion of sea behind us. The caption: My boyfriend's first trip to Coney Island! accompanied by the emojis of our respective flags. I wanted people to know—okay, I confess I wanted the jazz drummer, specifically, to know—that I had a boyfriend now, a man who was handsome and, somewhat exotically, Welsh.

It's possible, actually, that Caleb's disinterest in social media is advantageous. If he had an Instagram, it would only serve as yet another method of obsessively gauging our relationship's temperature; I'd waste precious time fretting about the frequency in which I was featured in his posts and the number of likes those posts received. I should be grateful there's nothing else to overanalyze or misinterpret.

And if Caleb knew how much time I spend adjusting contrast, structure, saturation, and shadow, or experimenting with Gingham, Lark, Rise, and Valencia, or drafting captions with a painstaking blend of candid and wry, I worry his respect for me would dwindle. Using social media, I become someone else—for better or for worse.

When I return from the bathroom, Rosemary is texting with a huge goofy smile on her face. I stare at her teeth until she becomes self-conscious enough to put them away again, her lips like a curtain closing. Who makes her smile like that?

"I'm going to a dinner in Park Slope, so I'm afraid I'll have to leave in five minutes or so."

"A date?" I ask pointedly.

"Not a date. Sorry, I don't mean to make you feel like I'm slotting you in or anything, I've just had plans with some college friends for a while. I honestly didn't think we'd talk for this long!"

I feel almost honored to have exceeded her expectations until I remember who, exactly, we are.

"Friend dates are the only kind of date I go on right now," she adds, seeming deflated.

I reassemble my features into an expression of concern, empathy. "I'm sorry, I didn't—"

"It's fine, I'm just being dramatic. It's a long story, but basically after a few years trying the long-distance thing, Caleb moved to New York but ended up desperately homesick most of the time.

Which I found totally exhausting after months and months of brooding. So I broke up with him. I didn't want to, but I thought it might snap him out of his funk and fight for us." Her voice has quickened, grateful, perhaps, for a fresh ear. Her friends are probably sick of hearing about Caleb. "But he didn't. He was just—gone from my life suddenly. I thought he'd go back to the UK, but he stayed. Why stay, if not to allow the possibility of getting back together?"

I'm tempted to ask, *If Caleb were American, if his accent were unremarkable rather than swoon-worthy, would you still want him?*

"I feel like our paths will probably cross again," she says, and gazes at me with unnerving directness, as if inviting me to validate or challenge this claim.

I do neither, saying instead in mock-horror, "Did you seriously drop in your romantic history at the very last minute? I have questions!"

When and how will your paths cross again? How certain are you that they will?

Rosemary gathers her bag and tosses her coffee cup in the trash and hops off her stool. "It's probably not as interesting as you think," she says with a sheepish smile. "I guess we all have our own little dramas."

"A cliffhanger!" I shout as she exits. A few people lift their heads from their laptops and stare me down.

After the door swings shut behind her, I text my father a series of small white lies.

Random question. I met someone at the bookstore today who might've been in one of your classes at NYU. Rosemary Pierce?

Three minutes later, my phone vibrates.

**I remember her! The 19th Century Novel.
Brilliant girl. Small world. Did she buy anything
interesting?**

No, I type, jabbing the keyboard with my index finger, **only a
condolence card.** Visibly bristling, I wonder how often, if ever, he
uses the word *brilliant* to describe *me.*

Yikes, he replies.

I delete the messages and then text Caleb: **Are you home?**

It feels suddenly urgent that I see him. I leave the café, hustle
toward the train station, and wait six minutes for the express train
to arrive. I'll transfer to the local at Ninety-Sixth Street, continuing north to Caleb's. I rarely spend time at his apartment, mostly
due to my beloved and needy Romeo and my lack of roommates.
Caleb's flatmate (his term) is a software programmer. I've only
seen him once but hear him often. He cooks and sleeps at odd
hours and seems to have only two musical modes: Mozart or
Metallica.

On the subway headed to wash heights, I add. **Thought we
could switch it up and hang in your hood!**

Caleb doesn't reply right away, but I remain on the train, I stay
the course, I'll surprise him if I have to.

Returning to Instagram, I scroll fast through people, places,
and things, turning the little hearts red when I like what I see. As
my finger brushes over a video and music begins to play, my stomach lurches as I hear a jazzy blend of bass and piano and sax—and
drums.

"Motherfucker," I say aloud. The person sitting next to me on the subway, a tall man in a leather jacket, gives me an alarmed look and shifts his body away from mine.

I begin watching the video and, in so doing, remember the unfortunate truth of Adam's great talent.

THE TWO STORIES I published about Adam were lies.

In them, his rejection of me was founded on a true and profound love, a feeling so sharp and deep it rendered him helpless, fearful, in the face of it. So he fled.

The truth is I have since suspected everyone who wants me is wrong for it, that they must be mistaking me for someone else.

The setting—cerulean seas, exotic birds, copious sunshine, hammocks in tucked-away corners on a luxurious cruise ship in the Galápagos Islands—leant itself to romance, but I was also sixteen and on a family vacation, which didn't. Adam had just graduated with his master's degree from a prestigious conservatory in Boston, where he lived; I was a high school sophomore. He was obnoxiously gorgeous in a sanitized, well-groomed, Disney-prince way that appealed enormously to teenage me. Adam kept to himself during the six-day cruise, but I still made sure to plant myself in his sight line whenever he appeared, flirting with the bartender and ordering virgin mojitos. On the last day, the cruise deposited us all on one of the islands. My parents opted for a hike, bringing Noah with them, and I opted for the beach—mostly because Adam had opted for the beach. I watched him settle onto a slope of sand, don a pair of giant headphones, close his eyes, and begin to air-drum. It was now or never.

Dodging his wildly slashing arms, I planted myself next to him and said, "What are you listening to?" Startled, his eyes flew open.

"Sorry!" I said. "Didn't mean to, like, scare you."

He laughed and said, "You don't scare me," before tipping his iPod in my direction. Brian Blade Fellowship, "Red River Revel." I knew nothing about jazz. I gestured at his headphones, asked if I could listen. He put them on my head himself, the pressure of his fingers both gentle and firm. I shivered; the music played; the song ended; I murmured my admiration and handed them back. We talked. He was on the cruise alone—he'd been touring Chile, Argentina, Peru, and Ecuador for weeks with his band and had set aside time to explore before his flight home. He'd always wanted to see Lonesome George, the world's most famous tortoise. (Only much later would I realize how lucky we were to see him alive.)

When I revealed to Adam, over the course of our conversation, that I was a published writer—which I technically was, after winning a kids' writing contest in *Writer's Digest*—he asked how old I was, and I told him.

"Sixteen," he repeated slowly under his breath, as if the word had at least three syllables. "Damn."

(I still wonder about the meaning behind that "damn": Was he impressed by my publication, or disappointed I wasn't an age-appropriate option to spend the night with?)

Adam continued looking at me for several long seconds with an interest and intensity I'd never experienced before. We were on a beach surrounded by barking sea lions. My hair was wet and matted from an earlier swim, but my cheeks must have been flushed and bright, my eyes must have been clear and glowing. But what I most vividly remember is the sound, the feeling, the fact, of the first time I was looked at like that.

After disembarking, I sent him a friend request on Facebook. When Adam accepted, I gave him my screenname on AOL Instant Messenger. A few hours later, he messaged me.

RedRiverRevel: Hey, Naomi. What does your screenname mean?

CallMeFrouFrou: It's kind of a niche joke. The doomed horse from Anna Karenina, plus the first line of Moby Dick

RedRiverRevel: Ah, so literary. how's life back on land treating you?

CallMeFrouFrou: Not particularly well. School sucks, I miss the Galapagos, it was a total fantasy

RedRiverRevel: I miss it too. that trip was actually the culmination of a lifelong dream of mine

CallMeFrouFrou: let's go back then

RedRiverRevel: I wish!

CallMeFrouFrou: you know what could've made the trip even better?

RedRiverRevel: what?

CallMeFrouFrou: if we'd hooked up

I had never even been kissed. *Hook up* could mean kiss, or fuck, or anything in between. I waited to see how he would interpret it, experimenting with whatever power I could glean from a few carefully chosen words. At the time it seemed only the sassiest, most assertive girls at school hooked up with the most attractive guys. I didn't have that reputation, not even close, belonging instead to a clique of somewhat prudish, studious girls who hadn't been kissed yet, either. But now I wanted to be something more, something else—mature, seductive, adult. In the novels I read, flirtatious dialogue always included a few suggestive questions, to start.

RedRiverRevel is typing . . . appeared, and disappeared, and reappeared.

RedRiverRevel: That's inappropriate, and you know it

I escalated.

CallMeFrouFrou: Fucking would be inappropriate?

RedRiverRevel: Yes. I'm eleven years older than you

CallMeFrouFrou: there are worse things

RedRiverRevel: behave

CallMeFrouFrou: make me

RedRiverRevel has left the chat.

But it happened again, and again, and again.

RedRiverRevel: how's school? have you been behaving?

CallMeFrouFrou: I never behave ;)

RedRiverRevel: well then you deserve to be pulled across my knee and taught a lesson

CallMeFrouFrou: oooh, do it

RedRiverRevel: didn't I just tell you to behave?

CallMeFrouFrou: cum teach me a lesson before someone else does

RedRiverRevel is typing . . . appeared, and then disappeared. Silence for hours and sometimes even days, until—

RedRiverRevel: You know I won't reply when you misbehave like that. Be good.

CallMeFrouFrou: Okay, but first tell me the truth. Do you ever fantasize about me?

RedRiverRevel: I'm not answering that.

RedRiverRevel: But if we were the same age, I'd take you on a date.

The tenderness of that last sentence kept me hooked. I didn't expect it, hadn't entertained the possibility, and so months passed like this—we sent each other links to ice hotels, tree-house hotels, and hotels beneath the sea, promising to travel there together; we talked about our families and our futures and our dreams. Mine seemed far away; his had already arrived. Soon we started speaking on the phone. "I don't need to be famous," he said. "I mean, how often does fame really happen in jazz? No one listens to it anymore, I just want people I respect and admire to respect and admire me, too, that would make me happy."

"Me too," I said. For months I huddled under my blanket after my parents thought I was asleep and listened to him describe musicians he played with, international venues he traveled to.

A few weeks before I turned seventeen, Adam posted on Facebook about his next New York gig. It was at the Blue Note, a club open to all ages, and I told him, entirely unprompted, that I planned to come. I informed my parents I was going to my friend Rachel's house and then took the subway downtown. I sat in the back, at the tables where the under-twenty-one set was deposited, in a black leather miniskirt and red V-neck sweater and thigh-high boots, wearing mascara and eyeliner and burgundy lipstick, sipping Diet Coke through a straw. Adam cocked his head as he drummed, angling his left ear toward his cymbals as if they were whispering to him, and my whole body buzzed and buzzed and didn't stop buzzing. After the set, I lingered, pretending to text, while Adam finished mingling with the musicians and hugging the other people he knew who had come. Once nearly everyone in the venue had shuffled out, Adam approached me. I don't remember the specifics, certainly nothing suggestive, mere small talk, his gratitude that I had come. What I do remember, vividly, is the sweep of his gaze—incredulous and amused and hungry all at once—as he took me in, and his hand on my arm. The way it lingered there. Our second-ever touch.

Then he removed his arm and said something about a bus ticket he needed to buy, right now, in order to go home. To Boston.

"You can stay with me," I heard myself say. "It's already so late."

My grandmother's brownstone, a mere three blocks away, swam in my mind's eye. I carried the key to its fourth-floor apartment with me everywhere then; my grandmother had very recently slipped it into an envelope for me. *Co-ownership of the writer's studio*, the note inside had read. It felt, at the time, like a true passing of the torch. With each successive year, she used the space less and less—the building was a walk-up, and her eighty-three-year-old body could no longer tolerate frequent climbs up three steep flights of stairs.

I remember Adam laughing. "Don't you live with your family?"

I'd tried to look and act older—but clearly, to him, I was still a teen under the jurisdiction of my parents. Bristling, I said: "I'm not staying with my family tonight."

And so Adam followed me there. We walked side by side, arms occasionally brushing; my whole body an electric field. **Sleeping at Rachel's**, I texted my mother from the bathroom after we arrived.

"Pretty sweet deal you've got," Adam said, standing in the middle of the bedroom. There wasn't a bed, just a couch and a desk and a sturdy wooden chair. The other room was a sizable kitchen my grandmother used only to make tea and toast. "What's this place for? Who lives here?"

"It's just—it's an office. For my grandmother and me. To write in."

I hadn't actually even used the key yet because I was afraid of not writing once I arrived. I wouldn't be able to forgive myself for taking the subway all the way downtown only to sit and stare at a wall.

"Lucky you." Adam pointed at the couch, then led me to it by the crook of my elbow. "Bend over."

I swayed on my feet. "What?"

"You heard me. Over the arm of the couch. Ass in the air. I said I'd spank you if you misbehaved, and you've certainly misbehaved. You've said lots"—he pulled my skirt down—"of naughty things."

My nose and mouth and chin were pressed into the musty couch cushion. I almost couldn't breathe, I was trembling with fear or with elation, I wasn't sure which, maybe it was both.

I heard him unbuckle his belt. Were we going to have sex? Did I want—

First I felt the leather against my ass cheek. He pressed hard, like he was attempting to brand me, and then crept a finger around to play with my clitoris. I moaned into the cushion, writhed, and then he took his finger away.

"You've been so, so naughty," he said. "I'll stop when you've learned your lesson. Just tell me when."

I couldn't believe this was the same person I'd been talking to for months on the phone about tree-house hotels and music and writing, about our families and our futures. I didn't know what roles we were supposed to play, and when. I'd wanted this, or something like it—but since when had Adam decided he wanted it, too?

The leather slapped my ass, and then his hand, and then the leather again. He alternated like that for five, six times before my ass cheeks really started to sting and throb, but I didn't tell him to stop, not yet, I was testing us both.

After the tenth blow, I told him I learned my lesson. I reared up and back against his chest, gasping for air, and he reached between my legs again and smiled and said, "Good, good girl."

I think I loved it. Being hit like that. Hearing his deep voice say my name. *You deserve this, Naomi, you know you deserve this.* I was wetter than I have ever been, will ever be, in my entire life. Did I deserve it? I had baited him, I had brought him there, I had been manipulative. I thought I had power.

And then Adam said, "There's no room for me, for us, to sleep here, I mean, to both fit on the couch, I really should get back, there's a two thirty bus I can catch," and so he caught it, and I slept on the couch alone, and when I woke up in my grandmother's office, the sacred space where she wrote, I was still a sixteen-year-old virgin who had never been kissed.

That evening, back in my bedroom on the Upper West Side, I logged on to AIM.

CallMeFrouFrou: that was fun ;)

RedRiverRevel: it was indeed. Are you having trouble sitting down?

CallMeFrouFrou: So much trouble

RedRiverRevel: good

CallMeFrouFrou: but are we going to fuck next time though

RedRiverRevel: good things come to those who wait ;)

And they did, sort of.

A few days later, he asked for a nude. I used my computer's webcam with Photo Booth to send one of myself bent over, ass in the air, breasts swinging, peeking over my shoulder, the majority of my hair covering my face.

RedRiverRevel: So sexy. I can't stop thinking about how red your ass was after I taught you a lesson. You were so wet too

CallMeFrouFrou: I can't wait for you to bend me over and fuck me

RedRiverRevel: yes, good girl, me neither.

Daily phone calls continued. They were chaste, even shy, on both our parts, but I wasn't bothered by this; I took it as confirmation that I meant something to him, that I was being handled with care. And then I turned seventeen, the legal age of consent, and I thought, *He's been waiting for this, been waiting for me, soon we will finally have sex, finally be together, outside, in daylight, off-screen. Soon, soon, soon—*

In the final weeks of my junior year:

RedRiverRevel: So I'm coming to NYC again next week for a gig, can I crash with you in that "office"?

CallMeFrouFrou: yes!! ;)

Sleeping at Rachel's, I told my parents. *We're working on a project for English and the only way we can finish it is basically if we pull an all-nighter.*

Adam asked me to help him parallel park his car, so I stood on the sidewalk occasionally yelling things like, "too far from the curb!" through his open window. Then we climbed the stairs to my apartment, together again at last. It was a Wednesday. I hadn't finished my homework yet, but I expected, by Thursday, I wouldn't be a virgin anymore.

"I should be back a little after midnight," he said after twenty minutes spent changing his clothes. "Sorry, I think you need an ID to get into this venue."

He was twenty-eight, and I was seventeen. So I waved and told him to break a leg, and finished my homework, and stayed awake until Adam came back to me around two thirty a.m., smelling like alcohol. I watched him gulp down three glasses of water before I asked, "Are you going to kiss me or what?"

He looked at me. "Oh. Yes." He put his hands on the sides of my face, gave me a peck on the lips. So quick and soft I barely realized what was happening—my first kiss!—until it was already over.

"I brought a blow-up bed with me," he said. "You can sleep on it with me or you can sleep on the couch, whatever you want—"

"Obviously with you," I said, suddenly near tears.

He noticed this and kissed me again. Deeper, longer. Full-lipped and probing.

On the inflatable bed, I snuggled in close. I wore underwear and a thin tank top, that was all. Adam was in boxers. He rested a hand on my breast, over the tank top. It didn't count as a real touch through fabric, I thought. Was he simply trying to further build anticipation?

When he continued not touching me, I said, "I'm going to apply to colleges in Boston."

"Cool," he said. "Where?"

"Emerson is one of my top choices."

"Writing program?"

"Exactly."

"That's awesome. I hope you get in. You'd love it."

I waited for him to register what this meant. He didn't.

"It would be cool to finally be in the same city," I ventured, "as adults." When met with silence, I added with forced bravado, "But I'm also applying to places out west, like California and Colorado."

"Boston has more attitude," he said vaguely, yawning. "But you should go wherever you'd thrive the most."

"Thanks," I said, confused, and proceeded to stay awake long after Adam's breathing steadied, long after he fell asleep.

He was still sleeping when I woke up for school approximately four hours later.

"I'm leaving," I said, poking his shoulder. "School."

"Remember to behave," he mumbled, a slow grin spreading, and then closed his eyes again.

It took him twelve whole hours to contact me.

RedRiverRevel: Hope you had a good day at school. It was great seeing you. Sorry I was so tired. Looking forward to next time!

And so I fell back into it for months and months and months. Adam was the first person I spoke to each morning, the last person I spoke to each night. He was essential to the rhythm of my days.

One morning in early November, I woke with severe stomach pain and staggered into my parents' bedroom to ask my father, who was the only one home, for help; doubled over in the back of a yellow taxi moments later, I willed the driver to go faster, faster, please, the pain was unbearable, radiating out from my stomach and up into my throat, pain so bad it made me vomit onto the ripped upholstery as the driver swerved in surprise, lamenting the smell—*Not an ambulance why didn't you get an ambulance?* he had said—and my father frantically attempted to mop up my mess with a small packet of thin tissues. At Mount Sinai Hospital on West Fifty-Ninth, an IV and pain meds and an ultrasound and then emergency laparoscopic surgery to remove an ovarian cyst. The surgeon said something like, *Worst-case scenario we might need to remove your ovaries do we have your consent*, and I must have given it because now at age eighteen, straddling the faint line between childhood and adulthood, I certainly wasn't thinking about future children of my own. But it's also true that I consented because I wanted to get it over with, and quickly—my father and I were supposed to fly to California two days later to visit Noah and my mother, who were temporarily living in Los Angeles; Noah was starring in a musical premiering at the Ahmanson Theatre. So, before succumbing to anesthesia, I asked the doctor if I would still be able to fly. *Travel at your own risk*, he said, glancing at my father, who nodded his approval. Our flights were nonrefundable, but either way, we'd been looking forward to the trip, to finally reuniting with the other half of our family, for months. Plus, I wanted to feel the sun and see the Pacific and upload enviable Facebook photos and maybe also make Adam miss me a little, or a lot.

Hours later, after emerging from anesthesia, I was informed I no longer had any ovaries. Then I was discharged, free to return home with fewer organs, and later that night, because of my sudden inability to bend over or use any of my stomach muscles, Rachel came over and cheerfully knelt on my bathroom floor, slathering shaving cream over my thighs and calves and running a razor blade down the length of each leg so I would arrive in California smooth and hairless and beach-ready. (I loved Rachel for so many reasons already, but that was the day I knew for certain she loved me back. She lives in DC now; we don't really speak, not due to ill will or anything, just due to—life, the way it moves.) I wore a flowing knee-length dress to the airport; it was the only article of clothing I could put on by myself. Until reuniting with my mother and enlisting her help in getting dressed, I was even forced to forego underwear. (For the record, I do *not* recommend going commando on a cross-country flight.) Unable to walk so soon after the surgery, my father also arranged for me to be pushed through the airport terminal in a wheelchair; on the plane, I kept dropping things and asking the cute guy next to me to pick them up. I told him about the surgery so he knew I wasn't just lazy. I was also on a lot of Percocet.

After landing, I texted Adam a picture of a palm tree and then left a rambling voicemail. *You won't believe this but I had surgery yesterday super randomly because I had a really bad stomachache and now I don't have, like, ovaries anymore, isn't that crazy, also I'm in California, okay, well, talk to you soon, call me back.*

"Sounds really scary," he said, calling me back twenty-four hours later. "But I'm glad you're okay. What's the recovery period like?"

Was I okay?

"Six weeks until the stitches in my stomach dissolve," I told him.

California happened. Noah was a star, deemed a certifiable "scene-stealer" in the *Los Angeles Times*. And though I couldn't walk comfortably or swim or bike or bend over to put on my own shoes or do anything, really, that I'd hoped to do in that sunny state, at the very least I got a little tanner lying by the sea, and at the very least I got to skip a few days of school. *It could've been worse*, I told myself whenever fielding another of my mother's concerned glances or pleas to "process the loss in therapy." *It could've been so much worse.*

But despite resisting any and all encroaching panic, it often snuck up on me anyway: the panic of narrowing options, of a future absence I couldn't fully understand yet. The experience most women take for granted—biological motherhood; their bodies performing properly—was suddenly cordoned off, inaccessible to me.

So I continued to resist, and resist—

Soon we were all back in our apartment on the Upper West Side, and due to suddenly being a menopausal eighteen-year-old, I started hormone replacement therapy (estrogen and progestin, a routine I soon normalized) and wrote my college application essay about the surgery, about the first bad thing that had ever happened to me, ever managed to touch my charmed life. It was, according to my grandmother, a beautiful essay—nuanced and crisp. "I'm so proud of you," she told me.

Exactly six weeks later my stitches dissolved, and—

RedRiverRevel: Hey, I've got another gig in NYC next Wednesday. Can I crash at your place? No worries if not, but I'd really like to see you

CallMeFrouFrou: yes of course, come!! ;)

Sleeping at Rachel's, I told my parents, giddy and bursting and trying not to show it. *We're working on a history project and the only way we can finish it is basically if we pull an all-nighter.*

My parents knew, they must have known, it was about a boy. But they didn't think it was *this* boy, a man, and so they kept pretending to believe my story about Rachel, kept saying *be safe* whenever I left the house.

Adam carried his suitcase up the stairs, made a few phone calls, and then left again. No kissing.

I watched *Before Sunrise* on my computer and cried when the sun came up on-screen.

Adam returned around three thirty, when I was nearly delirious from exhaustion, and fingered the scar inside my belly button with a strange reverence I couldn't help but imagine *meant* something, and fell asleep with his back to me. No further touch, no further meaning.

Around nine the next morning—I was already late for school—he rolled out of the inflatable bed and dressed quickly and made coffee and thumbed through his phone and said he had a bus to catch.

I stared at him, uncomprehending.

"I thought you liked me," I said, hating how it sounded as I said it. "I thought this was—something else. Why haven't you touched me, you said you wanted to fuck me! You said—"

"I'm sorry," he said calmly. "For giving you the wrong idea. I got carried away. I *do* like you, of course I like you, but you're—well, you know, and I just don't think it should happen. It feels—wrong. Like I'm taking advantage of you or something."

"But you're not!" I practically screamed. "I invited you here, I made this happen—"

"Hey, whoa, calm down, okay? Calm down. I want to be friends with you. Why can't we be friends? We enjoy each other's company, don't we, so—"

"A twenty-nine-year-old wants to be *just friends* with an eighteen-year-old?" I spit at him. "I must be really fucking fascinating."

He actually laughed. "Of course you're fascinating. I just—didn't picture this turning into a real relationship." And then he threw me one last bone. "At least, you know, not right now. Given the circumstances."

The circumstances.

I was, I suddenly realized, a girl who gave him a free place to stay in New York. I was the benevolent, accommodating host with a crush. I was necessary to him, essential, for all the wrong reasons.

And so I blocked his screenname and his phone number and moved to Colorado for college eight months later. *Watch me go,* I was trying to communicate. *I am not yours. Not so easily controlled.*

Toward the end of my freshman year, drunk in the disgusting bathroom of yet another frat party, I requested to follow Adam, who was private, on Instagram. We hadn't spoken in well over a year. While my request was pending, I perched on the edge of the moldy bathtub and typed his name into YouTube, searching for snippets, and eventually discovered a video of him playing at a Boston jazz club. It was posted by a woman whose name I then searched for on Instagram. Her profile was public. I executed a deep dive. There were photos of Adam everywhere, of him and her together; captions and time stamps confirmed she became his girl-friend in the months between Adam's second and final visit to my grandmother's office, to me. The discovery was shocking as well as inevitable, somehow—of *course* there was someone else, of course I hadn't been good enough.

The other woman was age-appropriate and pretty, and in photo-graphs it looked like they were in love, so I left the bathroom deter-mined to sleep with as many men as possible. Why not start right there, at the frat party? I charged down the stairs, intending to re-join the sweaty clump of gyrating bodies, but fatefully missed a step and tipped backward, bouncing cartoonishly down the remaining flight, and in the days that followed my right ass cheek turned black and blue and then purple and yellow, ultimately resulting in a literal dent, as if my ass cheek was a marshmallow someone pressed down that never popped back up again.

It was a weakness, but I would turn it into a strength: a better story.

Moving to Australia my junior year—ten thousand miles away from everyone I knew—allowed me to finally embody this better story, this better self. Giddy with newfound freedom, I casually told men in bars I had a dent in my ass from being spanked really, really hard. Quite remarkably, I was believed. The news rendered them simultaneously repelled and ravenous, and *then* I followed up by saying they could fuck me without a condom because I didn't have any ovaries and couldn't get pregnant. Many sets of eyes bulged in their sockets.

And so, after briefly relaying the results of our most recent STD test, we got down to business—in laneways splattered with commissioned graffiti in Melbourne and public parks smelling of eucalyptus and kangaroo dung in Tasmania and sterile high-rise hotel rooms in Sydney and a tent four hundred yards from Uluru at sunrise and below deck of a fisherman's boat in Byron and above deck on a racing yacht in Brisbane and inside the curve of a hammock in the Whitsunday Islands. I kept a notebook in which I wrote down all their names and the positions we tried and how many orgasms I had. I also wrote down where they were from and how old they were and how I felt after, if the sex or the conversation had made me happy or sad. It was a surprisingly diverse collection of data.

When Adam's name popped up on my phone the summer between my junior and senior year of college, months after returning from Australia, I found it very difficult, suddenly, to breathe.

I've been thinking about you, he texted. **I'm in New York, and was hoping we could get coffee.**

Instead of telling him to fuck off, or asking why now, so many years later, I wrote: **I've been thinking about you, too.**

I never stopped thinking about you, I did not write. *You ruined me,* I did not write. *Thank you for giving me something to write about,* I did not write. As it turned out, Adam was the first bad thing that happened to me, and the surgery was the second.

And so we had coffee. I was twenty-one by then, a woman, and I hoped Adam would realize this. I sat across from him and marveled at his face, still obnoxiously gorgeous but less Disney-prince and more lived-in; he had even grown a beard. It suited him. He asked about school, about my writing. *Good, good, all so good,* I told him, and later, outside the café, when he tried to kiss me, I jerked away and said I was *so* sorry but I had to leave, I had a date, the romantic kind. I'd always been too available to him, too eager to accommodate, so from then on I intended to prove I'd always be slightly out of reach. It was the only power I had left, and I hoped it would spur him to keep reaching, keep wanting. I considered it—growth, exponential functions—simple math.

I didn't have a date, of course. I went home that night and wrote another story about him, the first that was later published; it seethed with rage and yearning.

How was your date? he texted the next day. **Should I be worried?**
Yes, was all I replied.

Adam never mentioned his girlfriend, but I knew she was there, unspoken, unseen, and it made me, the idea of us, feel special, misunderstood, beyond judgment. We exchanged flirtatious messages for days, messages in which I often recounted my many sexual exploits with men who weren't him.

But then one night, feeling weak, I stopped playing the game. I called him on FaceTime and asked him to tell me why we hadn't ever become more than we were. I'd convinced myself a long time ago that his decision not to have sex with me was chivalrous, like he cared too *much*. But I'd recently begun to suspect I must have revolted him somehow, must have not been worthy. A plaything to be discarded. Still, I hoped he'd say: *Naomi, I was wrong; you're special; you're more than enough.* Even though Danielle told me again and again that I deserved better (did I?), I still wanted him to want me.

Now, when a man chooses to have sex with me, I am grateful and triumphant. Look—desire. Look—a conquest! When a man chooses to have sex with me a second time, I think, *Oh, weird, okay,* and then start the clock.

"I guess we intrigue each other," said Adam. "Nothing less, nothing more."

"Of course that must be it. I agree," I said, and then it was over, and—

I fictionalized our relationship and its eventual end as if it was equally significant for both of us. Giving myself closure.

THE SCREECH OF the train—a poor substitute for bass, piano, sax, drums—as it approaches the 168th Street station jolts me out of the past and into the present. My ill-advised decision to watch Adam's video lapsed into a thirty-minute scroll through his Instagram archives. I could have blocked him a long time ago, but I prefer having access.

Caleb still hasn't responded to my text, but I exit the station in Washington Heights anyway. After pressing the button for his apartment on the intercom, nearly two whole minutes pass before I'm permitted entry. As the elevator rises to the sixth floor, I use its dirty mirror to pluck a clump of mascara off an eyelash.

He opens his front door in a towel. "Sorry! I was about to hop in the shower when I heard the buzzer."

"That's fine, I'll wait in your room." As I move down the hall, Metallica throbs through the crack under his flatmate's door.

A month before I learned Rosemary's name, Caleb and I went for a five-mile walk from his apartment all the way down to Seventy-Second Street via Riverside Park. Around Ninety-Sixth, I bent to pick up a stick off the ground. It was thick and sturdy and at least a foot long. I had mentioned earlier that week that I was "into spanking," whatever that means, without telling him about Adam. With a goofy smile on my face, I slashed the stick through the air and said, "It's a spanking stick, see?"

Caleb blushed but nodded. I had been led to believe intriguing someone was the first step to keeping them. I didn't yet know what the second step was, or the third.

We brought the stick back to my place. It stuck out of my tote on the subway, looking absurdly like a baguette we might have picked up from a bakery.

Later, in my bed, I lay naked on my stomach and lifted my dented bare ass, a request. Caleb smacked me with the stick a few times, light and quick. I barely registered it.

"No, it's okay, you can really go for it," I instructed, and after slight hesitation, he did.

I suppose I was trying, then, to subjugate the memory of Adam, to domesticate and own it. But instead of feeling dumbstruck and then ecstatic and then dirty, like I remember feeling with Adam, I felt embarrassed and then deflated and then a little sad.

"Stop," I said. "Stop!"

Caleb stopped.

I rolled onto my back and pulled his body on top of mine and kissed him. I heard the stick clatter to the floor.

We never used it again, and a few weeks later, when I found it under the rug while vacuuming, I threw it out the window and into the alley.

My relationship with Caleb, pre-Rosemary, feels like such a long time ago.

Listening to the hiss of Caleb's shower through his thin walls, I search for his passport. The bedroom is orderly and spare—a twin bed, a desk, a small collection of books, a poster of John Coltrane, and a few creased, curling photographs of the Welsh countryside tacked to the wall. The passport is easy to find, tucked inside a brown envelope in the bottom drawer of his desk.

I thumb through pages, inspecting each faded stamp from border control at John F. Kennedy; visits in December and May and August spanning four years until his emigration. Each stamp corresponding to a memory of their togetherness. In Caleb's mind, I fear, New York will always be Rosemary's—when he turns a corner, boards a train, or enters a bar they once entered together.

I wonder what Rosemary's passport looked like during those years of long distance. Together with Instagram history, passport stamps—hers and his—would help me compile their relationship timeline. Who did most of the traveling? Who pursued, who was pursued? Can I supplant memories of her with memories of me?

We will turn that corner, board that train, enter a different bar. I'll attach myself to objects and places and people.

After putting Caleb's passport carefully back inside its envelope, I take off my clothes, stretch across the length of the twin-size bed, and await his return.

chapter four

ON MY NEXT day off, Saturday, my family treats me to a belated birthday brunch. Caleb is invited but can't come because he's busy preparing for a huge presentation on Monday. He apologized profusely and promised he was looking forward to meeting them, which I chose to take at face value.

"When are we going to meet this mystery man?" my father asks from across the table. "Are you sure he exists?"

"He's working on an important project," I say, emphasizing *important*. "But thank you for that predictable dad joke."

"What your father means to say"—my mother tosses him a glance both fond and exasperated—"is that we can't wait to meet him, whenever you're no longer afraid we'll embarrass you and scare him off."

Noah joins in, grinning. "It'll be a good test—can he handle the four of us?"

The waitress chooses this moment, bless her, to swoop in. Noah orders waffles and an iced coffee; my father, a cappuccino and a cheddar-bacon omelet; my mother, two poached eggs and a hot tea. I order a dirty chai, obviously, and then ask if I can substitute a few ingredients in an omelet.

"Substitutes cost extra," she says.

"It's her birthday brunch," my father says to the waitress. "So we'll spoil her."

My mother gestures at the paper crown she purchased and placed beside my utensils. "Sweetheart, why don't you put yours on?"

I reluctantly unfold it. Traditions, traditions, and lovely ones. I should be grateful.

After taking my order, the waitress smirks and veers away.

"The substitution queen," Noah says. "Have you ever ordered anything without asking if it can be changed?"

I point at his iced coffee. "It's twenty degrees outside. One of these days I'm force-feeding you some hot coffee, it's absurd you haven't even tried it."

"Hard pass. I like what I like."

"But hot is way more common at hotel buffets," I say. "What happens if there's no Starbucks or fancy espresso bar wherever you end up shooting your first film? I predict grumpy mornings."

"Enough, Naomi." My mother places her hand on my arm.

"Friendly banter only, put your claws away," my father says.

"Speaking of"—Noah clears his throat, effectively silencing us all—"I have some news. I've been promoted to a series regular on *Ghosts*!"

"Holy shit!" I blurt out, flicking my eyes from face to face. Neither of my parents look surprised, so I turn back to Noah. "Excuse me? Why am I the last to know?"

"Sorry! I meant to tell you, I just haven't seen you in a while."

"There's this new thing called texting, all the cool kids are doing it."

"Ha," he says, not laughing.

I take a deep breath, switching tactics. "Well, that's exciting, Noah, really—"

"Let's not get *too* excited," he interrupts. "I don't want to get my hopes up too much. They could still, like, kill me off in the writers' room. And then I'm unemployed—again."

"Writers *are* very powerful," I say, grinning, and then pause before adding something nice. "Optimistic and realistic. You're allowed to be both. I'm sure all your fans will be clamoring for more."

Cheeks reddeningly slightly, he thanks me and sips his iced coffee.

My father turns to me. "By the way, are you still working on that review?"

Oh, shit.

I forgot I told him, several weeks ago, that I was hoping to start pitching book reviews to magazines. At the time I reasoned it would be smart to have extra exposure, more bylines, even if it wasn't fiction. My father greatly approved, telling me that thinking deeply about the structure of contemporary novels would help me eventually craft my own. Both my parents believe I'm capable of publishing a novel eventually, but I'm unsure if their faith in me is justified or not.

"Yeah, still working," I say, despite most certainly not. "I'll let you know if I need another set of eyes." Rosemary—thinking about her, writing about her, monitoring her—occupies most of my time and energy now. I wish I could tell them about it. I never expected to become such a skilled liar, at least not *off* the page; I'm constantly teetering on the edge of confessing, but I anticipate what they would say, and I refuse to be dissuaded. At least not yet.

The food arrives. We all dig in, chewing for several minutes in a comfortable silence. Halfway through my onion-feta-spinach omelet, my father reaches across the table and hands me an envelope. My name is written in beautiful, slanting cursive. "It's from Grandma," he says. "Don't lose it. Maybe you can visit her soon?"

"We talked on the phone on my birthday," I say, a bit defensively. "It was nice." I open the envelope and discover five crisp hundred-dollar bills, apropos of nothing except once being born.

It's been at least two months since I last visited her. There are no excuses. I silently scroll through my weekly schedule of bookstore shifts, searching for space, as the waitress slides a chocolate chip muffin pierced by two burning candles onto the table in front of me. My family launches into a soaring vocal performance of "Happy Birthday," with Noah and my mother making it sound far better than it's meant to.

Why expend all that effort with no reward?

On the train home, I navigate to Rosemary's Instagram. It's become a habit, transitioning easily between my personal account and my anonymous one. Using the latter, I avoid implementing a distinguishable voice when captioning new photos of coffee and books; the account could ostensibly belong to a bot well-versed in hashtags. Remaining unobtrusive is the name of the game.

But Rosemary's Instagram Story, when I click on it, is the first to truly test my resolve. It's a photo of the Hudson River bike path; the geo-tag indicates she's in Washington Heights, and the caption reads, 14 miles later, with a bicycle emoji and a skull-and-crossbones emoji.

My hand spasms as I stare at the image more closely—searching each corner of the frame for another bike, for the curve of a spoke, for a shoe, a wisp of dark hair, a man-shaped shadow. How could Rosemary's decision to ride fourteen miles, from her neighborhood to Caleb's, possibly be a coincidence?

I text Caleb. **Hey you, just finished brunch with the fam, and they remain extremely eager to meet you, haha. What are you up to? How's the presentation prep going?**

Ten minutes later, he replies: **I'm eager to meet them, too! Prep is going okay, will probably need another few hours, but I'll come over later tonight if I manage to finish?**

Please do, I instruct him, adjusting my headphones. Then I press shuffle on my music library and turn up the volume.

I WAKE THE next morning with a sour taste in my mouth.

Caleb came over last night around nine. His hair smelled good, like he'd just showered. We had sex twice and each drank a cup of tea. I took my hormones and didn't ask him any clarifying questions about the bike path or the geo-tag. I was afraid of what it might mean to catch him in a lie and resistant, also, to behaving like a paranoid nag. No one wants a paranoid nag. Then I fell asleep without brushing my teeth.

The sight of him now, another body in my bed, no longer feels like a rare gift or a surprise. He stays here four, five times a week. It has started to feel normal; I might deserve it, might deserve him.

Caleb is still asleep, so I get dressed as quickly and quietly as possible, putting on the gold hoop earrings my grandmother gave me for my twenty-first birthday, as well as a pewter-gray sweater-dress she once complimented. Before heading out I touch his bare back, pressing gently against a pronounced knob of his spine.

He rolls over fast, nearly crushing my hand. "What time is it?"

"Nine thirty. I'm visiting my grandma, remember?"

"Right." He rubs his eyes. "That's so nice. You two have a really special relationship."

"We do," I say, pleased. "Hopefully you'll meet her soon."

"I'd like that. Will I be seeing you later?"

"Yes, but you need to be lying in this exact position when I get back," I tell him, "or there'll be consequences."

Laughing, he hooks an arm around my waist and kisses me goodbye. As he does so, I notice his phone, lying on the windowsill, buzz and light up with an incoming text. I can't decipher the name, but I'm fairly certain there's a *y* in it.

"Who's texting ya so early?" I say, attempting to sound offhand.

"Probably the Synergy group text." He yawns. "Jordan and Hillary are always sending memes."

Synergy is the name of his company, and Jordan and Hillary are two of his colleagues. Seems plausible. *Hillary* does, after all, end with a *y*.

"Ha," I say, too high-pitched. "Okay, well, see you later."

My grandmother's assisted-living facility is upstate, accessible via an hour-long ride on the Metro-North train. I hail a taxi from the station and, upon arrival, sign my name in the visitation log before taking the elevator to the third floor. To resist all temptation, I put my phone in my pocket and vow not to touch it again until I leave.

Walking down the fluorescent-lit linoleum hallway toward my grandmother's suite—it always feels like a hospital here—I pass a woman slumped in a wheelchair, staring at a bird feeder hung from the eaves just outside a window.

"A bully," says the woman in the wheelchair. Her face is darkening, and her voice, deep and scratchy, unsettles me. "He chases away the sparrows and eats all their food. It's a shame, how much I dislike him. He's very beautiful."

I mumble, "Oh, yes, sad," but don't stop to chat.

Moving down the hall, I knock on suite 308. Seconds pass slowly; no reply. I push the door—which is unlocked—open slightly, and poke my head in. "Grammie?" I shout.

Finally registering the sound of my voice, she turns, startled, to look at me from the reclined armchair in front of the television. It's blasting at an unnatural decibel. My grandmother is ninety-two. Her hearing aids—and her hip replacement and her adult diaper and her daily intake of six prescription medications—all keep her alive and functioning.

I brush my lips against her cheek. The skin is thin and rough like sandpaper. "Can we turn the volume down?" I ask. "So we can talk? Here, let me."

The screen has shifted jarringly from talking heads discussing the weather to a cheerful-looking blond woman on a manicured lawn—one hand on the back of a stroller, the other holding a bottle of pills.

"They should cast people with actual incontinence in these commercials," says my grandmother. "For authenticity. Look at this woman! She's never shit herself."

I laugh, even though the profanity concerns me—despite her writing a slew of dirty jokes over the span of her writing career, I've heard her say *shit* only a handful of times. I can't tell if departure from the norm indicates gleeful liberation or embittered surrender.

"So." My grandmother presses a button to reverse the recline of her chair, slowly folding into a seated position to look me in the eye. "Are you writing?"

"I have a few chapters, but mostly I'm in an input mode," I say lamely. "Researching, brainstorming, stuff like that."

When her thin, meticulously painted eyebrows furrow, my cheeks flush with heat.

"Words beget words," she says. "You know, I don't believe in writer's block."

"I didn't say I had writer's block! I'm just in the process of plotting things out."

She waves her blue-veined forearm, as if batting away my comment. "Where are my pages?"

During college we sustained a lively email exchange; words pinged over the two thousand miles between us. I sent chunks of text; she replied with suggestions and even praise. We were closer then. I wish I knew how to be more comfortable seeing her like this—diminished, disabled.

"I forgot. I'm sorry. I'll bring them next time."

"So what's this mystery project about?"

I exhale, reminding myself she has always been, and will always be, on my side. "So, for context, I recently found out why Caleb came to New York. He moved here for his ex, who's an American. She lives in Brooklyn and works in publishing, and I can't stop thinking about her. It wasn't what I expected at *all*."

My grandmother leans in. "What did you expect?"

"I thought he moved here for himself, you know, to further his career or choose a different kind of life. Experience living abroad. I didn't realize it was because of—love."

"I could ask why you said the word *love* with such disgust, but I won't." She laughs, shakes her head, pins me in her incredulous gaze. "It shouldn't be that shocking, Naomi. Most people do things for love."

"I know, but that's exactly why I'm freaked out. It sucks to be the girl who has to follow that kind of love. He basically sacrificed his entire life. For her."

"But every relationship is different. And that one didn't work out. He's with *you* now, not her."

Why won't she validate my perfectly reasonable concern?

"Well, the premise of the novel hinges on that insecurity, which I think is, like, a totally normal insecurity to have if you were in my position? So anyway, it's about a woman who becomes obsessed"—I'm gulping for air—"with her boyfriend's ex."

Now my grandmother is the only one who knows.

"What form does this obsession take?" she asks.

"She follows her around and eventually becomes her friend."

"Naturally." My grandmother laughs, and the sound, warm and buoyant, feels like permission. "Does Caleb know?"

"He will soon. Just waiting for the right time."

But what would telling him accomplish? Either he would love me enough to stay, despite everything, or he wouldn't. Loving and leaving are equally likely, and each would probably prove permanent. I'm not ready to narrow my options like that, not yet.

My grandmother steeples her fingers. "Do what you need to do. Caleb should understand your writing takes precedence. Over everything." She points at a drawer of her desk. "Know what's in there? The first story you ever wrote—I think you were six—about talking animals in a tree house."

I follow her gaze to the drawer of writings past.

"It was so imaginative, I've kept it all these years. Writing is your first love. Put it first. Protect it. And send me pages!"

I tell her I will. I make a promise.

FOR MY EIGHTEENTH birthday, my grandmother bought me a vintage typewriter. It was an Underwood No. 4, black and gold and elegant. It cost seven hundred dollars. I already had a MacBook and Microsoft Word, but my grandmother thought the typewriter would inspire me (*patience and perseverance*, she said) to write more slowly and thoughtfully. To be precise and hear myself think. But I used it only twice before returning, guiltily, to Microsoft Word. At the typewriter, the world was locked out; I had to type but sometimes couldn't. On my computer I let the world in, tons of open tabs on Chrome, for better or for worse, and the typewriter lived out the rest of its days on my bookshelf; it served as a bookend of sorts, as décor.

The truth is I'm a wealthy writer, insecure and bored.

My grandfather, after graduating from law school, learned he excelled at poker. It's not, in my opinion, a skill worth venerating no matter how brilliant or how patient your bluffs may be, and he went on to lose far more money than he ever won, but the irony of my grandfather's long tenure at one particular poker table was a certain blossoming friendship with the elderly man who sat to his left. The friendship resulted in three buildings in various states of disrepair bequeathed to my grandfather from the elderly "slumlord," buildings that subsequently resulted in my family's livelihood. My livelihood. My father's NYU salary, the checks from my grandmother's syndicated television shows and memoir royalties, and the trickling sales from my mother's (cruelly underrated) studio album available on CDBaby.com could not have been enough to sustain us.

"Just so you know, you can't casually use the word *slumlord*," I said snidely to my parents after they explained all this during my college years—not due to any linguistically ethical responsibility, but out of a once-repressed desire to shame them for something.

"Oh, shush, it's just us chickens here, I won't use it anywhere else," my mother said.

"That's actually what your grandfather called him," said my father.

The elderly man had no next of kin. He had alienated everyone. It was sad, but then we were rich. My family became landlords, a population of people universally loathed. When people complain about spiked rent costs, I join in, hoping no one recognizes the wolf in sheep's clothing.

The once-decrepit buildings were refurbished, though sometimes faultily, sometimes even illegally, and rented out. Their bad neighborhoods became popular after gentrification, eventually attracting the attention of mammoth real estate development corporations wanting to tear down the shabby seven-story building I grew up in and transform it into a shiny, sleek skyscraper piercing the clouds. There would be a gym, a pool, a penthouse, a doorman. By the time the real estate developer's offer had doubled and tripled, my grandfather had died of a stroke; we mourned the way you would expect to mourn a man generous with his pockets but not with his spirit—in other words, conflicted and guilt-ridden, with a sobering and small burial; my grandmother didn't even cry—and then both my parents took up the torch, assembling a team of lawyers and accountants to advise them. As proud artistic types, they saw this turn toward problematic capitalism as a great source of shame, but also of relief.

The deal, a land lease, was finalized five years ago. The developer would pay us seventy thousand dollars a month to lease the plot of land they would eventually raze and build upon. In ninety-nine years—*ninety-nine years*—our family would own the building again. ("In ninety-nine years, our grandkids will be in charge, I guess we're, like, legally obligated to procreate now," Noah joked then, before remembering my inability and turning red and changing the subject swiftly.)

Two years ago, the building I grew up in was officially torn down. My parents moved to a river town in Westchester to begin their lives as empty nesters and, in lieu of university, my brother moved to Hell's Kitchen with his best friend to be within walking distance of the windowless audition rooms where he has spent so many waking hours. I moved into the top floor of my grandmother's Greenwich Village brownstone.

A free fucking writing residency in New York and nothing to show for it.

Use it.

DURING MONDAY'S SHIFT, I stalk the stacks in search of books Rosemary has edited. I want to hold them. With each one, I navigate directly to the Acknowledgments page. Speak aloud, like incantations, all the words grateful authors have used to describe her: *incisive, shrewd, miraculous, invaluable.*

"Excuse me." A customer appears at my elbow. "There's no one at the register. I'm ready to check out."

Cheeks flaming, I slip the book Rosemary edited back onto the shelves and follow the customer to my designated post.

"Oh, I love *The Folded Clock*," I say. It's essentially a diary, albeit a carefully crafted one—intimate, meditative, witty, often wise.

The customer, a big-haired woman in gold satin pants, nods distractedly. "Yeah. Big fan of Heidi Julavits."

If it were socially acceptable, and if she didn't already look so disgruntled, I would recite aloud from a passage on page 212, in which Julavits muses about her partner's ex-girlfriends: "I have felt with these women a blood connection; these women have parted with a valued possession and now it has fallen to me. . . . And so I feel kinship, and gratitude. Also curiosity."

It hit me particularly hard when I read it recently. But the narrator, unlike me, doesn't do anything drastic. She only watches and wonders from afar.

After the customer exits, I glance at my phone screen. It's awash with notifications from my family's group text.

Thirty-seven minutes ago, Noah wrote: the first review of Ghosts is here! with a link to the *Entertainment Weekly* article attached. Noah is described as "compelling," and the season itself as "poignant and authentic."

Thirty-five minutes ago, my parents unleashed a torrent of exclamation points and congratulations. Now it's my turn to join in, gushing pride; it feels nice, tranquil even, to be swept up in someone else's joy. I'm happy for him, yes, it's true, but then I wonder—when did they last direct congratulatory exclamation points at me?

Scrolling through each of their Facebook accounts, I am petty and stubborn and single-minded. Check out this video of Noah's powerful rendition of Ed Sheeran's song "Thinking Out Loud" at 54 Below, my father wrote a week ago, alongside a YouTube link. Eighty-six likes, thirteen gushing comments.

It's Noah's final week of Broadway performances and your last chance to grab tickets, my mother wrote last month. Fifty-eight likes, five new confirmed ticket holders.

Two-ish years ago, my parents each posted a photo of me in my cap and gown. Happy day! my father wrote. Thirty-two likes. Kudos to our girl for graduating cum laude! wrote my mother. Forty-seven likes.

I once casually asked my parents to post my online publications on their Facebook pages. They said they planned on it but then didn't, and it would be too demeaning to remind them.

Three years, then, since I've done anything of note. So it's time to instigate a new scene, to extract new material. I can't accept oblivion or impermanence, I'm supposed to leave behind a legacy, I made my grandmother a promise. I can't make a baby, but I *can* make a book.

After cataloging a list of upcoming events—indie concerts, comedy shows, gallery openings, literary panels—I text Rosemary.

Hey, are you free tomorrow night? There's a cool talk about likability in literature called Bad Women. Any interest in checking it out?

I gulp my lukewarm dirty chai and wait until Rosemary's reply vibrates the desk. Wish I could, but I'm busy that night. Look forward to hearing about it, though!

Deflated, I text Caleb. Want to go to your favorite Ethiopian place for dinner tomorrow?

I'd love to, he replies three minutes later, but it's Becca's last day with the company. The whole office is having drinks to send her off.

I read the text three times. Could it be possible—?

No—it's perfectly reasonable, isn't it, that Rosemary and Caleb are busy on the same night, and it's kind of Caleb and his colleagues to make Becca's last day a memorable one, and of course Rosemary has a life I'm not privy to.

No worries, I write back to him.

More material is required now, more and more and more—if I can't have Rosemary in the flesh, I'll possess her on the page. *But this is the last time*, I promise myself. I need to know just a bit more before I retreat to my own imagination, before I keep my distance and stop being such a creep.

I scroll through her Twitter. Recent tweets span a range of topics—*New Yorker* fiction by a debut author, a plea for live music recommendations regarding an upcoming trip to Nashville, blasting a known misogynist in the media industry, and finally, a question posed: Twitter army, what are your favorite climbing gyms in Brooklyn? Trying to decide where to buy a membership!

A horde of acquaintances, social media strategists, branded content writers, and health and fitness editors chimed in. The consensus is Brooklyn Boulders Gowanus.

The revelation that Rosemary climbs feels unexpected but serendipitous, too, somehow. Unexpected because I assumed her workout of choice would be yoga or running or, of course, biking—*fourteen miles!*—and serendipitous because I once lived in Colorado, every climber's playground, and it would therefore be believable to say I was a climber, too. I never once ventured into my college's bouldering gym or elected to join any climbing trips in the mountains, true, because I was afraid to fail, afraid to make a fool of myself in front of more outdoorsy classmates, but it *had* always sounded like fun, and maybe now I am being given sort of a second chance.

VIA PROCESS OF elimination, I take a well-educated guess about Rosemary's exercise regimen. Twitter conveniently reveals she plans to attend book launches on Tuesday and Thursday, and since memberships are worthless unless you go biweekly, I predict Rosemary will stop by Brooklyn Boulders tonight, a Monday. Don't most healthy people desire to kick off their weeks with a workout? I wouldn't really know, I've never had a gym membership, but I do love to walk—often many miles a day, with headphones pulsing; it helps me think.

It only takes twenty minutes to get to the gym from work, so tonight is the night to push my relationship with Rosemary beyond books and barstools. I purchase a day pass and rent climbing shoes and fill out a waiver. I'm responsible, yes, for anything that happens to me.

"So rad you'll be climbing with us today, Naomi," the attractive man—bearded, tattooed, muscular—behind the desk says to me. "I'm River. We're a very tight-knit and supportive community here. We hope you'll consider a membership."

I smile at him while surreptitiously scanning the space. I would prefer to spot Rosemary before she spots me. In preparation, I practice configuring my face into a blend of surprise and amusement, an expression that communicates something like, *Whoa, fancy seeing* you *here!*

"Are the shoes supposed to be this tight?" My toes are squeezed and suffering. I rotate an ankle to get the blood pumping. "Is it supposed to feel this way?"

"You'll get used to it," River says cheerfully. "They have to be tight like that, you know, form-fitting, so you have more traction—"

"Naomi?"

Genuinely startled (the irony), I whip around, finding myself face-to-face with Rosemary. Her coat and scarf are still on. She must have just walked in.

"Oh, whoa, hey!" I say, unsure what to do with my hands. "Fancy seeing you here!"

"I should've *guessed* you were a climber!" She unbuttons her coat and taps what I assume is her membership card against a small machine on the desk. "But this must be such a letdown for you after Colorado, right?"

"Colorado?" River butts in. "So rad, dude. Such good climbing out there."

Ignoring him, I lower my voice and give a prepared speech. "Well, actually—this is kind of embarrassing, but—I've never done this before. Bouldering, I mean. Everyone at school was obsessed, but I guess I was too intimidated. I came to finally see what all the fuss is about."

Rosemary unravels her scarf, readjusts her tight ponytail. "Well, I can totally teach you the basics. I've only been climbing a few months, so I'm not amazing or anything, but still—I can help."

"I'd love that."

"Do you need to change or anything? I'm heading to the locker room, I can show you around."

I'm already in my workout clothes, so I ask, "Where are the bathrooms?"

"Same place. Follow me."

The gym is cavernous, a former warehouse. Loud music ricochets off the walls. If the average Equinox could be described as full of frat bros and sorority girls clinging to their prime via tread-mills and barbells, then the climbing gym would be a place where every type of campus outsider feels confident coming together to use their brains as well as their bodies. People of all shapes and sizes and colors—though the most successful climbers appear to be petite with ripped forearms and a sinewy back—rise and fall, slithering vertically and horizontally; arms and legs extend and then retreat, muscles tauten and release. Aware of the soft places on my body, I hike up my high-rise leggings. Tucking everything away.

There are two toilet stalls in the locker room. I go inside one of them, sit on the lid of the toilet, cough a few times to mask the sound of silence, and then flush. While washing my hands, Rose-mary wiggles out of her jeans and pulls off her blouse. As she swaps delicate lace cups for a utilitarian sports bra, I sneak a glance at her breasts. Without any significant manipulation of my own, Rose-mary is here, *half-naked*, in front of me. It's an effective scene, given our narrative, and so I take her in with an approximation of the male gaze because I'm seeing what Caleb used to see—and with a twinge of satisfaction, I remember undressing in front of him once, a couple of weeks after we started sleeping together, remember him saying, "Yours are the most beautiful breasts I've ever seen," as he reached out to touch them.

"It's actually so random that you're here," Rosemary says, ad-justing her tight workout shorts. "Isn't this technically the second time we've run into each other? Are you"—she gives me an exag-gerated wink—"stalking me?"

I let out an instinctive bark of nervous laughter and then, rap-idly calibrating, give her an exaggerated wink of my own. "Ooh, so what if I was?"

"It wouldn't be the first time," she says airily, unbothered. "This guy I went on a terrible date with a few months ago literally tracked me down to hand over his terrible manuscript."

"Are you serious?"

"Unfortunately."

When she wanders out of the locker room, I follow.

"You can share my chalk." Rosemary gestures at the pouch affixed to her hip, then points at the dozens of polyurethane rocks zigzagging up the wall in various different color schemes. "Every route's difficulty is marked by a piece of tape, see? That green one is marked a v0, for beginners, and that blue one is a v10, for experts. The rocks are called holds. I'll demonstrate how to climb the v0, but first I'll show you how to fall."

I plop down on the mat to watch, the pain in my toes nearly unbearable otherwise.

As Rosemary grabs a green hold with two hands, I notice the bulge of her biceps, the activation of muscles previously hidden beneath the sleeves of her sweaters. Next, she positions her feet on two tiny holds before pushing backward off the wall and collapsing onto the cushy mat, making contact first with her heels and then with her butt, gravity pulling her down and rocking her back. It's all very fluid. She doesn't look like someone whose toes are being squashed.

I imagine, and briefly inhabit, a different sort of scene: What if Rosemary, the more experienced climber, takes an unexpected fall? It won't be my fault—my body is not her body, my mind is not her mind—but it's possible I unwittingly distract her . . .

In the ambulance, I hold her hand and check her pulse. My finger on the leaping vein under her ear. In the emergency room, she asks for Caleb. I pretend not to hear, and so she asks again. She makes a fuss, she screams, she is beside herself—and so I call, and so he comes. He faces us both, rushing to her aid because I asked, and then she sees everything, she understands what I've done.

I'll write it down later, experiment with how it plays out on the page.

"Never let your arms flail," Rosemary says, interrupting all my fictions. "Just in case you land at an awkward angle. Keep them folded across your chest, like this."

I tentatively stand and approach for a better look. Seeing her splayed like that, vulnerable, with me above, I could step on her if I wanted. Easily break her nose with the pad of my climbing shoe. Her forehead is inches away from my left foot. A sudden ill-fated step, a loss of balance, a crunch.

I take two steps back, dizzy.

Rosemary leaps to her feet. "Ready? Your turn to fall."

I grab the same hold and imitate her movements. Soon I'm the one at her feet.

"Good," she says. "Now, watch. I'm sticking to the green v0 holds on the way up, but you can use any color to get back down. I wouldn't suggest jumping from the top unless you feel yourself slipping. If that happens, just remember how to fall."

I watch her crawl vertically upward, appearing both delicate and strong. A destroyer of binaries.

I follow in her footsteps. This time, she has given me permission. I attempt to curl my fingers and toes exactly as she did, to reach for the same holds in the same formation, to haul myself— exterior and interior, skin and soul—higher and higher above the ground.

"Keep your arms straight," she calls out as my elbows bend. "Most beginners drag themselves up by their arms, but your legs are actually stronger. Use them!"

My hip pops as I drag my left leg upward, but upon reaching the final hold, I'm delighted to so suddenly feel strong and accomplished and a bit badass.

"You did it!" Rosemary sounds genuinely thrilled for me. "Well done."

I toss a grin over my shoulder, grip the top edge of the wall with both hands, and hang there for a moment, suspended, as a satisfying ache spreads from my shoulder sockets down my spine.

"Climbing is all about using your angles," says Rosemary once I have safely returned to the ground. "Pivoting your body in the right direction to maximize balance and stability."

"You sound like a fitness manual," I say, smearing more chalk across my palms.

"Ha, well, it's just math."

I can't resist. "I guess that means your ex would be a pretty good climber, right?"

She bites her lip, breaks eye contact. "Maybe. I don't know."

In the long pause that follows, my hands start to sweat; casually I enter her personal space, slip my fingers into the pouch on her hip, and rub chalk across my palms.

"Come on," she finally says, "let's try a v1 now."

Though each hold is much trickier, I attack them with gusto. The muscles in my arms tremble, but I still succeed, refusing to fall unless it's intentional. My technique is appalling, but Rosemary is a good teacher. With her help, I'll become better.

"I took an action shot of you," Rosemary says. "Look."

Captured in her camera lens—my mouth slightly parted, right knee bent, left arm extended and reaching—I look determined, pliant, impressive. The best version of myself.

"You look so legit!" she says, correctly interpreting my expression. "I'll text it to you."

After a few more complicated climbs of her own, Rosemary's cheeks acquire an appealing glow; as she hooks a heel over a particularly tricky hold on a v5, another attractive man compliments her form.

"Thanks, Jake," Rosemary says, breathless, as she completes the route. "I've been working on this one for ages."

Modesty looks good on her, too.

When she returns to the ground, Rosemary introduces us.

"Jake Brantley, this is Naomi— Wait, I don't actually think I know your last name?"

"Adler," I say after a panicked pause. Close, but not too close. "Nice to meet you, Jake." I angle my body toward Rosemary. "I actually might be done for today. I'm exhausted! Do you want to get a drink? I feel like we both deserve one."

"Yes! There's a cool brewery down the block. I'll go change."

My leggings are smudged with chalk, but I wasn't organized enough to bring any other clothes. As I wait for Rosemary, I watch a woman with purple hair and a septum ring scuttle upside-down across an overhanging wall, defying gravity like Spider-Man. A few other people are watching, too, and when they all start whooping, I join them.

"Ready?" Rosemary reappears. "Let's go. See you later, Jake! Bye, River!"

AT THE BREWERY, we settle into a booth with a wheat ale for her and an IPA for me.

"That was surprisingly fun," I say. "No wonder so many people are obsessed."

"I know, it's gotten so trendy all of a sudden, hasn't it? I actually started climbing after my breakup. I was desperate to distract myself—I tried kickboxing, spinning classes, yoga. I spend so much time in my head or in a book that I forget what it feels like to have a body. Bouldering helps the most, so it stuck."

"That's great. Have any of your friends started climbing, too?"

"No," says Rosemary, momentarily avoiding my gaze. "My friends aren't super adventurous in that way, I invited them to join a few times but they kept coming up with excuses."

"They're missing out," I say, smiling at her, and in this moment I recognize an opportunity, a sudden opening, that I'd be a fool not to take.

By becoming her bookish friend *and* her climbing friend, it's possible to claim even more of her emotional territory, her trust. Of course, I'd intended to keep my distance after gathering sufficient material, but it has become clear that Rosemary needs something from me, too. I'm not sure what, exactly, but I aim to find out. If I continually orbit her, she'll grow accustomed to my presence, and perhaps even unconsciously rely on it, on me. I'll learn how to give her what she seeks.

"It's supposed to happen during this time in our lives, though, isn't it?" she muses. "Drifting apart due to different priorities, different paths. To be honest, I'm surprised it took this long. My friends never really understood my relationship with Caleb. They heard all about him, but by the time he finally moved and became a part of my real life, I realized how totally incompatible they all were. Caleb, well, he offered me a way out of the person I was. It's hard to explain. Before him, I'd always struggled to feel happy. And I guess my friends took that personally, which makes sense. But now that we've broken up, I can tell how relieved they are, how smug, and it's just—unbearable sometimes."

I open and close my mouth like a fish, unsure how I've bamboozled her into being so vulnerable. I hold all this new information close to my chest, keeping it safe, gratified to know she has granted me access. With Caleb gone, and her friends going, there's a vacancy in her life I aim to fill.

"They sound like shitty friends," I declare.

There's a bit of an awkward silence, and as we both reach for our drinks, I worry I've irrevocably offended her, overstepped my bounds. By insinuating she's a bad judge of character, I might have implicated myself, too. I instead need her to believe she's becoming better at choosing people, need her to see how I represent a new dawn of future friendships. It's time, now, for her to leave everyone else—the rooftop blondes, the Welshman with the sliced-bread smile—behind.

Rosemary finally speaks. "Maybe, maybe not, I don't know." Laughing somewhat harshly, she adds, "Or I could actually be the shitty one."

Willing to offer a conversational lifeline but tired of creating the perfect transition, tired of being careful, I ask, "How did your parents meet? Random, I know. But you mentioned Caleb offering you a way out of—"

"Not that random," she interrupts, setting down her glass. "I'm always curious about those origin stories. Theirs is pretty boring, but also sweet, I guess. They met move-in day freshman year at the University of Virginia. Inseparable ever since. So when I met Caleb at St Andrews, I guess some part of me was like, this is it, it's happening."

Seeking immediate relief, I crack the knuckles of my left hand.

"What about your parents?" she asks.

"Back row of an eighth-grade English class," I say. "They're New York natives, but then my dad's family moved to Los Angeles and they lost touch. Their paths didn't actually cross again until they were in their twenties."

I grew up listening to this story and interpreting it as such: serendipitous encounters are desirable, and engineered interactions are not. When I first told my parents how Caleb and I met, they exchanged a quick glance, and then my mother patted me on the shoulder sympathetically and said, "So much is changing out there." But online dating algorithms involve a certain amount of randomness and mystery and serendipity, too. Out of millions of single people looking for something resembling love and intimacy in New York, the probability of Caleb and me stumbling upon each other's Tinder profiles paralleled the probability of bumping into each other on some random street corner.

Rosemary's voice cuts in. "Ooh, I love these kinds of stories, how'd their paths cross again?"

"They literally ran into each other on Ninth and Second Avenue in the East Village. My mom was walking her huge Bernese mountain dog, Theo, and just as my dad turned the corner, Theo unleashed this absolute *flood* of diarrhea. My mom started frantically mopping up the sidewalk with these napkins she borrowed from the pizza place on the corner, and that's when my dad recognized her face and was like, *Linda Greenspan?*" My mother's maiden name is a relic, buried. I can't be identified with it. "She needed an industrial hose rather than a few napkins, but the rest is history."

"Wow, your dad has incredible timing." Rosemary giggles. "So memorable. No wonder they got married."

"Exactly." Too forcefully, I add: "It seems like no one meets in real life anymore."

"But we met in real life," she says, blinking at me.

I think of her Facebook profile, of @Language_and_Liquid, of locations tracked and photos studied—Caleb's arm around her shoulders in Washington Square Park, the purple graduation gown and blurry grin—and attempt to expel the twisting sensation in my gut.

"Cheers to our beautifully organic friendship, then." I raise my glass, and we clink our half-full glasses together.

I take another gulp before speaking again. "I'm jealous of how you met your ex." It's one of the truer things I've told her. My breath catches, releases. "I tried Tinder so I could finally have 'the boyfriend experience.' I thought it could be, like, a test run. It's impossible to be a perfect girlfriend the first time around, right, so I just expected it would end because of something I did or some way I fell short. At least I would have something to write about when that happened, a full spectrum of feeling, but sitting around expecting it to someday end paradoxically prevents me from actually *experiencing* it, which was the whole fucking point—" I can feel my jaw locking as the truth slips out between my front teeth; I drank too much too fast on an empty stomach; my beer, the menu reveals, is 9 percent alcohol, and yet, and *yet*, despite the danger of exposure, it's cathartic to share this insecurity, to be vulnerable, with Rosemary. It feels risky as well as right. The invisible string I've imagined dangling between us tightens, contracts.

"Whoa, hey, Naomi, listen, try not to think like that," Rosemary says firmly, reaching out to brush my shoulder with her hand. "Try and breathe for a sec, okay?"

I do as she commands, then say, "Ugh, yikes," with a hiccupping sort-of snicker to make sure she's aware I'm just as surprised as she is by my outburst.

"Plus, meet-cutes are rare, remember," says Rosemary, "the stuff of rom-coms, and I actually know a few friends"—*But the rare thing happened to you,* I want to point out, *why are* you *so rare*—"who married their Tinder matches! They're super happy and super in love. And who knows, Tinder might honestly seem cool and retro to your grandkids. Times change."

Again with the grandkids, again with the uninspired presumption I'm able to pass my genetic materials on into the next life. My family, plus Rachel and Danielle, are the only people who know the truth. I rarely share the fact of my inability because no one ever knows how to simply sit with it—they always want to fix the problem, fix me, coughing up the words *adoption* or *in vitro* or *surrogate*, words that provide alternatives but not solutions. I'll admit, sometimes, to feeling an unnamable, indiscernible sorrow so strong it embarrasses me. But maybe it's possible I'm only performing the emotion society expects. I can't be sure if my sorrow is organic, is mine alone. Either way: To procreate, or not to procreate? *That* is the question my body decided, circumventing my mind. But I don't need children, biological or not; I never did. It's what I would've chosen, surely, if I'd been given the chance to choose. Children are expensive, and often enough will also go sour, become bad, grow out of your control. Words, not children, can be manipulated and perfected and controlled, can someday perhaps even generate monumental, enduring ideas.

But I'm not ready to explain this to her yet, despite knowing that most friendships are born of confessionals. It's true—my desire to reveal exactly who I am feels nearly as urgent as the desire to conceal it. For now, though, self-preservation must overrule self-annihilation. Eventually the book will be written, and our relationship might even outlive the literary, occupying some sliver of the real world.

And so, I lead with a safer revelation. "But I can't help wanting a good origin story still! I guess that's the writer in me, you know, always wanting to play out some sort of narrative." *The Galápagos* was *a good origin story*, I remind myself, *but that was part of the problem, that was why*—

"Maybe you shouldn't think of your life as some kind of narrative arc," says Rosemary gently. "Isn't that kind of restrictive? Just live it." She pauses to take a sip, but something about the set of her mouth implies she isn't done. "Don't get me wrong, though. I really do hear you; it's tough for me, too, I'm also working on a novel. But the irony is, those stories you think are best—stories you've told yourself your entire life, stories you're desperate to turn into fiction—sometimes just aren't interesting and don't matter. I have real examples of this with my memoirists. Many of them don't know when they've hit gold, I have to point out that one little throwaway sentence on the seventieth page is actually the heart of their story, do you understand what I'm saying?"

"Uh-huh," I manage to say, "totally," but my vision is swimming, and my chest is tightening, and I feel like I might faint. Rosemary is a *writer*? Since when? Why didn't Caleb mention it? Had he somehow predicted how easily threatened I am?

Well, he's right. This is the most singularly damaging information I've learned. Ever since discovering how attractive and successful and sophisticated Rosemary is, I've comforted myself with the knowledge that at least I'm the first writer Caleb has dated.

But now I know Rosemary and I really are the same genre of person, and the irony remains: if Rosemary had never dated Caleb, had never loved him, if she was not exactly who she happens to be, then a discovery of this shared passion would, in any other context, have only served to further bond us.

But now I can't help but compare our worth as writers, as lovers, as women. Maybe everything about me invokes Rosemary, allowing Caleb to possess her anew. Is anything solely mine, or will I always dwell in someone else's shadow?

When my hands stop perceptibly shaking and my vision returns, I ask: "Wait—you're writing a novel?"

She nods as if writing a novel is no big deal.

"That's, wow, I mean—I'm surprised you didn't mention it when I said I wrote, too." I sense my voice hardening. "Why didn't you?"

"Oh, probably because I don't think of myself as a writer yet," she says, too airily. "And I won't, not until I have a few significant publications or a book deal in hand. That's when I can start using the word at dinner parties." She laughs, but it seems scornful. "People always ask, 'What do you do?' and if I say, 'Writer,' they say, 'What have you written?' See, it doesn't work."

She pauses to peel a piece of dead skin off her lower lip. It's disgusting, but also blasé, almost defiant.

"I'm an editor, that's my job, I needed a job, and being a writer just isn't—at least not according to my parents, who were always very specific about what I could and couldn't be. Anyway, my novel is just fifty consecutive rambling pages so far. I started taking my writing more seriously about a year ago."

"Fifty rambling pages honestly sounds like a good start." I smile at her. "Have you shared them with anyone yet?"

"No. Like I said, I want to finish something, and maybe even publish it, before I start telling people anything. I mean, even Caleb didn't know about it! I'd only write when he wasn't around, and then of course we broke up. But I actually started writing more freely after that."

Caleb's ignorance is another small shock. I've unintentionally acquired new knowledge of her, tidbits of her character that Caleb never understood. Rosemary is beginning to seem like mine, like she was never his. But if he discovers Rosemary is a writer, might she intrigue him all over again?

"So I'm the only person you've told? Honored!" I move my hand to playfully clink my glass against hers, but she doesn't meet me halfway.

"Ha, well, don't make me regret it." Rosemary studies my face for a moment, her eyes settling on mine. I try not to blink. "It's harder to reinvent myself with people I've known for so long. It feels different with you. I feel free, and, like, decontextualized. You're a writer, too. You understand."

There's that word again: *free*. I'm tempted to ask what she means by "writing more freely," to know exactly how she defines freedom, but instead I simply say, "Yes, yes, I do."

"I'm honestly terrified of admitting it to my colleagues. It's embarrassing!"

I push out some laughter. "Maybe a little bit. But on the bright side"—a tinge of bitterness enters my voice—"you'll have an army of industry people curious enough to read your book once you finish."

I need her to understand she has privileges, connections, I do not. *Ask yourself this,* I want to say. *How will you know you deserve it?*

She sips her beer. "Not necessarily. I've never been a confident networker. I don't want anyone to feel pressured to give me something I haven't actually earned. Nepotism is gross, and sliding my manuscript onto a colleague's very crowded desk would feel like that."

It's a surprising response, and an unsettling one. My obsessive self-reliance has allowed me to be merciless as I write; my whole self is at stake. I had assumed Rosemary would shamelessly rely on her network, like so many do—but maybe she is just as naïve and stubborn and self-righteous as I am, desperate to imagine it could be possible for her work to speak for itself.

I capitalize on her confession. "Well, I'd love to read what you have so far. One page or fifty. If you want an opinion outside the publishing world. What's your book about?"

"It's about surveillance."

My molars grind, a reflex. "Oh, cool, who or what is being surveilled?"

"No neat logline yet, but I'm planning to have several intersecting stories about women who spy on each other for a variety of different reasons."

"Sounds fascinating"—my heart pumps in arrhythmic repetitions of *what-the-fuck-holy-shit-what-does-she*—"and right up my alley, I want to read!"

"Thanks. I'd honestly love feedback from a bookseller! You're the true gatekeepers." She smiles at me, but I can't tell if it's genuine—does she actually believe we're equally influential? "But

I'm not ready to share anything yet," she continues. "I'm happy to read something of yours, though. Since I'm an editor by trade I can't really donate my time without compensation, but I do some freelance work for extra cash." She takes another sip of her wheat ale; foam pools on her upper lip. "I could probably swing a reduced rate, if you want an editorial letter? Sorry to be, you know—but I hope you can understand, it's how I make a living, so—"

My desire for validation is an insatiable ache. *Well-spotted, Rosemary*, I silently commend her. *You know how to prey on people, too.* Hers is a professional opinion, but also someone whose thoughts would prove most knotty and complex. In a sense, Rosemary is my ideal reader—and by feeding her a few careful pages at a time, I can control what is exposed and what is obscured.

"That would be great! And of course I don't mind paying, you're a professional, it makes sense that you can't just read for free."

Rosemary asks for my email address to send over information about her rates, but because it includes my real last name, an abnormally long pause ensues as I scramble for the right lie. Eventually I panic-blurt the address I used as a teenager. "Naomihorsesrule at AOL dot com."

Amid authentic laughter, an unavoidable flash of her teeth. "Holy shit, don't tell me you're a secret horse girl?"

My obsession with horses never used to be a secret—instead it was an undeniable fact, like the color of my eyes, like my own name—but after Australia, it became proof of something shameful.

"It was a phase," I tell Rosemary. "Doesn't every girl go through a horse phase? I read all one hundred Saddle Club books," I add, forcing a laugh, "and felt like an expert."

I used to love the way *rider* and *writer* sounded so indistinguishable spoken aloud. I liked being both. Nearly every story I ever wrote as a teenager involved girls and their horses, but after Adam and Australia, I could only seem to write about men.

"I couldn't afford to go through a horse phase," says Rosemary. The forceful bluntness in her voice could be intended as aggressive or matter-of-fact, and so I squirm in my seat, unable to detect the difference. "Isn't Georgina Bloomberg, like, the quintessential horse girl?"

"Few horse girls are Georgina-Bloomberg-rich, but yeah, I guess it's not a cheap sport," I say, somewhat evasively.

"God, what I would give for that kind of money, though." Rosemary's eyes become glazed, unfocused. "I love my job, honestly I do—I mean, my salary lets me *read*—but do you have any idea how much money it takes to write a good book, and how much time? More time than I have, more money than I make. I'm not one of those writers who can quit their day job and live off their inheritance until someday they manage to somehow hit it big and get a splashy film adaptation and begin really raking it in."

Rosemary's gaze lands on me. I don't know what, if anything, she has surmised about my circumstances beyond a history of horses, but I can't help feeling flattened, reduced. We've both hit a nerve.

"Yeah, that, um, makes sense," I say stupidly.

"Right, well, I'll shoot you an email soon." She reaches for her coat. "I should probably head out now, though, I still have a ton more reading to do. It never ends!"

"Thanks again," I call out.

On the subway home from the bar, I post the photo Rosemary took of me climbing on my (real) Instagram account. Sometimes I spend so much time in my head that I forget what it feels like to have a body, I write in the caption. Today, if only briefly, I remembered.

I add a rock-climbing emoji and a biceps emoji for good measure. As likes start streaming in, I get a text from Danielle: **Um excuuuse me, since when do you rock climb??**

Since today! She would, of course, find my sudden interest suspicious. **I saw a Groupon and decided to go for it. Don't you ever want to rewind and become a better Coloradoan?**

Who wouldn't want to rewind, become better, if given the chance?

I DON'T DESIRE money. No, that doesn't sound true. What I mean is, how can I desire—*desire* being an active verb—something I've always had? What motivates human beings other than some sort of lack?

As an aside.

If there wasn't any money then there wouldn't have been any horses, and maybe just maybe if there hadn't been any horses I wouldn't have met that man.

He wasn't a liar.

I remember well the truths he told to lure me there.

In Australia, I had grown accustomed to saying yes, grown accustomed to telling men they could fuck me—without a condom! Because I didn't have any ovaries! And couldn't get pregnant!

All true. In laneways, public parks, high-rise hotels. In a tent, a boat, a hammock.

In Victoria's High Country, as October bloomed into the most verdant of southern-hemisphere springs, there were nine horses in the field—munching on grass, tails flicking flies—just like the man said there would be. The man vaulted over the fence, beckoning me to follow. He even smiled.

The man on the other side of the fence that day was a stranger, yes, but also a horse person, and the latter meant more. It didn't matter that we met on Tinder. I had already met, and would continue to meet, men on Tinder. I would continue asking to be desired.

The Tinder man on the other side of the fence had an Australian accent, and thus far, men with Australian accents had treated me well, had done what I asked—and invited—them to do.

In his first Tinder message, the man, Lachlan, revealed he owned a horse farm a few hours from Melbourne. I revealed I rode horses, too. Then I Googled him and his farm and discovered he was a professional show jumper and a breeder, too. So when he invited me to come ride, I couldn't resist. We exchanged numbers, and over the phone, he gave me instructions about what train to take, and what station to disembark at, and what kind of car he'd be driving when he came to collect me. His voice sounded human and vulnerable. I remember he even hummed a little before ending the call.

On the train, I imagined what Danielle would say:

You were always the crazy one!

Of course you rode with an Australian equestrian you met on Tinder, you strange, spontaneous woman.

Of course this would happen to you.

Lachlan was idling in a red Toyota when the train trundled in. He was less attractive than his pictures had suggested. My body didn't buzz, and I couldn't decide then whether to be disappointed or relieved.

He waved. I waved back and, without pausing to consider what I was doing, got into his car. He smelled like sweat and cigarettes and, faintly, manure. On our way to the farm his family had owned and operated for generations, we bantered about my experiences in Melbourne and about his travels all over the world to compete; he laughed often and easily and didn't try to touch me, which seemed like a good sign.

When we arrived, I followed him into the pasture, slipping through fence posts like smoke. I had something to prove.

Neither of my parents were horse people—but unwittingly, they'd raised one. It started with police horses in Central Park; as a child I rushed their flanks, reaching out to touch every part of their bodies, and my parents, who paid attention, drove me to Vermont when I was eight for my first summer of sleepaway horse camp. In Vermont, I learned how to trot and canter and jump, how to trust I would land safely on the other side. I wasn't a graceful or subtle rider, but I was a fearless one. Each new horse ridden was like an achievement unlocked—when assigned the rambunctious, unpredictable three-year-old or the fancy, seasoned show jumper, I knew I'd proven myself capable. Wesley, my favorite, was athletic and enthusiastic. Anne said he responded exceptionally well to my legs and hands, so sometimes I pretended he was mine.

We always listened to Anne. She owned the farm. Her skin was weathered and tough; her gray hair was swept into a messy pony-tail. I worshipped her, even—and especially—when she shamed me to tears. The first time it happened I had improperly tied one of the Thoroughbreds to a fence post, so when the farrier came the spooked filly broke the fence post in half and made it two miles before Anne found her in a field with smeared blood on her chest and half a fence post dragging behind her. I was thirteen, and it was the worst of all the summers, spent traumatized and grovel-ing. But mostly, life at the farm was sickeningly idyllic. A dozen girls aged eight to sixteen lived together in the whimsical turreted house that Anne's husband, Paul, had built. June and July and August were humid and sticky and robust. I ate junk food and screamed curses at Nintendo 64 and galloped unsupervised in muddy fields and chucked horseshit into wheelbarrows and waltzed with my pitchfork and called to fellow horse girls through slats of wood. I was untrained and jubilant. Over the course of nine subsequent summers, I grew strong, my thighs and upper arms hardening. I had a body that was my own, performing only for me and the horses—at least for a little while.

In the pasture, the Australian equestrian introduced me to his nine horses. I don't remember all their names, but I remember watching Lachlan's hands carefully. I saw tenderness in the way he patted their rumps, stroked their necks. Suddenly encircling my hips, his hands were less tender. I remember squirming out of his embrace, turning to face him. "Are we going to ride?"

He nodded. "Which one do you want?"

I pointed at the first horse that turned its head in my direction.

"This is Indy," he said. He slung a halter over her head and handed me the lead rope. Indy and I followed Lachlan and his horse toward the gate in silence. My heart was beating fast. I remember entwining my fingers through Indy's thick ebony mane, hoping to stabilize.

When we reached the barn, he tied up both horses in the aisle and gestured at the door of a narrow, dimly lit tack room. "Go on in, then."

So I did. As I asked him what saddle I should use, and what bridle, he closed the door and turned off the light and pushed me against the wall and kissed me. We kissed for a few seconds. I didn't like it, but I remember thinking: *It's just a kiss, he can do that.*

"I want to ride," I remember saying.

He kissed me again, like maybe I was playing hard to get. I pushed him away, but playfully, trying not to upset him. "I came here because I love to ride—sorry, but—I didn't come for this."

I wanted to believe this was the only reason, wanted to believe I wasn't just reckless and dumb and desperate many, many miles from home.

He pinched my cheeks—I remember the stinging shock of it—as if scolding a child. "Okay, relax, we'll ride now."

Back in the brightly lit aisle, Lachlan tacked up both horses and led them into the barnyard and gave me a leg up, cupping his hands beneath my heel. His hands didn't linger when I jumped. I couldn't have gotten into the saddle without his help.

For a moment, he was invaluable. I remember that.

I hadn't brought any of my riding gear to Australia, so in my too-tight jeans and sneakers, I settled into the saddle. As Indy walked, I was lulled into a sort of bliss, and upon entering a sprawling field, Indy's ears perked and her muscles coiled between my thighs. I collected her energy in my legs and hands and fed it back, but quieter, and she relaxed. A cool breeze rippled the shadows, a reminder of my favorite Vermont days. I felt foolish for doubting Lachlan, for doubting myself.

And then I heard his voice floating toward me. He was saying, "You must have broken your hymen riding when you were young, right, you must have felt like such a dirty girl then, didn't you, losing your virginity to a horse?"

"Oh," I said, taken aback by the tonal shift, the sudden contamination of something pure. "I—I don't think that's what happened."

He shrugged and urged his horse forward as I tried to shake this off. I could handle provocative banter, even if I wasn't in the mood, I told myself—they were just words and didn't require accompanying actions. I could still make that choice.

We rode for another ten minutes or so before Lachlan veered onto a small winding trail in the woods. Dismounting, he tied his horse to a tree.

I halted Indy. "What are you doing?"

"Let's give the horses a break."

I blinked. "But we've only walked, it hasn't been very long."

"Indy needs a break."

His voice was harsher. I couldn't imagine doing anything other than what he asked. Indy was his. So I dismounted and watched, not quite comprehending, as he took the saddle pad off his horse and put it on the ground, like a blanket. As if we were about to enjoy some sort of romantic picnic.

"Come here." He sat on the pad, stretching his legs out in front of him.

"I don't want to sit, I came to ride, there are probably bugs everywhere, I'm terrified of Australian spiders, I mean, who wouldn't be, right, so—"

"Oh, come on, you're being so difficult, why can't you just relax?"

I didn't like the tone of his voice, but I sat, my back straight as a board, while he kissed me. He cupped my breast through my shirt. He moved his hand lower, toward the crotch of my jeans. I swatted his hand away and felt a strange urge to laugh.

I remember that well. The bubble of hysteria in my throat. I'd never wanted or needed to say no before. This was the first and only time, and it wasn't going well, he wasn't listening, I was no longer in control.

"I smell terrible," I babbled. "I don't understand why we can't just talk, you don't even know me, I smell so bad, I'm *gross*. Do you normally let complete strangers ride your horses? I would never let a stranger ride my horse, I'm actually surprised you did—"

"I have so many. I don't care if you ride one."

His horses were things, I realized then. I was a thing, too.

His hand returned to my crotch. As he rubbed, it felt good. I remember that particularly well, my body's betrayal. I didn't want it to feel good.

I removed his hand again. "I won't have sex with you."

"Why not?"

I stood up. "Because I don't want to."

"Sit down, don't get so fussed. Just sit."

I sat, but I was shaking. His hand moved back. His body moved, too, over mine, so I could no longer see the horses standing there. What could I have done? Stolen Indy and galloped away, Wild West–style, like some sort of deranged cowgirl? Should I have run? Wouldn't that have been dramatic? Was I being dramatic? Since when was sex something to be feared?

I tried to roll out from under him. I remember that, too.

"You want to. You're wet. I can feel it through your pants."

I was disgusted with myself and disgusted by him but mostly with myself. He wasn't a liar.

"I said I don't want to."

He sat up. I sat up. Maybe I'd won.

A moment of silence, punctuated only by birdsong, before he pushed me back down.

I remember wondering if the horses knew something bad was happening, if Indy would break free from where she was tied and attack him like in a movie, if she would kick him in the head, if she would bite him with large yellow teeth, if she would kill him. I wanted him to die.

But neither horse moved. They stood chewing on leaves, tails flicking flies, green slime accumulating around their mouths. Waiting for us to climb back into the saddle whenever it suited us.

I was done, then. I was tired of repeating myself, tired of caring, to no avail, about this one thing that I had, in fact, never cared that much about in the first place—or at least not while it was happening. Sex was either about to happen (anticipation) or had already happened (analysis). I had never been truly present during sex, or experienced romance of any kind, during. Ever since Adam refused to fuck me, sex had been a series of conquests. Perhaps this man and I had that conquering spirit in common, despite his disavowal of a crucial component: consent.

So I closed my eyes as he fumbled at my clothes, pulling and pushing my jeans aside, and moved within me. In that moment, I remember wanting the arm of a couch, the sting of Adam's leather belt. I felt I deserved, had even desired, that. I didn't deserve or desire this.

Soon it was over. Smeared all over the insides of my thighs. Without thinking, I remember sneering, "Was that it?"

He shrugged.

I pulled my jeans up from around my ankles and walked over to Indy and touched her muzzle. She snuffled into my hand, and it tickled. I tried to haul myself back into the saddle, but I couldn't. I was out of shape, inflexible, stuck.

Lachlan put his hands on me again, and with his help I returned to the saddle.

We rode back. He was friendly again now, attempting to make conversation, but I wasn't listening. The air felt humid and heavy. I wanted to shower. I wanted to leave. It was still such a beautiful day. I remember that.

When we returned to the barn, I tossed Indy's reins in Lachlan's direction and locked myself in the bathroom and washed between my legs and frantically Googled local taxi companies.

When the taxi arrived twenty minutes later, Lachlan didn't call my name or try to follow me out. Our transaction was complete.

The taxi driver was chatty and curious, asking lots of questions on our way back to the train station. I remember being bright, breezy, charming, as I steadied my voice and imagined a better story to tell him: Lachlan and I were old friends and lovers reuniting for a ride.

(And years later, I *would* imagine a better story, *would* override him by repurposing his name. He would become a fictional character, a front.)

"Beautiful day for a ride," the cabdriver said, and I remember it really was—

So you were raped, said Danielle, horror-struck, when I told her nearly four months later in the backyard of a house party in Colorado as we passed a joint back and forth between us. She's still the only person who knows.

Don't worry I'm fine it wasn't like a rape-rape I'm not super traumatized or anything, I told her. *I wrote it all down, and ever since then I no longer feel anything, really, at all.*

THE TRUTH IS, I have a real problem. It's called apathy. Unadulterated and lethal.

I chose it, began cultivating it, a long time ago. It helps me avoid pain. It's a miracle. I recommend it. But not if you're a writer—

writers are supposed to be exceptionally empathic, aren't we, and so my apathy is armor and Achilles' heel. What kind of writer writes because they feel *nothing*? Most writers write because they feel too much.

(But what motivates human beings other than some sort of lack?)

There are certain topics I'd rather not discuss (ovaries, horses, rape). During a conversation months ago about the random, irrelevant pregnancy of a random, irrelevant second cousin, I said, "Yeah hello can we please avoid blatantly insensitive conversations?" and my mother, her voice pitching into hysteria, wailed, "How could we possibly know it still bothered you this much if you never want to talk about it, if you never seek out support?" *Because I don't trust anyone with my sad feelings or thoughts, Mother, and so it's best to project lightness and exude indifference, to remain whole—*

When I'm in need of recognition, I usually just turn to books, where words, now immobile, are safe and private, inviting a different sort of intimacy. The first time I read the word *laparoscopy* was inside the pages of a novella: Ann Beattie's *Walks with Men*. I recognized the description—the strange dark stitches in her belly button, rippling like shadows, and the tiny scar above her pubic hair—as my own.

Unfortunately, apathy cannot be easily transmuted into empathy, either. Sometimes I cry reading a sad book or listening to a certain song or masturbating, but I am never not aware of the *absurdity* of the act—for what and for whom do we cry? What is the point? I can't be counted on to say the right thing when it comes to other people's sadness, either; I recoil.

But I keep trying—I write and write and write, hoping to fall into feeling—but all I ever seem to accomplish is yet another narrative where I remain as safe and cold and detached as ever.

What if I had subconsciously allowed the Australian equestrian to inflict harm—to prick me awake, alive? The truth is, I didn't ask to be raped. But maybe I looked at him and thought, *Do your worst, I dare you.*

A loss of control, granted. Brief yet absolute.

chapter five

DINNER IS FINALLY scheduled to introduce Caleb to my family. We have a six p.m. reservation at a midtown restaurant, so naturally both my parents send fussy texts by four thirty.

Ridiculous number of train delays, warns my father. **Leaving NYU now!**

From my mother: **Is Caleb meeting you at the bookstore? Or is he meeting us at the restaurant? If he arrives first, tell him to say the reservation is under our last name!**

I lock up the bookstore fifteen minutes early because I'm the only person here, and it's been a rough few days. Yesterday the manager, Peter, asked me to inventory six boxes of hardcovers, but I could barely lift the first. Forced to acknowledge my arms' refusal to be of any further use, I sat catching my breath on the floor of the storage room and texted Rosemary the kind of anecdote normally reserved for Danielle: **Apologies in advance because this is totally TMI, and maybe NSFW, too, but my arms are soooo sore I** could barely reach to wipe myself this morning. I added a poop emoji, for good measure.

Hahaha wow, I just experienced an actual spit-take, she wrote ten minutes later. I swear it gets better though! Your muscles are just in shock.

I believe you. Also don't forget to send me your rates! I had to jump through a few hoops—mother's maiden name, first pet, third-grade teacher's name—to restore my ancient AOL account, but thankfully it's up and running and ready to receive emails now.

After locking the door, barring any last-minute customers from flooding in, I empty the cash register—counting bills, tucking wads of twenties into envelopes—before programming the security alarm. (During my training shift two years ago, Peter explained multiple times how easy it is to trip the alarm if I don't vacate the premises in time. "I hope you're a sprinter," he joked, pinching my elbow; I didn't sleep that night for fear of humiliating myself on my first official day.)

I've since learned to enjoy the thrill of reaching for my coat and fumbling with the keys and turning off the light as the alarm trills its final warning.

At the restaurant, I'm the first to arrive and Noah is the second.

"I'm starving!" He shoves his backpack under the table. "Where's the breadbasket?"

"They haven't brought it yet. And hello to you, too."

My phone buzzes with a text from Caleb. Around the corner, he has written, and so I focus my gaze on the door, watching him enter the restaurant and thread his way in our direction through a maze of white-clothed tables. I wave him over and then notice my parents are closing in behind him. They all reach our table at the same time, like an ambush.

Caleb doesn't know who to greet first, but my father takes the lead and shakes his hand.

"He's even cuter in person," my mother whispers in my ear, then moves toward Caleb to introduce herself before I can reply.

"I heard you're responsible for warning the human race about impending doom," my father says after we've all settled in. "Will you let us know when to flee to higher ground?"

"Unfortunately I'm a mathematician, not a psychic," Caleb says. "I can describe every worst-case scenario for you in detail, though."

"Oh, I see. You went to the dark side to work for the insurance companies?"

"Dennis!" hisses my mother.

"It pays the bills," says Caleb, a muscle leaping in his jaw.

"He's joking," I say to Caleb.

"Of course I was!" says my father. "You knew I was just being facetious, didn't you, Caleb?"

"Oh," Caleb says. "Sure, yeah, I figured."

"Our family truly envies folks with quantitative skills," he says. My father is the sort of man who owns more than one bowler hat, frequently uses the word *hip* in conversation, immerses himself in meme culture so he can surprise his students with relevant allusions, and prefers words with four syllables or more, like *quantitative*. "So did you happen to take any literature courses at St Andrews? I'm sure my daughter mentioned what I teach."

"I didn't, unfortunately, but I do love to read."

"What do you read?"

"Why are you giving him the third degree?" I ask my father. "What a cliché."

"No, it's a good question," Caleb says, flashing my father a re-assuring smile.

Exchanging glances, my mother and Noah exhibit a sudden in-terest in the breadbasket, which has finally arrived. Their knuckles collide reaching for the same piece of focaccia. A murmured nego-tiation begins, buying Caleb extra time to prepare a reply.

"I've been reading nonfiction lately. *The Uninhabitable Earth* by David Wallace-Wells, *Between the World and Me* by Ta-Nehisi Coates."

My father nods his approval and asks a follow-up question, but due to being suddenly in the throes of a quite distressing recollec-tion, I don't hear it. Rosemary recently tweeted about *The Unin-habitable Earth*, quoting a passage that read, "It is worse, much worse, than you think."

A coincidence? I try to catch Caleb's gaze and search his face for clues. But he won't look at me. Together, he and my father choose a bottle of red wine. When it arrives, my father asks for five glasses and winks at Noah.

"In the UK you'd be legal," he says after the waiter departs. "In honor of Caleb, why not?"

Noah rolls his eyes, embarrassed, but accepts the glass.

"Noah got into Columbia last year," my father says. "He's tak-ing the year off to focus on acting, but I keep telling him he needs some variety, some intellectual stimulation. Right, Noah?"

Noah guzzles his wine like water and turns to Caleb. "Neither of my parents can grasp the possibility that I might not want to go to college."

"That's not fair," my mother says. "You know how proud we are, you *know* we support you and your career!"

"But education is a privilege, too, Noah," my father says, using his professorial voice. "Think of all the ways a psychology or litera-ture course could deepen your skills as an actor, expand your toolbox."

"If I hear *expand your toolbox* one more time, I'll start scream-ing," says Noah.

"So many people would kill for an Ivy League education, is all I'm saying," my father says.

I jump in. "I'm *so* sorry my school wasn't an Ivy and *so* sorry I couldn't follow in your hallowed footsteps to Yale."

"Always so dramatic! I've been gifted two dramatic children," my mother says, directing her gaze at Caleb.

"By nature and nurture," I say.

"Good one," says Noah, leaning across the table for a fist bump.

Before our building was torn down, while helping my mother pack boxes in preparation for their move to Westchester, I stumbled upon a sheaf of old yellowing letters my father wrote to my grand-parents in the months before I was born. I pocketed them, greedy for this undisclosed private piece of him: *Linda and I so appreciate your financial support as I finish my PhD,* one letter read. *Now that I'm on the brink of fatherhood, my career in academia—in the humanities, no less—has left me quite anxious about my present inability to support a family.* In his signature humor, he'd signed off: *Let us (symbolically, secularly) pray your future grandchildren will be doctors and lawyers!*

The irony, of course, is how neither grandparent made money pursuing medicine or law. A writer, a landlord. Would my grand-mother have had such a successful writing career if my grand-father hadn't been a landlord? I doubt it.

"Naomi showed me a video of you singing." Caleb angles his body in my brother's direction. "You're so good!"

Noah thanks him. Despite being accustomed to praise, he has

somehow remained, throughout it all, aggressively insecure and prone to intense fits of self-flagellation. It runs in the family.

When the food arrives, I busy myself cutting roast chicken into tiny pieces. My father's head bends toward Caleb's as their conversation sparks, flies; when the waitress returns to our table to confer with my father about a second bottle of wine, Caleb places his hand on my knee and squeezes.

It's too nice, too good. His touch should fill me with warmth but is, instead, oppressive—a reminder of all my lies of omission. I feel an inexplicable urge to provoke everyone present here, to test them, and myself.

"I've started my novel!" I blurt out. "I have a few chapters so far."

"That's wonderful," says my mother, just as my father says, "About *time!*"

Noticing Caleb's lifted eyebrows, the inquiring slant of his mouth, I quickly backpedal away from the edge. *Stupid*, I chastise myself, *dangerous.* "But I'm definitely not ready to show it to anyone yet," I add. "It needs a lot of work. I'm not sure where it's going or what it's even about."

Only my grandmother knows; she'll keep my secrets. Rosemary's royal-blue cotton dress and violet fingernails and nose ring are details I'll keep, for now, to myself.

"No rush," says my mother, in a tone dangerously close to pity.

When Caleb excuses himself from the table a moment later to use the bathroom, my parents immediately remark on his charm and wit and intellect. My first instinct is to bask in the pleasure of their approval, the satisfaction of knowing I've chosen well, but the praise congeals in my stomach within seconds, the deadweight of all my contradictions; what the *actual fuck* am I doing? I found a man who is charming and witty and intelligent, and now—

Physically uncomfortable, I shift in my seat and avoid my mother's gaze because the kind of writer I aspire to be wouldn't allow a meek moral sensibility to obstruct the story I intend to tell. The kind of writer I aspire to be is artistically ruthless, always putting the page first. I feel split in two by my own need, sometimes, to overlook his humanity, to strip him for parts and reassemble him into whoever will best serve the scene, ignoring the ways in which he is real and lovable and good.

Otherwise I might never write another word. Who wants to read about bland, unconflicted people who simply love each other?

Caleb will need to understand and to forgive. Once this book is done, I can be whole again; we'll be free to love each other fully and openly.

As the waiter circles the table to collect our empty plates, I fork one final piece of chicken into my mouth. Then Caleb returns from the bathroom, reclaiming his position by my side.

My mother asks for everyone's opinions on the dessert menu when it arrives, and miraculously we all agree on chocolate mousse and key lime pie.

Spoons dart in, then out, from all corners of the table, and just as the hefty bill arrives, my father slides his Amex inside the black-leatherette folder and invites Caleb to the upcoming Thanksgiving celebration my parents are hosting in Westchester.

"Oh, that would be lovely, thank you," Caleb says, with feeling.

Thanksgiving is ten days away. I already assumed he was invited—and planned to bring him either way—but the pomp and circumstance accompanying this official invitation is another satisfying stamp of approval.

After my parents depart for Grand Central and Noah veers northwest toward Hell's Kitchen, Caleb and I head southeast toward Greenwich Village. There's an icy wind blowing, but it feels apt. I put my hand inside the wool lining of his coat pocket and grasp his warm hidden fingers.

"That wasn't so bad," I say, and then after a beat: "Was it?"

"Not bad at all, everyone was really nice. You're all so close, too. It's nice to see. My family was never as—loose as that, not even before my parents got divorced. More private, closed-off."

I hold my breath and wait for more. Sharing, for him, is a rare event.

"I guess it would be easier if everyone in my family lived in the same country," he says.

Unsure if Caleb is hinting toward a permanent return home, I attempt to offer a solution: "If you and your family schedule regular phone calls, I reckon you'd get closer."

I've begun, slowly, to infuse my vocabulary with his: *reckon, rubbish, nob, queue, knackered.* One strange word at a time, I take him into me. Before we met, I was different. How is my own influence reflected? What has he elected to take? I want him changed.

"Maybe, but I'll see them soon enough, at Christmas. We'll catch up then." He shoves his hands deeper into his pockets, dragging my fingers down with his.

Back in my apartment, I lock myself in the bathroom and discover a new email from Rosemary. The email, quite formal in tone, lays out several payment options. I decide to give her twenty-five pages, which—at a rate of forty-five dollars an hour per five pages of substantive edits—will cost me 225 dollars. According to Rosemary, she has given me a 10 percent discount. If you can print your pages and give them to me in-person, I'd really appreciate it, she adds as a postscript. I probably shouldn't use the work printer for my freelance gig!

I send her a confirmation email and then schedule a time, post-Thanksgiving, to meet again, so I have a few weeks to brainstorm the safest pages to share.

ON THANKSGIVING MY mother recruits Caleb and me for pre-dinner tasks, one of which involves placing palm-size chocolate turkeys beside each porcelain plate. Hungrily, I eye my own turkey's tail.

It isn't Caleb's first Thanksgiving in the States—I've already seen the corresponding stamps in his passport—but this will be *my* first major holiday with a boyfriend in tow. I want it to be memorable.

A car horn beeps in the driveway. Through the dining room window, I watch a beefy man hop out of a van bearing the assisted-living facility's insignia. He hoists a wheelchair up and out of the trunk and helps my grandmother sink into it.

Rushing to her side, I kiss my grandmother on the cheek and take hold of the wheelchair, pushing it up a makeshift ramp and into the house.

During the meal I'm seated between my grandmother and Caleb and directly across from Noah. Over the course(s) of sweet potatoes and string beans, my grandmother and Caleb hit it off. She regales him with tales of traveling through Wales and Scotland before she got married, and Caleb peppers her with questions about her memoir, her experiences writing for television, her childhood in 1930s Manhattan. I periodically insert myself into their conversation until my grandmother focuses her full attention on me and asks how my writing is going.

"Super well!" I take another sip from my third glass of red wine.

"An editor is reading it right now, actually, so I'll have some professional feedback soon."

"Really?" Caleb and Noah and my parents and my grandmother all, remarkably, inquire in unison. Ten eyebrows arch.

I haven't given Rosemary any of my pages yet—and who knows what will happen when I do—but it slipped out anyway. I want to demonstrate progress. Rosemary is lucky—she's salaried, dexterous, upwardly mobile; I'm hourly, replaceable, in need of a conventional structure and something to say when people ask what I do. All the invisible hours spent on my book aren't represented on any payroll. It's the dream life inside my life.

Soon I'll privately clarify with my grandmother, but for now I mumble something about a woman I met at the bookstore, a friend of a friend of an editor, and then change the subject, asking Noah to describe a typical day on the set of *Ghosts Among Us*. Enthusiastically, he does.

My grandmother, clearly struggling now with the cacophony of intersecting conversation, fiddles with her hearing aid and smiles in the direction of whomever appears to be speaking until it finally becomes clear that she has given up, has resorted to sitting in silence and attempting, with her set of false teeth, to eat softer and less chewy bits of food.

At the end of the meal, Noah and my father help heave my grandmother onto her feet and into her wheelchair and toward the front door. The van has returned to bring her home. Before she goes, she gestures for me to lean down so she can whisper in my ear. "He's a nice boy, Naomi."

The words come out heavy, almost cautionary. Choosing to ignore this, I tell my grandmother I agree. I think Caleb is a nice boy, too.

On the Metro-North train back to the city, Caleb and I snag a six-seater. Two rows, facing each other. I spread out on one side, and Caleb spreads out on the other.

Noah, to my surprise, opted to stay the night in our parents' guest room. I love my parents, I do, but I reach my limit after a few hours—any longer, and I'll likely say something I'll regret. I ascribe my detachment to a superior sense of autonomy and independence, but sometimes, if I'm feeling particularly dark, I'll admit I might be jealous of the uncomplicated rapport they've cultivated and would prefer not to witness it. But it's true that from ages ten to sixteen, Noah didn't have many friends his own age. Our parents, as well as his middle-aged talent manager, were Noah's most trusted confidants after I moved to Colorado, and he was socialized by the adult actors he grew up around backstage, who never figured out exactly how to relate to him—was he a colleague or a kid? His childhood was punctuated and inconsistent: signing autographs by night and back in the school gym by day—a sheer-drop comedown from the thrill of a life lived onstage.

Everyone expects me to envy him, and I do, sure, of course, but why would I envy *that*?

A uniformed man with an unkempt gray beard clacks through the train carriage, asking to see my ticket. Once he punches mine and Caleb's and moves on down the aisle, something urgent lodges itself in me. "How long will you be home over the holidays? I forget."

"Three weeks. Leaving on December seventeenth."

It's a blow. I've daydreamed countless times about my first real New Year's kiss, about someone reaching for me at the stroke of midnight without a moment's hesitation. I'd envisioned us together at a party or a bar, reveling in our coupledom.

My cheeks ache from smiling, from suppressing disappointment, but I manage to stay light and playful. "You'll be in the New Year without me for five whole hours, then."

"True. I can let you know what the future holds!"

I wait for him to acknowledge our separation, my use of *without*, but he doesn't.

I twist a stray thread on my pantyhose as we both put our headphones in.

An hour later we pull into Grand Central. Both yawning, we move through the high-ceilinged atrium and toward the shuttle to Times Square.

Apropos of nothing except my own sulkiness, I say, "I'm pretty disappointed we can't spend New Year's together." *Like a* real *couple*, I almost add.

Caleb furrows his brows. "Well, you're always welcome to escape to Wales."

"Oh, I wish," I reply, knee-jerk, as we huddle around the same subway pole—and then, stunned, I realize what he has offered. My brain flicks fast through the connotations: Was it the sort of polite, offhand invitation people rarely follow up on, or did he only sound casual to offset the meaningful suggestion?

I wait a few seconds for a clarification, but it doesn't come. Maybe I'm overthinking it, maybe it's perfectly sincere; maybe I'm haunted by old doubts disinterred—unreturned texts, Adam's belt and drums, the sting of *I guess we intrigue each other, nothing less, nothing more*—

"C'mon, hurry, next train is in two minutes!" urges Caleb as we disembark the shuttle. He strides ahead toward the downtown platform, and without thinking I tug on his coattails, jerking him back, and he nearly drops his phone—pinching it, lightning quick, between gloved fingers.

"Catastrophe averted," he says, stupefied but smiling.

(*He was always bracing for something*, Rosemary said.)

I don't tug again.

IN THE DAYS leading up to Caleb's departure, I fantasize about strolling down the narrow cobblestoned streets of his hometown and across the hazy cliffs and green fields of the country he came from. I picture us drinking pints and wearing oversized sweaters in an ancient Welsh pub.

But I can't pay for it. Not on my own. I make twelve-fifty an hour at the bookstore, rarely managing to save more than half, and soon I'll need to allocate a significant chunk as payment for Rosemary's editorial acumen.

I call my mother to describe my fantasies—oversized sweaters, hazy cliffs—as longingly as possible.

"Sounds like a very romantic trip," she says with an edge to her voice.

"Well, he met my family, so now I need to meet his."

Too late, I realize how petulant I sound; when my mother offers to buy the flight, I wonder if she can sense my guilt and relief through the phone.

Next, I email Peter, requesting five days off work. Then I ask Noah if he can cat-sit for Romeo. (He can.)

Finally, I call Caleb. It's late afternoon, two nights before his departure. "Can you talk?"

"I can, but only for a second."

He's in the office finishing a model. The insurance company needs it tonight so they know how much to charge people to save their own lives. The earth warms, and catastrophe comes in all forms. Caleb is a hard worker—he sees nearly everything before it arrives.

"I have a surprise for you," I say.

"Surprises make me nervous."

I laugh. "I should know that by now."

"So please, put me out of my misery."

"I decided to take you up on your offer!"

"My—offer?"

Doubt shivers down my spine. "To visit you in Wales for the New Year? But, like, only if you still want me to, obviously."

In the brief pause that follows I think about my plane tickets, already purchased on the assumption that he is learning to love me, and feel a little nauseous.

"I mean, of course," he says after the longest two and a half seconds of my life. "If you really want to, you'd be welcome."

Even as my body loosens with relief, I wish he said something else, like, *I would love you to come*, or *It would be amazing to have you there*. I don't want to make this decision. I want him to ask me to make it. "I do really want to," I say.

"Great. Am I still staying at yours tomorrow night? Before I leave?"

Tomorrow is his last night in the States until early January. When I make a noise of assent, he says we can talk about it a bit more then, but for now he really, *really* has to get back to work. His tone seems to question why I couldn't have simply waited until tomorrow to inform him in person about my impending visit, but I'm not a patient person.

The only way to soothe my emotional whiplash is by putting it on the page. To make a scene. Why might Caleb still be so reticent about folding me any further into his life? *Her*, of course.

*I'm not a patient person, nor am I particularly cautious, either,
I write. I suggest Caleb and I eat dinner at the Italian place in
Carroll Gardens that Rosemary recently raved about on Twitter. An encounter between the three of us might force him to
make a choice, quickly and instinctively. I want his first instinct
to be me.*

*I'm in the process of ordering a bottle of red when she walks
in, flanked by one of the generic blond friends. Stunned, I drop
the menu. "Naomi?" prods Caleb as my mouth flaps open and
closed, soundlessly, like a fish.*

*"Erm, so sorry," says Caleb to the exasperated waiter. "We'll
just do the pinot noir."*

*In my defense, I didn't expect it to happen so soon. I was
prepared to frequent dozens more of Rosemary's favorite places
before getting lucky, but here she is, looking uncharacteristically
frumpy in an ill-fitting sweater, with several pimples dotting her
forehead.*

*The generic blonde spots Caleb first, turning red then white
then red again. She makes a big fuss of directing Rosemary toward the seat facing away from us, but Rosemary laughs and
shakes her off and, as most people would, turns to search for the
source of her friend's discomfort. She and I make immediate eye
contact, so I do the obvious thing. I smile. Appearing confused,
Rosemary smiles back—until she notices Caleb.*

*Before I can blink, she crosses the floor and, enraged, begins
repeating why and how and when and what have you done? The
whole restaurant has stilled, silenced—even the waiters by the
bar, even the cooks in the kitchen. I say, "I'm sorry, sorry, sorry, I
never meant to get so carried away, I really do admire you, all of*

that was real, I promise, I just felt threatened. Can't you under-
stand, wouldn't you feel threatened, too, if you were me?"

"It's over, Rosemary," Caleb is saying. "I'm committed to
Naomi now. Please stop making a scene."

In this version of the story, Caleb apologizes for his crazy ex
and then hurries us away from prying eyes, failing to register that
Rosemary's outburst was directed at me rather than at him. *I'm* the
villain here. I wielded the weapons of emotional destruction.

In this version of the story, Caleb and I just—move on. Is that a
happy ending?

I AM NOT a patient person. Nor am I particularly cautious. On Caleb's last night in the States, I suggest we go back out before he
even has the chance to remove his shoes. I steer us toward Fort
Greene via the C train and, upon reaching Lafayette, grab his hand
and pull him through the doors and onto the platform and out into
Rosemary's neighborhood.

The back of every woman's head looks like hers. Even the
blondes appear auburn-haired in twilight. I resist the urge to call
out her name. I resist this urge again and again.

I'm excited by, and dread, the prospect of a three-way
encounter—of *that* scene playing out off the page, and then spinning out of my control. Is it possible to desire anything I don't also
dread?

If Rosemary catches sight of Caleb and me together, delusions
will shatter. Hers, his, mine. I'll know, by simply seeing their faces,
if I've been lied to. Made a fool.

As we glide down the block where Rosemary lives, I can sense both our bodies—mine and Caleb's—fighting against the tide. When it's almost too late, I take him by the elbow and redirect his feet. I'm not ready to be a fool. Not prepared, either, to act upon new knowledge, converting potential energy into kinetic. I'd rather live here, inside my fictions, a little while longer.

I sense an unspoken relief as we cross the invisible boundary between Fort Greene and Bed-Stuy. There, we sit in a bar and each manage to finish an entire pint of beer without speaking a word. I wonder if he's thinking about her, too.

"You want another?" Caleb asks, breaking our silence.

"Oh, sure," I say, tracing a stain on the wooden bar.

Instead of signaling the bartender, Caleb cocks his head at me and thumbs my shoulder. "You okay? You've seemed kind of . . . in your own world lately. Preoccupied."

I look up, startled, and try to name a valid reason for what I've been accurately accused of. "I'm fine. Just bummed you're leaving, is all." Despite the stressful implications of Caleb's close attention, I'm gratified by his perceptiveness. He's a good boyfriend, he cares—

"But you're coming to visit." Caleb blinks at me. "So we won't be apart long. Two weeks is nothing!"

"I know that," I say, bristling, "but I'll still miss you. Just because *you're* used to long distance doesn't mean I am, I prefer living in the same place, where our relationship is *real*. Didn't you ever worry all the good times with *her* might be, I don't know, an illusion? Like, of course things were hunky-dory after so much time away, you didn't ever need to deal with the ups and downs of actually *being together*—"

Gasping for breath, I realize much too late the vitriol I've spewed and desperately try shoving it back down back into its hidden place. But Caleb's face is already dark and pinched; I've dragged Rosemary into the room with us. It's all my fault.

"You finished now?" he asks. "I don't know where that came from, or why, but my relationship with Rosemary isn't relevant anymore. I'd really rather you stop bringing it up." He sighs. "And you're wrong—after moving to New York, she and I *did* experience the ups and downs of being together, and guess what? Our relationship ended! Which you already knew. But thanks for the reminder."

At a momentary loss for words, I reach out to touch his shoulder in a gesture of contrition. He lets me. And several long seconds later, I manage to speak. "I'm really sorry, Caleb, I don't know where it came from, either. It just spilled out. I guess I get insecure sometimes. I think I'm honestly just cranky because I stayed up too late writing last night." The truth! "I'm exhausted. Can we skip the second beer and just head back to my place?"

"Whatever you want, Naomi," says Caleb. "Let's forget it."

Without looking at me, he tosses some bills onto the bar and strides toward the exit.

On the subway home, I can't help but feel panicked and conciliatory and needy. I touch his knee and his chest and stroke his hair, then reach for his hand and squeeze. He squeezes back, and I notice the flicker of a smile returning to his face.

I don't let go.

Back in my apartment, I ask him to fuck me on my desk. Sex solves almost everything, at least in the short-term. My desk faces a mirror, and I love to watch. As he thrusts into me over and over again the muscles in his ass clench, and focusing on that detail, on the rhythm of it, captivates me. I can hardly believe our bodies belong to us; I can't reconcile what I see with what I feel, and so as Caleb pulls and pushes at my hips, my mind drifts further and further away, and I begin imagining Rosemary is watching somehow, is our sole audience—would she be as turned on by us as I have been by envisioning the two of them? My orgasm erupts in a high-pitched whine just as Caleb slows and softens, and for a second I fear I somehow shared all of my thoughts aloud, but no, he's just tired, he says, just tired and anxious before his flight. He's sorry, but he can't finish. Stop apologizing, I tell him, it's fine, it's no big deal. We fall asleep for an hour or two, and then he's hard again, pressing himself against my thigh, and I sleepily adjust my body so he can insert himself. This time, he comes quickly but I don't. As he slides out and falls almost immediately into a deep sleep, I rub myself in languid circles until everything releases.

Hours later, I'm awoken by the sensation of Caleb's lips on my bare shoulder. "See you in Wales," I hear him say.

After he leaves, I sit up in bed and reach for my phone and text Rosemary.

I ARRANGE FOR us to meet at KGB Bar in the East Village. Well-known for its storied literary history, the bar seems an appropriate choice for a burgeoning friendship Rosemary believes was solely founded on books.

Before leaving my apartment, I slip a sheaf of printed pages inside my tote. A modified rendering of the book transformed into something Rosemary can, safely enough, read. I spent the entire day writing it. The ex-girlfriend is the narrator now, cultivating an obsession with her successor.

It's the story I convinced Danielle I was writing. Now it's no longer a lie.

Rosemary is the only person at the bar when I arrive. Her hair looks shorter, more geometric, in how it frames her face. She looks good, though less like me.

When I slide onto the stool beside her and say hello, she twists her body to hug me. Her shoulders are narrower than they look; wrapping my arms around them makes me feel like a troll. It's our first-ever hug, somehow.

"I just ordered a martini," says Rosemary. "What're you having?"

I have never in my life ordered a martini. What I really crave is a thick beer, something to guzzle, but I settle on a glass of white wine instead.

"Long day?" I gesture to the martini and its accompanying olive. "You're not fucking around."

"No, actually, it's been a great day, a great week—I'm celebrating!"

Flagrant announcements of happiness usually unsettle me. "What are you celebrating?"

"I've just been promoted!"

I say the correct thing, the kind thing, which is *congratulations*, though I'm unable to suppress something acidic as it climbs up my throat.

She thanks me. "It's more responsibility, obviously, but I hope it's worth it."

"It will be. Sounds like you're the only person I know who will be kicking ass in January. Winter stretches on forever after the holidays—nothing to look forward to."

"So pessimistic!" She swirls her martini, crosses her ankles.

"I'm in a good mood, so please put your negativity over there." She points at the exit.

It's a rude gesture, but I'm thankful for it—permission to move beyond the measured and honey-laced. I can do and say whatever I want because none of this is normal. Rosemary could have chosen to spend her evening with someone else, someone without ulterior motives. But is any friendship truly unselfish, truly genuine? Don't we surround ourselves with people who see us as we want to be seen?

"It's just a winter thing," I say. "I'm really fucking fun in the summer."

Rosemary laughs. "Another reason I can't wait for summer. So—did you bring your pages?"

Stirred by the prospect of a fresh injection of meta-drama, I tell her yes, yes, I did, and carefully deliver my prepared introduction:

"So I was inspired to write this because I recently found out Lachlan's ex is kind of . . . stalking me. I have no idea how she found out who I am because they don't talk anymore and all his friends live in Australia and don't talk to her anymore, either, but anyway—she started turning up at the bookstore pretending she was just a random, ordinary customer."

When Rosemary's eyes widen, I assume I've landed on a good hook.

"But she doesn't realize I know who she is and what she looks like, Lachlan never hid her existence from me, she must think I'm really dumb or something." I force a laugh. "I don't even blame her, not really, it's normal to be curious. If I were in her position, I might have done something similar, who knows. A few deep-dive Google searches, at the very least."

"That is *so* wild," says Rosemary. "Does she talk to you, or just skulk around?"

"She asks for book recs, and then I ring her up. That's it. It's kind of demoralizing, actually, to be her cashier." It's ironic, isn't it, how I'm only able to voice my feelings in fictional contexts. Finally, I hand her the sheaf. "So, in my book, I try to inhabit her. To imagine what a woman curious about her ex-boyfriend's new girlfriend might be capable of."

By choosing to direct her gaze toward everything I've feared she might discover, I hope any actual suspicion will melt away. Why wouldn't she take me at face value? But in the lengthy pause that follows, I wonder if I've overestimated my own power.

But then, as Rosemary carefully and calmly folds my pages inside her *New Yorker* tote, I know I've succeeded. "I'll read as soon as I have time, I'm totally intrigued!" she says, and then, avoiding my gaze, adds, "Oh, and do you mind paying me using Bankroll'd? It's an app, kind of like Venmo, an old college friend of mine's cousin created it—"

Excitement swirls in my stomach as she relays her account username and I copy it down. The information the app provides—who pays whom, and how often, and for what (the *what* often divulged via emoji)—is the most efficient way to determine the shape of a relationship between payer and payee.

"By the way, how's your writing going?" I ask, desperate to know. "Are you worried you'll have trouble finding time, now that you've been promoted?"

She pauses with one hand on her martini glass, shoulders instinctively rising, as if fending off an attack. "It's—going. I've always needed to carve out time to write, that won't change. I try to put in an hour every morning because then, if nothing comes out, I can still say my butt was in the chair."

Every morning? Jesus. By contrast, instead of taking advantage of my days off, I usually wake around ten most mornings and pad braless into the kitchen and spoon a bowl of Honey Bunches of Oats and spend hours envy-stalking book deal announcements by women writers under forty. I've recently become fearful someone else might have already written the book I'm in the process of writing, and written it better than I ever could.

"You sound like a drill sergeant," I say. "Your book will be written in no time. I still want to read it whenever you're ready to share, our projects are kind of in conversation with each other, don't you think?"

She finishes her martini, even polishing off the olive. "I mean, sure, I guess superficially they have thematic elements in common, but women watching other women is nothing new. It's all about how you spin it."

There's a slight vibration against the leg of my chair. Rosemary casts her eyes downward and rummages in her tote bag and removes her phone. Looking at the screen, her face cracks into a wide smile, another rare reveal of her teeth. It brightens everything in the room.

"Sorry, my promotion comes with a lot more after-hours email," she says.

I pretend not to watch as she types in her four-number passcode. One number is a 0, but I can't be sure of the others. When her phone unlocks, the screen displays three new texts splashed with my boyfriend's name.

A sound leaves my throat, the sort of low whine one might expect from an animal. I cover it up with a cough.

Rosemary hasn't noticed; she's still buried in her text messages, fingers moving fast, absentmindedly saying, "Sorry, I know this is rude, should only take a minute—"

Covering her mouth, she tries to disguise a goofy smile.

When did he text her? From the airport? From the onboard Wi-Fi? His flight took off less than two hours ago.

Frantic, I check my phone, too.

There's a text from Danielle—**What's our plan for the 23rd?**—and a text from Luna, asking if I can work a double shift tomorrow. No new texts from Caleb.

I'm frightened and elated and almost laugh. I've been writing bits of this story for weeks. Teasing it, toying with it. I created this version of her—or maybe she created this version of me? Here I am, impossibly entangled in a story I seem to have conjured and feeling more alive than ever. The book and my life, the book of my life and the life of my book, is crude and spiked and spinning out of control.

And then it ends.

Rosemary's phone soars back into the bag on the floor. She turns to face me.

"So, tell me what you've been up to. How's life at the bookstore? How's your boyfriend?"

Caleb's plane is nosing its way across the Atlantic. What will have changed when he lands on the other side?

I attempt to relax my face, unclench my jaw. "He's good. We're separated for a little while. Lachlan decided to spend Christmas in Australia."

"It's summertime there, isn't it? God, I miss warm weather. Is there a reason you're not going with him?"

I fan the fingers of my right hand across the sticky bar. Apply pressure. Hold steady.

"There actually is a reason," I venture to say. "We're going through a tough time."

"Oh, Naomi. I'm really sorry to hear that."

Perhaps out of politeness, she doesn't prod for details. But I fabricate them anyway. Certain elements of her own relationship's demise need to be deployed. Reanimating Caleb's words, as well as Rosemary's own, will remind her why they broke up—and by nipping in the bud any renewed intimacy between them, all three of us are protected. The status quo, preserved. I control the trajectory until I can write the perfect ending we all deserve. (A vision of Caleb and me at the altar, with Rosemary as maid of honor beaming by my side, flashes absurdly inside my brain.)

"He's been really homesick lately, and I can't help but resent him for being so unhappy. Which in turn makes him resent me for not understanding what he's going through. A cruel cycle, I guess." (*She hated my unhappiness*, Caleb had said.) "I need him to snap out of his funk and fight for us."

I let this last phrase—*snap out of his funk and fight for us*—drop into her lap, because it's one of Rosemary's own, paraphrased. She indulges in her nervous tic (earlobe, pinched), but I'm unable to discern the exact source of her discomfort.

"It's not our responsibility to heal our partners," she finally says. "Sometimes the best thing we can do for someone is leave them. But I'm not saying that's what you should do! I don't know enough about your dynamic, I'm only speaking from personal experience. Losing someone you love can sometimes push him to change."

Rosemary believes Caleb has changed. That much is clear. I remove my hand from the bar—applying pressure, holding steady—and return it to my lap.

With a tinkling laugh, I deflect. "Okay, enough about my

boyfriend woes. I know there's weird drama with your ex, but are you trying to date while you figure it out?"

"I wouldn't call it weird drama," she says, eyes instinctively narrowing. "But no, I'm not. Dating takes so much energy. I honestly don't have the time or desire."

It's a lie, or part of one. Rosemary *does* have enough time to date if she has enough time for me—she must instead be reserving her time in case Caleb comes to claim it.

"I should go," I say, too loudly for the small room, and with a wide sweep of my hand I manage to signal for the bartender and knock over my empty glass, hard, with the same gesture. It shatters like a bomb in the tiny bar. Shrieking, Rosemary leaps sideways off the stool as a few glinting shards pierce her lap.

"Shit, shit, I'm so sorry"—I paw at everything that gleams until red swirls on my fingertips—"let me—"

"I'm fine, it's fine"—she flaps her corduroy skirt so the glass dislodges and slides off; the bartender wearily emerges with a broom and dustpan—"but please just try to be more *careful*."

"I will," I say. "I must be drunker than I thought—"

"You're bleeding," she says gently. The blood has stained her skirt; I'm not sure she knows. I put my fingers in my mouth and suck away the blood.

Rosemary steps back, nose curling ever so slightly, and when the bartender slaps the bill on the bar, she includes both our drinks on her tab.

"You don't have to—" I say, hiccupping, but she waves me off, signing her name with perfect loops and lines.

"Get home safe," she says, "and remember to drink water."

Condescension, or care? I can't decide.

I board the Brooklyn-bound F train, traveling in the opposite direction of home. I need more time. My whole body is buzzing. When I reach the Delancey station, I text Caleb. I want my name to be all he sees when he lands. **I miss you already,** I type at 10:37.

At East Broadway, I scroll through our messages from the day before, and from the previous day, and from the previous week. There are only a few evenings he's unaccounted for. When he took a few hours to reply.

But I could be wrong—Rosemary could know two separate men named Caleb. Unlikely, but how ironic, how utterly insane, would that coincidence be? Another plot twist for the book.

Can't wait to see you in Wales soon! I type at 10:45, disembarking at York Street.

While waiting on the platform for the Manhattan-bound F train, going back in the direction I came from, I slip my notebook out of my bag and, upon realizing I don't have a pen, type into my iPhone Notes app: I'm frightened and elated and almost laugh. I've been writing bits of this story for weeks. Teasing it, toying with it. I've created this version of her—or maybe Rosemary created this version of me?

Thirteen minutes until the next train arrives. I open Bankroll'd, type in Rosemary's username, click PAY, and enter the three-digit number I owe. Then I navigate to her profile, which is public. It fascinates me to no end when people diligently guard their selfies or sunset shots on private Instagram accounts but allow an army of strangers to infiltrate their financial transactions.

Scavenging for clues, I rewind to July. That was when Caleb and I, after two months of dating, *entered into a serious relationship;* that was when I had no idea Rosemary existed, before she *came in with the cold.* That was also when it appears Caleb paid Rosemary for something involving the sushi emoji.

I didn't know he had an account. We never pay each other for anything—either we split the bill on the spot or alternate picking up the tab. It hasn't been a problem.

This is the only discernible evidence I have, but I'm not sure what it signifies. When Caleb told me about Rosemary's email back in October, he swore they hadn't been in contact for nearly a year—but why, if he wasn't prepared to be truthful, would he mention her at all?

Even as my pulse quickens, I decide against allowing a sushi emoji to torpedo my relationship—not yet. Not until I can conduct more research. Perhaps Caleb and Rosemary arranged to meet before I was officially his girlfriend, and perhaps he told her, over sushi, that he was interested in someone else. Caleb is a kind person—it's possible he wanted to give her closure face-to-face. And if so, he probably felt it was prudent to reveal just enough information to keep me informed without triggering any unnecessary alarm.

But then why would she email him again in October? Did she beg him to take her back? And wouldn't Rosemary have mentioned, in our conversations, the unfortunate fact that the ex-boyfriend she so clearly pined after was definitively dating someone new?

When the train finally arrives, I sit next to an elderly woman playing Sudoku with a pen. A confident move.

"Excuse me," I say, tasting my wine breath, "do you have an extra pen I could borrow? For a minute or two?"

She glances suspiciously at me. "I'm getting off at West Fourth."

"I am, too. I'll return it before then."

Sighing, she rummages in her purse.

With a pen finally in hand, I start scribbling. *The book and my life, the book of my life and the life of my book, is crude and spiked and spinning out of control . . .*

"What are you writing?" the woman asks.

My frenzied scribbling must've attracted her attention, like I wanted it to. I lift my head. "A novel."

"Wow," she says. "Good for you."

As we approach West Fourth, the train wheels shriek and the floor rattles beneath my feet and the woman asks for her pen back. She is very polite. She wishes me luck in my life.

ON DECEMBER 23, I meet Danielle at a jazz club in the West Village. Spending the eve of Christmas Eve together has recently become our (hallowed) tradition.

But when I walk in, my eyes immediately travel to the man behind the drum set. Old habits, as they say, die hard. It's not Adam, of course, but goose bumps rise, still, on my forearms.

"The point," Danielle whispers, following my gaze, "is to override your negative memories. One thing I refuse to let that fucker do is ruin jazz for you forever."

"Oh, he could never. It transcends. Caleb loves jazz, too. Overriding has already begun."

It's a quartet—sax, piano, bass, drums. The music lifts me up and sends me somewhere. At the start of the sax solo, I close my eyes.

When the band takes a break between sets, Danielle says she has a callback for a Shakespeare play.

"Fuck yes, Danielle! What's the show?" My enthusiasm means she can't accuse me of being unsupportive. But I still want us to succeed *in sync*—simultaneously reaching, within our respective industries, certain echelons of success.

"A tiny theater way off-off-Broadway, but it's something."

The shame of relief—she hasn't pulled ahead of me yet.

Remembering her detailed Halloween costume, I ask, "What's the role? If it's Lady Macbeth, you're officially clairvoyant."

"Not quite. Rosalind from *As You Like It.*"

The name shares only three letters, but any evocations of Rosemary stiffen my spine.

"The heroine!" I say, regaining control. "Super exciting. You'll kill it. It's perfect for you."

"Let's not get ahead of ourselves, it's only a callback." She sips her tequila and lime. "Thanks for saying that, though. Always open to an ego stroke. You gonna throw flowers during my opening-night bow?"

I clasp my hand over my heart. "Yellow roses, painstakingly dethorned."

"You're ridiculous."

"But also the best number one fan you could ask for?"

"Duh." She sucks on her lime wedge. "So! You excited to have sex in Caleb's childhood bedroom?"

"Jesus, so crude—"

"Oh, you love it."

It's true, kind of. Crudeness has often allowed me to exude nonchalance, to pretend I care less than I do. The night after I first slept with Caleb, I remember saying, "I've never fucked someone skinnier than I am, I thought his hip bones were going to impale me." Danielle and I were drinking wine in my apartment, and Danielle laughed so hard she spit hers out, and I immediately felt guilty because in reality I liked him and his hips and hyperboles, and wanted to keep seeing him.

"Okay, yes, defiling his bed is on the agenda," I say.

She laughs. "Please scout out some eligible Welsh bachelors and invite them to your wedding, okay? It's only fair."

"Let's not get ahead of ourselves," I mimic her.

"Do you still even notice Caleb's accent?"

"Sure do, mate." I dread the day I stop noticing, the day when he suddenly becomes ordinary.

Danielle tongues her straw. "How's the book, mate?"

"Mate, it's—" I pause. Curtailing my desire to vent—a desire I've never before suppressed in Danielle's presence—is proving more difficult by the day. I test the floor beneath us with all ten toes; it will hold. "Something happened a few days ago that sort of—blew the whole fucking thing wide-open, actually. I ran into Caleb's ex at a reading. She was standing *right next* to me, real and solid and breathing."

"No way! That's insane. Did you freak out and run away or, like, sniff the back of her neck?"

"You think I'm that much of a creep? No neck sniffs but at one point I spontaneously asked if she'd read anything else by the author."

"Damn, impressive improv skills. How'd you know it was definitely her?"

"I've seen her Twitter photo. It's a public account!"

"Praise be for public accounts." Danielle throws up her hands. "That's a wild coincidence, though. Like straight out of a movie scene."

"Or my book," I admit. "I might've plopped it into a chapter."

Lips curling into a smirk, Danielle gazes at me. Steady and unflinching. "Oh, I get it now. You *ran into* her." She makes quote marks with her fingers. "I'm sure it was totally random. I'm sure if I found her Twitter right this minute, I wouldn't find anything about the reading. I wouldn't find anything at all that could've tipped you off about any of her plans. Right?"

Blushing furiously, I massage my left hand with the fingers of my right and brainstorm a retort that straddles the border between truth and lie.

"Naomi, stop." She puts her hands on top of mine, wrenches them apart. "It's me. You know *I* don't care. I'm just saying I know what you're doing, and it's dangerous."

I blow out the breath I've been holding. "It's not a big deal," I say with a bravado I don't feel. "We exchanged, like, three words, she has no idea who I am, it won't happen again. I just wanted to see her, wanted her to look at me." In my head I'm already scribbling two wildly divergent scenes:

I'm glad he chose you, Rosemary is saying in the first. *He was lucky to have me, and now he's lucky to have you. I mean, does he have any idea how lucky he is? If it was possible to select my own successor, I would've chosen you, too.*

I don't understand, Rosemary is saying in the second. *What could he possibly see in you?*

"I think I know what you mean," says Danielle, interrupting the imaginary. "But it's not healthy, and you know it. It's human nature to be curious, but it's not *good*, it's not right, to take it too far."

"How far is too far?" My tone suggests this is a joke, but Danielle sees through me, often too well—though also knows better than to dig too deep, lest I unravel.

"The irony is she and I would actually have *so* much to talk about. I'm dying to ask her what Caleb was like when they were dating. If there were endearing but annoying things he did that drove her absolutely bonkers. I wish we could compare notes and kind of, like, affectionately roll our eyes at his expense. You know?"

"So, you're basically saying you want her to replace me as your best friend? No way. I will *fight* her."

"Shush, no one could ever replace you," I say, because it's true, and I owe her at least this much.

"Okay, good. Maybe you should stop stalking her now."

"Um, definitely not a fan of the word *stalk*, it's just some preliminary research for a character loosely based on her."

"Is *study* better?" she says, an impish glint in her eyes.

"*Took field notes* is preferable, actually." I emulate Danielle's tone, hoping to convince her it's silly and harmless, but despite this valiant effort, my body knows better—I'm still lying to my best friend, and although I haven't menstruated in seven years, my stomach cramps as if I am. I fear someday being (rightfully) called out for self-absorption; I wish I could, or even wanted to, stop. But I'm capable of becoming a better friend again, and soon, once I have what I need.

"And Caleb is okay with this?"

I take another deep breath, willing the cramps to stop. "Well, he doesn't know, like, the scope of it."

Her brows furrow. "I don't get it. How are you dating someone you can't talk to about it? Writing is what you do, it's who you are! I mean, *I* wouldn't date anyone who didn't 'get' me, who wasn't interested in my actress-self. It wouldn't be fair to them or to me."

I was prepared to defend myself from a wholly different line of attack—and so her righteous indignation on my behalf, rather than on Caleb's, is a shock. Why have I chosen a relationship where I have to hide? Why do I believe that's all I deserve, all Caleb deserves?

"I'll tell him everything eventually," I say, while also thinking,

Someday I'll tell you, too. "But I have to finish first. I need to know what it is I'm even working with."

As the bassist plucks a string and the pianist places a delicate foot on the pedals, Danielle wags her finger at me, a welcome return to playfulness. Then the drummer leans forward and launches us into a new beat.

chapter six

DESPITE OUR PRIMARILY Jewish ancestry and unwavering agnosticism, Noah and I visit my grandmother, the only Protestant in our family tree, on Christmas Eve. It's her favorite holiday and she's my favorite person, so it's simple. We celebrate.

Upon arrival to the assisted-living facility, Noah and I pass a group of elderly residents gathered around the baby grand piano in the parlor. A massive ornamented Christmas tree, and a few scattered menorahs, loom behind them. With some surprise, I realize my grandmother is in the crowd. She hates group activities. (*Glorified babysitting*, she has scoffed.)

We linger in the threshold as the pianist begins "White Christmas."

It's hypnotic, the blending of their voices. I close my eyes.

"My grandson!" I hear my grandmother call out between verses. The piano pauses on a bum note. "He's a singer! Noah, join us."

Bewildered but gracious, Noah leads the choir into "Have Yourself a Merry Little Christmas," which even I know by heart.

The applause, after, comes wild and quick. My grandmother grips her walker with both hands and leads us away as the choir launches into "Silent Night."

"I'm so glad you two are here," she says as we match her pace, shuffling down the hall and into the elevator and down another hall. "Everyone is going deaf in our dinky little choir, which makes it difficult to stay on-key. I regretted turning on my hearing aid until you saved us, Noah, with your dulcet tones." The recognizable grin that always prefaces her one-liners spreads across her face. "I suggested we sing 'Grandma Got Run Over by a Reindeer,' but for some reason it was voted down."

We both laugh loudly, which seems to please her.

"Oh, I have champagne for us!" she announces as we enter her suite. "And the dining hall donated some pastries. Come sit."

On a tiny table in the corner, beneath the window: a plate crowded with cinnamon rolls and chocolate croissants, three champagne flutes, a bottle of Veuve Clicquot. The display is often replicated whenever Noah and I visit her together, even on non-holidays, so it makes me sad, but I don't linger in this feeling for long. I wish our presence wasn't remarkable or rare enough to celebrate. I consider rejecting the coffee cake on principle and declaring my intention to return weekly forever. "I'll definitely have champagne, Grammie, thanks so much."

"I love chocolate croissants," says Noah.

The volume of our voices rises and rises until we're sure we have been heard.

"Eat as much as you want. Crummy pastries are included in this fine institution's yearly fee." The sarcasm in her voice bubbles over as she pours champagne into our flutes and then holds her own aloft. "A toast to my talented, wonderful grandchildren."

My cheeks are changing temperature. Noah and I glance at each other before clinking glasses.

"Tell me everything," she says as we fold into our chairs.

Noah finishes his croissant, slips his copy of the *Ghosts Among Us* script out of his backpack, and begins reading a scene aloud.

"My left ear is better," says my grandmother. "This new hearing aid is supposed to be the best in the world, but it's so staticky, it's garbage."

Noah and I switch seats so she can better hear him.

"So this scene takes place in a hot tub, and I'm supposed to be in love with this girl Bella, but she's heartbroken over Tyler, who was just killed in a motorcycle accident."

"Tragic." My grandmother scoffs. "Who writes this stuff?"

Noah's mouth twitches. He prefers to make the first joke. "I mean, it's not supposed to be high art."

"Oh, Noah, I was just teasing. It's very exciting. I see ads for it all the time, I hope it'll be a big hit." The cinnamon glaze on the tips of her fingers sparkles. "I just wonder if it challenges you."

"Every job challenges me." He gives her a wry smile. "Yes, *even* jobs where I have lines like, 'We make a great team' or 'I have a bad feeling about this.'"

I snort champagne through my nose.

"My personal favorite," says my grandmother, "is 'Don't you die on me.' Naomi, maybe you should ditch this novel-writing business and start a script?"

"I'm trying to blaze my own trail here, Grammie," I say through my teeth. "Can't do that if I follow in your footsteps."

"When are you going to let me read the first chapter?"

Noah gazes at me with new interest. "You have a first chapter? What's it about?"

I glance at my grandmother, willing her to follow wherever this conversation may lead. I can't just keep confessing.

"I'm not plotting it out, just seeing where the characters take me. I actually have no idea what it's about yet. But I know the narrator is keeping a big secret."

"You should base one of your characters on me," says Noah. "So when the film adaptation happens I can star in it and we can both make a bajillion dollars."

"Deal." I hold out my hand, and he shakes it.

"You two should collaborate on something," says my grandmother. "Maybe a play? No one in our family has written a play, Naomi, so you'd still be forging a new path there. And Noah could certainly provide a unique perspective."

"Maybe," I say, noticing a collection of stray crumbs and stains smudging the collar of her shirt. I attempt to swipe the crumbs off without detection or discussion, but my grandmother refuses to let it go.

"We regress, see?" She readjusts her collar. "Into infancy. It's ugly. I'm not living anymore. I'm existing."

I sit silently, unsure of how to respond, willing myself not to recoil—not this time, not from the person who loves me more than anyone else does—but I wish she hadn't said it, wish we could have carried on in the key of light.

"I'm sorry." What else can I say, or do? I attempt to rationalize. "But you can still write! And that's its own kind of living, isn't it? You can travel to faraway places, become someone else. Choose to live a totally different life inside the work."

Maybe someday I'll take my own advice to write outside the self, to stop stealing scenes. I'm reflecting life as I've lived it, sometimes even before it's lived, but maybe I should next aspire to embody a man, or an animal, or, fuck it, even Rosemary herself.

"I can't write anymore," my grandmother says. "Have you seen my hands?"

I look at them, really look at them, for the first time. Swollen and bulbous and misshapen, like someone has affixed a pump to the inside of her thumb, and blown, and blown.

"I can't hold a pen." She gestures to the remote. "I can barely even change the channel."

"What about dictation?" asks Noah the idealist. "You have so many stories to tell. We can write them down. Right, Naomi?"

"That's sweet of you both," says my grandmother. "But I'm done telling stories. It's time to listen to yours." She fixes her gaze on me. "How's Caleb?"

I allow her redirection. The conversation was becoming too fatalistic, too unnerving. "He's happy to be home, Wales relaxes him, I think the city is too overwhelming sometimes. Oh! And I'm not sure if Dad already told you, but I'm visiting Caleb for New Year's and staying at his mum's house."

"His *mum*? You're still American, Naomi, sorry to inform you," says Noah.

I flip him off, playfully, behind our grandmother's back.

"Your dad didn't mention it," she says. "Must have been very last minute."

"Such a jet-setter," says Noah, dry as firewood.

"Exotic boyfriend in an exotic locale," my grandmother chimes in.

"As if Wales isn't the least exotic place ever," says Noah. "You could be going to Mallorca or Morocco like a normal person."

"Wales isn't good enough for you? Your privilege is showing, cover that shit up."

Noah laughs. "Okay, okay, cease-fire."

"Meeting his family is a big step, though," continues my grandmother, holding my gaze.

"Yeah, it is, but if it goes horribly wrong at least I'll have some good material."

"Occupational hazard." Flashing a smile, she pats me on the arm. "Caleb has no idea how your brain works, does he?"

Unsure what she's trying to communicate, I toss back the rest of my champagne and excuse myself. In the bathroom, I notice all the gadgets my grandmother needs to perform basic bodily functions—nonskid mats, piles of adult diapers in packages, steel grab bars affixed to each wall, and, of course, the emergency cord in the shower—and a heavy melancholy descends. It smells like antiseptic and urine. I squat, thighs quivering from the effort, above the raised toilet seat.

It hurts to look inward, but it hurts to look outward, too.

Later, on the way to the parking lot, some of the remaining singers, milling around post-concert, smile and wave at Noah and me from their wheelchairs as we pass. Others don't seem to register any fresh stimuli at all.

"How many people do you think live here? Four hundred? More?" Noah gestures toward a group of women in wheelchairs arranged around a table strewn with puzzle pieces. No one speaks, but their fingers move with purpose. "I wonder how many of their grandchildren visit them. I haven't seen anyone else our age here."

"Who knows," I say. "Thinking about it depresses the hell out of me."

"Wouldn't it be fucked up if there was, like, some unspoken competition to determine which grandparent entertained the most visitors?"

"I don't think *entertain* is the right word," I say, laughing, and then immediately feel guilty for having laughed. How many brilliant retired doctors, lawyers, artists, scientists must live here, reduced to what they now are—the subject of a millennial's careless derision?

A FEW DAYS before the New Year, my parents drive me to the airport. My mother hugs me for too long on the sidewalk. Harassed by airport traffic patrol, my father yells, "Linda—we need to go. Now!"

Before their car pulls away from the curb, I turn my back on them to push through the revolving doors, and through the security line, and up into the air.

I spend the whole flight writing. Ever since Caleb gave me the notebook, I've prioritized writing longhand. Crossing out phrases I don't like, and then moving on. It feels so good to avoid pressing delete.

As I scribble, I imagine people watching from seats behind me. I keep the pen moving; I rarely stop. Strangers, like the elderly woman playing Sudoku on the subway, will come to obvious conclusions—*she must be a writer.*

The customs line, upon arrival to Heathrow, is long and slow. Trains to Cardiff depart every hour or so, but it looks like I'll miss the next one. If Caleb and I had flown together from New York, I realize we would have been funneled immediately into separate lines. He would be welcomed home, and I would be asked the customary questions. *What is the purpose of your visit? How long will you stay?*

Finally reaching the front of the line, I brandish my passport.

"Five days," I tell the uniformed woman behind plexiglass, trying to seem casual and matter-of-fact rather than prideful and giddy. "I'm visiting my boyfriend."

I belong to the club of international, cross-cultural transatlantic romances, I imagine saying, absurdly.

Halfway through the three-hour train journey, my stomach clenches and unclenches so relentlessly I think I might vomit. Before lurching down the aisle to find the bathroom, I ask the middle-aged woman sitting across from me if she minds watching my things. "Of course, love," she says, seemingly surprised by my American accent—perhaps because we've left the more touristy London behind. I want to tell her I'm not a tourist, that I'm visiting my *boyfriend* in his *hometown*, and thus have a legitimate reason to be on this train as it rolls through iconic, picturesque countryside, but rightfully I prioritize my digestive system. In the smelly lavatory, I sit on the tiny toilet for eight minutes, an eternity, until everything inside me quiets, calms. On the way back to my seat, I squeeze by a moderately long line of disgruntled passengers waiting to pee.

Finally off the train, I drag my suitcase onto the platform and exit the station and look up to see Caleb standing beside a gray sedan. A familiar face in a foreign place. Here he is: the man I've flown thousands of miles to see. Caleb scans each emerging body—dragging suitcases or hunched over from a backpack's weight—in search of mine. I enjoy watching him wait. We stand now on opposite sides of the same anticipation.

I can decide to be okay, decide to be happy. Visions of Rosemary's screen, splashed with his name, disappear. Maybe the thousands of words I just wrote—about Caleb's impending confession of his eternal love for Rosemary—can be replaced, rewritten. Maybe I've misunderstood.

We meet in the middle of the sidewalk. I grip his torso and bury my face in his chest just as he leans in to kiss me hello; my forehead collides with his chin. Giggling at the awkward entanglement, I tilt my head back so he can kiss me properly.

As we walk toward the car, my mind goes blank. It's been less than two weeks since we've seen each other, but I want to fill the space with enough light and sound to make up for the gap between us. I want my presence to change something in the air. I just can't think of how.

Caleb tells me his house is on the Gower Peninsula, about an hour away. "I know you've been traveling a while already, but hopefully the coastline views make it worthwhile." He gestures vaguely westward as we walk. "How was your journey?"

I tell him it was all fine. Other than my stomach issues, it was. "I wrote a lot," I say, hoping and dreading the inevitable follow-up question.

"That's great." He unlocks the car; it beeps twice.

Not so inevitable, after all. Maybe he already suspects I'm writing something that involves him. Maybe he, too, practices avoidance and repression. Maybe we're exactly the same.

"Liam went back to London this morning, bummer you just missed each other."

I shuffle through the names he has mentioned to me, people I imagine are important, and come up with nothing. "Who is Liam again?"

"My best friend since primary school. We went to St Andrews together, too. I talk about him a lot."

His voice is gentle, matter-of-fact, but I feel panicked, horrified, even, for having forgotten. I wanted to meet Liam, to muscle my way in, to become a real person in the eyes of my boyfriend's best friend. "Oh, duh! Sorry, I'm so jet-lagged."

As I reach for the car door, Caleb gently redirects my shoulders; I've attempted to climb in on the wrong side.

"Oops," I say, strangely delighted by yet another reminder that I'm finally here, in his home country.

Safely ensconced in our designated seats now, Caleb starts the car, exits the train station, and pulls smoothly onto the road. A short silence follows. He fiddles with the radio, and I sneak glances at his other hand on the stick shift, the pale, slender fingers. I've never seen him drive a car. We're accustomed to long subway rides home after the bar, the jerk and screech as we navigate dark tunnels underneath the boroughs, but here I can see everything—tall hedgerows, narrow dirt roads, slopes of green meadow, the line of blue sea as we round corners. It's beautiful in a way that feels fake, painted, like I can reach out and knock over the cardboard trees, the cardboard ocean.

Eventually Caleb takes a sharp right.

"This is my street," he says.

As we roll to a stop outside the modest Tudor, I register how tired I feel, and how heavy; I can't seem to get out of the car.

Inertia is certainly not a good way to start. As Caleb extracts my luggage and fumbles with his house key, I take a few deep breaths before willing myself to follow him through the doorway.

I wonder if Caleb will say something formal as I cross the threshold—*Here we are,* or *Welcome,* or *This is where I grew up*—but he doesn't. I wonder if his mother will appear, arms spread wide in welcome, but the house seems devoid of anyone but us. Caleb takes my suitcase and carries it up the stairs without sound. In the absence of speech, I want to say something like *This place is so cute,* or *I can't believe I'm finally here,* or *I missed you,* but I don't. I climb the carpeted stairs—passing framed photographs of Caleb as a round-cheeked infant and then as a pimply adolescent—and follow him into his bedroom, trying to take it all in at once. I want to touch and taste everything.

On his bed: a blue comforter. On the bookshelves: John Le Carré's *Tinker Tailor Soldier Spy,* Murakami's *Norwegian Wood,* a Harry Potter collection, some Penguin classics.

In the corner, a dusty saxophone. I point at it. "You didn't tell me you played!"

"Used to. I was in a band at uni."

This detail further deepens his character, so naturally I wonder why he never brought it up. Shouldn't everyone seek depth in themselves, in others?

"Why did you stop?" I ask.

"Math made more sense."

It's a practical choice rather than a romantic one, but there's a quiet dignity in it. Plus, I promised myself no more musicians.

Caleb opens his laptop and shows me a YouTube video of the band. "There I am," he says.

I watch his fingers move, his cheeks inflate with air. His eyes are closed; he looks peaceful. I could watch him play for a long time.

As the song ends, my gaze drifts to the opposite wall, where his St Andrews graduation photo is framed and hung. Caleb is holding his diploma with his right hand and squeezing Rosemary's shoulder with his left. I stare, forcing Caleb to look at it, to see.

He turns red. "I'm sorry if it's weird, but it's the only graduation photo I have. She came from New York to celebrate with me. It was a good day, but it was a long time ago."

During her Scottish semester, Rosemary must have been in the audience at Caleb's gigs, gazing up at him while he played. A fresh gust of envy blows in until I'm able to remind myself what, and who, he chose. Math, and me.

I'm the one in Caleb's home now, in his town, with what he has accumulated and accomplished spread across walls and tucked into corners, his whole life evident in the hiss of the Welsh breeze outside, the salty-sweet air from the nearby sea. Rosemary is three thousand miles away. I banish her.

Parting the curtains, I point at the tree outside Caleb's window, suddenly suspicious.

"It's a palm tree," he says, following my finger.

In Wales? No. On the flight, I envisioned a moody moor, a misty green hill, a Welsh chill. I don't want palm trees here, complicating my perceptions.

I venture downstairs to get a glass of water and, in the dark stillness of the kitchen, almost overlook Caleb's mother perched on a stool at the countertop, eating an apple. She flickers in and out of focus beside a ten-inch television emitting a bluish glow of muted newscasters.

"Oh, hi, Mrs. Morgan, I'm Naomi," I hear myself say. "It's so nice to finally meet you, thank you for having me!"

As her head swivels, I realize it must have been the anticipation of this inevitable meeting that ravaged my stomach on the plane. Was Rosemary close with Caleb's mother? Were they friends? For all I know, his mother could have been devastated about their breakup; she could still harbor a desire for their eventual reunion. Maybe she's wired to suspect me of something.

But I also know that if Caleb comes down the stairs and watches us speak, he'll appraise our chemistry. Its existence, or lack thereof, could alter his perception of me. I feel nauseous again.

His mother stands and hugs me, but without applying any pressure—her body merely brushes against mine. She is long and lean, like Caleb. Their hair is the same dark chocolate brown. "How lovely you're here, Naomi." Her voice comes out soft, slow. "And please call me Jen. How was the journey?"

"It was great!" I hear the high-pitched tones and feel the smile threatening to crack my jaw, but I can't recognize either as mine. "The views along the drive were beautiful, especially during sunset."

She looks beyond me, already losing interest, with brighter eyes. I turn and find Caleb standing by the refrigerator.

"Naomi's just saying that to be polite, isn't she?" Caleb's mother says conspiratorially. "The drive is really quite boring."

Unsure if I'm meant to rebut this statement, my mouth falls slightly open. "Oh, well—maybe—I—"

"She's joking, Naomi," Caleb says.

I force a laugh. Humor I'm good at, humor I can do. I must keep up.

"Is this your first time in the UK?" his mother asks.

I bristle in the space behind my eyes—the UK is one of the easiest places to get to from the United States, I'm not one of those ignorant Americans who doesn't desire to travel, what kind of person does she think I am?

"My grandma took me to London when I was a kid, we did a

lot of sightseeing." I keep my voice even and bright rather than prickly, realizing it's possible I've interpreted the question as condescending rather than simply curious or polite, which probably reveals more about my own privilege than it reveals about her opinion of me. I hope to redeem myself. "This is my first time in Wales, though."

"Well, I hope you enjoy yourself." Without looking at me, she pats Caleb's arm and moves toward the hall with the half-eaten apple in her hand.

"I love apples, too," I blurt out. "They're my favorite fruit, especially Honey Crisps. They're juiciest."

Caleb looks at me strangely, his eyebrows knitted together.

"I run," his mother says from the doorway, gripping the apple. Juice travels down her knuckles. "Apples are good for runners. Pectin gives me extra energy. Do you run?"

"I do."

It isn't a lie—she didn't ask how often or how passionately. Caleb and I ran, once, alongside the Hudson River in October. Leaves were changing in the park. I fished sneakers from the back of my closet, wore my only sports bra, and applied mascara to offset how unattractive I expected to look during and after. Caleb had longer strides but didn't leave me behind.

"Maybe we can run together while you're here."

The idea terrifies me. "Sure!"

His mother yawns. "Anyway, I'm off to bed. Goodnight and sleep well, you two."

When her bedroom door closes, Caleb turns to me. "Speaking of running, I'm going to take a quick shower. I went for one earlier and didn't have time before meeting you. Make yourself at home, obviously. There's another TV in the den."

I follow him upstairs and search my luggage for pajamas as he disappears into the bathroom. The shower whooshes on, and I move toward his bedside table. The key is not thinking too much, or at all. I hold his phone, sleek and silver. There are a few options. I've seen his fingers skitter across the screen countless times in a sort of figure eight, always beginning with the number one. A few numbers are possible.

I try 1, 9, 9, 1. The year he was born.

The phone buzzes, sensing an impostor, and I'm back where I started.

I try 1, 9, 9, 3. The year I was born, as though flattering myself could momentarily override the anxiety. But no—I'm not the answer, either. I have one more chance before the phone locks me out after too many failed attempts.

I try 1, 8, 6, 8. The year St Regulus—Caleb's residential college in St Andrews—was built. I did my research.

And I'm in. Just like that, everything laid bare. St Regulus—where he and Rosemary met—must still represent his best and most memorable years.

When I open his text messages, the first name is mine and the second name is hers. Brimming with dread I scroll backward, looking at dates and times, searching for context. I start reading, and the shower continues whooshing as my chest tightens, trapping air beneath my rib cage. I press the heel of my hand against my stomach, trying to release it, and imagine Caleb shampooing his long dark hair. I hope he uses conditioner. I hope he lets the water run for as long as I need it to.

The first messages are from July, around the same time I contracted that nasty flu. Caleb initiated their texts. He wrote: I'm sorry about yesterday. I didn't mean to hurt you and certainly didn't mean to make you cry. But I didn't know what else to say. I thought we finally had closure.

I understand, Rosemary wrote. But also, fuck closure. You'll never stop being a huge part of my life. I've missed you.

Likewise, he wrote, and something sharp twists in my stomach as I remember, vividly, the sushi emoji. It's contextualized now; I'm connecting the dots.

They began—tentatively at first, then gathering steam—to banter about her coworkers, about his job, about her sister's wedding in Nashville. I didn't know she had a sibling. We could have talked—and can still talk—about our siblings together. She was glowing, Rosemary wrote. It was beautiful.

I plan to write all of this down. My breath is coming in short gasps now, but I think this exchange might be normal, might not be a reasonable cause for panic. Isn't this what society should strive for, a tepid, infrequent politeness with our exes?

Caleb and Rosemary started making jokes, then making plans, then confirming a time and a place.

My heart flings itself against walls, searching for a way out.

On a Thursday night in October, before Halloween, Rosemary wrote: Grabbed a table in the back!

My teeth are chattering violently as if trying to escape my mouth. Where was I, and what was I doing, when Rosemary and Caleb sat together at a table in the back, drinking beers?

Later that night, at midnight, he wrote: It was so good to see you, hope you have sweet dreams tonight!

Doesn't this message imply Rosemary and Caleb didn't go home together? Consumed by a sudden, dizzying relief, I lower myself to the floor. I wish he hadn't wanted to give her something sweet, hadn't kept her ongoing presence a secret, but these aren't, in my mind, unforgivable betrayals. It could've been so much worse.

Beneath my shins the hardwood floor is cold and sobering. If I'd discovered real, potent drama and a bigger revelation, it might've justified everything I've done and felt. I struggle into an upright position, my fleeting relief overridden now by sour disappointment. But no matter, I can write something else, can change how it happened on the page, can escalate—

I keep reading, energized but wary about what I might unearth next.

Rosemary texted him again three weeks later. **How are you?**

The date catches my eye. It was the night Caleb joined my family for dinner. He replied to Rosemary's text at 7:20, so he must have excused himself from the table and texted her from the bathroom and then returned all smiles.

Things have been busy, but trying to power through before I head home!

When do you leave?

December 17th.

I'm sure it'll be so nice to be home. Please say hello to your family! I've been thinking about all of you.

Will do xx.

And then, on the day of his flight to the UK, he wrote her again: **Do you want to catch up again when I return? I would love to see you.**

I remember knocking over Rosemary's martini glass, the smell of her citrus-scented shampoo on the stool beside me. **I would love to see you, too,** she wrote. **We can celebrate my promotion!**

Ah, you finally got it! he wrote. **No one deserves it more than you.**

The word *love* dispatched twice like it's normal, like it's nothing, like it just makes sense.

And absolutely no mention of me at all.

Isn't this the revelation I've been waiting for? No need to escalate now—they already have. Within whatever remains between them, I don't even exist. I might as well be no one, mean nothing.

The shower trickles into silence. I frantically close out of their text messages and slip the phone back into its position on his bedside table, cheeks burning. When Caleb walks through the door, my fingers are dangling awkwardly near the lamp on his bedside table, so I make a big show of turning it off.

"You must be exhausted," he says. "We'll do something fun tomorrow."

All I can do is nod. I crawl underneath his sheets and lie down and turn to face the wall, still shaking.

Caleb climbs in beside me and kisses the nape of my neck and then falls asleep quick and easy. As his breathing settles, I turn over and look at him: the O his mouth makes, the hook of his arm underneath the pillow, his tucked-in knees. Reaching to lightly trace his protruding spine with my finger, I have a strange urge to shake him awake, to ask for promises or confessions. But I don't. Instead, I try to synchronize our breathing. There's nowhere to go. I'm here, in his country. What could I do—leave in the middle of the night, board a plane, return home in search of something else, something uncomplicated and drama-free? No. This is a worthy story now, isn't it? Indeed, I've been deceived. A plot twist I didn't even engineer.

As the night yawns on, lying stiffly in Caleb's bed, I can't decide if his concealment is truly punishable. Perhaps I've spent too much time constructing imaginary events rather than asking Caleb direct questions. But soon I'll demand the truth, rejecting his tendency toward reticence. And after we've shared all of ourselves, maybe he'll finally excise Rosemary from his consciousness.

I will be enough.

THE SUN BURSTS through a gap in the curtains. I blink back the morning brightness, orienting myself. Caleb rolls over and covers my body with his own. "Good morning! You're looking *brydferth*."

"Excuse me?"

"It means 'beautiful' in Welsh."

I want him to repeat it again, again. I want to bathe in the word as it leaves his mouth.

But then I glimpse myself in the mirror beside his bookcase. My hair is tangled; a small zit dots my chin. "No, I'm a mess."

Caleb laughs and kisses me, as if to prove I'm not.

"By the way, my dad invited us to his place today," he says, rising from the bed.

My eyes widen. "Oh?"

"I mean, we don't have to go," he says quickly. "If you'd rather do something just the two of us tonight, that's fine. But I guess it's nice he's making an effort."

A few months ago, lying postcoital in my bed, Caleb said he

feared becoming as aloof as his father, as neglectful of the people he was supposed to love. His confession, rather than alarming me, produced a small jolt of pleasure. He was confiding in me. This meant I was trustworthy. Perhaps it also meant we were happy.

"We should definitely go." I try not to sound overeager. "I mean, you're right, it'll be nice to reward him for the invitation."

I want to meet everyone who belongs to him—they will teach me how to become everything he desires.

After we get dressed, Caleb drives us to a few of his favorite places along the coast. Our first stop is a stretch of narrow cliff jutting over the ocean, almost otherworldly in its beauty.

"The last time I came here I was a teenager," says Caleb.

Rosemary never stood on this cliff where I stand now; he never brought her. We're making new memories. He'll think of me when he next returns here. I'm grateful for this knowledge but still want to scream over the crash of waves and wind, to say something dramatic I cannot take back.

I experiment with this urge. "I had a really weird dream last night."

The non sequitur seems to make Caleb uneasy. His fingers knead the fabric inside the pockets of his long coat. "What was weird about it?"

"It felt so real, I woke up sweating. It was about you and Rosemary. You went to some event of hers because she asked you to, and she kept introducing you as her boyfriend to the other people there, and even though you were uncomfortable you didn't correct her because you didn't want to embarrass her or make a scene."

Caleb's eyeballs flick upward. "Why are you telling me this?" His slight exasperation suggests he might be unconvinced by the dream's validity, and also by the spontaneity of the recollection.

"I'm telling you," I say fiercely, "because it upset me."

He pushes his palms out in front of him, as if fending off a rabid animal. "I'm sorry it upset you. I don't know why you would dream about something like that, try to forget about it."

"You haven't seen or spoken to her recently, have you?"

He heaves a dramatic sigh. "I haven't, Naomi, no. She did send me that email I told you about. Remember? But that was it. Now we're, you know, living separate lives."

I capture his gaze. "So you never responded to her email?"

Can he look directly at me and lie?

He pauses. "I think I responded to be polite, I'm not exactly sure, it was so long ago. I do remember wishing her well."

My attempt to inhale and exhale, like a normal person in a normal situation, fails. I cannot do this once-involuntary thing. I walk a little closer to the edge of the cliff and stare into the distance, trying to breathe.

"Should we head back to the car?"

Turning toward Caleb's voice, I'm compelled to ask: "Can we take a selfie first? With the ocean in the background?"

He presses his lips together. I've come to understand this is how he communicates impatience, but he nods and moves against me anyway. I dip my head into his shoulder and tell him to smile.

"I'm smiling," he says.

I take the picture. In the frame, two excellent liars.

"We look nice," he says.

We do. My hair is windswept and there's color in my cheeks, and Caleb looks, more than ever, like a man I shouldn't let leave.

Returning to the road is a treacherous downhill scramble using small, slippery steps cut from rock. I tempt the worst parts of myself by taking them too fast, cutting corners, refusing to use my hands. Halfway down, Caleb finally turns to check on me from several feet ahead.

"Careful!" he says. "Are you crazy?"

"Maybe a little."

"Jesus, Naomi, that would be a horrible call to your parents."

His concern is anger, not the right kind of concern. I nod and promise to go slowly.

In the car, he hums along with the radio while I edit our selfie on Instagram. I caption it Here in his homeland, absolutely zero complaints, which I hope also means *See how serious we are, see how cool my life is?*

"Before we go to my dad's, I'm taking you to my favorite place in the world," says Caleb.

It's a stone pub sandwiched between a red barn and a small church.

"You can see the ocean from that field over there," he says, pointing, as we bump down the dirt driveway. "Liam and I used to bring our pints and lie in the grass and watch the sun set into the sea."

Inside the bar, an assortment of scruffy dogs and humans of varying age are gathered around a roaring fire. The humans are wearing Wellies and drinking pints; bones have been procured for the dogs. The raucous level of chatter, the ease and familiarity between bar patrons and staff, feels as if I've intruded on a family reunion.

Caleb snags a spot for us beside the fireplace, on a ripped sofa covered in dog hair. Before sitting down, I ask where the bathroom is.

He points to the door where we came in. "It's a separate little building."

"An actual outhouse? How authentic."

In the bathroom's cracked mirror I apply more lipstick, plum red.

As soon as I'm back inside, Caleb hands me a beer and recites a brief history of the twelfth-century pub as I sink into the sofa. I appreciate his brevity and even manage to ask a few questions, even manage to smile.

A group of six locals—middle-aged men and women—soon join our conversation, intrigued by my American accent.

A face attached to a bushy gray mustache leans in. "How'd you find us? We keep this pub off the beaten track for a reason, you know! Tourists can't find us here."

Caleb rescues me. "She's here by invitation, Jack, but don't worry—I've sworn her to secrecy."

Jack grips his shoulder. "But the pretty ones, mate, you can't always trust them."

This comment should upset me, but I can't help feeling a little prettier.

"She's been properly initiated. Naomi, show him what you're drinking."

I tilt the glass toward the man. "Local Welsh ale, see?"

"Ah, yes, that'll get right into your bloodstream, that will," says Jack. "I reckon you'll be one of us when you finish."

I drain the glass and wipe my mouth with a dramatic flourish as the locals roar and applaud and then, finally, leave us alone.

As his warm breath swirls inside my ear, Caleb relays anecdotes about teenage years spent skateboarding and surfing, activities that seem to conflict directly with the studious, soft-spoken Caleb I've come to know. I try to reimagine him—if only briefly, if only for now—and soon we're laughing together. To preserve whatever mood we've created, I can't confront him yet. Caleb's body moves differently here—exuding confidence, loose and liquid. I've only ever seen him with rounded shoulders, an urban weariness. Here beside the sea, as the pub chatter builds and seeps into stone walls, I understand who he is and could be, and when he looks at me I feel a gush of warmth, like being baptized in his eyes. He's wearing an expression I've already written down—*with pleasant surprise or maybe with amusement, like I intrigue him. Are these akin to awe?* When did he last look at me like that? When did I last *deserve* to be?

I feel a sudden visceral longing for the early days, before knowledge of Rosemary took hold and inflamed my every organ—days when he snaked a spontaneous hand around my waist on the street or the subway, or how, in bed, we always fell asleep fused. We were poised for happiness then, weren't we? He was always pulling me close with his hands and eyes.

If we lived inside this pub, we could survive anything.

I think I'm becoming happy again.

THE PATHWAY TO his father's house is torch-lit when we arrive at sundown. Two black Labradors are pressed against the glass door ahead, barking. "Hi, boys," I call out. The dogs bark harder.

"One's a girl," says Caleb.

His father opens the door. "Hi, Naomi. I'm Henry. My girl-friend, Charlie, is around here somewhere."

The resemblance is striking; Henry shares Caleb's full lips and squinty eyes, his forehead creases and rounded shoulders. I suppress the urge to take his father's face in my hands and kiss the mouth I know so well.

"Nice to meet you!" I say. "Thanks for having me over."

Upbeat, staccato, straightforward.

"I didn't know you existed until yesterday," says Henry. "Caleb doesn't tell me anything. He's so secretive!"

This isn't meant to hurt me, I know. But it does. Something in my stomach dislodges and travels upward.

"I'm not secretive," says Caleb as the air thickens. "I live three thousand miles away."

His father ignores this. "Do you like chicken, Naomi? I know it's only four thirty, but thought you both might be hungry."

"I love chicken!" I yelp, my mouth settling into a stiff smile.

"I've been a vegetarian for three years, Dad," Caleb says, heaving a theatrical sigh that, frankly, seems out of character.

"Aw, shit," says Henry. "I'm sorry. I forgot. Charlie buys these frozen veggie burgers sometimes, let me see if there's any left—"

Before I can chime in to say anything else, Charlie rounds the corner, laughing about something dog-related. After pouring me a glass of wine, she steers us toward the couch and asks me to tell her about myself.

"Well, I'm a bookseller by day, and a writer by night," I say more pompously than usual, desperate to impress.

"Ooh, I studied literature at university, so I love to read. Who are your favorite writers? I was actually named for Charlotte Brontë, but Charlotte never suited me."

Grateful for her interest, and already predicting we'll get along, I recite a few classic and contemporary names from both sides of the pond—Rachel Cusk, Jane Austen, Zadie Smith, Miriam Toews, Ann Patchett, Toni Morrison, Virginia Woolf, Mary Gaitskill, Susan Choi—as she tips forward and generously refills my glass.

I hope Charlie will tell Henry how wonderful I am after we leave. I hope it'll serve as a conversation topic for a long time. I want to leave a good taste in their mouths.

The chicken Henry serves everyone—except for Caleb, who glumly nibbles a limp bean burger—is a bit rubbery, but I don't mind. He must have been too distracted by the joyful reunion with his son to properly cook the meat.

Tearing through the chicken breast with my teeth, I manage to swallow. Another moment passes before I realize Henry has spoken to me. "I'm sorry, what did you ask?" I'm sheepish but free, uninhibited. "This delicious wine distracted me."

"Oh, it's from the Loire Valley. My mate brought it back from a business trip. I asked what you write about. Caleb mentioned you're a writer."

Caleb didn't tell his father I sit for hours beeping bar codes and rearranging books, didn't tell his father I live for free in a Manhattan apartment and yet still fail to write as much as I could or should. Instead, he told his father that I'm a writer. His insistence on seeing me the way I want to be seen feels a little like love might feel.

I'm tipsy enough now to proceed uncensored, and it feels like floating. "I write about dysfunctional relationships. About how people disappoint each other all the time."

"There are certainly a few variations of dysfunctional," says Henry. "Just wait until you have children!"

I shift in my seat and do what I always do when confronted with the fact of my infertility—laugh nervously, make vague affirmations like *ha yeah totally I can't even imagine ha*, and then shut down, hoping someone will change the subject.

Thankfully, Charlie senses my discomfort—and perhaps Caleb's discomfort, too; after all, we've dated less than a year, with no impetus to discuss *that*—and jumps in, saying, "Well, before you leave, you'll have to tell us where we can read some of your stories. I'd personally love to."

I smile at her, allowing my gaze to slip from her face to Henry's, and then to my dinner plate, and then, finally, to Caleb. I haven't looked at him since taking my first or second bite. I've treated Charlie like a newfound friend rather than the woman who caused his parents' divorce, and Henry like another man I needed to charm rather than someone who made the man I hope to love. I've treated them like characters, soon to be written down, and am briefly ashamed of doing so.

I study Caleb's face, memorizing it. He's beautiful, and I'm lucky. Then I excuse myself.

In the bathroom, my face is wine-flushed in the mirror. Opposite the toilet, four photographs are hung on the wall: Caleb as a teenager nearly a decade ago, squinting into the sun in a Nirvana T-shirt, and then three professional portraits of a young boy in a blazer and khakis sitting on the front steps of their house. He has Charlie's brown eyes.

"We don't have any dessert," Henry says when I return to the table. "Sorry about that."

"Because you didn't think we'd make it to this point?" I meant to tease, though in the pause that follows my mouth floods with saliva and apologies and then—

Henry and Charlie exchange glances and laugh. Relieved, I swallow.

"We guessed arrival at four, departure at six, and now it's almost eight," Henry says. "You lot proved to be more entertaining than I expected."

"If you think I'm entertaining now," I say, "wait until you read my stories."

I'm too tipsy to immediately regret this.

With an impenetrable look on his face, Caleb rises from his chair. "You're right, it's late. But I'm glad we caught you."

"Caught *us*? Isn't it the other way around?" Henry pats Caleb fondly on the arm like his mother did the night before, but this time Caleb flinches.

"Maybe we'll visit New York this year," Charlie says as she slips each ecstatic dog a piece of chicken. "I'm dying to go. I've been bugging Henry about it for months."

"That would be fun!" I say.

After we all hug goodbye, Caleb fetches my jacket and helps tug my arms through the sleeves.

In the car, I ask Caleb about the young boy in the photos.

"Charlie's son. He's staying with his dad this weekend, but my dad is the one practically raising him. Probably making up for being so absent with me. By the way," Caleb continues, without emphasis or inflection, as if discussing the weather, "you were a hit, they really liked you."

Unsure of what I'm expected to say, we plunge into a silence I play music to fill. Perhaps I should have tried harder to be less likable, or disliked the right people instead of liking the wrong ones. Did I pass a test, or fail?

Gazing at the dark, narrow dirt road ahead, I wonder what would happen if something shadowy crossed in front of the car too suddenly to brake.

I've experienced a recurring nightmare in which Caleb dies and everyone important is invited to the funeral in Wales except for me. Rosemary weeps in the front pew, and Caleb's mother reaches out to me months later, still shrouded in black, to say, *So very sorry, I didn't know how to contact you, very little was known about his life across the pond.*

If we *are* fated to crash, I hope the collision succeeds in further bonding us without also inflicting any lasting damage. Just a few small cuts and bruises.

But of course, of course, the car eventually sweeps unscathed into his driveway. We're safe.

The lights are off, so his mother must already be asleep.

Undressing in his bedroom, Caleb suggests we take a bath. We've showered together before, awkwardly switching positions to stand under the stream, but a bath sounds old-fashioned and romantic. Caleb lights a vanilla-scented candle on the edge of the tub and we try having sex, but water sloshes over the sides and I almost burn my hair in the candle and the bottom of the tub is too hard on Caleb's knees as he kneels between my legs.

"At least we tried." Caleb laughs. "Maybe it's best if we stick to beds."

Deflated, I step out and towel off.

"I'll follow in a few minutes," he says.

Back in his bedroom, I'm alone with his phone again.

Anyone would do it, anyone would look. I choose to travel further into the past this time, before I entered Caleb's life, but evidence of these years is only accessible via email—either because he got a new phone, or maybe (and this seemed more appealingly dramatic) he'd been bitter enough, in the wake of their disintegration, to delete all previous communications.

I tap on his Gmail account and find how, a few weeks before moving to New York, he sent Rosemary this email:

I can't wait to say stuff like be there in ten or see you tomorrow, I can't wait to buy us spontaneous concert tickets instead of flights, I can't wait to walk home to you. We waited, we made it. I love you so much. See you so, so soon on your side of the pond xxx

When did Caleb first tell Rosemary he loved her? I'm desperate to know. How many months did it take him to be sure?

Because my breath has grown louder and more ragged, I don't hear Caleb's mother enter the room. "I didn't realize you two were home," she says from the doorway.

As I turn to face her, Caleb's phone is still in my hand. There's nothing I can do. Sudden movement will only spark suspicion, allow for accusation.

"Caleb took a really nice photo of us today. I'm sending it to myself so I can show my family." I hope my hands aren't shaking. I gesture at his phone with my free hand. "Do you want to see it, too?"

The lie falls out of my mouth before I've properly tested its weight. His mother nods and moves across the room.

Because the selfie was taken on my phone, not Caleb's, I need to withdraw from his open emails and sign into my (newly private) Instagram account—via Google, since Caleb doesn't have the app—and zoom in on the photo itself in the next three seconds.

Angling the screen toward me, I start pawing at it.

"Okay, um, hold on, okay, yeah, here it is," I murmur in a panic, finally holding it out for her to see.

"Ah, yes, you both look lovely," she says, and then looks away. It's over. "I'm putting the kettle on. Do you want a cup of tea?"

Nearly breathless with relief, I forget to adjust my enthusiasm to tea-appropriate proportions. "That would be amazing!"

She shoots me an amused glance before leaving the room.

I put his phone back where I found it. *Stop*, I tell myself. *Stop*.

IN CALEB'S SMALL town, the New Year's Eve tradition involves dressing in costumes, drinking in pubs, and then, just before midnight, flooding the cobblestoned streets en masse toward the beach to watch fireworks burst over the sea.

In New York, the holiday always signifies tight sparkly dresses and overpriced parties, high heels and even higher expectations.

We spend the late afternoon perusing thrift shops for last-minute costumes. Caleb purchases tie-dye snow pants and a fuzzy lime-green vest. I squeeze into a lace ball gown, donning opera gloves and cheetah-print ski goggles, and turn a slow circle in front of a floor-length mirror.

"Sexy," he says, tugging on a curl of my hair.

On the street, adults dressed as jellyfish, as Darth Vader, as cowboys and ninjas, strut past. I post videos on my Instagram Story so people will see how cinematic my life has become. I can't share my wonderment with Caleb—for him it's tradition, not novelty. But I still expect camera crews and to hear someone scream *cut*.

At 11:50 we walk down to the beach in a coagulating mass of bodies, trying not to get tangled in dangling costume appendages, and stake out a spot on the sand. The countdown begins. *Ten, nine*—rowdy teenagers bump against us from both sides—*six, five, four*—someone screams, "Apocalypse Now!"—*two, one*—and Caleb kisses me and kisses me under all that noise.

Walking back uphill, we're silent and stumbling. Caleb suggests another drink. The pubs are still packed. A year has ended, another has begun. I'm drunk and weightless and woozy, floating through crisp air. We settle on barstools next to a witch and a vampire bride and order two more beers.

Halfway through his beer, Caleb begins to slur.

"I hate my job, Naomi," he says. "I feel like I'm wasting my life. It's what I went to New York to do, it was the first job I got and I'm grateful, but it's not—it's not—"

No, I want to tell him, *don't ruin it, don't start—*

"—not what I want, I don't want it anymore."

I run my fingers through his long dark hair, so soft and silky, and don't reply.

"I'm sorry, I know I shouldn't complain, but it's just—sometimes I wonder what I'd be doing if it had been different. I love being here, being home. It feels—right."

My lips are dry. I lick them.

"I fucked up my life, Naomi," he says. "I fucked up my life for her."

My first thought is, *I need to write this down.* How absurd. How could I? My hands are still in his hair. I scratch his scalp instead, knowing how good it feels, and then drag my hands away. I need him to understand—why doesn't he understand?

"But you didn't—I mean— Your life isn't fucked up," I say. "Is that really what you think? If you hadn't moved for her, we never would've met."

"You're right," he says, stricken. "I'm sorry, I didn't mean it like that—my life is so much better with you, I'm so glad we met, I'm so glad."

He grips my shoulders and kisses the corner of my mouth. I recoil, and then say his name—sharp and cold, like chewing ice. He loosens his grip and looks at me. It's time. I no longer have the energy to carry this hurt alone. I want to make a scene—and within it, to also extract a really fucking credible explanation, one that might save us.

"You lied to me."

His eyes flick around the room, a trapped bird. "What are you—what are you talking about?"

"I peeked at your phone. It's shitty, I know, but something felt off, and you lied. You've been seeing Rosemary behind my back. I know everything, I've seen the messages."

"Oh, fuck. Naomi, *fuck*." He dips his head into his hands and takes a deep breath. "I don't—I don't know what to say. I'm so sorry I didn't tell you, okay? I'm so sorry." He presses his palms into his kneecaps and lifts his gaze a marginal distance to my chin, nostrils flaring. "It's true that I've been talking to her and—I saw her a few times, but it wasn't a lot. It was three times. You know that already, don't you, that it was only three times?" Frantic now, he begins to repeat himself. "I'm so sorry I didn't tell you, I'm so sorry, I didn't think you'd understand."

"But I *would* have understood!"

I imagine kissing Caleb in the doorway of my apartment and telling him to have a great time and merrily waving him off. *Say hi to Rosemary for me*, I might have said. *I trust you.*

"Let me—please let me try to explain?"

"Okay, fine, explain."

He switches—as he should—to the past tense, but my shoulder

blades still feel tight, primed for fight or flight. "I thought we could be friends. I thought maybe we owed each other friendship, after all we went through. Our relationship ended for a lot of reasons, but one was I was no longer attracted to her. I don't see her that way anymore. Nothing happened when I saw her, okay? We just talked."

"Late at night, with beers, you just talked." I cross my opera-gloved arms against my chest, suddenly feeling very cold. "What happened at the end of the night? No kiss goodbye?"

"Naomi, no! None of that. I swear."

My upper lip trembles. "Does she know about me?"

"Know—about you?"

"I mean, does she know you have a girlfriend? Someone who flew three thousand miles to meet your family?"

He slides his beer a few inches to the left without looking at me.

"I didn't mention it," he says slowly. "This might seem strange to you, but we only talked about our families and our jobs. Mundane stuff. Really. Our love lives never came up in conversation."

"That's a lie." I sound more assured than I am. "Tell me the truth."

"It is the truth! I swear. I actually saw—well, it was kind of awkward. She got out her phone to show me a picture of her sister's wedding, and I saw a Tinder notification pop up. She seemed embarrassed, but we ignored it, it wasn't important, it wasn't the point. We've moved on."

"You need to tell her you have a girlfriend. She needs to know. Tell her right now."

"But—that would break her heart," he blurts out, and a strange sound vibrates in my throat. Now I know. She still loves him, and he has allowed her to, and his first instinct is, and has always been, to protect her. My stomach churns.

"What about my heart, Caleb?" I shout. "What about my fucking heart?"

The vampire bride and the witch angle their bodies in the opposite direction, away from the quarreling couple we've turned into.

Caleb doesn't reply for a long time. I finish my beer, staring at the wall.

This moment, I realize, might definitively end the "boyfriend experience"—*I thought it could be, like, a test run. It's impossible to be a perfect girlfriend the first time around*—I told Rosemary about, an experiment that had turned into reality, into my actual life. How will we recover? Emotional cheating, snooping, secrets, and lies are not the foundation I'd dreamed of. But maybe I deserve it, maybe I manifested it all. The climax could be happening right here and now; Caleb will probably admit it all—*yes*, he still loves her, and *yes*, he's sorry, and *yes*, he didn't mean to lead me on, had never even intended to bring me here to his hometown, it was all a mistake.

"Naomi, I'm so sorry," says Caleb finally. "I'll tell her, if you want me to. I promise I will. I'm sorry I lied. I was afraid you'd take it—well, the wrong way, like this. But obviously, well, that's no excuse. I'll never lie to you again." He takes another breath. "Naomi. I love you. Please forgive me."

Snot—mine—drips onto the bar. Am I crying? *Pull it together, this is embarrassing, don't be such a cliché.* I toss some coins on the table. The queen's silver face scowls at the ceiling. I gather bunches of ball gown in my hands so it doesn't drag on the floor and start walking even though I know there is nowhere to go.

Caleb leaps from his seat and grips my elbow. *How could you say it like that?* I want to scream. *How can this be the first time it's said?*

This is how I'll always remember it, the feeling of finally being loved—only said to stop someone from leaving. Desperate, thoughtless, conditional.

He squeezes my hand, but I pull it away and gesture to the bathroom, where I'll attempt to stitch myself back together. I splash cold water on my cheeks, sit on the toilet lid, open Rosemary's Instagram. Curiosity and guilt have liquefied into a viscous seething disgust she doesn't deserve. What to do with it? Nowhere to set it down safely. Her face—those ugly teeth, those gorgeous green eyes—beams into the room, a face Caleb has, in actuality, *rejected* in favor of my own. It finally hits me: I've won. But after so much drama and angst prefacing this climax, hasn't it simply . . . fizzled out? What happens now?

I go back out. My face is blotchy, but it's over now. I can decide it's over.

"Naomi, are you sure you're okay?" Caleb's face is wide and pale, like the full moon. "Please talk to me."

"I think I will be. Let's go back."

This won't be the reason our relationship ends; it's too pathetic. If it has to end someday, it will be on my terms, and under my control. It will be written.

In bed, Caleb's body wraps around mine like a comma. Our bodies overheat fast, slick with sweat, but neither of us move out of each other's arms.

chapter seven

THE FOLLOWING MORNING, I lie in bed next to Caleb and search the contours of my body for any of the expected signs, the *bumps and bruises.* I'm loved now, apparently, so where is the evidence?

By the time I wander sleepily into the kitchen, Caleb's mother has already left for her run. There's a note tacked to the refrigerator: *Lovely meeting you, Naomi! Hope you enjoyed your time here and hope to see you again soon, in NYC or Wales. Xxx Jen.*

"That's nice of her," I say to Caleb, pouring myself coffee.

"I actually wrote you a note, too." Licking his lips—his nervous tic—he hands me a sheaf of lined paper. "When I'm back in New York we can talk about it. If you want."

Intrigued and terrified about what it might reveal, I resist the urge to snatch the letter from him and devour it. With a shaky hand I pick up my mug and take a few slow sips and put the mug down and then, finally, take the letter from him and shove it deep into my pocket. "Thanks," I say. "I'll read it when I'm alone."

I don't want to give up any power I have by saying I've already decided to forgive him. By writing it all down, he clearly knows how best to win me back; I enjoy feeling like a prize earned.

When Caleb offers to drive me to the train station in Cardiff, I elect to take a taxi instead—unsure if I'm punishing him, or punishing myself. In the back seat I watch the green fields roll by and suffer what feel like palpitations of grief, but for what, exactly, I can't name. I preemptively wrote this betrayal, but a part of me trusted that our relationship was solid and strong and tender, maybe even boring, in the way domesticity can often be; I'd hoped I just had a dark, overactive imagination and a propensity for self-sabotage, an unwavering belief in my own unsubstantiated deficiencies.

But I can no longer pretend. It's all true. Something is wrong, and—

—*when a man chooses to have sex with me a second time, I think,* Oh, weird, okay, *and then start the clock*—

Oscar Wilde was right, it seems, when he suggested life imitates art; perhaps the only consolation is this odd power I now seem to wield.

After the train pulls in at Heathrow, I board my flight and make eye contact with three attractive men in my vicinity and wonder if I could have made a better choice. But all of them are capable of hurting me, too, in myriad and distinct ways.

I smooth the pages of Caleb's note and begin to read:

Dear Naomi,

I'm so sorry for lying and for hurting you. I'm furious at myself. Throughout our relationship you've been honest and open, and I've been afraid to be. I let my past affect the best thing in my life: us. I need you to know that I love and care about you more

than you probably know. Rosemary was a stupid crutch for me:
she's the only person in New York who has known me for a long
time, and it has been comforting to talk to someone who under-
stands my past life. But that's no excuse, and I guarantee it won't
happen again. I wrote Rosemary an email this morning to tell her
I'm in a serious relationship now, and explaining why it wouldn't
be wise to remain in contact. I wish to prioritize your feelings, and
our relationship, from now on. I truly believe we have so much
room to grow together. I want to grow with you. Please forgive me.
Much love xx, Caleb

I reread until my eyes grow irritated and dry. I blink frequently, and in quick succession, to create lubricating tears. Flushing everything out. The man in the seat beside me pointedly angles his body toward the window, as if expecting me to ask for something he isn't willing to give. *I'm not crying,* I almost tell him. *It isn't real, you can relax.*

Caleb's note feels heartfelt and maybe even like an epiphany, like he realized while writing it that I might actually be enough after all. But how can I be sure the letter wasn't driven by a fear of being alone again in a still-foreign city, or by the shameful stigma of returning to an ex? I give him so much—by choosing me, he gets a cat and family dinners and regular sex and affection.

I fold the letter until it's a tiny square that fits in the palm of my hand.

Best-case scenario: his betrayal allows us to reset, to start over. Maybe what I wanted all along was to test my value to him, to know if he would fight for me. I want to be worth fighting for.

—*I thought it might snap him out of his funk and fight for us*—

Didn't Rosemary want the exact same thing from him?

As the fact of my success and her failure sinks in, I don't feel as triumphant as expected. Frankly, I feel a little sad that the only person who would understand is the only person I can't speak to about any of it: *her.*

The plane lands then, bumping down the runway at top speed. My least favorite part of any flight is sensing the brakes shudder beneath me. How ironic would it be to survive seven flawless hours of flight only to crash and burn upon returning to the ground?

JFK has relatively new self-service kiosks at international customs. I position myself in front of a camera lens when the machine tells me to and try to look pretty so I can post the photo to my Instagram Story and broadcast my triumphant return.

In the Uber Pool from the airport, I text Caleb. I read your letter. I'm sad this happened, but I'm grateful for this note, and happy you're being honest with me. I think we'll get through this. I definitely want to check in with you about everything when you return, but for now, I want you to know that I love you, and forgive you.

Three words I've waited so long to hear, and to say aloud, and of course to write, appear alien now. As if I've never seen them in this particular order before.

It's close to three a.m. in Wales, so I don't expect a reply until morning.

After the Uber drops me off, I climb the stairs and turn the key in the lock and enter my apartment. Romeo rushes around the corner and wraps himself, mewling, around my legs. On the kitchen table, Noah left a note.

I have at least three scratches on various limbs thanks to Romeo's talons, which I'll be invoicing you for soon, but other than that, he's really fucking cute.

Redirecting energy toward my empty fridge and growling stomach, I waltz into the supermarket five minutes before closing time and begin to aimlessly wander the aisles. Sensing the reproachful gazes of exhausted employees, I accumulate cereals and tea and linguine and pesto and eggs and bananas and garlic hummus and celery and a bag of chocolate-covered pretzels. On the checkout line, I invent other errands to run. I don't want to go back to my apartment yet; I prefer to be among people. Despite the two heavy bags the cashier hands me, I take the long way home, and in doing so pass a beer shop I've never seen before advertising British imports. I wander in and peruse the shelves until I recognize a familiar bottle of Welsh golden ale. The label is a dragon's face, its tongue wreathed in fire. I picture Caleb opening my fridge and finding the bottles, a pleasant surprise, when he returns.

I will become worthy of love and well-equipped to describe it.

I buy a six-pack.

After lugging the bags home, I light a candle and unload the groceries—positioning the beer front and center—and crack open a window to air out the apartment. Clutching a steaming cup of chamomile, I open my computer and consider changing my Facebook profile picture to a photo of Caleb and me on the beach in Wales, but ultimately decide not to risk it. Even though the bulk of my profile is private, and even though Rosemary still isn't aware of my real surname, I feel it's too risky a backdrop. It's possible she could stumble upon my profile in some other way unbeknownst to me. I often feel like a Naomi Adler, rather than an Ackerman, these days. The more frequently and the more deeply I've written this version of myself down, the quicker I've turned into a more dangerous—but more purposeful—version of myself.

Naomi Adler is my id. I'm satisfied to give it, to give *her*, a name. She is not me.

I post the photo to Instagram instead. Missing this beautiful place already! I caption it. Shout-out to my guy for showing me around.

I would normally roll my eyes at any caption involving the phrase *my person* or *my favorite human* or *my man* or god forbid *my guy*, but now more than ever I need the possessive clause.

Once in bed, I listen to some moody music ("Somebody Else" by the 1975; "All My Friends" by Dermot Kennedy) and read an article about a motel owner who spies on people through a small hole in the ceiling of their rooms. Then I take a few BuzzFeed quizzes ("What Kind of Bagel Are You?" "What Emoji Are You?"— poppy seed and eggplant, respectively) and then, via a series of ill-fated clicks, I end up on the Reddit Relationships message board. It's an amalgamation of unreliable narrators. Searching for contrast, I immerse myself in the shitty circumstances of strangers.

Then I condense my own story, all the inciting events, into three paragraphs. Our relationship was lovely for months, I type to anonymous strangers on the Internet, because the specter of his ex-girlfriend hadn't yet arrived.

(*And also because I wasn't behaving in character, because I was going against all my instincts, because I was trying to feel—*)

It was too good to be true, I type, describing the lies, the secrecy, the table in the back where Rosemary and Caleb sat drinking beers. Then I describe the confrontation and quote Caleb's apology letter, before asking anonymous strangers on the Internet: Was I right to forgive him?

Then I press post.

*A stupid crutch . . . We have so much room to grow together . . .
Throughout our relationship you've been honest and open . . .*

I squirm remembering this line, despite knowing my actions
are justified. My book's function isn't to betray or avenge—it's
only an expression of my inner life, my fantasies and fears, so it can
be argued that I *have* been open and honest—and soon, hopefully,
all that honesty and openness will be printed and shared. Someday
Caleb will read everything I've thought and tried to feel—and if
he can't forgive me for writing it all down, can't understand the
need to first sort myself out on the page, then we shouldn't be together. Right?

Only when I reveal my worst self, and am forgiven for it, will I
be certain I am loved.

After a few minutes of obsessively refreshing the message
board, I notice Valentine_bandit has commented: I think you
need to make a choice between two hurts: constantly wondering if
it will happen again—which will erode both the quality of your relationship as well as your own sanity—or breaking it off to ensure it
won't.

Valentine_bandit has a point.

"We should break up," I announce to my empty bedroom, testing how that feels.

"Never mind," I say, tossing my voice again into the empty
room. Reaching for Romeo as he lounges beside me, I press my
hands into the soft space on his belly where I can feel his heartbeat,
the little body rising and falling, but my hands must be too heavy,
too insistent, because he edges out from beneath all ten fingers and
slinks off.

My book, I realize, is the ultimate defense mechanism; I model catastrophes, too. Writing down every worst-case scenario allows me to forgo their effects, to skip right over the pain. I will already be prepared, armored against hurt—*told you so*, from my future self.

The plot will move forward as planned. I text Rosemary.

Hey, hope you had a great holiday! I'm planning to climb tomorrow, wanna join?

Rosemary's response pops onto my screen ten minutes later.

Yes! Tomorrow is great. I also just finished reading your pages. We can talk about it after we climb?

My stomach lurches, then settles—a viciously betrayed person wouldn't agree to go climbing with their betrayer, would they?

My phone buzzes again.

Your pictures make me physically ill with jealousy, but I'm so glad you're back, texts Danielle. **Five days is too long. I hardly know ye anymore!**

Ok, drama queen, I type, **let's hang out when I'm not so jet-lagged! I'm going to stay in and do some writing.**

She won't doubt it because she believes in me. And how have I repaid her for the unwavering support? Lies.

But it'll stop soon, I chant to myself, digging a nail into the crepey skin between my thumb and forefinger. *Soon, soon.*

Yes, but until then, no more "accidental" run-ins, remember? she writes with a winking emoji. **Behave yourself.**

———

My STOMACH WON'T settle during the next day's shift. Even as I manage to laugh at Luna's snide comments about overhyped authors and about Lit Bro's latest habit of describing in granular detail the plot of every single Philip Roth book, I can't help obsessing over what Rosemary will think of me now that she's read my work. Will she like me more, or less? If it's the latter, we won't remain friends. I know this for a fact. No two writers can ever be truly close if one doesn't respect the other's work—it's emotionally impossible. So much more is at stake.

When my shift is finally over, Luna—perhaps sensing my restlessness—offers to lock up.

"Where you headed?" she asks.

"Oh, just dinner with my brother," I say before rushing off.

To avoid the frightening prospect of Rosemary seeing me naked, I arrive at the climbing gym early. Beelining for the locker room and changing into a V-neck T-shirt advertising my alma mater, I'm momentarily proud, puffing out my emblazoned chest, until I realize what the shirt represents. Other climbers will assume I'm better than I am, will be disappointed or disdainful when I'm not what they expect.

Still, I want Rosemary to find me in action, not waiting around, and so I choose a friendly-looking v1 with large holds for my fingers to slide into.

The final two holds require a certain blend of physics and fearlessness I can't seem to muster. I hang with straight arms as my left foot scrabbles for purchase and my right hand reaches—but in vain; I let go, falling as I've been taught.

When I make contact with the mat, I hear a man's voice. "Dude, you've gotta trust the wall and get that hip tucked in. You were so close. Want the beta?"

Warily, I spring to my feet and face him—Jake. One of the men Rosemary introduced me to last time. "What's that?"

"Oh, it's the best way up the wall. I can show you?"

I shake my head. "Thanks, but I'd rather figure it out on my own."

"All right, whatever." He cocks his head at me. "You're Rosie's friend, right?"

Rosie? I frown at him. "You mean Rosemary?"

The name-butcher nods. "Yeah, is she coming today?"

"Supposed to be," I say, lip curling, and turn to hop back on the wall. I'm still only slightly off the ground when a tiny blond woman with a pixie cut and a forearm covered in tattoos—several faces, mouths wide-open in simulations of a scream—points from the ground and says, "You have to get both feet on that hold at the same time."

Unsolicited advice, it seems, is the norm. "How? There's literally not enough surface area."

"There is," she says. "Trust the wall."

I'm beginning to realize climbers might be as bad as, if not worse than, Equinox bros. Self-satisfied and peacocking, but also friendly? And genuinely invested in watching me succeed? I don't trust it.

Grimacing, I accept her first tip and then her second, and succeed.

Below me, I notice Rosemary has arrived and is applauding; her hair is partly covered by a tie-dye bandanna.

"Look at you!" she says. "A natural. You don't even need me anymore."

"False," I say. "I still need you."

Feeling emboldened, I approach a slightly overhanging wall to attempt a v2 despite my inferior form and wobbly v1s. Gravity works on me as I wriggle my way up and up and sideways. Stretching my left arm from a friendlier hold toward a tinier and more unforgiving hold, my overworked, weakening finger muscles refuse to grip. I start toppling. When I attempt, frantically, to fall the way I've been taught, my body tilts forward like a rag doll instead. On the way down I smack my forehead, hard, on the edge of a hold and crumple to the floor, moaning.

"Oh, *shit*, dude," I hear someone say with alarm. "That didn't look so good."

"Naomi!" Rosemary's face hovers above mine. "Are you okay?" She presses gently on my forehead. "There's a bump forming already. Does it hurt? How many fingers am I holding up?"

She makes a peace sign.

"Four," I say. I want to be scrutinized, the recipient of Rosemary's focused attention a little while longer.

"Oh no. Can you stand up?"

"Maybe. It's, like, throbbing. My head, I mean. The bump." Stumbling a bit as I get to my feet, I place a steadying hand against the wall. "Fuck, I might've twisted my ankle, too."

"Someone get her some ice," Jake says.

"And a glass of water," Rosemary says.

It's not the scene I envisioned, but this unexpected alternative might lead somewhere better.

I sip the water and press the ice to my forehead and experience a gradual numbing.

I prefer numbness. Always have.

"Rosemary, don't you live nearby?" Jake asks, and I wonder how he knows, if he's been inside. "Maybe you could take her there and make sure she's okay? I'm happy to help out, too."

It's a clumsy offer, one with clear ulterior motives, and so I grip her arm, reclaiming her attention. We both want her.

"That sounds nice," I say. "I'm feeling a bit light-headed. But I don't want to intrude—I can also just go home?"

"No, it's okay, you can come with me," says Rosemary. "Fort Greene is only a few minutes away if we Uber. You can lie down until you feel better, okay? I'm so sorry, I feel responsible, I should've been spotting you!"

"That sounds good," I say, and then: "It's not your fault."

As I gingerly remove my climbing shoes, my toes begin to breathe again and my heartbeat quickens. What will Rosemary's apartment reveal? I'm eager and impatient and can no longer feel any pain.

Jake's plan pays off; he finagles his way into the Uber, too. We set off, an odd trio. I'm sitting in the middle, much to Jake's disappointment. My right leg is pressed against Rosemary's left leg; my left pressed against his right.

"How are you feeling right now?" Rosemary asks as we speed through the dusky streets. "Any better?"

"Not really. Do you have Advil at your place?"

"Of course."

"Pain is productive, though," Jake says. "If you don't let yourself feel it, you risk ignoring a more serious problem."

Irritated, I twist toward him. Determined to make him feel small. "Sorry, what's your name again?"

"Jake," Jake says.

"You look like a Jake."

"Do I?"

I can't decide whether to flirt with him or to insult him.

"Okay, so, look: every Jake in every rom-com is the heroine's best friend from childhood who gets friend-zoned early on and spends the rest of his screen time vainly trying to convince her otherwise."

Jake's mouth falls open, momentarily speechless, as Rosemary's burst of laughter vibrates her whole body. I can feel it against my hip.

"That was mean," Jake says. "How hard did you hit your head?"

He's not wrong; I backtrack. "Hard, I guess."

"You're a writer," Rosemary says, as if I need another reminder. "Subvert the genre. Save the Jakes from their fate." The car stops in front of her modern, industrial-chic building. "Here we are."

I perform a first impression. "Wow, this is—so sleek."

"Ugh," she says, interpreting the comment the way I had hoped. "It embarrassed me at first, like, hello, gentrification, I'm ruining the quaint neighborhood! But it was miraculously within my price range and I fell in love. There's so much light. Perfect for all my plants."

If her salary is anywhere between forty and sixty thousand (not counting the freelance work), then her price range could conceivably be—

"Do you need help walking?" Jake asks me.

"There's an elevator," Rosemary says. "Another perk. I'm on the top floor."

I watch over her shoulder as she types in the building's entry code: 0229. I turn into a silent chant, *0229, 0229*, committing it to memory. Just in case. Leaning on Jake, I hover my ankle above the ground.

The elevator is barely large enough to comfortably fit three people. I can feel Rosemary's hot breath against my exposed collarbone.

The elevator dings. We exit. I limp toward her front door as she slides the key in the lock.

"I thought your apartment would have a fancy entry code, too," I say.

"Oh. Nope. Just a normal key."

Rosemary and Jake exchange a glance. Did I not sound as casual as I thought I had?

Inside her home—inside her home!—I'm struck, first, by the abundance of greenery hanging from the high ceiling, crowding every windowsill, and flanking each side of a turquoise couch and an off-white armchair. Some are nearly five feet tall, long-stemmed; fronds sway in the breeze through the open window. On the glass coffee table, a stack of magazines fans out across the surface—*Harper's, The Paris Review, Afar, The New Yorker, Bon Appétit, Vogue, Vanity Fair.* Also on the table: a green-wax candle, pine-scented. Rosemary leans down to light it, and shadows soon flicker on the cream-colored wall opposite.

"Where's your bookshelf?" I ask. Its absence is palpable.

"Oh! In my bedroom." She laughs. "You looked genuinely concerned for a second. What's that famous John Waters quote? 'If you go home with somebody and they don't have books, don't fuck them.'"

"I love—books," says Jake, blinking rapidly.

Oh, Jake, you poor thing.

"Good to know," says Rosemary, mouth contorting to probably prevent herself from laughing in his face.

"You're responsible for so many lives." I gesture at the plants. "They're thriving."

I'm not a plant person. They look nice, yes, immediately brightening both the room and my mood, yes, but I don't know what else I should say. It seems obsessive, though, her plant thing, and obsession I can understand.

"I wasn't always into plants," she says. "But Caleb once took me to this giant greenhouse in the UK with a tropical biome and a Mediterranean biome, and every plant was categorized and defined by their special skills, I was fascinated by it—"

Can plants have skills? Why didn't Caleb bring me to this greenhouse, too?

"—and so I started buying aloe plants to use on my skin and mint to chew on and it made me feel self-sufficient and resourceful and kind of witchy."

"Any witchy plant facts you want to share?" I ask. "I'm always on the hunt for a good metaphor."

"So here's an interesting one if you're an etymology nerd like I am—*willow* is actually derived from the same word as *wicked* and *witch*. Oh, and *mimosa pudica* folds up its leaves when touched. Pretty resonant, right? I'm probably going to put that in a story."

I file this away.

"I can't believe we're still talking about plants," Jake says.

Normally I would have agreed with him, but after watching Rosemary lovingly finger a fern, I choose allyship. "Is this conversation beneath you in some way?"

He shakes his head and turns to Rosemary as if she can save him. "So, who's Caleb?"

"Her ex-boyfriend," I say before she can reply.

"Let me get you that Advil," Rosemary says, faux-chipper.

Sitting on the turquoise couch, I feel the fabric rush to hold me. "Is this memory foam?"

Rosemary shouts a reply from the kitchen. "Yeah, I have an astonishingly bad back for someone in her twenties."

Jake sits beside me and deigns to bounce up and down a few times. "Very comfy!"

I want him to disappear, now.

Rosemary returns with a glass of water and two smooth pills. I remember the pain, which has subsided to a dull throb; still, I touch the bump on my head and finger the curve of my ankle, eliciting sympathy. "Thank you." I swallow them. "Seriously. For taking me here and making sure I don't fall into any concussive naps."

She laughs. "No problem. Should we call someone to take you home later? Lachlan, maybe?"

"No, that's fine," I say quickly. "His boss is taking the whole office to some fancy steak dinner. I don't want to bother him."

Caleb is, of course, a vegetarian.

She shrugs and turns to Jake: "I'm making a Negroni. You want one?" When he nods, she turns back to me. "I'd offer you one, too, but, you know, the Advil—"

"Do you mind if I go lie down for a bit?" I gesture to her bedroom door, which is ajar.

"Oh." She hesitates. "Sure, just don't fall asleep."

Limping in, I stretch out on the comforter and stare up at the ceiling, surprised to find a skylight perfectly framing a sliver of moon. An airplane, its lights flashing, zooms across the square of visible night sky. Blink and you'd miss it.

I redirect my gaze to her crowded nightstand: lavender candle, a small cactus, a pair of silver hoop earrings, shea butter hand moisturizer, two beat-up paperbacks: *Break.up* by Joanna Walsh (unbelievably on the nose, no?) and *Transit* by Rachel Cusk. Both boast an array of neon sticky notes. I thumb through the pages and read the sections she has underlined:

From *Transit*: "Like love, I said, being understood creates the fear that you will never be understood again."

From *Break.up*: "A love story comes only after the end of love, whether it ends one way, or the other, and, until the story's told, love is a secret, not because it's illicit, but because it's so difficult to tell what it is."

I type each quote into the growing document in my Notes app, then scroll and scroll through the details I've collected, satisfied with my growing catalog of her.

Next, I open the drawer of her nightstand as quietly as possible. Inside, an assortment of ChapSticks, some crinkled receipts, pencils worn down to the nub, and a pink vibrator the size of my thumb.

Nearly identical to the one Caleb gave me for my birthday.

Seized by a rush of white-hot anger and hurt, I realize it's likely—isn't it?—that both our vibrators came from the same source. The alternative—Rosemary roaming around Babeland after her breakup, sad but hopeful, fingering an array of different colors and sizes—doesn't sit right in my stomach.

I click it on, testing its capabilities. Seven speeds, not eleven. Mine is clearly an upgrade.

Feeling for the first time like a dirty intruder, I put the vibrator back inside the drawer and shut it away, trying to breathe. Coincidences, coincidences, that's all. Every self-respecting woman I know owns a vibrator of some kind.

I search for something else to look at, to consider. My gaze moves to the opposite wall, where there's a startlingly large photograph of St Andrews taken from high above the town. I imagine, in her dreams, Rosemary swoops over the town like a bird, identifying every spot of land where Caleb kissed her.

The intimate murmur of voices beyond the bedroom door—joined by the tinkling of ice in glasses and the hiss of a cocktail being poured—is a kind of lullaby, and Rosemary keeps up a constant stream of chatter. I'm certain that by disallowing any lingering, easily misinterpreted silences and keeping her voice chipper, she doesn't want Jake to kiss her.

Their conversation remains climbing-related for now, so I tune them out. Fluffing a pillow, I tug the covers down and wiggle my way under them, cocooned by her soft pale pink sheets. Underneath, any sounds I make will be muffled. Closing my eyes, I become the bird Rosemary embodies in her dreams. When heat pulses between my legs, I listen. I open the drawer again, soft and slow, and retrieve the vibrator. To appease the small part of my brain screaming, *Hygiene! Hygiene!* I apply pressure only to the crotch of my underwear. As it pulses through fabric, I visualize Rosemary wrapping her legs around Caleb's back as he enters her slow and deep, his lips brushing against her collarbone. Before long, a low whine escapes my lips. Caleb and Rosemary have been in this bed together.

Now I'm here, too. Defiling those memories. They'll never lie together again, here or anywhere.

ROSEMARY'S VOICE CUTS through my sleep fog, but faintly, like she's calling from a faraway shore.

I flutter my eyes open, panicked. "Shit, I must have dozed off." I can feel the vibrator curled inside my fingers. I hold it tight, concealing it beneath the comforter like a weapon.

"You're fine, it's only been fifteen minutes. Jake just left." Rosemary grimaces at me. "I didn't think you'd actually get under the covers. You worked out and got all sweaty. I'll need to lug my sheets to the laundromat now."

I try to look wide-eyed and abashed, like a naughty puppy. I cannot lose her now, not over some dirty sheets. "I'm really sorry, Rosemary. I wasn't thinking. I can give you some quarters? For laundry."

"Okay. Thanks." She unfolds her arms and massages her eyelids and sighs. "I'm sorry, I didn't mean to snap at you. It's been a long day. It's not a big deal. Don't worry." She gestures toward the couch in the living room. "Shall we finally talk about your book? I owe you your feedback."

"Yes, please. Gotta get my money's worth!"

I realize this is the wrong thing to say as soon as I've said it, despite being factually correct. I meant it as wry and flippant, but maybe I also meant to shame her a little, and in so doing, forgot the rules of my own game. As Rosemary's jaw tightens, I can sense an invisible barrier wedging itself between us—personal/professional.

But isn't she the one who first erected that barrier by charging me actual money?

"Of course," says Rosemary, smooth and sweet now. "I'll get us another drink—oh, right, the Advil—"

"It's fine, I won't drop dead. Just a few kidney problems when I'm old."

She doesn't laugh.

"I'll follow you out," I say, gesturing to the bump on my head with my free hand. "Gotta go slow."

She nods, turning on her heel, and as soon as she disappears out of sight, I slip the vibrator back inside the drawer, which was left slightly open. She must not have noticed.

I hear the sound of a wine bottle being uncorked, a glass making contact with countertop. Without remembering or really even caring about the state of my head or ankle, I swing my legs out of bed and join Rosemary in the living room.

Her hands are trembling a little as she hands me a glass, red liquid sloshing like a small contained tsunami. Something is clearly wrong, but I'm not yet sure if it has anything to do with me.

We sit and sip for a while. Despite being inches apart on the couch, she doesn't seem to register my presence at all. Eventually, I shatter the thickening silence. "So. Start with the bad stuff, end with the good stuff?"

She finally laughs. "So you don't need to be buttered up first, noted."

As she extracts my pages from her tote and hands them to me, I notice an alarming amount of red-ink marginalia. Scanning my faux first page, I almost can't believe I wrote it:

My boyfriend's new girlfriend, Naomi, has the same thickness to her eyebrows as I do. The same wavy auburn hair and pear-shaped hips.

I'm peeking through the stacks at the bookstore where she works, watching her gift-wrap a mug with Shakespeare's face on it. Mugs are geometrically difficult, much more unwieldy than the perfect corners of a book, and for a moment I pity the grimacing girl white-knuckling the Scotch tape. Then I recover, remembering who she is.

In photos, we looked so different; it was a lie. She must use too many filters, an excessive play of shadow and saturation.

When photographed, I press my lips together while Naomi chooses to flash all her yellow-tinged teeth. This unpleasant shade could mean I'm prettier than she is, but who knows? Maybe her yellow teeth suggest the kind of unassailable confidence that would appeal to Lachlan, especially after enduring so many of my halfhearted attempts to be happy.

When I finally muster enough courage to approach the cash register, I ask if she has any recommendations for books set in Australia. "My boyfriend is really homesick," I say, just to fuck with her a little.

The long pause that follows, in which she blinks at me a little too rapidly, indicates a successful provocation.

Finally, she offers several suggestions. "Um, The Slap by Christos Tsiolkas—that one more's modern—or Helen Garner's Monkey Grip or for a real classic, Peter Carey's True History of the Kelly Gang."

"I'm impressed! You know more Aussie authors than the average New York bookseller."

Naomi smiles without showing her yellowing teeth, which must mean it's false, forced. "We stock Carey's, but I'd need to order the others."

"Oh, could you? That would be great. Both of them." Work a little harder on my behalf, I wish I could say.

After I pay for Carey's in single dollar bills, I grab a slice at the pizza place across the street and stalk Naomi on Instagram. Given her public account and the overwhelming number of #TBT posts, it's clear she is absolutely desperate for validation.

By the time Naomi's shift ends, I'm ready to rock. The Clark Street subway station is only a few blocks away. I trail her there, and we enter the same train car heading uptown. Bodies in suits *shove in at Wall Street, and those huddled near the doors squeeze closer together. In the scuffle, I manage to stand a few inches away from Naomi. When the sleeve of my sweater grazes her denim-jacketed elbow, I wonder if we'll look at each other. But her gaze never rises. Being two inches taller proves advantageous—I'm able to peer at her screen as she scrolls through artists, albums, finally settling on Gang of Youths' "Let Me Down Easy." With a twinge of discomfort, I realize Lachlan used to blast this song every time we cooked together, chopping onions to the smash of a cymbal.*

As I'd hoped, it's shaping up to be excellent material for a book. Later, I'll scribble down some details—her pear-shaped hips, the Shakespeare mug, her yellowing teeth, the Australian rock band, her denim-jacketed elbow brushing against the sleeve of my sweater. The beginning of my book. I've found, I think, a worthy story to tell. Until now I've only written short fiction, twenty pages or less; I've never felt intrigued enough about any-one to sustain a steady accumulation of words. But now, finally, life has begun to interest me. To prove the believers right and the nonbelievers wrong—I fall into both categories, depending on the day—I'll write a novel, generate a plot, and maybe, over the course of it all, find a way to bring Lachlan back to me.

Throughout the twenty-five pages, as the ex-girlfriend, "Penel-ope," returns to the bookstore again and again, expertly playing the part of a loyal customer, a tentative friendship founded (duh) on the concealment of identities and intentions develops between the two women.

By inverting certain details, I've thrown Rosemary off the scent; believable lies often skew as close as possible to the truth.

Worst-case scenario: she assumes I'm obsessed with *myself* rather than with her.

"I love how this piece is evolving into a story about the relationship between the two women," says Rosemary. "At first I was frustrated by the relative thinness of Lachlan's character, because I wanted to understand why he was such a prize, you know? But now I understand it was an intentional decision. He's auxiliary, a projection rather than a person."

Grateful that any inadequate character development has been ascribed to shrewd authorial intent, I nod in agreement. Accepting credit where it is (not) due.

Rosemary continues, consulting her notes. "Right now, though, the friendship between the women feels a bit one-sided. I'm not sure Naomi would—oh, very clever by the way, very Ben Lerner of you." She pauses to smirk at me. "Anyway, I'm not sure *fictional* Naomi would be so quick to embrace this new friendship. I would build to it a bit more, exploring what Naomi gets out of it. Is she kind of lonely herself? Does she actually *know* Penelope's true identity and is just as curious about her?"

What do you *get out of it, Rosemary?* I want to ask.

Maybe she isn't yet aware of how meta it has all become. How does she truly not realize I'm reenacting a version of our own origin story? People see what they want to see, I suppose, and filter out the rest.

"Cool, that makes sense." In my notebook—lavender, sateen, monogrammed, still the best gift—I scribble *make it build.*

Rosemary plows on: "Right, so, the pacing so far is excellent. I kept thinking, *Penelope can't possibly get away with that*, but then she does. And in the meantime she's burying herself in all these lies, it can't end well."

I write *end well?*—the question mark is important—in my notebook.

"But you'll need to make sure all the tension doesn't leak away as the narrative evolves. I think a reader will expect and also desire a surprising reversal or twist of some kind, too. A seesaw of power—who's up, who's down. Do you know what I mean?"

"Oh, yes, totally."

But I don't have any twists planned. I don't need to. The events I've set in motion are likely to produce one without any further interference on my end.

"So I'm obviously a fan of books about writers, but not everyone is, so if Penelope's justification metric for stalking Naomi is her fiction, and her desire and desperation for a good story drives the action, I feel like there needs to be a bigger existential question underneath."

As if for dramatic effect, Rosemary picks up her glass and slowly drinks from it. Sip, pause, sip. When the glass returns to the coffee table, she licks her red-stained lips and resumes speaking just as my nervous system shifts into overdrive.

"Penelope admits her life is stagnant, right, and until now, relatively charmed. So choosing to stalk her ex-boyfriend's new girlfriend gives Penelope an edge, some friction to brush up against. It's paradoxical how having money and privilege and a supportive family makes her feel almost as if she doesn't exist."

Oh.

"So does Penelope manufacture events to write about because she doesn't believe she's an inherently interesting person on her own? Is that her motive for creating drama—to fill the void? To *exist*, if only to herself?"

My mouth is dry. I need water. "Oh, I'm—"

"It's okay!" Rosemary notices my distress. "You don't have to answer these questions right now. Just something to think about as you write—"

But I do think about it, all the time—

"—because Penelope has never written with a symbolic gun to her head, and I think she's jealous of those who do. Naomi, for example, has a job but still worries about paying her bills, while Penelope flounders around trying to 'write a book' using her parents' trust fund. Her jealousy is misplaced and problematic, obviously, but it *is* true that there's a different sort of compensation in having too little time and too little money. And so often, art made under those conditions has an undeniably exquisite savagery. I mean, existential terror is honestly kind of a luxury. Penelope is terrified she won't ever have what it takes—which, in her mind, means experiencing *real* difficulties—to make truly incredible art."

Unconvinced she could have gleaned all this from my pages, I blink at her.

Could she have? Or was this bubbling up inside her already, and my work simply granted her the opportunity to finally say it?

But why should I need to be terrified in order to make things? I wish I could say without reserve: *If you're so obsessed with not having enough money then maybe you shouldn't live in a one-bedroom in Fort Greene, maybe you shouldn't buy a dirty chai every day, there are ways, you know, there are ways*—But how would she respond?

You have no idea what I do simply to survive. Allow me a luxury, allow me a latte. You move easily through life, creating drama where there is none. Your circumstances have affixed childproof bumpers to all of life's sharp edges—

She wouldn't be wrong.

Is it possible to resent my family for providing literally

everything I could ever want or need, thus dampening any opportunity to face a single character-building hardship?

But you did have hardships, a small voice ventures to say. *You don't have ovaries. You were raped. Adam—*

Those aren't hardships, a bigger voice chimes in. *Someone took out your ovaries to make you better. You wrote about your rape; how traumatized could you be? And Adam never even fucked you. There are worse things. There are worse things. There are—*

I can whine all I want about the shame that accompanies immense privilege, but then I would be yet another whining asshole. There will always be those who whisper my greatest fear behind my back:

A rich writer can write a good book and a poor writer can write a good book, but the poor writer writes her book against all odds, working and wanting twice as hard, and that makes a poor person's book worth twice as much, and more—

What, and when, have I ever wanted enough?

And so now I imagine friction where there is none because a frictionless life is deadening.

I close the journal and compose myself. "Were you ever bored? Did you care enough to keep turning pages? I don't know if it's good enough to keep going."

"Oh, absolutely. I can think of many words to describe this, but *boring* isn't one of them."

I'm afraid to ask for the other words. "Okay, phew. It's the most fun I've had writing in a long time." And to nail it home: "Both women are actually two different, warring versions of myself."

"Like you and your id?"

I nod, happy to be believed, and try not to guess how she might one day—once it's published—react to my original draft, to the character she inspired. What qualities of her depiction will Rosemary find most offensive? She might surprise me by empathizing with how and why my fixation began, and then bristle at descriptions of her (vampiric) teeth.

But imagine being the subject of such fervent scrutiny, such exalted reconstruction—how could anyone hate a person who makes them feel that special?

I change the subject, saying brightly, "By the way, I love that giant photo of St Andrews in your room, the town looks so regal from up high. I have a similar tribute in my bedroom, a cool painting mapping Melbourne's tram lines. It's part of a series—the artist paints nearly every major public transport system in the world."

"Oh, great concept. Every city's heartbeat. Obviously the MTA fucking sucks," she says, tossing her hair over her shoulder, "but I still love it. So many stories, a constant cataloging."

I couldn't have articulated it better. "Have you seen the Senegalese man who teaches everyone about West African music while he plays his drum? It's called a *djembe*, apparently. I've seen him on, like, four different train lines."

She shakes her head.

"You probably will soon, then," I say, and move on. "I guess the only downside to my map of Melbourne is how it's a constant reminder I'm here and not there. I miss it so much. I loved being— separated from my life, like I could try anything, *do* anything, be a totally different person. And if it turned out badly, it wouldn't even count. It wouldn't follow me home, to my real life. Kind of like hitting pause for a few months. There's a freedom in that."

"You mean, a freedom in having no consequences?"

I look at her. "Exactly."

"I know what you mean," she says, and I'm glad for it. "I miss

St Andrews, too. Except my life there *did* follow me home." Her spine compresses and curves as she sinks back into the couch cushion. "The last time I went back there was for Caleb's graduation, and I'm not sure I ever will again."

Inching closer to the precipice, I plan to leap off in a tidy nosedive, with her flailing behind. "What do you mean?"

"I can't untangle memories of St Andrews from memories of Caleb. They're synonymous. And I really need to move on, so I can't return. Not for a long time."

Because I need receipts, I follow up with: "So you don't think you'll be able to work things out with him?"

"He isn't open to that." Her eyes begin to water; she swipes at them with her sleeve. "I'm sorry, god, I feel like such a mess."

"Oh stop, it's fine, you can vent if you need to, that's what friends are for." I almost choke on the cliché as it slips out.

Rosemary drinks a quarter of her glass. I watch the liquid move inside her throat. Coming up for air, she belches and covers her mouth without uttering any apologies or excuses. "I've wasted so much time thinking we'd get back together. That's what he said when we broke up—*'who knows what the future holds.'*"

I can sort of understand why she made the assumptions she did, but wasn't it also naïve to imagine things would work out after so much had ruptured between them? Wasn't it narcissistic to think Caleb couldn't find someone else to love?

"Two nights ago I left him this wacky drunken voicemail at two a.m. saying we should give it another try—"

I never noticed this; it must have happened after I looked through Caleb's phone and found what I needed to confront him—

"—and then he finally called me back yesterday to say he's been seriously dating someone else." She no longer cares about wiping her tears away; she simply lets them fall. "I always thought it was weird he was never free to meet up on weekends, and now it makes sense. Weekends were reserved for her."

She has finally conjured me in her mouth—Caleb's new girlfriend. *Reserved for her.* I want to bask in all the weekends that belonged to me, but I can't overlook yet another lie. In his letter, Caleb said he emailed Rosemary. But now I know he called. No paper trail, no receipts—nothing documented. How will I ever be sure what was said? As devastated as Rosemary seems now, it's possible he made her some sort of promise, keeping an illusion alive. *Who knows what the future holds.*

Or maybe he only wanted one final pure and private conversation, voice-to-voice, to say goodbye. I could forgive him for that.

"I should've asked what was going on a long time ago, but it was easier not to know." Rosemary pinches her earlobe so hard it blooms red.

"I'm so sorry," I say, surprised by how much I mean it. Then I take a breath and test the ledge. "But maybe it's for the best?"

She finishes the rest of her wine. "Maybe I'll feel that way eventually. But not right now. Caleb was my first real boyfriend, which might explain why it's so hard letting him go."

Mine too, I want to shout. *Look, we are the same!*

"I understand," I say delicately. "But you have to trust there's someone out there who will be better for you."

When she falls silent for a while, I don't know what to do with my hands. What would a friend do? Hug her, then encourage a full-body sob in pursuit of catharsis? I initiate a hug. She goes limp in my arms.

"I'm exhausted," she says as we break apart. I can take a hint.

"I'll head out. Give you some space." I grope around on the

floor for my tote bag. "Thanks again for reading and editing so thoughtfully. Please send your work soon, too!"

She swallows. "Sure, I will—but I can't, you know, pay you or anything."

Her face reddens, and ironically I sense mine reddening, too. Sex, death, money: no one likes to talk about any of it, except as it pertains to writing fiction, where it's safe.

"Oh geez," I say airily, "you don't need to pay me, *I'm* not a professional editor. Just someone with a lot of free time, I guess." I squash my hands between my thighs to prevent from wringing them. "I'm actually a good reader, though. At least according to former classmates."

She smiles. "I believe them."

I ask one final question. "Do you mind if I borrow some books? I've been meaning to read Rachel Cusk and Joanna Walsh for a while, it's so serendipitous they're on your bedside table."

She tells me to go ahead, that she just finished them, that they were great. I return to her bedroom and take them. If Rosemary never sends me her writing, we'll have at least one other reason to meet again. I could choose to leave her alone, but it doesn't seem like she wants me to. I'm the one who initiates, true, but she always agrees to hang out—if she didn't enjoy spending time with me, she surely could've ghosted by now. We have no mutual friends! We don't live in the same borough! I'm incapable of single-handedly preventing her authors' books from being sold in my bookstore! None of it is up to me. I have no power, except on the page.

Outside in the hallway, I stand with my ear pressed against the door for a few minutes. She could call someone, or put on loud music, or release a primal scream—and if she does, I want to be there to hear it. And to maybe even scream back.

chapter eight

THE FOLLOWING WEEKEND, Caleb presses my apartment's buzzer. He promised he would come directly from the airport, and now he has. I buzz him in. The strident sound always sends Romeo diving for cover underneath my bed. "It's Caleb, it's your buddy," I reassure him, brushing mascara onto my lashes and painting my lips cherry red.

I open the door as Caleb rounds the corner, startling him. With his fist hanging in midair, poised to knock, he remembers to say hello. And to kiss me. His lips are cold, corpse-like. I cut the kiss short, telling him why.

"In my defense, it's nineteen degrees outside. I'm guessing you haven't left the house today? Explains why you're not wearing any pants." He swipes at my bare thigh.

"Busted," I say.

He removes his hand. I wonder if it's because he felt me tense and shrink away. The door to my apartment is still open with him

only halfway in. His letter, my tears, our messy scene in the bar—
we haven't forgotten yet.

I move aside to let him enter. He closes the door behind him
and goes to my bedroom and takes off his shoes.

"I'm glad you're back," I say.

"Me too."

Caleb opens his suitcase and begins to unpack, sliding a few
boxers, socks, T-shirts, and the sweatpants he sometimes wears to
bed inside the empty drawer I've allocated for him. As he does, it
strikes me how much of his stuff already lives here, scattered
around my apartment. His toothbrush and razor and shaving
cream usually crowd the bathroom windowsill alongside my facial
moisturizer and toothpaste and tweezers. Without either of us
having acknowledged or announced it, this space—my space—
has become ours. Why haven't I noticed before? It's evidence of
faithfulness. If he planned on leaving me, he wouldn't keep so
many of his things here.

Assessing that danger levels are low, Romeo rushes out from
under the bed and weaves through Caleb's legs, purring. The man
of the house, returned.

I grab two bottles of Welsh golden ale from the fridge and twist
off their caps.

"Look what I found!" The foam rises too fast as I present it to
him, threatening to dribble onto the carpet. I instinctively wrap
my lips around the bottleneck and suck it all down. "Oops." I wipe
my mouth. "You can have this other one."

"Wow, am I still in Wales?" He laughs, faux-incredulous. "Can't
believe you found this here." He takes a sip. "Thank you."

"You're welcome. Thought it might ease your transition."

"It will. It has." He kisses me again. His lips have warmed.

I don't pull away until a siren whines outside the window, breaking the reverie. "I've been doing a lot of thinking the past few days."

He lowers himself onto the couch and looks up at me warily. I perch on the opposite end, twisting my torso toward him.

"First I want you to know how much your letter meant to me," I say. "But it still takes a lot of time to rebuild trust, as well as hard work on both our parts. Are you sure that's what you want?"

"Of course." His voice is tinged with impatience. "How I feel about you hasn't changed."

"That's good," I say.

He rubs his eyes, which are red-rimmed and watery. I've never seen him cry, nor even approach the verge of tears. He's probably just tired and jet-lagged. That would make more sense.

"Did Rosemary respond to your email?" I ask, despite now knowing it was a phone call instead. Let it be his last lie.

I watch his shoulders drop. "She did. I wasn't going to reply but—she asked if I was happy."

When he pauses, I can't help resenting him for it. He's allowing me to entertain the possibility of doubt. "What did you tell her?"

The smile he directs at me is both fond and pitying. "I said I was."

I release the breath I've been holding and allow my body to sink into the couch cushion. For a long minute we sit slumped next to each other without moving or speaking.

Could it be true that Rosemary herself is the friction I've yearned for? Her existence, the romance of their past, made Caleb even more interesting and desirable to me. When we started dating, our relationship seemed too good to be true, and it was. Then enter this, enter *her*, and suddenly I was embroiled in someone else's story; influencing it became a sort of perverse power. I can't even remember what our relationship felt like in the early days, without Rosemary as a reference point.

Maybe all three of us are meant to scrub clean, to rid ourselves of this triangulation; maybe we're supposed to be happy now, floating free and forward, unburdened of the past.

I sit with this for a moment, seeking to untangle all my wants.

Caleb leans down and grabs my heels. Drawing them into his lap, he begins to knead my skin with his thumb. My feet aren't smooth or soft—they're calloused and neglected from traversing the city in uncomfortable shoes. I savor the sensation as he presses harder, deeper. His movements methodical.

We move from the couch to the bed. He takes off my underwear and begins rubbing me. I moisten quickly, holding his gaze as I squirt onto his fingers. Excited, he flips me over and enters me from behind. We move together until he comes inside me for the first time. He usually ejaculates on my breasts, stomach, thighs. Feeling him soften inside me is so intimate I almost laugh from the shock of it.

"I'm going to shower," he announces, sliding out, and we're no longer connected. I don't shower as often as he does after sex. I don't understand the urge to be so constantly clean.

I hear the water turn on, the swish of the shower curtain. On the windowsill by my bed, I spot his phone. Then it vibrates.

Even though there's nothing to be afraid of—it's all over—I'm still afraid. To spike my blood pressure, I reach for it. One more time, I promise myself, just once.

Rosemary's name, back on his screen, feels inevitable; nausea rushes in as I read: I intended on giving you and your girlfriend the space you requested, and even though I've wanted to reach out every single day since we last spoke, I haven't. But something disturbing happened last week, and I'm feeling very shaken. I think hearing your voice, just for a minute, would help.

The nausea has relocated from my throat to my mouth. I swallow bile as it rises. What disturbing event could she be referring to? As my pulse throbs in my fingertips and blood roars loud and thick in my ears, I delete her message and block her number.

It no longer exists. Caleb will never see it. I'll be safe. Surely Rosemary's pride won't allow her to follow up again by phone or email, won't propel her to come knocking on his door. The only way Caleb will discover I've blocked her number is if he attempts to call her—and if *that* happens, well, I've already lost.

It's for the best, I reassure myself. *She can't lean on him anymore; she needs to learn to lean on someone else.*

Later that night, as Caleb and I fall asleep holding hands, I reluctantly but undeniably comprehend how letting go of her is the only prerequisite for a future of holding him here, like this, with his pulse leaping against my palm. Maybe I really can, maybe it's finally time. The shape of our narrative arc has solidified; now I just need to figure out how it should end.

AT A COCKTAIL bar known for its varied collection of Latin American spirits, I grab spicy palomas with Danielle and tell her everything—or almost everything.

"So Caleb was seeing his ex-girlfriend behind my back and lying about it, and—"

"Omi*god*, they were fucking?"

"Oh, no, he wasn't cheating, it never turned physical." I lick a splash of paloma on my thumb. "I know this because I snooped on his phone. I kept telling myself I was crazy and nothing was going on until finally I decided to settle my suspicions once and for all. And I was right! They were in constant contact."

"Holy shit, I can't believe—"

"Wait, let me finish. So I confronted him in Wales and he was super apologetic and wrote me this beautiful letter and said all the right things, so I decided to forgive him."

Danielle exhales and sucks on her teeth. "Jesus, Naomi, I'm honestly shocked. He seemed so good, so *different* from other men." She shakes her head. "How fucking disappointing."

"But he is good! He apologized, and weirdly it all kind of made sense—his reasons why, I mean. I wanted to tell you earlier, while it was happening, but I was afraid of exactly this. You seeing him differently. Because we're doing better now. Really, we are."

Really, we are.

Danielle grips my arm. "I think Caleb is wonderful. You know I do. But I'm worried. It takes time to rebuild trust, and sometimes— sometimes it just never comes back. That's all I'm saying."

But what if it was never there to begin with?

The truth is I have since suspected everyone who wants me is wrong for it, that they must be mistaking me for someone else—

I catch myself doing this more often lately: mentally flipping through the pages of my own book, searching for evidence to explain myself to myself. If I once wrote it down then it must, in some inexplicable way, be true.

"We're going to do our best," is all I manage to say.

"So Caleb forgave you for snooping?"

"What? Yes, of course." A peevishness enters my voice. "I know some people think snooping is a symptom of bigger problems, blah blah blah, but I had a bad feeling and I was right. There *was* a bigger problem. And now it's over." I confirmed everything with Rosemary, my primary source, but I don't tell Danielle that.

"I'm not judging you or anything. It's just hard to draw that boundary for yourself once you've started. You sure you won't get the urge to snoop again?"

"Yes," I say, defiant. "I won't."

"Okay, well, you know I'll support you no matter what. What's the situation with his ex now? Did they stop talking? Did he tell her he loves you? If he didn't"—she makes a fist and menacingly punches the palm of her hand—"it's up for debate whether or not he's keeping his balls."

"He's allowed to keep his balls."

"Good." She reattaches her lips to her wineglass for a few long seconds. "On the bright side, this is amazing material for your book."

"That's the plan!" A high-pitched laugh escapes my mouth.

"I mean, it's *exactly* what your book is about." She arches an eyebrow. "Kind of a self-fulfilling prophecy, right?"

Remembering what I originally told her—*I started spitballing possible plots, like—what if she was still in love with Caleb and tried to sabotage us*—I find myself provoked, oddly, into defending Rosemary.

"Oh, I don't blame the ex at all, she didn't even realize Caleb was dating anyone until the New Year—"

"What the fuck? He never *told* her about you? Okay, that's it, he definitely needs to watch his balls!" shouts Danielle, punching the palm of her hand again, and a glamorous blond couple who look disturbingly like brother and sister pause mid-smooch to glare at us from a cozy table in the corner.

Gleeful and giggling about the sudden attention—such an

actress—Danielle retrieves a small box of Altoids and offers one to me. "Want one?"

I accept, rolling it around on my tongue until my mouth smells wintergreen.

Later, back in my apartment, I scroll through Rosemary's blog until I find the section where Caleb is introduced—to be reminded what he's worth. I'm drawn into her giddiness, watching as she begins to fall in love.

Before Caleb, I was desperate and frenzied and hopeful. But *with* him—how had I felt then?

I reread my own pages. *He made me feel new,* I wrote.

I'll try to remember this.

DAYS AND THEN weeks pass as my relationship normalizes—becoming content, domestic. It's what I always wanted. Caleb and I have sex every other day in various positions and try a new bar or restaurant weekly and say *love you* whenever we part ways and make it through two seasons of *The Americans*, a show about fake identities, while drinking red wine out of coffee mugs.

"This is going to blow up in such a delicious way," says Caleb as credits roll after the season finale. I laugh a little too loudly and turn off the light. Caleb drifts into sleep as I stare at the ceiling, wondering if things will blow up in a delicious way for us, too. But isn't my top priority, now, preserving the contented domesticity we've built, at long last? I can simply mail the books I borrowed to Rosemary's office when I'm done with them. We shouldn't see each other again. I haven't plotted anything new—the story is stagnant—but I'll finish it eventually, I'll use my imagination, surely I have enough material by now.

Right?

Still wide awake at two a.m., I lock myself in the bathroom and open my ancient AOL account, just in case there's something to see.

There is. An email from Rosemary sits in my inbox, time-stamped at one a.m. Either she's also a night owl or was too anxious to press send until after dark.

The subject line: at long last!

Goose bumps rise on my upper arms as I open it. In the body of the email, she wrote: Please feel free to tear this apart. A Microsoft Word document is attached. A surprising choice. PDFs, locked and inflexible, seem safer. Word documents are easily modified. Sent to people you trust.

I download the document—which is untitled, surprisingly—and begin. How could I not?

After reading only five hundred words of her eight-thousand-word story, I confidently but lamentably deem Rosemary's writing both exquisite and savage, two adjectives I've coveted in my own work for as long as I can remember. (The prose in her blog, I remember thinking, was *sharp* and *clean* and *rigorous* but lacking *a certain singularity of voice*—but now it seems she has grown into someone formidable.) There's something hypnotic and lulling but also urgent and volatile about her sentence structure now, about her voice. Like treading water in rough seas. All I can do is keep my head above water. Is Rosemary a better writer than I am, objectively? Will she be more successful? Does she deserve to be?

Her story is from the perspective of a young girl on a hike with her parents and their Bernese mountain dog; as the elevation steadily increases, the dog jerks out of its harness and runs off. The meat of the story involves the family's slow disintegration as they weave desperately through trees in pursuit of the animal while, unbeknownst to them, they are surveilled by some mysterious entity, too. It's haunting, and after reading it I can hardly breathe. But something also doesn't sit right with me about this particular interpretation of surveillance—didn't she mention she was writing a book about women watching other women? Where was *that* book?

And of course I can't help but wonder, briefly, if her choice of dog breed was influenced by the story I told her about my parents meeting on the street—and if so, was it an unconscious or intentional decision? And if the latter, what might she be trying to communicate? For the first time in a while, I'm paralyzed about how to proceed.

It takes another hour for my heartbeat to slow down enough for my body to even consider the possibility of sleep, but eventually I'm able to.

The following morning, I'm awoken by Caleb puttering loudly around the apartment—the clinking of breakfast dishes in the sink, the soft purr of his briefcase zipping closed.

"You were up late last night," he says evenly when I join him in the kitchen.

I could have sworn he was out cold when I slid back into bed. "Couldn't sleep," I say without looking at him, and pour myself coffee from the French press. "I didn't want to wake you, so I came in here and did some writing."

"Will you read me what you've been working on?" Caleb asks. "I'd love to hear it."

I turn away from the open refrigerator toward his voice, incredulous. He hasn't asked to read anything of mine since our first date, since courting me with compliments. Uneasy and elated and confused, I ask, "You really—want me to?"

"I don't ask about your writing as much as I should." He shrugs. "I don't want to be the kind of boyfriend who gives you a notebook without actually expressing any interest in what you put inside it."

I squirm a little, terrified by the sudden thought that he might have peeked inside already. But how can I say no? Maybe this is exactly what I've been waiting for permission to do. "Okay, sure. If you want me to read a little bit, I can."

I select a few paragraphs recently written about Wales. Rosemary doesn't appear at all. I take a deep breath.

"On the flight, I envisioned a moody moor, a misty green hill, a Welsh chill. I don't want palm trees here, complicating my perceptions. I venture downstairs to get a glass of water and, in the dark stillness of the kitchen, almost overlook my boyfriend's mother perched on a stool at the countertop, eating an apple."

I pause. "Should I keep going?"

His gaze drifts toward the notebook. My accomplice. "Erm, it's a little close for comfort, as you can imagine. But go on."

"If my boyfriend comes down the stairs and watches me speak to her, I imagine he'll appraise our chemistry. Its existence, or lack of, could make or break his perception of me." I turn the page and read on. My whole body is buzzing. *"I feel nauseous again. My boyfriend's mother stands to hug me. Like his, her body is long and lean; their hair is the same shade of silvery-blond."*

"Nice job making me nameless and blond." Caleb's voice is light but sharp-edged. "No one will ever be able to guess it's me."

"Fictional archetypes," I say. "It's more interesting to re-create and dramatize the dysfunctional—"

"Can you please not write about my family, though?" he interrupts. The tone of his voice is steady, reasonable. "And can I not be

Welsh? Because I am literally Welsh. Make me Dutch or Italian or something. Everyone loves Italians."

A vein in my wrist flares a darker blue. I assume this is my blood pressure, rising. "That's fine, I won't. I'm sorry, I wanted to process that trip somehow, it felt significant, meeting your parents, and so I fictionalized—"

"You just said that." Caleb thumbs his eyelids and sighs. "Look, I don't want to fight about it, I'm just telling you it makes me uncomfortable, okay?"

I clasp his hands in mine, squeeze. "Hey, look at me. I hear you."

You interest me enough to write you down, I want to tell him. It's the best compliment I could ever give, and so I try to locate a line that might prove to him that, sometimes, the novel serves—if you squint—as a sort of love letter.

"My boyfriend's body moves differently here—exuding confidence, loose and liquid."

The next lines—*I've only ever seen him with rounded shoulders, an urban weariness*—might hurt, so I skip down. *"Here beside the sea, as the pub chatter builds and seeps into stone walls, I understand who he is and could be, and when he looks at me I feel a gush of warmth, like being baptized in his eyes."* I look up now, holding his gaze, and read: *"If we lived inside this pub, we could survive anything."*

Finally, Caleb gives me the hint of a smile. "Well, fuck, now I miss the pub."

"I miss it, too," I say, and kiss him.

He rubs my back in one smooth stroke before heading out the door, saying he'll see me later after we both get off work.

When the door closes behind him, I exhale in relief. No delicious blowups, and only one ultimatum: no writing about his family. But I have four thousand words set in his country and don't intend to waste them. So I take out my laptop, type all four thousand words from the notebook into Microsoft Word, and then email it to my grandmother, explaining how it's "loosely based" on my trip. Her opinion will help determine whether the work itself is worth flouting Caleb's request.

Remember? Writing is my first love. *Put it first. Protect it.*

I'M READING JOANNA WALSH'S novel behind the register at work when a reply from my grandmother arrives. Well, technically two replies, as it seems she'd accidentally pressed send too soon.

> Finally, an Ackerman original! I was beginning to worry
> you'd given up writing for good. Distraction from the remna

Thirty seconds later:

> This ridiculous contraption! I meant to write: from the
> remnants of a day—physical therapy, soft foods, existential
> agony—is sorely needed. I'll read ASAP!

She isn't kidding. Her next email arrives four hours later. To allow myself to digest the verdict in some semblance of peace, I avoid making eye contact with customers.

I'll get to the point, begins her email. It's good. Your characterizations are unflinching and incisive; the narrator acknowledges her own fatal flaws even as she dissects others. If it's indeed "loosely based" on Caleb, then yes, it might hurt him if you publish it. He will forgive you, or he won't. So what? Your writing is too important to allow anyone else to control what and whom you write about. P.S. In anticipation of your upcoming literary success, I'll postpone upping my morphine levels.

Her humor has never been *this* dark, but now is not the time to wonder why.

Knowing in my bones what she has suggested I do, I chew off a hangnail and then text Rosemary. **I really loved your story. When shall we meet to discuss?**

A man around my age in a backward baseball cap approaches the register holding Michelle Obama's memoir, which is a welcome distraction from continually side-eyeing my iPhone for Rosemary's reply. After completing his transaction, I decide I'll further disguise the characters in my story, lending them plausible deniability. Caleb's family will be Irish—Wales and Ireland share *misty green hills* and *moody moors*. Not much needs to be rewritten.

That corner of the world is essential to his character, I'm prepared to argue. *He needs to hail from a rocky island adrift in the northern Atlantic.*

After my shift finally ends, as I set the alarm and reach for my coat and fumble with the keys, my phone buzzes inside my back pocket. Outside in the cold, I huff warm air onto my palms and rub them together and then check my texts.

Wow, that was fast, texted Rosemary. **Thanks for reading, and for your kind words. I'm swamped these next few weeks—can I get back to you when things settle?**

Kind words? Her tepid formality is a bit suspicious. And *a few weeks?*

Is she avoiding me or genuinely busy? The former flatters my sense of self-importance, despite also being absolutely devastating in its implications, but after Googling her again (for the first time in weeks, I might add) and noticing her name and job title crop up in another recent book deal announcement, the latter seems more realistic, and yet—

Attempting to ease my paranoia regarding whether the "disturbing" event she texted Caleb about involves me, I download the Headspace meditation app.

Breathe in, and then out.

ROSEMARY BEING "SWAMPED" doesn't work for me. A couple of weeks pass in which we don't speak. I sent her a *Harper's* essay I enjoyed recently, but she hasn't yet responded.

"Damn, we're late to the game this year," says Luna as we open boxes of Valentine's Day cards to cram into the spinner toward the end of our shift. "Valentine's Day is in less than two weeks."

"People actually buy cards two weeks in advance?" I feign disdain. "Usually there's a mad dash on the thirteenth."

"Heteronormativity strikes again."

I always did my best to ignore Valentine's Day during my reign of singledom, mocking it to anyone who would listen, but now that I'm finally eligible I do in fact intend to celebrate my new coupled status somehow. In the absence of a fancy dinner reservation I certainly won't ask for or expect, I would happily accept a card and flowers and wine and maybe some chocolate, and also multiple rounds of amazing sex while laughing together about how stupid it all is. *But what a great excuse for flowers and chocolate and red wine!* I'll say airily, after a third consecutive orgasm.

(Cool and fun and low-maintenance, see?)

Before the end of my shift, I use my employee discount to surreptitiously purchase no fewer than four cards with varying levels of sentimentality from *I'd share my dessert with you* to *You give me tachycardia!* When the day comes, I can make a game-time decision about how expressive I want to be.

On Saturday night, five days before Valentine's Day (oh god, am I really measuring time this way now?), Caleb and I see a jazz show and play a halfhearted game of pool at the Fat Cat with Danielle and the new guy she's dating, who is wearing a polo shirt and sporting a floppy hairstyle reminiscent of college lacrosse-bros. Not my type (or hers, for that matter), but I'm still envious of the easy way they interact after only a month of knowing each other— inside jokes, glances exchanged, his hand on the small of her back. In public, Caleb and I are still, somehow, disconnected: glances are thrown but don't land, almost as if we're each waiting for the other to make the first public display of affection. If Caleb has ever felt as insecure about my feelings for him as I have about his, our hesitancies and manifest ambivalence would make so much sense. I wonder, briefly, if this might actually be the case. He could be far more sensitive than I give him credit for, picking up on something shifty and unsettled in me.

When we were single, Danielle and I used to play a game at whatever bar we happened to be drinking in: we would assess couples and make an educated guess about how long they'd been together. Was it a first date, a third date, had they already fucked, was one person hopelessly in love while the other assumed it was only a fling? I swore by my guesses. I never approached and asked—of course not—but something in my gut just knew how two people in love would look.

If a stranger could see us in bed clutching our mugs of red wine, could see our feet intertwined beneath the covers, could see the gentle way Caleb rubs my back once, twice, after we turn out the light, it would be different.

Caleb leans over the pool table, his shoulder blades lifting underneath his cotton tee, and angles the cue. I applaud when the balls scatter.

Now it's my turn, and in a moment that seems to defy all physics, one of the balls bounces off the table after I hit it and hurtles toward a group of clearly underage NYU students playing Ping-Pong.

"You trying to kill somebody?" slurs one of the boys, sloshing his beer as he ducks out of the way.

"Sorry," I mutter, going to collect it.

"My little Terminator over here," says Caleb, mussing my hair. "You're the worst pool player I've ever seen."

Caught off guard by this unprompted affection, I smooth my side part and wonder if he's beginning to read my mind.

"Fair." I gesture toward the bathroom. "Be right back."

The lock is broken on the flimsy stall door. To avoid making contact with the dirty toilet seat, I hover a few inches above with my ass in the air, grasping the handle and pulling in tight to preserve my balance, and through the crack between the door and floor, a parade of identical kitten heels clack by. I imagine the kitten heels are all single and desperate, for love or attention or at least some free drinks, and do not envy any of them.

After flushing and exiting the stall and washing my hands, I stay hidden in the dimly lit hallway outside the bathrooms, no longer in the mood to socialize. I want to go home. I'm bored of this place, of these kinds of nights, even of—dare I say it—domesticity; I want—

It's a Saturday. Maybe Rosemary is in the West Village, too. At a snug wine bar, or a farm-to-table restaurant, or catching a movie at the IFC Center. There are so many places to be. But in the past month, Rosemary hasn't uploaded any new photos to her grid. I've watched a few Instagram Stories, starved for news, but each one was boring: her plants growing, a rhubarb pie she'd made, the spines of her latest book haul. It's possible her promotion is sucking up all her free time and energy, but still— wouldn't most women, after learning of their ex's new relationship, attempt to prove they're doing well and moving on by going to cool events and meeting cool people? I check her profile for updates.

There's a new post! Uploaded two hours ago. I pinch the screen with two fingers and, greedy, zoom in for a closer look.

"Are you, like, waiting?" asks a girl struggling to stand upright.

"I'm not in line," I say without looking at her.

As the girl lurches toward the bathroom door, I retreat even farther into the shadows and recognize, in Rosemary's photo, the elegant staircase of the Metropolitan Opera captured from the grand tier level. The red velvet curve of the carpeted staircase is beautifully framed. Newly minted opera fans, reads the caption.

But it's *fans*, plural. On a hunch, I check to see if Rosemary has been tagged in anyone else's Instagram photos recently, and voilà, there she is: her slight shoulders in a green, velvet, floor-length gown, her pretentious white opera gloves, her hair.

Her hair! It's no longer the same color as mine—she has dyed it black. Though the color suits her, Rosemary looks so different from the person I've come to know. Who is she trying to turn herself into? With her face slightly tilted away from the camera, Rosemary places a white-gloved forearm on the banister. It looks forced and awkward, but she's beaming. The caption of the photo is fond and teasing, suggesting a certain established intimacy: It's this native New Yorker's first time at the Met! I've already shamed her enough, so let me just say how honored I am to be her guide.

The man who posted it has a public account on Instagram, so I dive in. His name is Oliver. According to his bio, he works as a freelance filmmaker and photographer. It's a sexy career when done right, but how many people self-identify as "photographers" on social media these days? All you need to do is point and shoot and add a filter.

I scour Oliver's profile—mostly dramatic, shadow-shrouded portraits of elderly people—for photos I can be certain are of him. Will he be uglier or sexier than Caleb?

Oliver, as it turns out, is fit and broad-shouldered with a nice, easy smile, but a painfully average face—nothing special, nothing alluring. The opposite of Caleb.

Is Oliver her rebound, likely to expire soon, or is he the person she was always destined to meet?

I decide to send her another text, fuck it. She might think I'm needy, or bothersome, but fuck it, just fuck it. There are worse things I could be.

Finally finished Joanna Walsh's book! I've never even been through a breakup but damn, feeling RAW af now. Cusk is up next. Let me know when you're free, I want to return the book and talk about your story!

Then I put my phone away. She'll respond, or she won't. No use checking every five minutes. No use. And so I return to the pool table, this time as a spectator, and wait until we all grow tired enough to call it a night.

Finally, hours later, we do. Walking home holding hands, Caleb casually mentions he started searching for a new job.

"Really?" I stop on the street and turn to look at him, startled and pleased.

Despite confessing his dissatisfaction weeks ago in the Welsh pub, he hasn't attempted to transform the circumstances that brought him here, not until now. His job is the last remaining link to the life he shared with Rosemary—and soon he'll sever it. With Caleb's credentials, acquiring another job shouldn't be difficult. We haven't yet discussed the possibility of future visa problems, but I don't mind. Surmounting obstacles sounds preferable to banality and convenience.

I imagine a radically different life: a spacious flat near Hampstead Heath and a sun-drenched home office to write in while Caleb works at a reputable company or university in central London. I imagine traveling to Sussex or Edinburgh on weekends, and to Paris or Florence or Barcelona during the longer holidays. It sounds lovely; a future worth striving for.

I reward Caleb's sudden agency with an enthusiastic and sustained blow job when we return to my apartment. He strokes the back of my neck with his thumb and shudders into my mouth and clutches my hair as I finish him off.

Later, once he's asleep, I check my phone, hoping Rosemary has responded, and she has.

When Caleb's cock was in my mouth, she wrote: **Glad you enjoyed Walsh! Sorry I've been MIA. Are you free Monday?**

ON MONDAY, INSIDE the Cobble Hill wine bar Rosemary suggested, I don't recognize her at first, not until an ebony-haired woman catches my eye and pats the stool beside her. I forgot all about her new hair color. Slipping onto the stool, I place Walsh's paperback in her hands. Then I acknowledge the dye.

"Some of my friends hate it," she says, sweeping strands off her forehead. "I can tell."

"The same unadventurous friends who won't go climbing with you?"

She blushes. "Touché."

"Well, I don't hate it," I say, and order us each a glass of red.

"Thanks," says Rosemary. "How have you been?"

I shrug and say I'm doing okay, writing a lot, selling books. "All pretty mundane. What about you? It's been a while."

Rosemary, who must have picked up on a latent accusation in my voice, rushes to defend her absence. "It's been a crazy start to the year, I've been so busy with work and family obligations. Plus I actually started seeing someone. You know how it is at the beginning of a relationship—it's easy to get caught up in it. I'm guilty of that."

"Ooh, details please," I demand, recalling the photo at the Met Opera.

"His name is Oliver, we met literally two weeks after Caleb called to end things. It's only been a month, but since we have such an intense connection we're giving it a real shot. Making it official."

"That's awesome," I say with genuine enthusiasm. "How did you two meet?"

"Our mutual friend threw a party. Oliver went to NYU, too, but

I didn't know him well back then. Apparently he had a crush on me. To distract myself from everything that happened with Caleb I agreed to go on a date with Oliver, and we just . . . clicked."

"Sounds like it was meant to be," I say through my teeth. Truthfully, I was hoping she'd been forced, as I had, to wade into the waters of Tinder or Hinge or OkCupid to find a mate, but no—it seems as if love always arrives organically for Rosemary.

"I think so, too. Oliver is so uncomplicated and caring and optimistic, he wakes up every morning excited to start the day. Caleb is so brooding in comparison. It's like a weight has been lifted."

Poor Rosemary. The lady doth protest too much, clearly trying to convince herself she isn't still heartbroken. It's impossible to move on this fast. The story of Oliver can't possibly live up to the story of Caleb, the story I memorized and held up, enraptured, to the light. *Moors and mist, hidden passageways, riverside towns—*

Rosemary looks directly at me. "Oliver shouts his love for me from the proverbial rooftops, you know? I've never experienced anything like it."

"But Caleb moved for you," I say, lest she forget. "Isn't that the highest rooftop? The loudest shout?"

How can she be so ungrateful? This is revisionist history.

"Don't get me wrong, Caleb is a wonderful person. I'll always care about him. But he was withholding. When he moved here, he made it seem like a sacrifice, not an act of love. That much is clear to me now. It took me so long to *see*."

I'm caught between the urge to defend the man I've professed to love and the urge to run from him. To take her word for it. But then I realize her sudden hostility and bitterness must be prompted by discovering Caleb has a new girlfriend. Nitpicking his alleged flaws is clearly how she self-soothes, and if Rosemary believes

Caleb blocked her, this is the narrative she'll likely cling to in order to heal.

Rosemary signals for another glass of wine. "I still find it difficult to forgive him for screwing up my timeline. I know this might sound crazy, but we were twenty-one when we met, so if we'd stayed together we'd probably be married by now, and I envisioned being pregnant by thirty-one."

> do we have your consent
>> estrogen and progestin, a routine I soon normalized
>> was I okay?

"Wow," I say, "that's, um, so specific."

"I know I'm supposed to want to put my career first now, considering my promotion and all"—she casts her eyes upward—"but I feel this ache whenever I imagine being a mom. Caleb and I talked about all of that." Rosemary sighs, and I'm pleased to notice a familiar wistfulness has reentered her voice. "All of it was something we discussed."

Rosemary and Caleb—with soft voices, assured and loving—once reached a decision about their shared future; I imagine two chairs huddled together at a mahogany table with candles lit and a bottle of wine uncorked and a vase of flowers, fragrant. When have Caleb and I discussed anything significant that didn't begin with a tentative dangling clause, that wasn't triggered by a miscommunication or a lie? I wonder how many months passed before Rosemary and Caleb began to make certain promises. Long distance likely rushed things a little, but Caleb and I still might have missed a pivotal signpost of our own a few miles back.

"Lachlan and I feel the opposite," I say, despite knowing

nothing about Caleb's views on fatherhood, despite having avoided the topic like the plague. "I think it's a bit irresponsible to bring children into this world. I mean—think about climate change! Life on this planet is going to get so much worse."

"That's a really macro way of looking at it. The micro way is— just acknowledging that I really want to. Why should I deprive myself? For the greater good?" Her eyes flash. "Humans are so hypocritical, there are a billion ways to negatively contribute to the world. Whether or not I have a kid won't single-handedly change anything."

I'm ill-equipped to argue.

So I change the subject, launching us directly into a discussion of Rosemary's writing. It's the reason we came to this wine bar, after all, and it feels good, really good, to be utterly absorbed in someone else's thoughts, someone else's fictions, for a blessed while.

As per Rosemary's request, I fully intend to tear the story apart—but not before praising her first. Putting her at ease. And so I say how impressed I am by her adept and generous examination of the fictional family portrayed from all angles.

When Rosemary cracks a smile, I'm free to begin plucking at details that don't work and questioning motives and strengthening plot twists and making necessary cuts. "The marriage of content and style wasn't as cohesive," I say, "because there's something a little too convenient about the Bernese mountain dog wiggling out of its harness at the narratively opportune time, and a little too convenient about a family finally able to face their demons and divulge dark secrets while floundering around a literal dark forest."

"Hmm, all good points," says Rosemary, scribbling in a small black Moleskine. "Thank you so much."

By becoming indispensable, and demonstrating my value, I'll continue to prove myself deserving of her time, her attention, her friendship.

"It's seriously my pleasure." Unable to resist prodding, I ask, "So is this, like, an excerpt from your novel? Or a stand-alone story you're going to submit to literary journals? Or are you pivoting from your novel and working on a story collection now?"

"So many questions!" She laughs. "So your third theory is correct, I needed a break from the novel, it was getting to my head and putting me in a dark place. It's—hard to describe."

This particular genre of anxiety is well-trodden territory. Thrilled she has led us here, to confide in someone who gets it, I jump in. "I feel the same way about my book, trying to stay inside Penelope's stalker-y head is really unsettling, especially given how meta it is. You know, like"—I quickly clarify—"stalking myself, observing how I might be perceived. It's all pretty dark."

"That does sound exhausting, but not what I was—"

I'm no longer listening to her, no longer engaged in a dialogue; I have too much to say.

Dirty chai, tote bag, vampiric teeth.

Green, velvet, floor-length gown, dyed black hair, ankle-high brown suede boots, Bernese mountain dog.

The details are piling up.

"It is exhausting, but I need to keep going. It's more interesting than my life," I say. "It's *become* my life."

Rosemary looks alarmed in a way that suggests concern rather than suspicion. "You're wrong. It's not your life. You can always stop and work on something else, something light. You're talented. Trust yourself a bit more."

Some criminals return to the scene of the crime, hoping to be caught; I think I know why.

"So I actually read Lachlan part of my novel for the first time last week," I say. "I didn't want to hurt him—I mean, I actively-present-tense don't want to hurt him—but I think it's inevitable that I will."

Will I eventually stumble upon something better, a narrative I can promise myself won't hurt anyone I love? I don't want to hurt anyone I love. But the person I care most about not hurting is me.

I lift my gaze to Rosemary's chin; it seems like the safest place. *Absolve me*, I wordlessly beg. *Absolve me*—

"What about this particular story feels so necessary to write?" she asks softly.

"Maybe because I'm trying to exorcise the worst parts of me. Once they're *out there*, they'll no longer be *in here*."

"But won't it always be *in there*—all of it, forever?" She taps the side of my temple lightly with her finger.

It's a shock, electric, and even after she is no longer touching me I feel the imprint of her finger like an itch and am compelled to keep confessing. "I don't know," I tell her.

"You're not a bad person."

"Okay," I say, feeling weak. "I trust you."

"Good. You should. Remember that self-flagellation becomes boring and narcissistic after a while. And I don't think you're boring or narcissistic. Just remember Lachlan's feelings and sensitivities are his own; you're not responsible for them. Your responsibility is to yourself and to your work. That's how I frame it for myself, at least. If he loves you, he'll hopefully understand."

Her advice sounds eerily identical to my grandmother's. Merely being in Rosemary's presence as she utters it is dizzying and deep and surreal. She is unknowingly giving me permission to write down whatever version of her—and of Caleb—will best suit my narrative needs.

Rosemary is still talking. "Do you know that famous quote by the Polish poet Czeslaw Milosz? *When a writer is born into a family, the family is finished.* Well, I don't believe in it. I think a family can be reborn that way, made immortal. Even if its ugliness is all the author chooses to describe. Maybe your relationship will be made immortal, too."

I'm so stunned by this assertion, seemingly extracted from the unutterable depths of my own brain, that I blink at her several times before finally managing to say, with an ironic smile, "But I still feel an insane amount of dread all the time."

"Maybe all this dread is something your body is trying to tell you. So many writers have said their work is powered by the force to find out what they think. So if you're still not sure how you feel about Caleb—oh shit, I meant to say Lachlan, sorry." She laughs, all lightness, but it's too late; my stomach is already twisting. "Freudian slip."

What does the Freudian slip reveal? Caleb was most commonly in her throat and on her tongue for years, so it might be a force of habit. Or she knows who I am and why I'm here and what I've done. Staring at a fixed point—a bottle of Malibu behind the bar— lessens the nausea; the world steadies itself.

"What I meant to say is maybe your writing is revealing the truth to you. I finally read *I Love Dick* by Chris Kraus and came across an amazing quote, maybe it will resonate with you, too. Kraus quotes Ann Rower—hold on." Rosemary swipes through her phone, then reads the quote aloud: "*Every time you try and write the truth it changes. More happens. Information constantly expands.*"

"Wow, chills."

"Right?"

"I haven't read it, but now I want to."

Rosemary offers to let me borrow it. "I recommend reading it on the subway, the prudish stares are an added bonus." She chuckles. "Anyway, I'll bring it with me next time. Maybe the four of us can grab drinks?"

I'm slow to comprehend. "The four of us?"

"Oliver, Lachlan, me, you. Like a double date. Our friendship exists in a sort of vacuum, haven't you noticed that?"

I search for an answer that might convince her the vacuum is, in fact, essential. "Well, sure, although"—fumbling a bit here—"I don't really think it's necessary for all my relationships to intersect. Or even preferable!" I add, as chirpily as possible.

Rosemary presses her lips together as a nearly imperceptible shift of her stool permits a few extra millimeters of space between us. After a long silence, she speaks. "That's not how I organize my social life, but okay. I just thought it would be fun."

She can't be upset with me, not for long, I need to win her back—bridge those extra millimeters—to erase any and all suspicion, and so—

"I lied to you," I say. "Before."

She cocks her head, piercing me with a gray-green gaze. "Lied about what?"

"About children. The truth is, I don't like talking about it because I can't have them. And that's why it would hurt, to not write, because that's all I can make."

"Can't have them—how?"

She looks genuinely stumped, and I deride the stumped. A failure of imagination.

"I am lacking the parts required," I say, almost pleased with myself. Look how caustic, how high-functioning, an infertile menopausal twenty-five-year-old can be!

"Oh, fuck." She pauses. "Still not exactly sure what you mean. What happened?"

"Surgery when I was eighteen. It could have been worse. The cyst could have burst inside me, but it didn't. They had to remove the ovaries—"

"—like what happened with Lena Dunham?"

Celebrities are reference points for certain unknowns, this I understand, but I can't help rolling my eyes at how quickly she made the connection. "No, that was different," I say, shaking my head. "I still have a uterus. Lucky me."

Rosemary gnaws on her bottom lip. Other women might smile with eyes full of pity, might awkwardly pivot away from the woman who will never have the chance to choose, but Rosemary manages to meet me with the required amount of compassion. "That's really heavy, Naomi. I'm sorry. I had no idea, obviously, but I wouldn't have brought it up, you know, if—"

"Don't worry about it," I say, even though I want her to worry, and to wonder, even a fraction as much as I have worried and wondered.

"I hope you know you don't have to lie anymore," she says. "I hope you know you can talk to me about this stuff."

"Thanks, but in the future I'd rather write about it, to be honest."

"It *is* easier that way," she agrees. When the check comes, and I rush to pay for our drinks, she doesn't protest. "Let's exchange again soon," she says before we part. "You're a great reader."

"Likewise," I tell her. The irony of it, and the inevitability, too, makes my chest tighten.

On the subway home, I play "Loch Lomond " by Runrig, wanting to be consumed by a familiar yearning. As Donnie Munro croons *and I'll be in Scotland afore you*, I close my eyes.

chapter nine

ON THE DAY before Valentine's Day, I direct my gaze toward a few hapless-looking men wrestling with the card spinner.

"Told you so," I say to Luna. "Mad dash on the thirteenth."

One of the hapless men ceases spinning and approaches the register.

After ringing him up, Luna turns to me. "He bought two of the *exact same* card."

"I'm guessing one for the wife, one for the mistress."

Luna laughs. "Straight guys are the worst." Then: "Well, Caleb is okay."

"Honestly a winning endorsement from you. What are you doing tomorrow, by the way? Any plans?" I'm genuinely curious, but I also want her to ask me the same question.

"Umm, most likely eating ice cream and watching *The Sopranos*— Oh! Did I tell you I finally started fucking the woman who owns the bike shop downstairs?"

"Wait, I thought she was married—like, to a man?"

"Newly divorced," says Luna, wiggling her eyebrows. "So she's coming over to watch Tony hit on his therapist with me." The phone rings then, and there's a tonal shift in her voice as she answers it: "Lit House, this is Luna speaking, how may I help you? Mhmm, yes, of course, let me quickly check on that for you—"

I busy myself changing the music currently thumping through our speaker system—Michael Bublé somehow snuck onto the Spotify playlist, how fucking dare he—until Luna gets off the phone and finally asks about my plans.

I only broached the subject for the very first time last night. Caleb was standing at the sink with his back to me, rinsing out a wineglass, and I was sitting at the kitchen table, thumbing through my phone. "I know it's cliché and kind of basic," I said into the space between us. "But, well, Valentine's Day is in two days, and I was wondering if you maybe wanted to celebrate it?"

Caleb turned off the faucet and turned around and shot me an amused, tender glance. "Of course," he said. "Why not?"

Relieved, I suggested trying our luck at the underground cocktail bar a few blocks from my apartment.

"Sure, let's show up around five and try to beat the rush," mused Caleb. "I can leave work early."

This small sacrifice was pleasing; it was a date.

When I tell Luna this now, she rolls her eyes. "How romantic. Are you going to wear red and pink? Is he going to place a single rose between his teeth?"

"Oh, shush," I say. "I'm thinking of it more like an anthropological study, you know? Observing the lovesick species out in the wild."

This turns out to be accurate. At the cocktail bar, we arrive noticeably underdressed. Around us, men awkwardly tug at their ties and women adjust the hemlines of their minidresses. Still, we manage to snag a high table along the wall. I order something obscenely fruity with lots of muddled mint, and Caleb orders a hot toddy, as if we're living in entirely dissonant seasons. Over ninety minutes, we consume three eighteen-dollar cocktails (each) and talk about normal things as if it's a normal day.

Once we're alone and back in my apartment, I give him the card about tachycardia. He laughs and thanks me (though later I catch him Googling it) and hands over a box of chocolate-covered strawberries from Edible Arrangements. We each eat several of them before climbing in bed and turning on the TV and fumbling around in the dark. It feels good, and right, and easy.

But is good and right and easy all there is to want? Is it enough?

Caleb, as always, has fallen into a deep sleep after orgasm; I touch the curve of his shoulder and allow a warm rush of tenderness to take hold of me. It's nice but scares me a little, too, this softening, so I reach for my phone and log in to @Language_and_ Liquid, a routine that peculiarly continues to bring me a modicum of comfort. I want to know exactly how Rosemary and Oliver celebrated *their* love.

Rosemary hasn't posted anything on her grid, but there's a new Instagram Story from two hours ago. I click on it and am confronted by a startlingly zoomed-in photo of a mushroom pizza. While it seems like every other couple in Brooklyn made reservations weeks ago, we decided to spontaneously try our luck at Roberta's, reads the caption, and a mere eighty-six minutes later, we were finally seated! All hail these cremini and shiitake beauties. Definitely worth the wait. ☺

Playful and spontaneous was clearly the vibe she was going for. I imagine she drafted it sheepish and blushing—not wanting to care or be caught caring about Valentine's Day, but *still* caring, in spite of herself.

Oliver's Instagram is up next. New post:

A picture of Rosemary smiling with vampiric teeth bared, her black hair organized into an immaculate topknot. She looks radiant. I wish she didn't, but she does. The caption: Best month of my life & she's the reason why. But it feels like we've known each other for years!

In the dark, sans audience, I mime sticking a finger down my throat. The gesture, however ridiculous, still feels cathartic somehow. Caleb wouldn't be caught dead typing something like that.

(But how would it feel if he did?)

I put my phone facedown on my bedside table and try to quiet my mind, to vanquish all thought, to sleep.

DAYS HAVE PASSED and passed, nights bleeding into mornings, and I'm still keeping tabs on Rosemary's new relationship on Instagram, square inch by square inch. Even when Caleb lies beside me, I tilt the screen and dim its backlight, surveilling in plain sight.

As winter recedes, and Pisces season finally comes to a close, Rosemary's and Oliver's Instagram posts increasingly reveal a connection that appears authentic and adventurous. They've gone to obscure museums, art galleries, and far-flung city parks; they've already traveled to the Berkshires, and even Montreal, on two separate weekends. In one photo, Rosemary's arm is slung across the shoulders of a girl who appears to be Oliver's teenage sister. And she continues showing off her teeth, such a rarity in the past. Oliver must have been behind the lens. It's beginning to look like love, and I'm still envious—despite the fact that Rosemary's new relationship could single-handedly alleviate my guilt. Haven't I done Rosemary a favor by taking Caleb off her hands and allowing her to pursue a deeper connection with someone else? If Rosemary discovers who I am, I'm prepared to say, *Look at how happy you are now, I'm responsible, I gave you this life.*

But I'm resentful of her happiness, too. I admit it. I'm resentful and relieved and bitter and glad. Rosemary is supposed to be devastated, as devastated as I would've been if it had happened to me. She wasn't supposed to fall in love—she was supposed to be sad and alone. (So why do I still feel an illogical jolt of dopamine every time I see Rosemary smile in Oliver's direction when he films her on his Instagram Story, as if she's a real friend I'm happy to observe has finally found love after being burned?)

But if her newfound happiness suggests Caleb is no longer a prize worth pursuing, it would invalidate nearly everything I've written down, and believed, and felt.

No—Caleb is *mine*, now; doesn't that mean we simply make more sense than he and Rosemary ever did? I'm tempted to show him photos of Rosemary and Oliver, prepared to say, *Look at them and now look at us, this is how it* should *be.*

Perhaps Caleb and I will fade from Rosemary's narrative. Perhaps her story will unfurl, leaving us behind.

This idea doesn't pacify me. I want to remain part of her story, even if only abstractly, with our narrative arcs irrevocably entwined. I refuse to be forgotten.

Oliver's Instagram, upon even further examination, reveals a high frequency of visits to a collection of bars and cafés on Williamsburg's Metropolitan Avenue. As a freelancer he treats them each like an office, so it's easy to craft an encounter.

On a rare sunny afternoon in late March, after my shift ends, I enter a café filled with natural light. Potted ferns hang from the ceiling underneath a skylight. With my journal and a pencil, I settle at the table adjacent to his, awarding myself a full view of his average-looking face. I notice, too, how his broad, sinewy shoulders are so unlike Caleb's bony ones. I watch Oliver's muscles move beneath the thin cotton.

While at the register ordering a dirty chai, I gaze undetected. Every few minutes he exhales loudly and squints at his computer. A camera strap peeks out of the backpack at his feet. I can't see his screen, but I assume he's editing photos.

After a half hour of working side by side, I drop my pencil at an angle, hoping it rolls in Oliver's direction. If he's a good person, he'll pick it up and return it.

He is, and does. I make sure our hands brush during the exchange.

"Oh, thanks! I'm such a klutz."

"No worries," he says without looking at me.

I clear my throat, wanting more. "Do you happen to know the Wi-Fi password?"

Thanks to a cardboard sign at the register, I'm already aware this café doesn't offer it. But I can't think of another way to hold Oliver's attention.

"They don't have Wi-Fi, it's why I like it here." He finally meets my gaze. "No distractions."

Marginally chagrined, I ask if he's familiar with the area. "I just moved and am in desperate need of a place to do research outside my apartment. Do you know of anywhere else I can go?"

He names a few names. "Slowshare has the most seating, if that helps," he adds. "And a punch card. If you prove your loyalty, you'll be rewarded with free coffees eventually."

"Excellent. I'll take what I can get. Are you loyal?"

"I am."

"Why don't we go there together right now? You can prove it to me." I'm a rusty flirt, but still curious to know how he'll react—if Caleb fell in love with Rosemary and *then* fell in love with me, surely Rosemary and I must share certain lovable qualities, and by that logic, Oliver might be intrigued by me, too.

He blushes, eyes widening. "Oh, I think maybe we misunderstood each other, I wasn't suggesting that, I have a girlfriend, so—"

A wisp of air leaves my lungs. "I didn't mean it like that," I insist, backpedaling. "But either way, you pass with flying colors. Above-average loyalty."

He forces a laugh. "Good to know. Anyway, I have to get back to work now, but I still recommend Slowshare!"

With no other choice, I repack my tote and leave clutching my dirty chai, waggling goodbye with a few free fingers. Only a small exchange, but he seems to deserve Rosemary's praise, seems worthy of her, and won't be lured away.

My phone buzzes then with an opportunely timed text from Caleb. I scan it for a quick reminder the man I love is mine; why should I care, still, about Oliver's above-average loyalty?

Caleb's text includes a Ticketmaster link, followed by: **Want to go? Doors open at 8.**

Caleb needs his concerts. They loosen him up, allow him to emote. Our best conversations always come after an encore. **Meet you there!** I reply.

THE CONCERT IS at the Music Hall of Williamsburg. Caleb and I arrive early enough to see the opening act, a woman with bubblegum-pink hair carrying an acoustic guitar. After her first song, she addresses the audience: "Does anyone have a special skill? Come on, don't be shy—doesn't everyone in Brooklyn at least *pretend* to have a special skill?"

After an extended silence, someone brave, maybe obnoxious, shouts, "I do!" and the singer invites him to join her onstage. After the man executes a flawless headstand, the crowded room erupts into cheers and a wave of people clamber onstage to perform their own special skills. I notice, obscured in shadow in a corner of the stage, two men wrapped in an embrace. It's clear they're making some sort of point, intentionally or not, offering a counterpoint to the theatrics, but still, it occurs to me then, and feels truer than most things, that sincere and lasting intimacy is also a special skill.

When the singer notices them, she demands we all follow suit. "Hug whoever is standing next to you! Make new friends!" Laughter sparks around the room, bemused and uneasy, but no one moves; some people even appear legitimately terrified by her instructions. But then, suddenly, a ripple of movement: two people offstage embrace, and then two more, and then everyone is hugging all at once, like we've won a war or maybe an election, and I imagine even the most cynical person in the room must be moved. I look at Caleb, who, instead of looking back at me, looks incredulously around at everyone else, and a knot develops in my stomach and in my throat. I need him to touch me, and quick, because if he doesn't, I might dissolve or shatter into something untouchable.

"Hey." I tug on his arm, playful rather than insistent. "Hug me."

He does.

As people drift apart, lapsing back into spectators, the singer announces her intention to embark on a silent crowd surf and then leaps backward into a sea of hands. People giggle and whisper and shush one another as she moves like a human sacrifice, held aloft above the crowd; I hope she'll be passed all the way to the rear of the venue where Caleb and I stand, but when she gestures back to the stage and all the hands obediently change course, I know we won't be reached.

As her feet land back on solid ground, she shouts over the triumphant collective roar about the main act, who will be performing after a short break, and then exits stage left.

Caleb angles his body toward me. "That was so strange! We're paying to see her sing, not fuck around."

"I liked it. She was trying to connect and shake us up a little."

Grimacing, he turns to face the stage. "Thankfully she's just the opener."

Our divergent perspectives seem significant here. Pressing my lips together, I turn to face the stage, too. We stand like rigid soldiers awaiting instruction until Caleb reaches for my hand, a reminder or a plea. I squeeze until my heartbeat pumps into his palm, until my fingers cramp and sweat—until I see a flash of Rosemary's face in profile under the swirling stage lights, a shock of shadow and light roving across her features.

Every muscle in my body seems to spasm all at once. I realize I've bitten my tongue only when the metallic taste of blood blooms in my mouth. Swallowing it down, I drop Caleb's hand as if relinquishing a burning object, pivoting so quickly I nearly give myself whiplash. "I'll get us some beers," I say over my shoulder, heart pounding.

Given the choice between fight or flight, it seems I've chosen the latter—to protect rather than destroy in service of my immediate happiness, swerving away from potential narrative drama. (But what does that say about my commitment to the plot?) Sneaking away toward the bathrooms—not the bar—I watch Rosemary notice Caleb. Her face exhibits zero evidence of surprise, which confuses me. Even though I'm desperate to watch their encounter unfold, I can't risk sticking around. As she moves toward him, her lips rearrange into a thin and confrontational line.

In the bathroom I lock myself in a stall and take shallow breaths and press a finger to my tongue to slow the bleeding. I didn't anticipate this plot twist tonight of all nights, but it could prove a pitch-perfect climax for my book if I'm ready to enable it. Should Rosemary and I scream a litany of abuse? Should the crowd turn away from the performance onstage and toward our performance offstage? Am I supposed to get slapped? Is someone supposed to cry?

Again and again, I'm alternately entrapped, or liberated, by my own unexamined impulses.

I'm so tired.

I lower the toilet seat and sit on it because I'm a coward and a hypocrite and there are, after all, certain things I can't, or won't, do for art.

A few minutes pass. The door opens and closes, voices intermingling with the sound of a running faucet. The music vibrates in the walls, the floor, through the soles of my feet.

A girl shouts from one toilet to another: "You're *kidding*!"

"I'm not!" comes the answer, amid a fit of giggles.

I flush the toilet, a waste of clean water, fuck it, fuck it, and go to the sinks. A figure in a black denim dress is lifting a tube of lipstick to her mouth and leaning toward the face in the mirror. Slowly she paints her lips red. I approach the row of sinks and turn both faucets, hot and cold, to achieve the desired temperature before washing my hands.

When the figure in black denim straightens, we make eye contact in the mirror.

So I make a joke. "We really have to stop meeting like this, Rosemary."

For what feels like forever, she stares without blinking, as if straining to place me.

"Oh," she says finally, "what are the fucking odds!" Pulling a paper towel out of the dispensers, she swipes away a clump of mascara under her eyelids. "I really love this band. I love them so damn much that I bought myself a ticket and came alone. So get this—Caleb is upstairs, of *course*. And so is his mystery girlfriend!"

Mystery girlfriend. "Holy shit, Caleb is here?" I squeak. "Did you talk to each other?"

It seems obvious now. Rosemary must have already known Caleb's affinity for this band, this genre, this venue, and so she came here to track him down.

"I tried. For like a second. But we couldn't hear each other over the music, and—I don't know. I'm just sad." She slips the tube of red lipstick back inside her black clutch. "I sent him a text a couple months ago, something friendly and normal, but he never responded. And just now he swore he never got it, but that's, like, impossible unless his new girlfriend deleted it or something, which would be totally psycho. I don't see him dating someone like that. Clearly I have to accept he doesn't want me in his life at all. In any form."

I seem to have forgotten how to speak.

"Want to help me track down the mystery girlfriend?" asks Rosemary, showing off her teeth and peering at me, it seems, a little longer than would be normal. "Apparently she's buying them drinks at the bar."

She knows she knows she knows flashes through my brain, and a torrent of words rush out of my mouth. "You're fucking with me, aren't you? Let's get it over with, let's end this now, then I'll explain everything—"

"What are you talking about? End what?" Her eyes widen. "Oh, I get it. Now you're fucking with *me*." Laughing, she adds, "So are we going to the bar now? I seriously need some whiskey."

I'm confused but relieved, and in attempting to backpedal, make sure to laugh, too. Hard. "Sorry, I'm kind of high," I say, thinking fast. "Lachlan and I smoked before we got here—bad idea—it makes me paranoid about literally everything—"

"Clearly," says Rosemary.

"Ugh, I don't feel well." Face burning, I rush into the nearest toilet stall—*what have I done*—to stick a finger down my throat and gag loud enough to justify an abrupt exit.

I'm feeling really nauseous all of a sudden, I text Caleb. **Not sure why but I really need to go home. Meet me outside in 2 min? Sorry!**

"Naomi, do you need help?" Rosemary's voice, then a knock on the stall door.

"Nope," I choke out, then gag again for good measure. "Just need to let it all out. You don't have to stay with me!"

She doesn't. "Okay, well, feel better. I'll catch you at the bar." I hear the door swing open and close.

I wait thirty more seconds before exiting the stall. Then I start running. I'm moving so fast I knock someone's purse off their shoulder and spill someone's beer.

Caleb is outside, smoking a cigarette, when I exit. Lately he has only smoked when stressed.

"Are you okay?" he asks as I approach.

I shake my head and start walking briskly down the avenue. Falling into step beside me, he matches my pace with no further questions asked. I'm grateful.

"I threw up," I tell him once we're three blocks away. "Maybe it's something I ate? I feel a teeny bit better now, though, it was so stuffy and hot in that place, this fresh air is amazing, let's take the bridge, I'd rather be outside." We redirect our feet. "What about you? Are *you* okay? You're smoking, so—"

"I saw Rosemary," he says, no longer patient. "She was *there*, she came up to me while you were gone and started yelling, no, *crying*, about how she expected me to at least . . ." He trails off, then looks at me sideways. "I swear I didn't know she was gonna be there!"

"*Really?*" Despite trusting him in this moment, I imbue my voice with a measure of suspicion, hoping to demonstrate some sort of moral high ground before it becomes clear, to both of us, that I have none.

"Of course, we haven't spoken at all! And, well—this is awkward, but—she said she texted me recently, and I didn't get it, and I wouldn't have responded anyway, but it's so weird that I didn't see it, and since I know you have my passcode—"

"I blocked her," I say without thinking. We're on the Williamsburg Bridge now. "I'm so sorry, it was wrong, but it scared me, I was angry she wasn't leaving us alone. I mean, she must still love you, that's why she was there!" Cyclists and a few other night-walkers and the clanking J train pass us by on their separate tracks. Two tiny figures, us, must be visible but fragmented through gaps in the red-steel barrier. It's a mile across. "Nothing good would've come from it, you have to know that."

He takes a final drag before tossing his cigarette off the bridge and into the water. "Jesus, Naomi, you really need to stop going through my phone. I mean—*blocking* her is so controlling and deceptive, you realize that, right? What happened to trying to trust each other?"

"I'm really sorry," I repeat. "It won't happen again, I swear. I saw her name pop up on your phone and I panicked. It's still raw. The betrayal." *Lest you forget, Caleb.* "You could change your passcode right now, if that would make you feel better—"

"No, that's not the point." He shakes his head. "It's just, the irony is—I actually made you an extra key yesterday."

"A key?" I repeat, uncomprehending.

He takes an envelope folded into quarters out of his back pocket. "It's for you, to my apartment. I thought it might be time."

He hands it to me. I finger the key-shaped lump inside.

"We go back and forth so often, so I wanted you to feel welcome."

"Oh," I say, swallowing. "Thank you!" I remember, also, to say: "I'll make you one, too."

"Only if you want to. I didn't do this to pressure you. It's not about that. I want you to trust me. Can I trust you, too?"

"Yes, you can." I badly want to deserve it. Another J train passes, loud and fast. The bridge rattles beneath our feet. "You didn't mention my name to Rosemary when she confronted you, right?"

"No." He furrows his eyebrows. "Why do you ask? I already told you, she knows you exist, but I still like to keep certain things private—"

Relief loosens my limbs. "No, that's fine, I'm glad. I don't want any crazy exes coming after me."

"She's not crazy—"

I give him a calculated smile. "Yeah, okay, I was just kidding."

To sidestep the developing tension, I say I have a song stuck in my head.

He takes the bait, as relieved as I am to deflect. "Which one?"

When I start to hum it, he conducts with his hands. Fingers moving effortlessly through air before being rearranged to strum an imaginary guitar. We both laugh our way into Manhattan, leaving our conflict behind on the Brooklyn side of the bridge.

Back in my bathroom I brush my teeth, and tweeze my eyebrows, and take off my mascara, and enter the bedroom to find Caleb with his lips slightly parted, perched on the edge of my bed with my notebook in his hands.

My shoulders and arms jerk instinctively as if to grab for it, but I'm too late. His torso is rotating toward me now—impossibly slow and impossibly fast, all within the space of a second. I can see the whites of his eyes.

"It was on your bedside table," he says softly, pointing to where I left it. "I've been interested in the rest of your book. I didn't think it would be—like this. I'm so confused." He begins to read jumbled excerpts of my first chapter aloud: "*I finally found a photo his ex-girlfriend took of him, on a desolate beach somewhere on the Irish coastline.*" He licks his fingers, turns the page, and continues to read. "*I imagined Rosemary and Caleb holding hands on drizzly roads or Dublin parks or windy beaches, her putting a finger on equations in his notebook and asking what he intended to solve. They were ripening into characters I could write down, and use, and maybe even keep.*"

"Caleb, stop." I'm panicked, wild, pulling threads out of my skirt. "Let me explain—"

"I'm not fucking done," he says quietly, still flipping through pages. "You need to listen. *When she stands and strides toward the*

bathroom, I duck my head and fish inside my purse for a tube of lip-
stick. When my fingers close around it, I enter the bathroom, too."

His mouth, in its ultra-thin line, spits more syllables:

"Calling my boyfriend while staring at his ex-girlfriend's back
through the window feels risky. I like it. What the fuck, Naomi? Is
this real? Did you actually follow Rosemary? Speak to her?"

"No, no." With slick fingers I grip my own thighs like a lifeboat.
"It's fictionalized, I stalked her on Facebook once, you know, out of
curiosity, but no, I've never followed her into a bar or anywhere
else." My face is burning. "Do you really think I'm capable of that?"

What kind of writer would I be if I wasn't? (Incapable, incuri-
ous, the opposite of myself.)

"What am I supposed to think?" he shouts. "A lot of this isn't
fucking fictionalized! It's my life, Naomi. When I said it was okay
to write about me, I meant more along the lines of using something
I said, or setting a scene somewhere we once went together, or—I
don't know—"

"I take whatever I need for the story I'm trying to tell," I say,
more coldly than intended. "These breakup details are actually
pretty universal, they're not unique, this happens to almost anyone who moves somewhere for another person."

"Then why even bother writing about it? You're not making any
sense. You're contradicting yourself." He seeks my gaze, demands
it. "I promised I wouldn't speak to Rosemary anymore. I kept my
word. I thought we were moving on."

"We are, we can!" I hear myself pleading now, the most unap-
pealing of sounds. "Look, Caleb, when you told me about Rosemary for the first time, it triggered something—a desire to, I don't
know . . ." I trail off for a moment, fighting to find the right words
and locate the truth. "I'm inspired by things from my life. Didn't

you know what you were getting into when you decided to date a writer?" My lips are dry so I lick them. It stings. I lick them again. "If you can't love my writing, if you can't at least respect it, then you can't truly love me. We're a package deal."

"Maybe you should try and use your imagination for once," Caleb says. "Isn't that what writers are supposed to do?"

His words cut, as he intended them to. I take a deep, shuddering breath. "This is fiction."

"Should I call Rosemary right now and ask?"

He has to be bluffing. I grind my teeth together.

"If you don't believe me," I say with forced bravado, "maybe you should leave."

My whole body is shaking. *Don't leave; it's a test, it's just a test—* I grip the edge of the closet door to steady myself.

Caleb stands and moves across the room, heading in the direction of the open bedroom door, and for a moment I believe he's leaving, that soon he'll truly be gone.

But then he is gripping my shoulders, and pulling me in, and crushing my head against his chest, and stroking my hair. With my nose and mouth pressed against his flannel shirt, oxygen arrives only in tiny pockets of air; I angle my head to gasp through the space underneath his armpit. He shifts his weight and holds me there for a long time, longer than I can remember being held by anyone.

"I didn't mean it," he says, sounding scared. "I'm just—I was in shock, I was upset. I'm still upset. But I'm not going anywhere."

"I'm sorry, too," I say, because I must. "I should've told you earlier, but I was afraid of how you'd react." This statement is the truth, the *truth*!

Soon I'll reveal the full extent of it, but not yet. I can't overwhelm him.

Only when I reveal my worst self, and am forgiven for it, will I be certain I am loved.

I move to the bed, peeling my spine backward and horizontal vertebrae by vertebrae, and press my thumbs down on my closed eyelids.

A hand, Caleb's, scratches my arm from wrist to elbow.

"I sometimes think you don't have faith in me," he says quietly. "I feel as if the things I say or do are never the right things to say or do, are never what you want from me."

Where have I heard this before?

"I do have faith in you!" I say. "I'll get you a key, I'll make it tomorrow, I'm sorry, okay? I'm sorry—"

"It's okay," says Caleb. "Stop apologizing! It's going to be fine. Now I know."

Caleb brings me tissues when I ask for them, and then we lie on my bed with our hips and knees touching. It's enough, for now. It's enough.

Tomorrow, I'll write it all down.

In the morning, I spoon some cereal and take my hormones and brush my teeth and text Rosemary. **So funny running into you last night! Sorry I was such a mess—no more edibles, lol. Did I miss an epic smackdown between you and the Mystery Girlfriend?**

No epic smackdowns, unfortunately, Rosemary replies an hour later. **Which means I'll have to write one.** ☺

Naturally! Would obviously love to read that scene when you're done.

Give me a few weeks, she writes.

chapter ten

M Y GRANDMOTHER IS sick.

My father calls to let me know. Pancreatic cancer, fast-moving and deadly.

As I Google "pancreatic cancer survival rate elderly" behind the desk at work, my father tells me she isn't considering treatment. It takes me approximately five seconds to process what that implies.

I dig a sharp jagged thumbnail deep into my palm, almost as if to scoop out a sliver of my own flesh. I don't stop until the pain is biting, localized, intolerable. My grandmother is just being dramatic, she must be—I know she'll try to fight. She has always loved being alive.

"I hope you can understand," my father says. "She made her decision."

I clear my dry throat. "So we're just going to let Grammie kill herself?"

A woman approaching the register with an armful of books

swerves away, alarmed, and focuses her gaze on a display case of literary-themed mugs.

"That's a dramatic way of looking at it." My father sighs. "Lacks nuance."

"Is there a more accurate phrase?" Panicked, I think of all the things my grandmother will never see me do. And then, in realizing I'm only thinking of myself, swallow down the shame.

"She's almost ninety-three," says my father. "Her hearing aid is so awful she can't participate in conversation. It's isolating. And her fingers are too swollen and arthritic to even write. Shall I go on? The treatment—it would be too intense. She doesn't want it."

Overwhelmed by the thought of a world without her, I fall silent, and my father misinterprets it, my preemptive grief, as acceptance. He ends the call.

Even if I vow to hold the entire hearing-aid industry hostage until they produce a superior model, it's my grandmother's swollen fingers, her inability to write, that depresses me—what kind of life is that?

Still, after my shift, I call her, hoping to be the only person in the world capable of convincing her to fight. We are, in so many ways, the same.

When she answers the phone, I'm breathless with relief; a part of me feared she might already be gone. "Dad told me about—well, he said you're sick, and I just don't understand—why you won't even try some sort of chemo?"

"Oh, sweetheart, I'm sorry, I really wanted to tell you myself. But I didn't know how. So your father said he would." Slow and heavy, she exhales. "Given the prognosis . . . it just doesn't make sense. What kind of life would I be preserving? I'd rather know

when and how it ends. Without too much pain. Morphine helps!"
She pauses. "You can understand, can't you?"

I can, I really can.

"No, I can't," I say. "It's stupid—"

"*Stupid?* That's a one-cent word, do better."

"You could live another year, or more! It's happened! I was
reading some studies—"

"Exactly. A long, long year. I don't want to suffer every day of
the year."

For once, I have nothing to say.

"It's okay, Naomi. I'm not scared. I'm just tired."

I stay silent and morose as I pass crowded bar after crowded bar,
all advertising happy hour specials. The irony doesn't escape me.

My grandmother speaks again. "Can I ask you to do something
for me?"

"What is it?" I ask, almost rudely.

"Finish your book. I want to be around when you do."

Inside my purse, I roll my silver key—*co-ownership of the writer's studio*—back and forth between my fingers. "I still have a lot of
writing and editing to do."

"Write how it ends, and deal with the rest later."

After a long pause, I tell her I'll try. And then, while descending
the stairs to the subway station, I add, "Especially since procrasti-
nation will have deadly consequences."

Miraculously, my grandmother laughs. "Exactly."

CALEB HAS BEEN peppering me with relentless texts—**just checking in!**—ever since I told him about my grandmother's diagnosis a
few days ago. His kindness and care are smothering; I'm not sure I

deserve either. I didn't even cry when I told him. I'd already armored up, becoming untouchable and numb. Maybe that's why Caleb is so concerned. Maybe he somehow sees right through to the heart of it, to the hurt. Maybe, as he said, I'm constantly underestimating him.

You still want me to come over later? his most recent text reads.

I reply in the affirmative before hopping into a scalding shower to shave my legs and underarms and inner thighs and belly. Then I make myself a cup of tea and sit at the kitchen table, still dripping. Romeo weaves through my legs and yowls when a water droplet catches him on the ear.

Blowing gently into my steaming mug, I allow myself another moment of procrastination-disguised-as-research. Navigating to Rosemary's Instagram, I notice her tiny profile photo has flamed pink. I click on it, discovering a screenshot of an email she posted a few minutes ago.

Most of the text is censored by red squiggly lines—an Instagram editing feature—but the words she draws attention to read as follows: We love your piece "Surveillance in G-Minor" and feel absolutely privileged to publish it in—

My vision swims. Tiny pinpricks of white light.

Absolutely privileged to publish! privileged to publish! publish! short-circuits my brain.

How is it possible that Rosemary—who recently confessed how nervous she was about putting her work out there, about owning her identity as a writer—has suddenly decided to make a definitive debut? Did something I said encourage her to submit? Or maybe (and this alternative comforts me very much) Rosemary is only reposting an email sent to one of her authors, or her friends, or her colleagues. After all, no one's name is visible in the screen-shot. Maybe Rosemary is just a really supportive person, happy to shout other people's successes.

But deep in the pit of my stomach, I know this isn't true, and that the story must be hers. "Surveillance in G-Minor" strikes me as an odd title for the piece about the dog and the forest and the family, although I suppose the very best titles are meant to intrigue us, to draw us in, perhaps complicate our perceptions.

I allow myself a tiny nugget of pride. I must, really, be an excellent reader if my feedback contributed to this story's forthcoming publication.

But who, then, is "absolutely privileged" to publish her? *The New Yorker*, or an obscure online magazine no one actually reads?

What I do next is entirely unplanned. I might soon regret it, might soon punish myself for it, but it happens, it happened.

In response to the photo, I type: Such a tease . . .

Then I press send, somehow resisting the urge to add *when can we read it* and *where can we read it* and *what the fuck do you mean by G-minor?*

And there it is, my bubble of text—three words with that psychotic-looking ellipsis, the potential start of a dialogue between Rosemary and the anonymous bookstagram I've now activated to do more than simply lurk and observe and record. Maybe she'll think the person behind it is a man, lonely and creepy and awkward.

Exactly three minutes later, Rosemary's response materializes on-screen. My breath catches.

Don't you consider, she has written, an anonymous account commenting on a post about surveillance gloriously ironic? 👀

I don't reply, hastily logging out.

When Caleb delivers himself to me an hour later, we tumble

onto my bed. He kisses my neck, removes my jeans and under-wear. We roll around, knocking knees and clutching desperately at each other's shoulders. I fuck to forget the psychotic ellipsis, the dread. I don't know what Caleb fucks to forget. (There are many possible catastrophes, according to his calculations, but how can you forget something that hasn't happened yet?)

Afterward, he brings me tissues to wipe his semen off my stom-ach and says, "Oh, I forgot to ask how your workshops are going."

For a panicked second, I blink at him. "My—workshops?"

"Yeah." He blinks back. "With Luna. Right?"

I crumple the soiled tissues in my right hand and recover quickly. "Oh, duh, right! They've been going really well. Her feed-back is amazing, it's been really useful and fun."

"Workshops" with "Luna" have been my alibi for any evening spent with Rosemary because Luna is a writer, too, an essayist—though I haven't asked about her work in a while.

Now I need to keep Luna and Caleb apart, lest he start asking her questions. But that shouldn't be difficult. He rarely visits me at work.

How much longer will I even work at the bookstore? What else might I want to do with my life?

I can feel it, my narrative, nearing its end; for months there's been a constant buzzing in my abdomen, a sustained adrenaline rush, but nothing lasts—except words, written down.

OVER THE NEXT three weeks, I write as fast as I can, frequently logging several hours a day in the café across the street. To avoid dirty looks from patrons or staff regarding the length of my visit, I pointedly approach the register to make additional purchases at ninety-minute intervals: iced dirty chai latte, seven dollars; a blueberry chocolate chip scone, three-fifty; a mozzarella-and-tomato baguette, nine-fifty (plus tax).

Then, finally, I send to my two best readers.

For my grandmother—a rough, rough draft from the beginning to the almost end. I've stopped short of the final chapter because nothing I've thought of feels quite right. I'm hoping to gauge, from her reaction, some sort of hint regarding how to craft the climax. For Rosemary—a text, first. **I don't know how much time you have these days,** I venture, **but I will happily pay you for another critique!**

We haven't spoken since the concert, and to be perfectly honest I miss her, which feels unexpected, and dangerous. I want her to want me in her life. I want to have made enough of an impression. It frightens me, all this sudden wanting; someday soon I'll most certainly need to choose between her and Caleb. And it surprises me to realize that the choice is no longer so obvious.

A scene I've previously envisioned (us, at the altar) shapeshifts into something new; this time it's Rosemary in the white veil and me, maid of honor, beaming at her side—although it's not entirely clear who the groom might be.

I'm surprised by how soothed I feel, writing it down; inexplicably, the scene seems to suggest a kind of absolution.

Forty-eight hours (much too long) later, Rosemary replies. **Sure! I'll try to read ASAP.**

This time, I send an excerpt featuring my origin story: Adam. I want to be understood in a different way.

But my grandmother reads faster—time is of the essence now— and calls me a few days later. "You did it!" she greets me.

"Ha, yes, but I'm not sure if it's any good."

"It will be. I must say, my favorite scenes were between the women. And as for the boyfriend, well"—there's a long pause as she breathes shallowly on the other end of the line—"their relationship seems lovely and normal. So it's unfortunate, the narrator's instinct to self-sabotage, now that she's finally in love."

Struggling to digest this, I resist the urge to ask, *How can you tell she's in love?* Pulling Romeo onto my lap, I bear his weight and feel grounded—if only briefly.

"Well, I think she has this—fear," I say, finally trying to articulate my own. "That she's incapable of love—not just of *being* loved, but of properly lov*ing*. So she behaves in ways that make her unlovable, see? When she's rejected she'll know why; she'll still control her own fate."

"Quite the hypothesis! But no one is incapable of love, that's ridiculous." A slyly suggestive omniscience animates her voice as she asks, "Can you relate to your protagonist?"

Nothing gets past her.

"A little bit," I offer, exhaling. "I guess, maybe, my book is a version of that. If my own relationship ends because of everything I've done and what I've written, then how could I allow myself to love a person who would someday leave?"

She lets me sit with this for a moment. And then she speaks again, gentle but direct: "If given the choice between being in control and being in love, what do you choose?"

I remain silent. Is there a way to be both?

"Let me get back to you on that," I say eventually, and force a laugh—hoping she'll drop it and finally let me off the hook. "Thanks for reading, Grammie," I continue, as chipper as possible. And then, as the dark truth of what little time we have left settles in my stomach, I add, "I don't know what I'll do without you."

"You'll be fine," she says, and then, laughing, "But if you reread my memoir enough times, it'll be like I never left."

This isn't goodbye, not yet, so I don't say it. "See you soon!" I say instead.

I make it sound like a command because it is.

MY APARTMENT'S KEY is silver. Caleb's key is gold. I love hearing them tumble against each other in my purse. I love the soft click of each key fitting perfectly into each lock.

Today, the smell of sautéed vegetables and roast chicken wafts under my apartment door and into the hallway, perfectly capturing the illusion—or the reality—of what it might be like to live together from this day forward, for better or for worse, in sickness and in health. Such good luck, finding him. My boyfriend.

(*He's a nice boy, Naomi,* my grandmother had said.)

When the door swings open, the sight of Caleb at the stove makes my heart twist. Voices from *Slow Burn,* a podcast he likes, pulse through my speakers. "Smells amazing," I say.

He turns down the burner and then the speakers. "Hi! It's almost ready. How was your day?"

"Pretty good," I say, popping open a can of cat food. The sound makes Romeo appear instantly. I coo at him, then shuffle into the bathroom, strip down, and scoop his litter box. I imagine dislodged and dirty dust particles rise and settle on my skin and in my hair during this procedure, so I only ever scoop naked, just before showering. It's a ritual.

The water rains down. I massage my scalp with dandruff shampoo as soapsuds churn around my toes, suckling at the drain. With my eyes closed the pressure of my fingertips alleviates something inside me, shaking it loose, and with a dazed clarity—*something shadowy crossing in front of the car, too suddenly to brake*—I finally know the end.

The protagonist's boyfriend, in the final chapter of my book, will die in a mysteriously tragic accident, unwittingly forging a lifelong bond between the two traumatized women he leaves behind. In spite of all the lies and deception, all the feints and misrepresentations, there is forgiveness, and healing, and a happily ever after. I get clean, and then cleaner.

As I turn off the faucet, it seems even more obvious—no other solution is possible. Death is a vessel for the excretion of every ugly, conflicting emotion; it also offers the opportunity to evade, no questions asked. I'll award myself what I really want, if only ever on the page.

After drying off, I stand naked on the bathmat and with a frenetic speed draft the chapter outline using the Notes app on my phone until—in the midst of evoking a shared grief—an AOL notification pops up on-screen.

Rosemary has emailed about the Adam excerpt I sent her. I really love this, she has written. It's raw and vulnerable and moving. If I may also be very blunt, it's better than what you sent me last time. More of this!

I sit and reconcile her backhanded compliment with the words *moving* and *raw* and *love* until Caleb calls to me from the kitchen. Moving into the bedroom, I put my phone facedown on the bedside table and change into sweatpants and a T-shirt before going to join him.

Caleb smiles when I enter. He plates our food, lights a vanilla-scented candle, and screws the cap off two amber ales.

We sit and eat the meat and the veggies, and I decide to be real this time. Allow myself to confess *one* specific detail. "Caleb, how would you react if—I told you, um, if I said that—I can't have children? Biologically, I mean." My voice comes out so quietly that for a second I assume he didn't hear me, and am relieved.

Caleb freezes, fork halfway to his mouth. "What're you talking about?" His voice quickens. "Are you okay, are you sick?"

I sense the empty spaces inside me so distinctly. "This isn't totally relevant to our relationship at this exact moment or anything, I mean, it's a conversation that'll probably be more important down the line, you know, in the future, as we get more serious, *if* we get more serious, and basically—well, the issue is, I don't have any ovaries." I catch my breath. "I had this—surgery. As a teenager. To remove a cyst. But it went wrong, wasn't working, so they removed the ovaries, too. So I—or we—you know, well, we could, like, adopt. If it comes to that. Someday in the future, obviously. Like I said."

Caleb puts his fork down and stares at his food for a long, uncomfortable minute as I count each breath—in, one, out, two, in, three, out—and prepare to be told how I'm physically incapable of telling him the truth, how I'm a liar, how I'm untrustworthy— (*there is no other possible solution*)—

"Wow, Naomi," he finally says. "That's just—wow. I'm really sorry." He swallows. "I don't know what to say, exactly. That's really tough. And you were so young! I wish you'd told me— earlier. But I guess I get why you didn't."

Gawking at him, I scramble for the right words. "I would have, though. I would have if you'd asked, if you'd said, *I want to have kids someday,* I would've told you immediately. But you didn't."

He puts a hand on my knee. "I know. It's okay. It didn't exactly come up, you're right." His eyes flash. "I'm still not ready to talk about it, you know, with any real seriousness, that whole thing, but, well, someday—"

"*That whole thing*, meaning—babies?" I say, feeling so weightless and relieved that I start to laugh.

And then he starts to laugh, too. "Well—yeah. But it's not an impossible situation! I mean, it's difficult, obviously, but we'll figure it out together, if we need to. Down the line."

"Right, yes, exactly, down the line," I repeat, trying not to doubt, even though Caleb's confident allusion to our perceived future together is downright contrary to the fear-based, avoidant ending I've awarded us.

My left hand twitches suddenly, as if moved by the urge to revise, and so I sit on each splayed finger until the feeling goes away, numbs.

THE SMELL OF dark-roast coffee pricks me awake the next morning.

"What time is it?" I mumble, disoriented.

"Seven," Caleb whispers, attempting to get dressed without turning on the light. "I've got an early meeting, but I'll see you tomorrow night."

"Tomorrow?"

"Yeah," he says, brows knitting. "I think I should just—have tonight to myself. I have some work to catch up on, and—I also haven't been sleeping well. I need to reset, or something. But I'll come over tomorrow."

"Oh, okay." I say, blinking at him. His sudden desire for space might be connected to the information I dumped on him last night—which would be understandable. He needs to process, doesn't he? "Sure, I understand. We both need our me-time. I hope you feel better. Text me later?"

"Of course," Caleb says before he leaves. "I love you."

"I love you, too." I readjust my pillow and nestle back in. I planned to spend my day off doing absolutely nothing writing-related. For so long I've been full-speed ahead, and now, finally, I can rest for a while. Over the next few hours, I alternate between aggressive games of Words with Friends (but with strangers), You-Tube rabbit holes, and rereading my published stories for an emergency injection of pride.

Around six p.m., Luna texts me. **You know you left your note-book here, right? A customer found it on the floor. I'll lock it in the safe tonight! So you can get it tomorrow.**

On the *floor*? My stomach clenches, and for a moment I feel, absurdly, how I imagine a mother might feel losing sight of her own child at a crowded playground.

I could've sworn I saw a flash of lavender in my tote bag yesterday, but maybe I'd imagined it. I text Luna back. **Omg, I didn't even realize it was missing. THANK YOU!**

I trust she won't read it—it doesn't have the forbidden allure of a diary, and besides, she's been totally consumed by Sally Rooney lately.

In bed, I play the word *BIKE* with a stranger called Marisa L (72 points, landing on a triple word *and* a triple letter), send Caleb a photo of Romeo peeking out from inside a paper bag, and then finally fall asleep.

chapter eleven

THE NEXT DAY, after I'm reunited with my notebook, I settle into the swivel chair behind the register and ring up three white men buying, between them, eight novels written by white men.

"I'm slipping Audre Lorde into their bags one of these days," says Luna after they leave, hunched over a newly delivered box of hardcovers.

"Ha, yeah," I mumble, and then—distracted by a sudden and unpleasant intrusive thought—ask, "The customer who found my notebook . . . what did they look like?"

Luna looks at me, eyebrows raised. "Uh, I don't know? A woman. Decently attractive. Black hair. Short-ish. I wasn't paying close attention."

My stomach flips. "Did she have weird teeth?"

Luna wrestles with the box—it's exceptionally well-sealed—before finally slicing open a flap. Books cascade out, clunking against the floor. Cursing, she inspects them for damage. If a book gets damaged, we discount it. Peter, who rarely appears unless it's to shout at us before major holidays, will shout.

"I'm not a dentist, dude, I didn't exactly ask her to open wide and say *ahh*," says Luna, laughing, but after observing my face, asks, "Is something going on? You're really pale."

My feet have fallen asleep now, tingling like little beads of electricity, and so I stomp them on the floor. Left foot, right foot, left again, to return to feeling. "I do feel kind of sick. Can you take over the register for a sec? Need the bathroom."

"Oh, TMI," Luna says as she waves me off.

In the bathroom, I lean against the mirror and check my phone for text messages with exclamation points or accusations or threats; none have been delivered.

Is it possible Rosemary was spontaneously in the neighborhood yesterday and hoped to pop in to tell me the contents of her email face-to-face? But still, why wouldn't she mention if she was planning to visit?

To quiet all these crowding thoughts, I text Rosemary, hoping her response will assuage my anxieties. **I got your email—thank you so much for reading, and for being so kind! It means a lot. Looking forward to getting another drink as soon as you're able.**

I don't expect an immediate response—it's past lunch, so Rosemary probably won't have another free moment to engage until her workday is officially over. I settle behind the register and will myself to stop speculating; maybe she *wasn't* the customer who found the notebook. If she was, all hell would have broken loose by now. Lots of women have black hair, dyed or otherwise, and her teeth are definitely too vampiric for Luna to overlook.

Slowly, my heartbeat returns to its normal rate.

Five minutes before closing time, a woman buys one of the

books I've recommended—Elif Batuman's *The Idiot*—on our Staff Picks table, stacked high by the back wall. Luna and I keep track of which Staff Picks sell the most copies; we want our tastes confirmed. The table includes recs from staff who no longer work here, and sometimes, when it's slow, I read their recommendations and wonder where they've moved on to, what they're doing now. Would they still recommend the same stories?

When I finally leave the bookstore, the sun casts the sky pinkish-orange and the air is redolent with spring. I tie my jacket around my waist and start walking toward the Brooklyn Bridge. I finger the keys—silver and gold, mine and his—inside the zipped left pocket as they thwack against my pelvis. It's always tourist season on the bridge, and I watch them take photos of one another as I cross the river. A few women climb onto railings to get the perfect shot, and I think of how easily they could fall. Cyclists scream at pedestrians wandering unwittingly into the narrow bike path.

I take a selfie. My first in a while—I don't think of myself as someone who takes selfies, plural; the occasional one, sure, if the occasion calls for it.

My hair appears redder in this light; my face, whited-out and ethereal from overexposure. Liking the way it looks, I post on Instagram with a mermaid and sunset emoji: Felt cute; definitely won't delete later.

Once I'm off the bridge, it still takes another four hours to walk to the border of Hamilton Heights and Washington Heights. I'm wearing sturdy, capable boots, but I've never walked this far in the city before; by the time I reach the Upper West Side, heat flares in my knees. I push on anyway, taking pleasure in a close examination of the neighborhoods changing, shifting, bumping up against each other: Whole Foods melting into barbershops melting into wine bars melting into dollar stores melting into Whole Foods again. I purchase a bottle of Argentinian Malbec, Caleb's favorite red, at a liquor store on 163rd, and then climb to his fourth-floor walk-up. I angle the key in the lock.

Oddly, it doesn't click open. So I push my shoulder against the door and jiggle the knob. Nothing happens. I can't remember if Caleb has a dead bolt—but why would he even use it? I blow out a breath and look around me, shifty and embarrassed, hoping no one saw me fumbling. No one did, so this time I knock thrice with a bit of rhythm, a bit of personality, to alert him that it's me. Silence, stillness.

I check for yellow light visible through the crack under the door. It appears to be dark inside, but it's possible that Caleb is sitting in his bedroom in the back, playing music or a podcast on his headphones. Loud enough to ward out any and all unwanted disturbances.

Maybe his roommate is home? I knock again before emphatically ringing the doorbell I've been previously warned not to touch. Both men hate hearing its tinny whine.

When nothing happens, I try calling him. It rings and rings and goes to voicemail, which he has never personalized; instead, I'm greeted by an automated, apologetic-sounding female voice. I don't leave a message. No one except my mother leaves or even listens to voicemails anymore.

Are you home? I text him. **I'm at your place and for some reason can't get in.**

I calculate the amount of time it might take for a person's eyes to drift toward their phone and read their messages and shuffle to the door. I wait five excruciatingly long minutes before calling again.

Automated message.

Fear unzips along my spine. Has something terrible happened to Caleb? Is it possible the ending I've written for him has manifested somehow? Do I really have that kind of power?

Getting a little worried now, I write. **Where are you? Hope you're okay. Please call me back when you can!**

Hungry now—starving, actually, it's ten thirty and I've consumed nothing but coffee since one fifteen—I wander into the takeout falafel place on the opposite corner. There's a long line, so I check Twitter for distractions.

Rosemary still hasn't responded to my text. Maybe her Twitter account will hint as to why. In her mind, has our friendship run its course? Maybe she's the kind of person who ditches their friends entirely as soon as they start a new relationship. And if so, wouldn't it be for the best?

I type her name into the search bar, but nothing comes up. Weird.

Impatient, I bypass Twitter and Google her full name instead.

None of her social media accounts appear as search results but, oddly, *Vogue* magazine's does. Its most recent tweet has gone viral, or at least as viral as literary works do. Thousands of likes, hundreds of retweets—many of them by other writers and media giants I admire. Dry-mouthed, I click on the accompanying link and am redirected to the esteemed magazine's website.

The essay I'm staring at is titled "Surveillance in G-Minor," and the author is Rosemary Pierce.

A whine of shock and envy escapes my lips. Here it is, out in the wild at last.

"Motherfucking *Vogue*," I mutter. *That's* Rosemary's debut publication?

The man ahead of me understandably edges away from the

auburn-haired woman cursing to herself while waiting for falafel, but no need. Abandoning my spot in line, I lurch toward the restroom.

Locked inside a stall, under the fluorescent lights, I read:

My ex-boyfriend's new girlfriend is writing a book about me. A novel, actually, in which we become friends under false pretenses. But this part is fact, not fiction: she lured me in with books and beers, pretending not to know who I was. She pretended she was no one, when in fact she was someone very specific.

But I suppose I was an easy target—lonely, aimless, in need. She slid a pedestal under my feet, and I stepped onto it, tired and grateful.

Before you judge her, or me: I'll explain how it started.

She stood across the street from my office in a chunky maroon sweater and sunglasses, watching me leave. The sunglasses were, in retrospect, a halfhearted disguise. She must have wanted to be known, wanted to be watched, in return.

It was 6:35 p.m. when I crossed the street, popped a breath mint, flipped off a driver honking inside his black BMW.

My ex-boyfriend's new girlfriend remained in the same spot, pretending to look for something in her tote. Where did she imagine her reconnaissance would lead?

She hovered too close to me, mere inches away, on the Fulton subway platform. I resisted the urge to ask her—a stranger still!—what she wanted from me. I might even have been willing to give it, but not for free.

Months before she held vigil outside my office, I stood on the corner of my ex's street and watched as he exited his building with a woman. They held hands and I held my breath, desperately hoping I'd be noticed, and desperately hoping I wouldn't be. I never saw her face.

Boarding the train at Fulton, I sensed the auburn-haired stranger staring behind those ridiculous sunglasses. I allowed us to make seemingly arbitrary eye contact exactly twice, but of course all I saw was my own face, reflected in the lens. When I exited at Lafayette Avenue in Brooklyn, she followed. I walked down the street, took a left, a right, then punched in a code to enter my modern, industrial-chic building. The stranger couldn't follow me anymore, but I wanted her to, I was desperate to be observed—I just didn't know, yet, how it would feel to be.

Have you ever been written about? Or stumbled upon a character that eerily resembled you? I promise it's a profoundly surreal and disembodying experience, gratifying and unsettling all at once—especially when facts and fictions, opinions and observations, are all jumbled together.

I began to doubt what I knew about myself, what felt true to me. I often mistake fiction for reality, but the boundary feels particularly tenuous now.

But still—imagine being the subject of such fervent scrutiny, such exalted reconstruction! How could anyone hate a person who makes them feel that special?

I can't.

My ex-boyfriend's new girlfriend got a lot right in her novel, but she also got a lot wrong. "Rosemary" is a fiction—enticing, true, but false and flimsy. She could never truly capture me. I belong to myself.

I can't breathe, I'm not breathing, I keep reading, I almost drop my phone in the toilet.

The end of the essay leads us right here, to this moment:

If she reads this, I hope she'll write us both a better ending.

Bile rises in my throat; I bend over. When the nausea leads to vomiting, and my knees hit the floor, someone in the next stall over tentatively asks, "You okay in there?"

Obviously not, you fucking idiot, I want to say. I'm kneeling on the sticky, disgusting floor of a restaurant's bathroom, vomiting into a toilet speckled with pubic hairs (not my own).

But I manage to grunt a reply. Communicating the necessity of being left alone, unbothered.

I wait for them to flush, wait for their shoes to clack away, before emerging to wash my hands and face. In the mirror, my skin is wan; blood vessels burst in spooky red tendrils underneath my eyes. I fill my mouth with water, then gargle and spit. I do this three times.

She has taken my words and made them hers. The protagonist cannibalized by the antagonist—or is it the other way around?

What it means is I've lost all control.

How long has she known who I really am?

She needed enough time to write this, and submit it, and publish it.

Maybe she wrote it recently in one long feverish night and sent it off the very next day, eschewing the slush pile altogether by slipping her essay into the hands of a senior editor she knows. Using her arsenal of connections, it wouldn't have been impossible to expedite its publication.

I remember the text I deleted—**something disturbing happened last week, and I'm feeling very shaken . . .**

Was that when she began connecting the dots?

I skim more of my memories for moments when she might have been alone with my notebook, when greed or paranoia or curiosity moved her to read, and later to take.

You know you left your notebook here, right?
A customer found it on the floor—

Of course, of course. How stupid, how careless, I'd been.

What's left of our story for me to tell? Is it possible Rosemary has written several more pieces about us, or will this *Vogue* essay be the extent of her revenge—*if* revenge is, indeed, what this is?

An image pops into my head: the two of us sitting side by side, co-writing our story from dual perspectives. It's so absurd and enticing and impossible that I laugh out loud. The sound, high-pitched, skitters across the bathroom tile.

Maybe it's true that what I always wanted from her was commiseration, sisterhood. Our shared experiences of loving Caleb, of being loved by him, of trying to write it all down. We could have made a list of everything we shared.

I log in to @Language_and_Liquid, desperate for clues. In the last twenty-four hours a few other Instagram accounts have requested to follow, but I've made them wait, heightening (I hoped) their hunger. The majority of requests my anonymous account receives tend to be lingerie-clad bots, other lame bookstagrams, or D-list rock bands desperate for acknowledgment and indiscriminate in their strategies to earn a follow-back. Today's offerings seem to be a blend of all three, but my eye travels immediately to @LiteraryConfessions13. I accept the request and click on their profile, noticing how their own followers top out at a whopping zero. Only a few photos have been uploaded, and as I realize what they depict, my teeth start to chatter.

Each photo exhibits notebook pages displaying my own familiar scrawl, heavily annotated by a red pen. But my handwriting has the faded look of having passed through a photocopier, and on the photocopied pages, cuts have been made, different word choices have been suggested, sentences have been reordered. Certain words and phrases, too, have been circled or underlined—*St Andrews* and *follow* and *moody moor* and *math* and *private* and *Caleb* and *want* and *writing* and *Rosemary*—with multiple exclamation points leaping in the margins. The caption of one photo: You aren't an interesting enough monster. And another: You're writing your book as a way out, but it won't work.

And another: The Plot is never the point, but yours ended in the bookstore. I stopped by to ask about some unsettling coincidences. I wanted to see you, wanted you to look at me. But it must've been your lunch break, or your day off. Of course. To justify my presence, I wandered through the store and stumbled upon your notebook—lavender, sateen, monogrammed. So distinctive. Actually, what I mean to say is: during my deliberate, careful search for evidence, I found exactly what I was looking for.

Your coworker was distracted. She didn't notice me snatch it from your cubby by the storage room, nor did she notice me standing in an empty aisle reading it—the first time I really, truly, honored my paranoia.

For so long I chose to ignore the deleted text and provocative prose and confusing dead-end Google searches of your name. I even convinced myself the disturbing parallels between your fiction and my reality were symptoms of an overactive imagination, or a sort of narcissism on my part—which is a truly destabilizing thing to believe about oneself, I assure you, but somehow you led me there.

And then of course came that concert, where you were sloppy and revealing and I could no longer look away. Was it on purpose? Were you tired of being careful?

And finally: In another life, we might have actually been friends.

I stop reading, stop looking, click out and away. The phone feels too hot in my hand, so I put it in my pocket. The heat lessens, but the weight of it still presses my feet down onto the dirty restroom floor.

The thought of Rosemary paging through my notebook and judging my scrawled rough drafts is enough to send me back to the porcelain god for another round of dry-heaving. Unsure if I still have a chance to defend myself, I desperately navigate to her Instagram account. All that's left of it is Rosemary's tiny thumbnail photo and three words: User Not Found. In the white space where her photos used to be: No Posts Yet. I search once more for her Twitter, and then her Facebook. Nothing. She's a ghost.

Instead of rejoining the falafel line, I exit the restaurant and cross the street and grab a premade nasty-looking sandwich from a bodega, put it inside my tote bag, and rush down the block back to Caleb's apartment. Maybe he returned from wherever he was, maybe I can warn him, maybe I can explain. His sudden silence could just be a coincidence, his phone might be off, or—

I pound back up the stairs, the plastic bag with my sandwich and Malbec slapping against my thighs, and resume ringing the doorbell.

Finally I hear the sound of a dead bolt being slowly unlocked. *Thank god*, my body says, sinking deeper into the floor. *Thank god*. When the door opens a smidge, Caleb's flatmate, large headphones slung around his neck, peeks through the crack. Deflated but still relieved—he is better than nothing, better than no one—I open my mouth.

"Oh," he says, looking annoyed. "Uh, hi, Nadine."

"Naomi! My name is *Naomi*." We've only met once, but seriously? He can fuck right off.

"Right. Sorry. Are you looking for—"

"Caleb, yes," I say, breathless. "Do you know where he is?"

"I'm, uh, pretty sure he said he was going to your place a few hours ago—he took the day off work."

"Oh thank god," I say aloud, on the verge of tears.

Running back down the stairs, I hail a yellow taxi to take me downtown. It'll be close to fifty dollars, but I have so much to tell him. It can't wait.

I take out my sandwich.

"No eating in car," the driver says. "Please, thank you."

I slide over, hoping to locate his blind spot, and take another bite. As he pulls onto the West Side Highway and begins to fly through all the neighborhoods it took me hours to walk through—Whole Foods, dollar store, wine bar, barbershop, Whole Foods—I realize I left the bottle of Malbec on the floor outside Caleb's apartment in its black plastic bag. I start laughing. When he finds it, I imagine he'll laugh, too.

On my phone screen, no new text messages or phone calls from Rosemary or Caleb.

If Rosemary believes Caleb has known about my novel and about our burgeoning friendship this whole time, even believes he has *allowed* and encouraged me to befriend her for fiction, she won't want to speak to either of us ever again. I feel the truth of this in my bones.

I peer out the window. The river rushes past on my right; this I intuitively know even if I cannot see through the nighttime blackness. In my childhood, I always fell asleep quick and easy in the dark backs of cars, but now my body is a vibrating electric field the whole way home.

You're writing your book as a way out—The Plot is never the point—

No, it was always the point, I admit to myself, dragging a finger in a figure-eight down the window's cool glass. To plot, and obsess, and construct, is to escape from

estrogen and	*cymbals*	*tails flicking flies*
RedRiverRevel is typing . . .	*progestin*	*sterile high-rise hotel rooms*
	Should I have run?	

Once we reach my block, I ask to be let out at a particularly endless red light. "I'll walk the rest of the way," I tell the driver. He unlocks the door once my payment is approved. I tumble out and run. My knees and hip flexors protest. *Thirteen miles,* they scream. *Enough movement, enough.*

When I reach the top floor, there is no suffusing smell. My key in the lock, the swinging open, and then a memory: him at the stove, stirring.

My apartment looks tidier. It could be a surprise. He could be surprising me with this act of service. His love language. Is it true what people say—a clean home, a clear mind?

I walk through each room looking for him. *Thank you,* I'll say when I find him, *but you didn't have to do this, you scared me, did you know that I was scared?*

There aren't many rooms, this of course I know.

In the bathroom, my facial moisturizer and toothpaste and tweezers stand alone in a neat row. His toothbrush, razor, and shaving cream are all gone.

I suck down as much oxygen as possible and retreat; my body, slack and heavy and lumbering, bumps up against corners.

In my bedroom, the bed is made and the pillows have been rearranged. Romeo is sitting on the comforter with his paws facing out in perfect parallel symmetry, like a sphinx. When he blinks at me, I wish we could communicate telepathically: *What did you watch him do, why did you let him leave, why were you the only one granted a real goodbye?*

On the shelf at the back of my closet, the absence of his shirts and pants. My clothes, refolded and redistributed, to fill the spacious shelves. I back up and away from the emptiness.

Entering the kitchen, I spot the hard copy of the censored version I gave Rosemary on my burnished wooden table—*I'm peeking through the stacks at the bookstore where she works, watching her gift-wrap a mug with Shakespeare's face on it*—which must have been marked up by the same red pen. At the top of the page, in cursive, she's written, *This version is better.*

I turn in one last circle as if it's possible to sniff her out, as if Rosemary herself might crawl out from under the table and scream, "Did you think you were *invincible*?"

My notebook must have passed through both sets of hands—my fingerprints, and her fingerprints, and his fingerprints, still lingering on the same surface. The two of them must have met and discussed the evidence, before Caleb arrived here to deliver it. Every encounter with Rosemary was meticulously documented.

I check Oliver's Instagram. It's the last, and only, place Rosemary can still be found. How would Oliver react if he knew his girlfriend met up with her ex-boyfriend to plan and execute revenge for an intimate joint betrayal? Would he feel, as I have, that nothing he and Rosemary share will ever come close to what she has shared with Caleb? If Rosemary no longer appears on Oliver's Instagram, no longer makes cameos in recent photos, it'll be obvious that she has officially returned to her first love. The trauma of being rewritten, then, would have served as the catalyst for their reunion.

User Not Found, Instagram informs me. *No Posts Yet.*

It's over now, isn't it? All traces of her, gone.

I imagine an army of people out there, in the process of being turned against me.

Removing the lavender, sateen, monogrammed notebook from my tote bag, I set it down on the table, too. It was *mine*, it was supposed to be private, supposed to be loyal, but now my initials beam up at me accusingly.

Was it worth it, Naomi Amelia Ackerman? Was it?

With my worst self finally revealed, no one has decided to stay. I suppose I can't blame them.

The stack of pages is bookmarked by a key. I flip to the place Caleb has directed me to—the middle of an excerpt from our story—and remove the silver key. Mine, and once his.

In the margins, he has scrawled:

Do what you need to do, I can't and won't stop you. But please don't contact me again. Let me live.

His words collide with my own: *Writing is my first love. Put it first. Protect it.*

I take a wineglass from the cabinet and fill it with water and chug. Most of my water glasses are dirty. I hear the whir of the dishwasher, which Caleb must have loaded before he left. The absurdity of it, the displaced care.

Choking on water as it flows down the wrong pipe, I start to hiccup, violently. The sound feels apt—my inner turmoil, externalized.

But somehow I can't accept this is how it ends.

Should I have run?

I've been running all evening—why stop now?

I feed Romeo and, still hiccupping, pound back down the stairs and get on the C train bound for Fort Greene. A confrontation, a smackdown, an explosion. Hasn't that always been inevitable? I'm behaving in character.

Caleb erected a boundary I simply cannot breach, I owe him that much, but Rosemary and I are still in a sort of communion— how could we not be? We've been writing toward each other, hoping to be read, to be reached. Haven't we?

I wonder if I'm fated to stand on the corner of Rosemary's street and watch Caleb hold her hand as I hold my breath, desperately hoping I'll be seen, and desperately hoping I won't be.

Maybe what I've always wanted from them is to be deserted, shaken, bereft. Forced to feel.

Could this be what Rosemary meant when she accused me of writing "as a way out"?

(*It won't work*, she wrote.)

On the train, people are loud and drunk and happy. A man in a trench coat strokes his panting three-legged dog as a teenage couple wearing matching paint-spattered overalls points and coos. An emaciated blond woman devours a sandwich as the gap-toothed man sitting beside her explains why the Old Testament is better than the New. The train shuttles past High Street, Jay Street, and Hoyt; my hands are cold and clammy; I wipe them on my knees.

When Rosemary's stop, Lafayette, arrives, I exit, walking the familiar path. Brownstone, moonlight, lamplight, industrial-chic.

The street is empty and quiet. Approaching her building's keypad, I remember my silent chant—*0229, 0229*—and press the 0, and the 2, twice.

And pause.

On the page, my narrator is desperate and defensive and asking, always, to be absolved. Should I allow her to be something else instead? Maybe it's finally time to seek out a new story, rearrange all the ingredients of a life. I have another in me, don't I? Please— this can't be all I ever make. All I ever am.

A cacophony of voices and laughter rings out on the street behind me; spooked, I back away from Rosemary's door and bolt for the nearest shadow. Six people stream by—no one I recognize. They're loud and drunk and happy, too.

I start to sob with my whole body. Doubling over with the shock of it.

One girl, willowy and stooping and lagging behind her friends, whips around to find the source of the sound and looks directly at me. For a moment I think she's going to be the second person in less than two hours to ask me if I'm okay, but then she doesn't. She continues on, continues forward.

I stand on the dark street for a while and let myself feel it.

———

THE SUBWAY IS quieter now. Everyone but me, it seems, has reached their destinations. Homeless men stretch across the seats, draped in blankets and dreaming.

If she reads this, I hope she'll write us both a better ending.

What would that even look like? I try to imagine.

Back home, Romeo greets me at the door like a dog, and in the quiet hum of my apartment, I make blue-ink slashes across *St Andrews* and *follow* and *moody moor* and *math* and *private* and *Caleb* and *want* and *writing* and *Rosemary* and then attempt, finally, to write my way (back) in.

acknowledgments

To my inimitable agents, Callie Deitrick and Wendy Sherman, for their passion, advocacy, and sound counsel. I had a special tingly feeling from our very first phone call—partnering with you both remains one of the best decisions I've made. Special thanks as well to Jenny Meyer for your foreign rights expertise, and to Katrina Escudero for your savvy and enthusiastic support in the film/TV world.

To Lexy Cassola, my brilliant and insightful editor—thank you for being my ideal reader. I feel immeasurably lucky to have had you as my guide throughout this process, and I'm so proud of what we accomplished together. I'm also grateful for the hard work and care of the whole team at Dutton/PRH, including Hannah Poole, Tiffani Ren, Alice Dalrymple, Katy Riegel, Susan Schwartz, Ryan Richardson, and Andrea Monagle. Thank you as well to Vi-An Nguyen for the book cover of my dreams!

I'm indebted to my English teachers and writing mentors over the years—from MCS to JJHS to CC to NYU—who nurtured and challenged me as a writer, reader, and human. I especially want to thank Bryan Hurt and Steven Hayward for their warm mentorship at Colorado College, as well as Jonathan Safran Foer, Hannah Tinti, and David Lipsky at New York University for their vital feedback on excerpts of this novel.

To my absurdly talented NYU MFA cohort—I truly couldn't have dreamed up a better group of people. Thank you all for reading many pages and providing such invaluable insight as well as writerly camaraderie in *and* out of class. Special thanks to Elizabeth Nicholas, Raven Leilani, Angela Qian, Maria Lioutaia, and Maria Mazarro.

To my very first writing group(s) in NYC—exchanging work with you all was a joy and a privilege. I especially want to acknowledge Kwame Opoku-Duku, Tabitha Laffernis, and Dana Wilson.

I began submitting stories to literary journals as a teen, so my heartfelt thanks to every tireless editor who published me over the past decade and made me feel like a real writer.

To the dear friends from every phase of my life who cheered me on while I wrote this book (and tolerated me talking incessantly about it), you know who you are, and I love you all. Special shout-out to Sarah Hupper, who has kept me giggling and grounded throughout our decades-long friendship, and Rachel Duboff, who always responds with care and wisdom to my lengthy WhatsApp voice notes and is one of my favorite people to talk books with.

To Owen for your love, encouragement, and patience, and for not running as fast as you could in the opposite direction when I told you I was a writer on our first date.

To Paulette, Gary, and Neeny for nurturing me as I grew.

To my fiercely generous and loving parents, Douglas and Lynne, who read to me from day one. I'm so incredibly lucky to be your daughter—none of this would be even remotely possible without you both as my ultimate support system. To my hilarious and multitalented brother, Nicholas, for inspiring me daily, and for being the best travel buddy I could ask for.

And finally, to my late grandparents and earliest cheerleaders—Joan, the most inspiring of women, and to whom I've dedicated this book; Gilbert, who kept a disintegrating piece of paper in his wallet with my first ever poem written on it; Gloria, who spent hours kneeling on the floor listening to me tell stories about my dolls; and Norman, the original writer in the family, who inspired and encouraged me to "just *finish* it!"

about the author

Caitlin Barasch earned her BA from Colorado College and her MFA from New York University. Her work has appeared in more than a dozen publications, including *Catapult, Day One, The Forge,* and *Hobart.* A former bookseller, Caitlin currently teaches creative writing at the Writers Circle. She was born and raised in New York and now lives in Brooklyn. *A Novel Obsession* is her debut novel.